FORBIDDEN UNION

Sharia's eyes opened, violet and silver in an equal and incredible mixture. She was not surprised to find Kane holding her in his arms. She had dreamed this before, had experienced this instant as surely as she knew her own heartbeat, her own rippling timeshadow. *You feel like my dreams of you. Hot. Powerful. Perfect. Do you taste like my dreams, too?*

Her thought caressed Kane as surely as her translucent silver hair combing through his living timeshadow and her hands threading deeply into his black hair. Slowly he lowered his head until his lips could brush over hers. He meant it to be for only an instant, a glancing caress. But the instant passed and he was still touching her. Timeshadows overlapped hesitantly, then with greater certainty, twining sweetly as each color sought its complement. Reality expanded in a silent sentient explosion. Then she was tasting him and he was tasting her, their mouths joined in a wild pleasure.

The knowledge of what they were doing battled against their mutual need. The torrential, tantalizing rightness of each completing the other was a siren call that became more irresistible with each sweet instant.

Also By This Author

Writing as Ann Maxwell

Shadow and Silk
The Ruby
The Secret Sisters
The Diamond Tiger
Fire Dancer
Dancer's Luck
Dancer's Illusion
Timeshadow Rider
The Jaws of Menx
Name of a Shadow
The Singer Enigma
Dead God Dancing
Change

Writing as Elizabeth Lowell

Winter Fire
Autumn Lover
Only Love
Only You
Only Mine
Only His
Untamed
Forbidden
Enchanted
A Woman Without Lies
Forget Me Not
Lover in the Rough
Tell Me No Lies
Desert Rain

EVERYBODY LOVES ANN MAXWELL!

WRITERS LOVE ANN MAXWELL!

"Ann Maxwell's voice is one of the most powerful and compelling in the romance genre. She writers intense stories, and her readers are equally intense in their response. She has contributed much to the definition of the modern romance novel."
—*New York Times* bestselling author Jayne Ann Krentz

"No one has a voice like Ann Maxwell. She is stellar!"
—Stella Cameron, author of *Sheer Pleasures*

"Ann Maxwell may be *the* most talented, evocative writer in the genre. I pick up her books for more than pleasure. I pick them up to be inspired."
—Suzanne Forster, author of *Blush*

CRITICS LOVE ANN MAXWELL!

". . . Weaves together past and present, tosses in tidbits about archeology without impairing the story's non-stop action or putting a crimp in the romance. Maxwell's control of her material and unabashed willingness to entertain make this book a success."
—*Publishers Weekly* on *The Secret Sisters*

"Only Ann Maxwell could have brought this story to such explosive life. . . . An unforgettable sensory experience, this splendorous tale of adventure is everything a reader could wish and much, much more."
—*Rave Reviews* on *The Secret Sisters*

YOU'LL LOVE ANN MAXWELL, TOO!

TIMESHADOW RIDER

Ann Maxwell

Pinnacle Books
Kensington Publishing Corp.
http://www.pinnaclebooks.com

Prolog

Throughout the history of the Fourth Evolution, azirs sometimes appeared to men and women. The people so blessed usually go mad and die, for condensations of the *other* are inimical to lives rooted in linear time as our lives are.

Yet there are legends of two people who did not die when azirs condensed to walk by their side. Kane and Sharia were from the near-mythical planet Za'arain. They were of the race of Kiri, the clan of Darien, and the family known only as "five."

They were also lias'tri, all their lives and times bound together in a unique whole.

Legends, you say. Myths.

Perhaps. Yet azirs are condensing again, even as we breathe, and they are neither legend nor myth. If you hear the azir's unspeakably beautiful song shiver through your timeshadow, you will seek out those legends and myths. You will gather them to you like a lover.

And you will dream.

If you awaken in another place, another aspect of time, you have dreamed the dream of Kiri, Darien and five. If you don't awaken. . . .

Ah, well, that is always the risk, isn't it?

One

Za'arain was dying.

A million years of serenity and power. A million years of science and art. A million years of intelligence and ambition, pragmatism and compassion. An achievement forged by billions of individual lives, individual dreams. Disintegrating. It was in the very air. Za'arain's silver skies were thick with imminence, seething with despair.

Sharia ZaDarien/Kiri did not notice the people who shrank away from her as she hurried through the glass-walled maze of the Kiriy compound. Her white robe and clearly displayed hands marked her as a five, tabu. By all custom she should have been in her suite, dreaming deeply, waiting for the moment when she would either live as Kiriy or die among all the cascading timeshadows of the *then* and the *now*.

But custom, too, was disintegrating. The dying Kiriy had spoken in Sharia's mind, summoning her with neither ritual nor courtesy. The Kiriy's need had overwhelmed everything except the pain of the disease consuming her body, the same disease that had struck the capital city without warning, the same disease that was destroying Za'arain.

The Kiriy's glass-walled audience room was empty of all but a handful of Sharia's Darien cousins, men and women almost as sick as the Kiriy herself. Sharia froze in the doorway, shocked by the change in the ruler of Za'arain. It was something more than the wasted body or the mahogany skin bleached to pale red. The Kiriy's eyes were open—

Her eyes. Open. Silver. Human. For the first time in Sharia's memory, the Kiriy's eyes were not covered by the Eyes of Za'ar. The large, twin crystals were on her forehead, their violet fire reduced to a pale lavender reflection of former glory. The Kiriy's emaciated five-fingered hand came up and pulled the silver band holding the Eyes back over her own. Instantly the color of the Eyes deepened.

CHILD OF MY SISTER. COME TO ME.

The Kiriy's body had been claimed by sickness, but her mind-speech was like freshly cut glass, slicing through Sharia's emotions to the core of Darien strength beneath. She walked forward carefully, stepping around the Kiriy's attendants. Sharia yearned to ride their living timeshadows, to comb the spreading darkness of disease from their time/then and heal their time/now; but some of the attendants were mature fives and so was she. They were forbidden to touch one another. The punishment for transgression was Za'ar death, the last death, death in the *then* and the *now* and the *always*.

"All that I am is yours," said Sharia clearly. "How may I serve the Kiriy of Za'arain?"

SHOW ME YOUR NECKLACE.

Sharia blinked, surprise clear in her translucent silver eyes. She reached inside her white robe and pulled out a chain. A large jewel flashed and turned, suspended from the iridescent black links of a metal that had been forged light-years and za're-placements from Za'arain. Though the jewel was black, it was almost transparent. Marvelous colors scintillated in its depths, pure colors with no darkness, brilliant as the Eyes had once been brilliant.

The Kiriy made a sound that could have been anger or despair or satisfaction as she watched the pouring wealth of colors within the gem.

EVEN THE EYES OF ZA'AR COULD NOT SEPARATE YOU FROM HIM.

Sharia did not respond, because what the Kiriy was telling her made no sense.

I WAITED TOO LONG TO EXILE YOUR OTHER HALF. BUT I WEPT
FOR YOU AS NO ONE HAD WEPT FOR ME BEFORE I WAS KIRIY
AND CURSED WITH THE EYES. ZA'ARAIN HAS SENT SO MANY
INTO THE DARKNESS IN ORDER THAT WE AND THEY MIGHT SUR-
VIVE. ZADYNEEN ZADARIEN/KIRI, MY LOST-SOUL, MY TABU
SOUL. EVEN HIM I SENT AWAY, COMPELLED BY THE EYES. I
WEEP FOR THE DUSTMAN WHO WAS ONCE THE FORBIDDEN HALF
OF THE KIRIY OF ZA'ARAIN.

WE HAVE FORBIDDEN TOO MUCH IN THE NAME OF STABILITY.
IN THE MILLION YEARS SINCE THE EYES PULLED US FROM THE
MUCK OF ATAVISM, OUR GENES HAVE CHANGED, MORE FIVES
BORN, MORE AND MORE OFTEN, MORE AND MORE POWERFUL.
BUT THE EYES ARE CHANGELESS. THE DUST IS NOT. I HAVE
SENT MY OTHER HALF INTO THE DARKNESS AND NOW IT IS COME
TO ME AGAIN. CHANGED.

DISEASED.

AND IT IS DESTROYING ALL THAT WE HAVE WORKED FOR. THE
EYES OF ZA'AR WILL CLOSE. THE ATAVISM WILL BE UNLEASHED.
BEWARE THE PSI-PACKS FORMING.

With a small sound Sharia went to her knees. The Eyes were
all that stood between Za'arain and unspeakable savagery: Kiri
psi-packs hunting human prey; Za'arain destroyed beneath an
upwelling of Kiri atavism that could only be described in night-
mares.

YES. EXACTLY. A DUST RAIDER WILL COME AND TRY TO—
"Dust?" asked Sharia numbly. "I don't—"

I KNOW YOU DON'T. HE WILL, THOUGH.

"He?" repeated Sharia, wondering if the Kiriy had succumbed to madness as well as disease.

KANAEN ZADARIEN/KIRI.

Sharia could not prevent her sudden rush of emotion at the
sound of Kane's name. Kane, who had cherished her when every
other being in the Kiri compound had shunned her. Kane, who

had protected her from her cruel four and six cousins. Kane, who had taught her to laugh and use her protean Darien mind. Kane, whose warmth had pervaded her senses, eased her loneliness, shown her that she was alive.

Kane, who was Kiri, Darien and five. Kane, who had been exiled by the Kiriy to ensure that the Great Tabu would not be broken. Mature five touching mature five. Catastrophe.

DO YOU WANT TO SEE HIM, CHILD OF MY SISTER?

Though Sharia's voice was disciplined, the force of her answering *"Yes"* came from both her lips and her mind.

The Kiriy flinched. THEN TAKE THAT CURSED CRYSTAL IN YOUR HANDS AND CALL TO HIM.

"But—"

NO. I DON'T HAVE THE STRENGTH FOR ARGUMENTS OR EXPLANATIONS. THE DUST RAIDER COMES, THE EYES WILL CLOSE. KANE MUST COME—AND QUICKLY! YOU MUST FIND THE EYES, TAKE THEM UP AND LIVE OR DIE. IF YOU DIE, KANE MUST TAKE UP THE EYES; FOR HE, LIKE YOU, HAS THE BEST CHANCE OF SURVIVING THEIR TIME-WRACKED DEPTHS. HE, LIKE YOU, HAS THE BEST CHANCE OF DEFEATING THE DUSTMAN WHO COULD HAVE BEEN KIRIY.

IF KANE DIES TRYING TO WEAR THE EYES, THE DARIENS WILL GATHER. IF ANY OTHER FIVES HAVE SURVIVED, THEY WILL BE THE FIRST TO TAKE UP THE EYES. IF THE FIVES ARE DEAD, THE SIXES AND FOURS MUST TRY. A NEW KIRIY MUST BE FOUND. ONLY THEN WILL CIVILIZATION LIVE AGAIN ON ZA'ARAIN AND IN THE JOINING, CHILD OF ZA'ARAIN'S GREATNESS.

POOR, LOST CHILD. WITHOUT THE PLAGUE THE JOINING WOULD HAVE SURVIVED ZA'ARAIN'S DEATH. BUT THE PLAGUE CAME, HIDDEN IN TIME AND A DUSTMAN'S BASTARD EYES.

Sharia did not understand the voice speaking so hugely in her mind. She felt it sinking into her, spreading like shock waves through her, an irresistible shaping of her mind beneath the power of the Eyes. Yet some small part of her writhed and tried to evade the imperative, for if Kane broke exile and returned at her call he would die the final death. She could not bear that, knowing that he was not alive in time/now or the *now*, that he would never live again, ever, in any time. Za'ar death was not a simple resting between lives. Za'ar death was final.

KIRIYS NEVER WASTE WHAT CAN BE SAVED. WHY DO YOU THINK I EXILED RATHER THAN EXECUTED KANE? IF THE EYES ARE CLOSED HE WILL NOT DIE THE LAST DEATH WHEN HE RE-TURNS TO ZA'ARAIN, CALL TO HIM.

Head bowed, Sharia felt the Za'ar imperative sinking into her mind. She did not fight it. She could not. At some level she had never stopped calling to Kane since he had been exiled ten years ago.

The Kiriy knew that and used it, for she was dying and had few choices left, none of them comforting. She fought ruthlessly for her people's survival with every bit of her rapidly waning power. Even wearing the Eyes, dealing with her niece's inno-cent, too-powerful mind was rapidly using up the Kiriy's small reserves of strength. The Kiriy's frail body shook with the force of the demand pouring out of her mind.

IF IT COMES TO DUST AND KANE, YOU MUST REMEMBER: HE IS FORBIDDEN TO YOU! GO WITH KANE, FIND THE EYES, BUT NEVER TOUCH HIM. NEVER. WHEN TWO FIVES LIKE YOU TOUCH, THE BOUNDARIES OF ZA' ARE DISTURBED. THEN TIME AND LIFE FLOW TOGETHER, DESTROYING EVERYTHING. CATASTROPHE. THAT IS THE TRUTH OF THE GREAT TABU. IT WILL BE TRUTH AFTER THE EYES CLOSE. IT WILL BE TRUTH WHEN ZA'ARAIN IS DUST. IT WILL ALWAYS BE TRUTH.

NEVER TOUCH YOUR FORBIDDEN SOUL.

Abruptly the Kiriy's body went slack. She lay back in the alabaster alcove, spent by disease and the difficulty of trying to force her niece's powerful mind to accept an unwanted com-mand all the way down to the level of reflex. She hoped that the Za'ar imperative had been stronger than Sharia's deeply buried need to touch Kane. Once there would have been no doubt that a Za'ar imperative would hold. But Kiris had become Dariens over time, and Dariens had become fives. The power of Sharia's mind was unique in all of Za'arain's history. Kane's mind was also unique in its power, and capable of joining completely with hers. Neither of them knew it. The Kiriy hoped that neither ever would. If they did, it would be the last thing that they would learn before they died the final death . . .

. . . And took with them into Za'ar death every psi who had ever lived or would live, the *then* and the *now* and the *always* released from za' until it all imploded, shredding timeshadows beyond any hope of rebirth or renewal in this or any other dimension of time and za'.

Sharia watched the shallow movements of the Kiriy's chest for a long time. When no more words came to ring hugely in Sharia's mind, she turned and fled to her suite. There she sat without moving, cupping the odd gem in her palms. At first she felt helpless, knowing only the impossibility of reaching out across space and linear time to Kane. Yet the Za'ar imperative and her own deepest desire kept driving Sharia back to the gem's torrential colors.

She did not count the minutes or the hours or the days of linear time piling up around her like winter leaves. She ate when she was too weak to hold the stone steady, drank when she must, and poured herself into the endless colors turning deep within the alien jewel. She called to Kane through all the levels of her Darien mind that were accessible to her. There was no answer, no whisper or shout returning, no shift of color into meaning, nothing to separate one anonymous minute from the next.

Finally there came a moment to mark the end of Za'arain's history, wrenching Sharia from the depths of her fiery gem. A terrible psychic cry shattered her concentration. The Kiriy's timeshadow was thinning, energy radiating out of time/now into times/other, those unnamed and unknown dimensions where life gathered between births. The Kiriy's rich timeshadow convulsed as it was torn from time/now and rooted irrevocably in the *then*.

The Kiriy was dead.

Sharia lay dazed, exhausted by her long, fruitless search and its shattering end. Soon someone would come to take her to the Eyes of Za'ar as custom and tabu decreed, a four or a six leading the chosen five to death or greater life. Then she would take up the Eyes and would either live as the new Kiriy of Za'arain or unravel among the endless, rippling timeshadows of the universe.

No one came, neither four nor six. All that reached Sharia was a distant sense of fear and triumph—and then the massed Kiri minds writhed in agony and despair as they sheared away from each other, unable to maintain civilized unity without the guiding Eyes. Kiri minds slid backward down the long darkness of linear time while savage atavism glided upward to meet them on deadly clawed feet.

The Eyes of Za'ar closed.

The gem in Sharia's cupped palms blazed fiercely, as though freed from a stifling veil. Blinded by alien light and compelled by the dead Kiriy's Za'ar imperative, Sharia called to Kane from every level of her unique mind. She called while ordinary Za'arains became mobs that rose and flooded the streets in a frightened, destructive tide, leaving only shards of civilization in their wake. She called while the city's psi-dependent machinery was first damaged, then destroyed. She called while Kiri atavisms burned into sudden life, Kiris looking out at the world from savage violet eyes.

And as she called she felt fives die one by one, each death sending dark ripples through the colors of her timeshadow until finally the last fives of Za'arain were dead. Save one. And still that one called out to Kane.

Only Sharia's own need to survive ended the channeling of herself into the call. The jewel finally slipped from hands too weak to hold it. The crystal swung heavily on its chain, gorged with light and colors and life. Slowly Sharia realized that with the death of the city's machinery, both food and water had stopped coming to her isolated rooms. If she were to continue calling Kane, she must care for herself. She must put aside customs and tabus engrained into her almost as deeply as the need to drink.

But the Za'ar imperative the Kiriy had thrown like a spear into Sharia's mind was deeper, more urgent, than mere thirst.

She pried open the door and went out into corridors of the Kiriy compound that had been tabu to her since the onset of her fertility ten years ago. She held her five-fingered hands before her, an unequivocal proclamation of Za'ar tabu.

The six- and four-fingered Kiris flinched away from her, squeezing against the wall to allow her free passage, no chance of touching. Part of their reaction was custom; while fives were not always expressly tabu to fours or sixes, Kiris simply did not touch mature fives at all unless the Eyes declared one to be a five-fingered Kiriy's mate. If custom weren't enough to hold back the Kiris in the compound's rainbow halls of glass, there was always primal fear. At the darkest levels of their minds, the Kiris knew that a five unbridled by the Eyes was a thing of deadly power.

Water was just beyond Sharia's room, which faced the Kiriy's courtyard. Though the capital city of Za'aral was disintegrating around her, the massive, artesian dance of the sacred fountain would not waver. She would walk into those drenching crystal mists and fill herself with water.

But even as she went from Kiriy halls to the fountain's sacred white courtyard, she found the water's silver beauty bleeding into horror. The dead and the dying were everywhere, timeshadows knotting and writhing, silent screams shredding her control. She fought against the lure of riding the agonized timeshadows down to the knotted beginnings of disease and unraveling that knot, bringing health in the wake of her ride.

The farther she went into the fountain's mists, the more strongly timeshadows called to her in all their tangled colors. After a decade of isolation as a mature five, the timeshadows had an elemental allure to her. She knew the feel of the disease's energy, knew that she could cure its dark draining of life. Weeks before the Kiriy had spoken hugely in Sharia's mind, she had healed the onset of the disease in her own body, riding her own timeshadow back to the moment of incubation and outbreak, and then she had delicately smoothed out the tangles until life flowed unhindered and her timeshadow shimmered with vitality once again.

A wave of wounded timeshadows broke over her. Suddenly she could no longer turn aside from their desperate colors. A single thought freed her translucent hair from its discipline. Silver hair flowed out, seeking and finding the troubled currents of life. The instant of contact was excruciating. Sharia screamed but did not hear her own cry. She was riding a wild Darien timeshadow, combing its colors until there was no darkness, unknotting tangled lines of energy. She released the vibrant timeshadow and flowed into another, riding it down to the beginning of disease, combing, healing, releasing.

The cycle repeated itself endlessly as her own life-force ebbed; and even then she continued to heal. Time did not exist. Za'arain did not exist. Only a Darien compulsion existed, draining Sharia of life as surely as disease had drained the Kiriy.

Colors shattered around her, cutting her until she screamed. Pain tore her from the healing trance, hurling her back into time/now. Blood ran down her back from a fresh wound. She opened her eyes and she saw healed Kiris watching her. Some of them had violet eyes. Others blinked, and then their eyes, too, were violet. The violet-eyed Kiris flowed soundlessly toward each other. And then they turned toward her, a five, a powerful mind that the psi-pack must either kill or rule.

Instinct older than the Eyes of Za'ar rose in Sharia. As the pack closed in to claim or kill her, she fought in a way and with a ferocity that took her Kiri cousins off guard. Her long hair swept out, hurting instead of healing, disrupting rather than combing. Then she fled through the fountain's mists, coming out at an unfamiliar point in the huge, circular courtyard. She ran through the first open door she saw, seeking the safety of her own room.

But she had been raised a five, in isolation, and soon she was lost in the ancient circular maze of rooms surrounding the courtyard. She ran until she reached a dead end. There she turned at bay, her back to a glass wall scaled by time. She looked at the sky through a ruined ceiling. Beyond the clamoring of her own survival instincts she sensed death with every too-rapid beating of her heart, every silent slide of blood from her fingertips onto surfaces smoothed by the passage of her Za'arain ancestors.

Sharia tried to still the frantic demands of her body for air, tried to hold her breath in order to catch the sound of death coming toward her, tried to listen for the mindless growl of her Kiri cousins hunting her. Pack hunters, prowling and snarling, dripping blood and death.

With a low sound Sharia looked at her hands and felt savagery in her own mind, a hot seeking for a breach in the cage of her will. The blood she wore was her own. She had not killed. Yet. She could feel it coming, though. She could feel the grief and the rage uncoiling in her, black flames burning toward a feral freedom. The unique culmination of a million years of linear time was sliding through her fingers, a brilliant culture was bleeding through cracks in the *now* as surely as blood sinking into pavement stones.

Yet she must survive to find her way out of this maze and take up the Eyes, giving Za'arain a chance to live again. She was the last five alive on Za'arain. She knew that as surely as she knew the feel of her own blood dripping from her five-fingered hands. She had heard Kiri whispers, Kiri revelations, mad Kiri laughter in her mind as fives had died one by one in their private rooms across the face of the planet.

There had been no real reason to blame fives for the catastrophic plague that had brought down Za'arain, no reason to kill them rather than fours or sixes. But the Kiris believed that something had to be responsible, that a great culture did not

fall without blame being assessed among the ruins. Next to the
Eyes of Za'ar, fives were the central mystery of Za'arain, forbidden to touch on pain of unknowable catastrophe. Since catastrophe had come, it must have come from a breach of the
Great Tabu. Therefore all fives had to die.

A low, feral sound vibrated through the cool wall at Sharia's
back. Her cousins were coming, burning their way through a
million years of civilization seeking the Kiri passageways impregnated in the compound like time itself. She could heal herself again as she already had. She could survive to hide for yet
a few more twists and turns, a few more hours. But why bother?
Why not just slide softly, hotly into the rage that was uncurling
in her mind and testing the bars of her discipline? Why not turn
and confront her tormentors? Why not die rending their
timeshadows, tearing a hole in time/now and letting their lives
leak through?

Sharia pulled on the fine black links that hung around her
neck. Delicate, unbreakable, the jewel's chain emerged from the
concealing folds of the once-white robe she wore. The crystal's
colors called to her at a level deeper than atavism. Her silver
eyes focused on the gem, reflecting the silent, sleeting hues
within the crystal, her eyes consuming the living colors with a
hunger that had never been appeased since the day she had
awakened and found two necklaces beside her pillow. Both
necklaces had been rare, extraordinary, complementing each
other. One light, one dark, each with a wealth of colors turning
in its still center. She had kept both crystals for a time, worn
both. Then she had sent the light one out to the stars.

She turned the clear, black crystal slowly, cherishing its endless colors, calling to Kane yet again, wanting to sense his presence just once before she died. She wondered if somewhere far,
far away Kane held the transparent brilliance of a crystal in his
palm and thought of the Darien cousin he had taught to smile.
She would never know, now. She did not even know if Kane
had received the crystal that she had sent, a condensation of all
colors from a timeshadow rider, a silent thank-you for the laugh-

ter that he alone had brought to a childhood all but strangled by tabu.

Kane. Come to me. Come to me!

The sounds of Sharia's savage cousins drifted through translucent walls. Soon they would see her, a shadow within the wall. Soon she could die. Or she could heal herself and live for a few more hours, watch again the infinite fascination of colors turning within a crystal as black and transparent as space.

For an instant longer Sharia dreamed within the crystal, then she hid its blazing facets within bloody folds of cloth. She tried to gather herself, but her mind still reached for Kane.

You can't call him if you're dead. Heal yourself. Fight. Live!

Sharia rode her own timeshadow with an ease that would have astonished her aunt, the dead Kiriy. Throughout all of Za'arain's long history, there had been very few Kiris who could ride even the wakes of former timeshadows, much less ride the torrential living shadow itself. There had been no one to teach Sharia how to use her mind. No one had dared. Except Kane. He, too, was Darien and five. He understood the patterns of nonliving wakes as deeply as she understood the living timeshadows themselves.

He had brought her plants and pets to heal, urged her to control the multi-edged gift of a timeshadow rider's mind. He had known that some day she would be given to the Eyes of Za'ar. He had hoped that learning to control her own mind would increase her chances of surviving the instant when the Eyes sucked her into an infinity of seething, overlapping timeshadows.

He had cared, and now she would never touch him again.

The thought shocked her. After all the years of tabu and isolation, she thought that she had accepted Kane's irrevocable absence in time/now. She had not. She had merely tolerated it. She hungered for Kane in a way that transcended everything that she was—Kiri, Darien and five—and she knew she would die without him.

She could not heal herself endlessly. Her strength was not

that of the sacred fountain, rooted in millions of years of linear time. She could, however, take down into darkness with her some of her savage Kiri kin. Perhaps, just perhaps, the death of those cousins who had most easily embraced atavism would ease Kane's job when he returned and took up the Eyes in hope of dragging Za'arain back out of the muck it had fallen into. She owed Kane that much and would have gladly given him more.

And she owed it to psi-hunters to teach them that timeshadow riders could kill as thoroughly as they healed. Even a five. Especially a five.

The smile that Sharia wore was as much a warning as the hammered silver of her eyes. With every heartbeat, years of civilization slipped away from her, years and then more years, an endless cultural timeshadow reaching back down linear time into savagery . . . freeing it.

Black flames licked upward through Sharia's core, freezing flames which burned through inhibitions. For the first time in her life her inner eyelid flickered down, transforming the landscape with atavistic light. Violet eyes looked out on a world where living timeshadows burned like jeweled flames. Atavistic eyes.

Psi-hunter eyes.

She pushed away from the fractured glass wall and ran into the sacred courtyard again. Acres of satin stone swept in all directions, stone as white as her robe once had been. The single huge artesian fountain leaped. The sound was that of an immense river falling over the chasm between time/then and time/now. The fountain had been both symbol and shrine of Kiriy and Za'arain. Here the present joined invisibly with the past, the rain of a million million yesterdays slaking the thirst of today while today's rains ran down out of time/now to be reborn in a million million tomorrows as silver drops dancing beneath Za'arain skies.

Sharia tore off her hooded robe, freeing her body and her hair in the same savage motion. She threw the bloody garment aside. Wearing only the black necklace Kane had given her, she stood beneath the chill waters of condensed time. Today's blood was washed away, pink water sliding through the cracks in the ancient, radiant pavement, water draining into the future. The grime of the recent past slid from her body. There were no injuries beneath to mar her pale, luminous skin. She had healed herself for this, to stand naked beneath the thundering water of the *then* and to consecrate herself to death in the everlasting *now.*

"There! Near the fountain!"

The voice had once belonged to Kiri Dirneen, the woman who years ago had taught Sharia to understand the elegant ideographs of Za'arain. The Dirneen of Sharia's childhood was gone, though; the Dirneen of today was half wild, wholly savage, gripped by fear and a greed for power that would not be exorcised short of death.

Sharia stepped out of the veiling mists. Her hip-length hair shimmered and lifted with each movement of her head, shedding the water from time/now and the *now* with the ease that only a rider of living timeshadows knew. Translucent, silver, as fluid as the water it so closely resembled, Sharia's unbound hair floated on currents that only she could sense. Living currents rippling through time. Tendrils of hair fanned out, seeking other currents, other timeshadows, other lives . . . other deaths.

She laughed and held out her arms to the shifting, amorphous mob of people who had tracked her down.

"Come to me," crooned Sharia. "Touch me. *Touch death.*"

Her Kiri cousins hesitated, but only for an instant. With a savage growl they began running toward the only living five on Za'arain.

Two

The Wolfin lightship groaned like the quasi-living being it was. Kane felt the cocoon around him shift, becoming a fluid restraint that protected his body from the backlash of forces seething around the ship. The za'replacement symbol had glowed orange in the homing crystal, warning that the upcoming transition would not be an easy one. He had ordered Jode to take it anyway, despite the fact that there were lavender za're-placements scattered within six ship-hours of the orange site.

The ship closed with the difficult za'replacement point. Conflicting forces sleeted through Kane, tearing at him, making every bit of his large body ache. For an instant Kane wanted to groan with the Wolfin ship. Then the ship shuddered and reappeared in time/now, all forces balanced again. Quietly the lightship sped away on its predetermined course.

The cocoon peeled from Kane and vanished into the couch, freeing him. He stood and stretched, his knuckles brushing against the resilient, textured ceiling. Wolfins were among the biggest of the Fourth Evolution peoples and built their ships accordingly. Even so, Kane found himself a bit cramped. He was careful not to complain, though, any more than he complained about the crude, timeshadow-tangling eccentricities that the Wolfins built into their sentient machines. The Wolfins were proud of their technological accomplishments. A man who wanted to pass as the grandson of Wolfin colonists would be the last person to complain about the Wolfins' sometimes bizarre technology.

And for Kane to criticize the most sensitive, sophisticated machines that the Joining had to offer would be to raise the question of where he had seen better ones. There was only one possible answer: Za'arain. Kane did not want to connect himself with that forbidden planet. In the Joining, Za'arains were considered to be deadly, inhuman combinations of gods and devils. No one in the Joining even knew the galactic coordinates of Za'arain. Or if they did, they did not live after putting those coordinates to use. Za'arain's isolation was enforced by the most potent weapon in the known galaxy—the Eyes of Za'ar. Kiriy weapon. Za'ar tabu.

Za'ar death.

"That was a tough one," said Jode as the pilot's cocoon retracted. He looked up at Kane who was standing and stretching as though nothing had happened. "Even your Wolfin body must have noticed it."

Kane rubbed the back of his neck and flexed his powerful shoulders. "I felt it."

"Does that mean you're going to be more reasonable about the next one?" asked Jode curtly.

Kane hesitated. He closed his eyes, searching his mind for the source of the uneasiness that had been riding him with unsheathed claws for several weeks. In the last few days it had become intolerable. With a muffled curse, Kane rummaged through his mind again, asking, demanding. Why? he thought. What in all the billion suns is driving me across the face of the known galaxy? Why did I put ship and crew through an orange za'replacement just to save a few hours when I don't even know where in time I'm going?

Jode looked up sharply. The Jhoramon psi-master's austere face became even more grim as he measured his captain's flaring psychic unease. Jode did not attempt to initiate the more intimate communication of mindspeech. Kane had never offered it in the four years they had been together. But now, at this instant, the captain's questions rang as clearly in Jode's mind as they did in Kane's.

There was no answer in either mind.

"I don't know if I can be reasonable," admitted Kane.

Jode's black eyes narrowed as he studied his captain. "You're acting like an azir's chewing through time to get to your soul. What's wrong?"

"Azir," muttered Kane. "Myth."

"Don't count on it, Captain. The Dust is full of them."

Kane shrugged. His long, five-fingered hand raked through hair that was filled with hidden currents of energy and vagrant gleams of light beneath the black dye he used to conceal his Za'arain heritage. "I don't know why or how or what, I simply know all the way down to the bottom of time that something is wrong."

"The bottom of time." Jode closed his black eyes, then snapped them open again. "An odd phrase for a Wolfin."

Kane made a casual, dismissing movement with his hand, though the effort not to show his unease was great. Some habits were nearly impossible to break. Patterns of speech were one. Patterns of speech a Za'arain exile could not afford. Like the memories he could not afford—a child/woman's laughter following him through the galaxy, haunting him, a sound as beautiful and unattainable as the color of time itself. But he would not think of Sharia. He could not. Forgetting was all that had kept him sane.

"Not all Wolfins ignore time as a dimension of reality," he said to Jode in a casual voice. "Colonists, in particular, are prone to heresy. In fact, both of my parents—"

Kane uttered a sharp sound of pain and grabbed for the crystal concealed beneath his tunic. The jewel was suddenly alive, tormenting him. There was an endless instant of agony, worse than any orange za'replacement, worse than anything Kane had ever known except the instant when Za'arain had vanished from view as a lightship hurled him into endless exile.

The agony passed, freeing Kane. He straightened slowly and realized that Jode's lean body was levering him back onto the captain's couch.

"You're Wolfin in one thing, at least," muttered Jode. "Stubborn to the living core of your bones." But there was fear and affection in the Jhoramon's voice. "Lie down and stop fighting whatever your mind is trying to tell you."

"What do you mean?" said Kane, breathing quickly, feeling sweat cool across his skin. "That wasn't my mind."

"Then what was it?" demanded Jode, fear racing through him in a cold explosion. "What's riding you?"

Kane's body convulsed again as the hidden jewel resting against his chest stabbed deeply into his timeshadow, twisting it. He forced his hand to go beneath the black tunic. With fingers that trembled he dragged out the gem he had kept concealed from everyone, a treasure to warm the coldest nights of exile. He yanked, but the silver chain did not give way even to his strength. Cloth ripped, though. The pale, transparent crystal spilled out, blazing with colors—and riddled with terrible shards of darkness.

"Lias'tri!" hissed Jode. Relief glowed in his voice like sunrise until he saw the blackness laced through the stone. "Oh my cruel gods—she's dying." Compassion transformed Jode's harsh face, softening bleak lines and planes with an emotion he had never before revealed. "No," he said gently, trying to hold Kane down. "Don't get up. The pain will get worse before she— before it's over."

"What are you babbling about?" asked Kane harshly, evading Jode's sinewy grasp with the easy power that only a mature Za'arain knew.

"Your lias'tri."

"Lias'tri," snapped Kane impatiently, "is a word without meaning. What is lias'tri?"

For the first time in their four years together, Kane saw that the pilot's quick mind was truly stunned.

"You don't know?" asked Jode. "How in the name of sanity can you wear that crystal and not know?"

"Not know what?" snarled Kane, pacing the control room like a caged predator. Urgency was riding him again, razor claws unsheathed, ripping through him. He had to be—*somewhere*. He had to be there now. Yet the nearest reasonably safe za'replacement point to anywhere was hours away.

Too long. Too far. Urgency raking through the currents of time. Timeshadows twisting, knotting.

Kane turned, prowling the deck with savage grace. At each step the crystal burned and coruscated across his chest. Jode watched, compelled by the incredible colors pouring through the lias'tri gem. And then he realized that the black shards were thinning, fading, gone.

Jode made a sound of pure disbelief. "That. Can't. Be."

"What?"

"The blackness. It's gone from the crystal!"

Kane looked down at the blazing gem. Colors seethed and flashed back at him. "Black? It's never black."

"But it was. When you ripped it out of your tunic, there were fragments of black. That's why you were in pain. Your lias'tri was dying."

The last of Jode's words were lost in Kane's low cry of agony. His hand had clenched around the crystal. He swayed, fighting to shed pain the way a timeshadow rider shed the infinite *now.* He was partially successful, driven no further than his knees by the hammer blows of agony. When his sweat-slippery fingers parted, the crystal swung free.

"Look," said Jode, pointing at the crystal.

Shards of black lanced through the colors once again.

Fear crawled over Kane, as cold as the sweat dripping from his body. He moved with the speed of death itself. A hard bronzed hand wrapped around Jode's wiry arm.

"Tell me," snarled Kane.

"She's dying," said Jode simply.

"Who's dying?"

"The woman who sent you that crystal."

"Sharia?" demanded Kane, his long fingers closing with crushing force on Jode's arm. "Are you trying to tell me that Sharia is dying?"

"If Sharia gave you the crystal, yes."

"How do you know?"

The psi-master's black eyes closed, unable to bear any longer the sight of Kane's dawning comprehension. Feeling the death of a lias'tri was a terrible thing. Watching a friend writhe with a lias'tri's death throes was little better.

"The black within the crystal," said Jode, his voice hoarse. "First shards, then gaps, and finally a veil of . . . absence . . . dimming the colors of her life."

"I don't believe you," said Kane flatly, abandoning the inter-culture courtesy of the Joining that had become almost as ingrained in him as the speech patterns of his natal culture.

Jode's eyes opened as black as midnight water on a moonless world. Kane flinched from the grief and compassion he saw there. Wordlessly Jode opened the soft fabric of his tunic. Against the smooth blackness of his skin rested a pale, transparent crystal. Colors turned in the gem's center, but they moved only slowly, like echoes of living color rather than the reality itself. A haze veiled the clarity of both crystal and colors. Unwillingly, Kane's hand lifted toward the jewel. He had to know it with more than just his eyes. He had to know it with a timeshadow wake rider's subtle binding of the *then* and *now*.

"May I?" asked Kane, his voice tight.

Reflexively Jode flinched from permitting Kane to touch the dim lias'tri crystal. Then the Jhoramon man sighed, understanding at last that Kane knew little about lias'tri and believed even less.

Kane's finger brushed briefly against the odd gem. There was a vague sense of laughter, fragments of conversation in a language he had never heard, the smooth brown beauty of a woman's body. Ice moved through Kane's blood as he realized that he was riding the wake of a dead woman's timeshadow.

"She died more than nine years ago," said Jode, his voice as colorless as the haze within the crystal. "I could give you the weeks and the days, the hours and the seconds if you wish."

Kane knew no words of apology and regret to equal the pain in his pilot's voice.

"The winnowing?" guessed Kane, using the comspeech word for the epidemic that had swept through the planets of the Joining.

Jode made a weary gesture of agreement. "The winnowing."

"That can't touch Sharia," said Kane, his voice calm and absolutely sure.

"She's been immunized?"

"No, she's—" Kane stopped abruptly. There was no word in comspeech that equaled the Za'arain concept of a living timeshadow rider. Frowning, Kane searched for a comspeech analog. "She's a healer," he said finally. "Disease can't take root in her timesha—" With a silent curse, Kane rephrased his statement. The Za'arain word *timeshadow* existed in comspeech, but only as an obscenity so vile that it was rarely used. "Disease can't touch her body unless she permits it," said Kane.

Jode's glance returned to Kane's crystal. With a startled sound the psi-master leaned closer. As he watched, shards of black faded, leaving an unblemished crystal behind. "Fascinating," he murmured. "Has this happened often?"

"No. Never."

"I wonder what's hurting her," murmured Jode to himself.

Kane did not answer. He did not even hear. A chilling idea had come to him. What if the Kiriy had died before her expected time? Was Sharia even now being offered to the Eyes of Za'ar? Was her struggle to survive being reflected by the agonizing fluctuations of the crystal he wore?

Grimly Kane reviewed everything he had ever learned of the Eyes of Za'ar. Though only one in one hundred Kiriy aspirants survived, nothing in his memory pointed toward a slow, hard-fought death. Kiris simply prepared themselves, came into the presence of the Eyes of Za'ar, and lived or died within seconds of taking up the two violet crystals. There was little pain. Nor was it Za'ar death. No timeshadow energies exploded into other dimensions, shredding beyond recovery the delicate, tenacious patterns of linked yet discreet lives stretching through time.

No, it was not the Eyes of Za'ar that were causing Sharia pain.

"Are you positive," asked Jode carefully, "that your lias'tri is immune to the winnowing?"

"Yes."

"It would take a very skilled healer to survive. The disease is extraordinarily complex," said Jode, his voice neutral.

"Sharia is like no one I've ever known. Once I brought a mangled—" at the last instant Kane substituted the name of a common Joining pet, "—jhora to her. The silly creature had somehow evaded the traffic restraints. There was nothing left of the soft little body but reflexes and pain. I had no hope that the jhora would survive, but the child who loved it was crying." Kane frowned, remembering. The child had been his cousin, a red-headed Darien four, and very gentle. "Sharia rode the jhora's—" Again, Kane swore silently, cursing the seething emotions that had made him lose control of his speech patterns. "Sharia healed the jhora as it lay dying in my hands."

Jode listened intently, remembering the question he had always had about the oversized stranger who had saved his life four years ago. Jode had introduced himself as a Jhoramon psi-master and lightship pilot. Kane had said only that he was a trader of Wolfin descent. There were times when Kane's accents could not be pinned down; the man was the same way. As a captain Kane had no peer. As a companion he was an enigma.

"What about the people around your Sharia? Have they been immunized?" asked Jode.

Kane's mouth flattened into a cruel grimace. Za'arain immune? Not in this or any other dimension of time. Nothing from off-planet was permitted to touch Za'arain's hallowed soil. Not people. Not ideas. Not vaccine. Nothing.

Except lightships carrying exiles out to the stars. Could those ships have carried something back? Something so small that it had evaded the notice of the Eyes? Had the virus of the winnowing finally come to Za'arain?"

"No," said Kane slowly. "Only a healer of Sharia's innate skill would be immune. And those she healed, perhaps."

"Did your colony have many such healers? Enough to hold the structure of civilization together while the winnowing raged?"

"No." Kane's voice was very soft, very final. "Healers such as Sharia are only born once in a million years."

"Then your planet is probably in the grip of the winnowing," said Jode, his eyes compassionate and his voice calm. "A minor healer would have no chance against the disease. I know. My brother had some talent for healing as did my grandmother. Even working together they couldn't shield us." Jode read the fear on Kane's face, felt it burning at the edges of his mind. "Don't worry so, my friend. Colonies are very resilient. Their people are accustomed to largely governing themselves. Anarchy won't reign for long. Your lias'tri is probably looking for a safe place even now, somewhere to hide until chaos passes by."

"S/kourat," breathed Kane. Horror was clear in his voice as he remembered the savage ruins of a civilized planet where human predators stalked their human prey in the name of inhuman gods. Four years ago Jode had been that prey. Only Kane's deadly skill as a fighter had kept the skinning knife from Jode's throat. "Do you mean that my planet is like S/kourat?"

"Not at all," said Jode, his voice and mind reaching out, trying to soothe the potent, dangerous mind so close to him. "S/kourat's government was ten thousand years old. Inflexible. The people had no idea how to care for themselves when the government fell. A colony world wouldn't be like that."

Kane's laugh was a terrible thing to hear. His mind burned with black flames. *S/kourat is not Za'arain. There was no atavism on S/kourat to rise and rule minds. If S/kourat slid into barbarism in the years after the winnowing, how much more quickly would Za'arain slide back on the bloody claws of psipacks? Months? Weeks? Days?*

Hours?"

Were violet-eyed Kiris even now stalking Sharia through Za'arain's time-smoothed streets? Were they catching her, wounding her? Was she killing them and then healing herself again and again? How long could even a timeshadow rider of Sharia's skill survive?

Is that what his mind had been trying to tell him? Is that where he had to go?

"I don't know!" screamed Jode with his mind and his body, reeling from the mindspeech that Kane had unknowingly projected with overwhelming force.

Bronzed fingers closed around the psi-master's arm. With casual strength Kane hurled Jode onto the pilot's couch. Simultaneously, a lance of energy from Kane's mind merged with the Wolfin ship, putting it on full emergency status. Bone-jarring sonics trembled through the ship, sending crew members beyond the control cabin racing for the safety of their cocoons. A flick of Kane's mind held Jode's cocoon open.

"Hear me, pilot," said Kane in a cold, clipped voice. "I'm giving this ship a destination. If you do anything to hinder it, I'll shred your timeshadow until there is nothing left, not even a single color."

Kane had used the Za'arain word timeshadow precisely, pronouncing it as only a Za'arain could.

Jode heard the certainty in the alien syllables, and knew that he would never be closer to the final death. "I hear you," said the Jhoramon carefully. "Give me the destination. If your lias'tri is attacked while you're meshed with a Wolfin computer, even a Za'arain god couldn't untangle the result."

Kane's mouth turned up in a cold smile. "What do you know of Za'arain gods?"

"More than I did a few minutes ago. More than I want to." Then, softly, "Trust me, my friend. If it's possible to save your lias'tri, we'll save her."

Kane hesitated for a split instant, then one of the most closely kept secrets in the galaxy burned across Jode's brain. The psi-master reeled again at the force of Kane's untrained mind. The coordinates were clear, unforgettable. Though the contact lasted only an instant Jode was sweating as he addressed the quasi-life that was the brain of the Wolfin lightship. Immediately the ship changed course, speeding toward the nearest za'replacement point at full emergency power. Jode turned to Kane. He wasn't surprised to see a weapon in his captain's hands.

"You're a better pilot than I am," said Kane. "You can make Dani do things no one else can."

"Only because you refused to let me train your mind."

"I had too many secrets to allow you in my mind," Kane said flatly.

"I know. Now."

"Yes, now you know. You're going to let me into your mind, pilot."

"I can't keep you out," Jode said mildly.

"I don't want to hurt you."

Jode sighed and made a graceful gesture of acceptance. "I know. But she's your lias'tri, and you'll do whatever you have to. I did the same. It wasn't enough." Jode's face changed, showing a core of determination like the finest Wolfin steel. "I won't fight you, Kane. I want your lias'tri to live."

"Even if it means risking our lives?"

Jode's smile was thin and reckless. "Death is an old friend. I've been trying to visit him for nine years."

Kane smiled in return; it was a predatory rather than a reassuring gesture. "You may get your chance. You're going to take this lightship through the closest za'replacements between here and the coordinates I gave you. Orange, purple, yellow, red—it doesn't matter. We're getting there if we have to ride the Great Timeshadow itself. Do you understand me?"

"Should be a memorable trip," muttered Jode.

"I could ride your mind and make sure you don't choose an easy, distant za'replacement over a dangerous, close one." Kane looked at the black energy weapon in his hand. He slipped the gun back into its harness with the same casual speed that he had drawn the weapon in the first place. "I won't ride your mind. I trust you," he said, looking at the dim crystal on Jode's chest, ghost of a warmer past. "But," he added harshly, "I still don't understand lias'tri."

"You will." Jode watched Kane return to the captain's couch. When the Jhoramon spoke again, curiosity and caution mingled oddly in his voice. "Are you truly Za'arain?"

"Yes."

"And your lias'tri?"

"Yes."

"Those coordinates?"

There was silence. Then Kane said softly, "Za'arain."

"Za'arain," sighed Jode, despair and wonder in the same word. He closed his eyes and murmured a prayer for the dying in his own language. Then his eyes opened, focused inward. Between one breath and the next, he merged his awareness with that of the sentient lightship.

Dani. Jode's thought-command brought the ship fully alive.

Kane sensed the difference instantly, felt the currents of mind swirling and seeking, testing the limits of the ship's knowledge and abilities, extrapolating, choosing. Life shimmered over metal—a life more sensed than seen, tugging gently at the edges of Kane's awareness. As always, he marveled at Jode's finesse. Kane could have—and had—commanded the Wolfin lightship, but the psychic backlash varied from painful to agonizing. Like men living in a desert, who thought that oceans were a myth, Wolfins did not believe in nonlinear time. Za'arains, however, believed in time above all else; their minds were uniquely constituted to experience it. And for a Za'arain, merging with a machine that made no concessions to the multi-dimensional nature of time was like going through an orange za'replacement without a cocoon.

As though summoned by Kane's thoughts, his cocoon slid upward, folding him into a soothing fluid embrace. His mind was still free, however, still vibrating with urgency. He did not know how close he was to Za'arain in time. Spatial distance was irrelevant. Planets only a few light-years apart could be separated by many za'replacements. Planets across the galaxy from each other could by joined by a single za'replacement. The Joining was braided together by za'replacement nodes, not by lightspeed. Though Wolfin lightships could outpace light many times over, speed alone was not enough in a vast universe shaped by time as well as space.

Even the stubborn Wolfins finally had bowed to that reality. Though they did not believe in timeshadows—the energy wakes that all living things left on time and matter—Wolfins had learned the hard way that unless something living was on board, a ship could enter a za'replacement and appear anywhere in the galaxy. It took an immaterial, living timeshadow to anchor the material reality of the lightship to its own linear time.

Pain arced through Kane, black flames burning deep within the lias'tri gem, within him. His powerful body tightened like a drawn bow as his psychic scream radiated through the sentient ship. The pain passed quickly, leaving nothing, not even sweat, for the cocoon's tender embrace lapped over Kane's body, renewing him. The cocoon could do nothing for his mind, however. It turned blackly, savagery awakening beneath the restraints of a million years. *How far? Za'arain. How long? Sharia.*

It was the same question, really.

Delicately, ruthlessly, Kane's mind reached out to the lightship's homing crystal. Within that extraordinary construct shimmered all the known za'replacements, tiny molecules of color warning of transitions that were easy or hard or deadly, as well as all variations in between. Za'arain's location in space and time was represented by a shimmer of silver. The ship was a blinking silver dot. There were no easy lavender or purple za'replacements between the ship and Za'arain. There were not even any blues or greens.

Za'arain lay within darkness. Only one node was within light-years of the planet. That node was very close, too close, well within the planet's gravity well. The node's marker burned deep gold, an incandescent flame warning of dimensional energies unleashed, seething, deadly.

Kane was not surprised to see the planet and the za'replacement so close together in space. Nearly all stars and planets had gold za'replacement nodes within their wells, for gravity was an aspect of time. No sane pilot had ever put his ship into a gold node.

Yet it was the only possible choice if they were to reach Sharia while she still lived.

Good-bye, my Za'arain friend, whispered the psi-master's mind. With no more warning than that, Jode hurled the ship into the gold za'replacement.

Pilot, lightship and Za'arain screamed as one.

Three

For no time, for all time, an unleashed hell of realities without limit or number raged around the lightship. Kane felt his timeshadow twist and flex and then lick outward like an explosion of wildfire. Dimensions replaced each other dizzyingly, former and future timeshadows of the *then* and the *now* and the *always* writhing like streamers of plasma in a nova. Under normal circumstances, living timeshadows knitted themselves through a za'replacement without conscious aid, seeking their inevitable position in time/now with the ease of pieces of iron attracted to a powerful magnet.

But there was nothing normal about a gold node. In a gold za'replacement, the conflicts—among time and space, matter and energy, mind and linear reality—were so great that timeshadows unraveled.

Kane suffered the chaotic energies, dimly aware of the lias'tri gem as a center of sanity within the raging universe. Colors sleeted around him, through him, through the jewel burning coldly against his skin. He could not ride living timeshadows—but like the Wolfin ship's mind, the lias'tri gem was not living. Not quite. And Kane knew the jewel's timeshadow as intimately as he had ever known anything. Though Sharia had worn it for less than a year, the wake of her timeshadow on the gem was as vivid as fire burning in the heart of winter. He could not read the wake, because Sharia still lived. He could appreciate it, though. And he did. For him, Sharia's timeshadow wake had a beauty that surpassed words.

Kane reached instinctively for all the colors that poured through him, gathering those that were an aspect of lias'tri, discarding those that were not, braiding colors one with the other until the lias'tri gem's unliving, undead timeshadow wake was intact. The jewel became like a seed of linear reality dropped into a supersaturated solution of time; linear time crystallized out, and the *now* was limited to a single overwhelming probability once again.

The ship burst out of za'replacement. Thunder belled across Za'arain's silver skies, hammer blows of sound that rent the atmosphere and made the ground itself tremble. The ship shrieked endlessly, but Kane did not hear. He, too, was screaming. His body was as torn apart by material forces as his mind had been by time. The Wolfin ship was disoriented, shuddering, life-support systems no longer operating.

Half a world away, Sharia's voice rose in a terrible cry. Her crystal flared blindingly, colors running wild, sleeting through dimensions, tearing apart reality.

"An Eye!" shouted the man who was reaching for Sharia's throat. "She wears an Eye!"

Sharia heard only at a distance, for her whole being was focused in the exploding instant of unprecedented timeshadow awareness. She healed her own writhing timeshadow almost reflexively, having done it many times since the mob had finally trapped her by the fountain. She defended herself silently, touching people with her long hair, twisting their living timeshadows until people screamed and fainted and other pack members took their place. Even now she still fought against killing her cousins. She still hoped that they would tire of their futile beating on her and slink away among the ruins. But the Kiri pack had not lost its taste for blood. It never would. With a feeling of fear, Sharia realized that the self-healing was not enough this time.

Something was tearing at her, draining her life, a wound deep in her mind that even she could not heal. Soon she would not be able to sustain her own healing, her own life.

With a feral snarl Sharia loosed her control over the black flames of savagery burning at the center of her awareness. Her translucent silver hair lifted eagerly, riding currents of time that only she could sense, seeking all the colors of life. She lashed out indiscriminately, tendrils of her hair touching every living person within reach, a deadly silver whirlwind slipping through the Kiri pack's four- and six-fingered hands.

Those Kiris Sharia touched died, their timeshadows strangled in the grip of an unleashed Darien five.

The pack hesitated, then disintegrated with cries of fear and despair. Sharia stood in the midst of death, her hair a wild silver corona around her. Shattered colors raged out from the lias'tri jewel, colors stitched through with black lightning. Pain swept through her body, bringing her to her knees.

As she fell the crystal swung outward. Dimly she realized that it was the jewel rather than her own body that needed healing. But she could ride only living timeshadows, and the crystal was not alive. Not quite. Yet something about it called to her, coaxing her, whispering to her of a nexus between quasi-life and life that a desperate Darien five might ride.

With a cry of despair Sharia rode her own living timeshadow back and back, years peeling away as she sought the danger to the jewel's quasi-life in time/now, hoping that she would find and conquer the danger in time/then before the *then* consumed her. That was a living timeshadow rider's nightmare—if she rode her own shadow too far back into time/then, she would lose her balance and die.

Sharia felt it all slipping away, the colors and the currents, the timeshadow's braided beauty sliding faster and still faster, running through her fingers like blood or time, unstoppable, faster and faster. A single current caught her attention, a branching of the multi-colored torrent of her timeshadow. The branching marked the place where her life-force translated into . . . something. Her colors slid through dimensions, hungry dimensions, colors seeking . . . something. No. Someone. The tendril branching out from her timeshadow was changing even as she watched. Expanding. Colors and more colors, currents and eddies, electrifying life. Not quasi-life. True life. Alive.

Hurting. Someone was hurting. Someone whose torrential timeshadow felt more beautiful to Sharia than her own life. With a silent cry she poured herself into the exquisite, potent timeshadow, healing it with what little strength and consciousness remained to her. It was easy, incredibly easy.

And dangerous. Incredibly dangerous.

Yet Sharia fought to remain among the pouring colors, needing to know more of the strange timeshadow, needing to feel more, to twine as deeply with it as time with life itself. She didn't have the strength. Unconsciousness folded around her like a benediction, softly separating her from the enthralling timeshadow.

Sharia's body slumped onto the radiant white stones. Spray from the fountain washed over her, making her silver hair and body gleam. On her breast the lias'tri gem scintillated with every color known to life and time.

The Wolfin lightship groaned and shuddered wildly as Kane's mind swept out, holding Dani's quasi-life in an unflinching grip, forcing her systems to function once again. Cocoons flexed and resumed protecting fragile life, peeling away gravity's thick embrace as the ship's engines flared at full emergency thrust, dumping speed as metal screamed. At a distance Kane sensed Jode's awareness, a flickering, pulsating turmoil of colors shot through with pain. Before Jode came to full consciousness, Kane ruthlessly made a series of adjustment in Dani's energy patterns. Sweating, swearing, Kane rode the ship's quasi-living timeshadow, unraveling and knitting up braided colors with equal determination. The ship screamed and writhed. Kane ignored it. This was one Wolfin ship that was going to recognize all the aspects of time. Never again would the life-support systems fail merely because a za'replacement contained more than the usual five dimensions.

Finished? Jode's dry thought skated over the edge of Kane's awareness, leaving overtones of amusement mingled with something close to awe.

Yes.

May I take Dani in? You're squeezing her to death. That's not really necessary. She's a cantankerous construct, but rather lovable, all things considered.

Lovable? Not to a Za'arain mind!

Jode's mental laughter was like his body, black and smooth, rich with unexpected strength.

Gratefully, Kane gave Dani back into Jode's affectionate keeping. A determined Za'arain might be able to crush cooperation out of a Wolfin machine, but the price was time's own headache and a sulky lightship.

As Jode's mind spread through the ship, Dani stopped shuddering. Below the level of conscious awareness, Jode made thousands of tiny, reflexive adjustments to the ship's sentient machinery. The descent smoothed, though the ship was still burning through Za'arain's skies at a rate just short of suicidal. The cocoons remained wrapped around their human cargo, nurturing and nursing bodies that had been battered in the instants when the ship had gone crazy within the gold za'replacement.

Kane's cocoon had little more to do than to stand between him and the reverse thrust of the lightship's powerful engines. Kane's body was refreshed, revived. Even the headache that had come from dealing with a half-mad Wolfin machine could not diminish Kane's wonder at his physical well-being. He knew that he had not imagined the physical pain and the physical forces smashing him when the ship had slammed back into time/now deep within Za'arain's gravity well. He knew that he had recovered *before* the cocoon had resumed its normal functioning. He knew that even with the cocoon working at maximum efficiency, he should still be in pain; Jode was, though the Jhoramon's disciplined mind handled the ship exquisitely despite his body's complaints.

It was impossible; but somehow, somewhen, something had healed Kane, taking pain and leaving a marvelous wake of pleasure. He had never felt more vivid, more alive, radiant with perfectly balanced energies.

Shut up, Za'arain, complained Jode with a corner of his mind. *You're distracting me and making Dani jealous. Just because your lias'tri is a healer doesn't mean the rest of us don't hurt.*

Sharia couldn't have healed me. She can't heal at all unless she physically touches a living timeshadow.

Jode's laughter left an astringent taste in Kane's mouth.

You really don't understand lias'tri, do you? retorted the psi-master, his mixed feelings of surprise and sardonic satisfaction clear in his mindtouch.

Why does that please you? returned Kane with a thread of savagery.

The idea of knowing more than a god is . . . amusing.

I'm not a god!

Tell that to Dani. She's building altars and burning incense right now. As far as she's concerned, you passed a major miracle getting us through that gold za'replacement.

But we both know that Dani isn't very bright, pointed out Kane, sarcasm flickering like a whip through his mindspeech.

The ship balked, power stuttering.

Gently, cautioned Jode, laughter turning wickedly in his mental touch, *or Dani will see if a Za'arain god can fly without benefit of a not-very-bright ship.*

With a stifled curse, Kane withdrew from Jode's mind. Or tried to. Kane realized uneasily that he had not even been aware of entering the Jhoramon's mind in the first place. It was more than a matter of Kane's customary absolute control of his own mind and emotions having been shattered by the unexpected pain blazing from the gem that he had worn in perfect peace for nine years; it was the fact that, having been let free from restraints, his mind was . . . stretching.

Kane struggled silently to stuff his awareness back into its habitual shell, to live shut down as he had in the years since he had left Za'arain. The shell did not want to close. Having tasted freedom, Kane's mind was reluctant to return to self-imposed half-life.

There's a better way than going to war with yourself, offered Jode. *I'll teach you if we survive your lethal planet. Unless you have more secrets you must keep from me . . . ?*

The psi-master's calm thought eased the tension that had been creeping through Kane as he struggled against his own mind. With a sigh Kane thought, *No more secrets.* Then, almost below the level of thought, *I hope.*

Jode winced and closed his mind against Kane's powerful presence. The pilot did not want to be caught in multi-leveled mindspeech with a psi whose lias'tri might be mortally wounded at any moment. That mistake would ensure a one-way landing on the unforgiving surface of Za'arain.

Where? Jode's thought was single-level, as emotionless as a recording made by a primitive machine. There was just enough contact for simple mindspeech.

As delicately as he could, Kane gave Jode the coordinate for the shuttleport in Za'aral, coordinates that Kane had stolen from a Za'arain shuttle's limited mind on his way out to exile ten years ago. And now he was returning from exile, breaking one of the two great Za'ar tabus. When the Kiriy sensed his presence on Za'arain again, he would die. Za'ar death, death without rebirth. But there was no other choice. He could not leave Sharia to die alone and afraid.

No sooner had the coordinates passed to Jode than Kane convulsed with a terrible pain. At first Kane thought that the Eyes had discovered him, that he was being torn from his living timeshadow, colors shredding, dissolving. Then he realized that the pain was not his, not quite. His gem was changing again, dark within light, Sharia wounded. Dying.

Now! Get us down now!

Kane's demand scored across Jode's mind, making the pilot scream. Kane did not care, for he too was screaming, dying.

Using old Wolfin knowledge, Dani examined her conflicting imperatives and their ramifications in the order of their importance—save the woman called Sharia, save Kane, save herself that Jode and the crew might live, land on a planet instantly where it was death to land at all. The ship saw nonexistence at every outcome. At inhuman speeds Dani assessed her imperatives in light of the information that an angry Za'arain had forced into her quasi-consciousness. All but one of those possibilities ended in certain nonexistence. The remaining possibility offered a modest survival opportunity.

Calmly Dani took the raging energy of a Wolfin lightship on emergency power, increased that power until it teetered on the breakpoint of self-destruction—and flashed toward a nearby gold za'replacement. She could risk it for a short time. A very short time. A billionth of a unit.

Reality disappeared, consumed by sleeting energies. During the split instant when the ship was out of time/now, Dani reoriented herself, dumped energy like a star going nova and popped back out into time/now. After a few minor adjustments in arc, the ship was perfectly positioned to ride her incandescent tail in a long spiral down to the surface of Za'arain. Smugness radiated throughout the Wolfin ship. Though dangerous, nonlinear time was a very useful dimension.

Jode felt immaterial many-legged ghosts walk up and down his arms as he realized what had happened. Kane had taken a quasi-living Wolfin construct, taught it to recognize at least some aspects of multi-dimensional time, and in doing so had inadvertently created an entirely different order of intelligence.

A feeling of assent washed over Jode, a ripple of near-emotion transmitted through the net of mindtouch joining him to the ship. It was the first time that Dani had touched Jode any more deeply than at the most superficial level of his awareness. Jode no longer knew what the ship was, but he knew what Dani was not. She was not stupid.

Dani was feeling a good deal less smug as she seared her way through Za'arain's silver skies. Nonlinear time was an amusing reality, yes, but it was also very difficult. She was not nearly as clever as a Za'arain. She would have consulted Kane, but her new awareness told her that Kane was not feeling very clever right now. Certainly not clever enough to teach her how to survive the slipface between today and yesterday. The difference between time/now and time *now* was impossibly elusive.

It was also the difference between living and not living.

Kane's sweat ran into the cocoon where the salty, mineral-rich moisture was absorbed and returned to him as much-needed water. He lay rigid, helpless, trying to control the baffling pain ripping through him. He knew without looking that the crystal he wore was not clear. He could feel the cracks of darkness radiating through it as though they were radiating through his own mind.

Because they were. The cocoon was trying to heal the uncanny bruises spreading across his body, bruises that appeared as though fists or feet were battering him. Even as the cocoon succeeded in healing or ameliorating the physical manifestations of injury, his timeshadow remained tangled and unyielding, black cracks radiating.

The immediacy of Kane's agony faded, leaving him in control of his mind if not his beaten body. He touched the cocoon with a tendril of awareness. Obediently the cocoon offered him a view of the landing field. Empty. Za'arain's single shuttle must be on the inner moon. The ground was leaping up with dizzying speed. Za'aral's fantastic spires and spider bridges were beginning to emerge from the surface of Za'arain.

At Kane's silent command the view shifted until a single, vast compound condensed. Iridescent colors ran over the massed silver buildings like rainbows called from a fountain by Za'arain's magnificent sun. The view kept enlarging. Far below, in the center of white satin brilliance, Kane saw the last of a pack of Kiris flee toward the cover of the Kiri compound. Within the shimmering crystal shadow of the fountain, the pack left behind most of its members, dead, and a Darien five, dying.

Dani, get as close to that fountain as you can without injuring Sharia. Quickly!

The ship shuddered as Dani used Za'arain knowledge to override her built-in Wolfin imperatives. Many orbits too soon, she swept down, cutting a flaming swath across the city with her star-hot exhaust, and at the last possible instant before self-immolation switched over to her normal atmospheric-power mode.

The sudden change between propulsion modes resulted in a devastating implosion. Cocoons protected the ship's inhabitants, and Dani's rugged construction protected her own crucial brain centers. The city of Za'aral, however, was not so fortunate.

The outer spires of the city exploded into countless glittering shards. Almost all of the inner spires were webbed with fracture lines, testament to the ship's terrible descent. Dani swept across the radius of destruction toward the compound that was Kane's destination. The center of the vast compound was untouched. The ship had calculated well, knowing that her own survival was at stake.

As gently as a snowflake, Dani settled into the sacred center of the Kiri compound. The violence of the ship's passage through space, time and planetary atmosphere had left Dani's skin incandescent. Heat peeled off her in great waves that met wind-driven mist from the fountain in a hiss of instant evaporation. White satin pavement scorched and cracks raced outward as ancient stones that took the weight of the Joining's most modern spacecraft.

Let me out!

The ship ejected Kane's cocoon with a feeling of relief. It was not enough, though. The Za'arain mind was not so easily gotten rid of. Kane remained aware of Dani on a level that she could not evade. Irritably the ship stabilized her body on the fragmenting pavement, waiting for whatever her unwelcome god would bring next.

The cocoon opened, freeing Kane. Although he was beyond the steam ringing the overheated ship, the air itself was hot enough to make him choke. Quickly he plunged into the cooling mist, racing around the fountain's immense, turbulent silver core. The cocoon had healed Kane's body sufficiently that it responded to his demands. It was a false healing, though; he sensed injury somewhere, nagging at his strength, his time-shadow shuddering in slow disarray.

Kane burst out of the mist's soothing, concealing veils at the point where he calculated that the pack had brought down Sharia. There were bodies scattered everywhere: Darien bodies with translucent hair in every color of the rainbow. Kiri skin gold and red, brown and black, green and lavender and every-thing in between. Za'arains one and all. A million years of care-ful breeding had resulted in diversity, not sameness. All the colors of the Za'arain mind. Kiris in their six- and four-fingered modes, in their serenity and vaulting arrogance, their compla-cency and staggering artistic achievements. Kiri paradoxes lying dead beneath the sacred fountain's shifting caress.

But nowhere lay a Kiri with smooth, pale silver skin and hair as pure and translucent as the fountain itself. Nowhere lay a Darien with five-fingered hands and an enigmatic gem burning against her breast.

The absence of Sharia ripped through Kane. He had been so sure that she was here at the fountain waiting for him, sensing his presence at levels that had nothing to do with consciousness. He grabbed his lias'tri gem, afraid that he would see its colorful certainties flickering dimly beneath a veil of darkness. There was no change in the crystal, no colors draining into death.

Sharia!

The cry came from Kane's mind and body equally, but it was his mind that knew the answer. He spun and ran toward the fractured compound walls surrounding the immense fountain. As he emerged from the fountain's mists he saw a trail of blood.

He bent, touched it—knew it for Sharia's in a single rending instant of timeshadow awareness. The chaotic, painful impressions were an exquisite relief; they told him that Sharia was still alive, her timeshadow energies still inaccessible to him. If she had been dead, her blood would have been a revelation of the circumstances of her death, her life, her very mind, for Kane would have unraveled the timeshadow wake of her blood as easily as Sharia had knitted up her own living timeshadow.

Then the naked reality of Sharia's blood burned through a million years of restraints, exploding down through Kane's cultural time as quickly as a thought, bursting through to the instinctive responses of the dark eons when psi-sensitive Kiri packs had roamed the face of a planet not yet known as Za'arain. Rage and blood-hunger raced up from the deep past, feral imperatives ripping through Kane, tuning his body and reflexes until he was what he would have been a million years ago—the deadliest predator ever forged out of a cruel evolution.

Fragments of mist burned blindingly against the silver sky. Kane's inner eyelids closed in a reflex far older than Za'arain civilization. Instantly the light level became perfect for psi-hunting, neither too bright nor too dark; and currents of time swirled, glowing. Sharia's blood trail glistened with jeweled clarity, silent and compelling.

Kane flexed his hands unconsciously, an atavistic memory of claws stirring beneath thick layers of time and civilization. His memory held other things, too. Fangs no longer gleamed beneath his lips, but the feral snarl remained unchanged. Few Kiris were born fully furred, but skin still rippled in primal response across Kane's skull and down his spine. Deep in his brain, chemicals were released to carry messages older than even a Darien five's memory.

Casually Kane's hands ripped off his clothing, allowing his skin and hair to sense the undiluted presence of Za'arain washing over his body. There were messages in the lush air, chemical signals of fear and blood, madness and death. Kane absorbed them through his nostrils, his mouth, his skin. His black hair stirred restlessly, seeking currents of time.

He knew there were other Za'arains in the mist. Some of them were Kiris. Psis. He could taste them, feel them in his mind. Psi-hunters. Kiris were always born with a formidable weapon: timeshadow awareness. It was what made them Kiris, no matter whether they were born among the Kiri aristocracy or the other, less-gifted, less-driven races of Za'arain.

But Kane was more than Kiri. He was Darien. He could ride the wakes of once-living timeshadows with an ease and power that no Kiri could attain. On Za'arain, the very earth was infused with timeshadow wakes left by long-dead Za'arains. Those wakes could be manipulated. To a skilled, powerful psi-hunter, the city itself could be a weapon.

Kane was Kiri, Darien and five. And he was unleashed.

Four

Silent, sure-footed, powerful, Kane glided swiftly across the satin pavement toward a body huddled in the mist. The psi-hunter was Kiri, dying, violet eyes glazing as blood rushed from her torn throat. Kane waited by her, sensing the timeshadow knotting, transforming the woman from a deadly psi-hunter into a nonliving reality whose wake could be read by a short-haired Darien five. By Kane. Though atavism prowled with unheated claws deep in his mind, he waited for the last of the life to drain into time. Then he bent and buried his lean fingers in the woman's dead hair.

Impressions sleeted through him: faces and fear, past laughter and recent screams. The psi-hunter had hunted alone, and successfully. The brutality of the woman's memories both sickened and lured Kane. The siren call of mindlessness was unbelievably potent. It promised a savage cessation of intelligence and time, complete annihilation to the very core.

Eyes violet, Kane fought the hot seduction of atavism. Instinctively his hand went to the lias'tri crystal that was all he wore. As he brought it level with his eyes, splinters of color slid into his mind, twisting, spinning, shimmering, slicing through to that which was still Kane.

With a terrible cry, Kane let icy awareness return to him, chilling the savagery sliding hotly through his veins. After coolness came the long memory of culture stretching like a timeless rainbow between the bestiality of the past and the intelligent imperatives of the present.

Shuddering, Kane returned to sanity. It was a different sanity, an uneasy alliance with atavism; but it was not the unleashed atavism itself.

"Kane . . . ?"

In the instant before he recognized Jode's soft voice, Kane's atavistic reflexes re-emerged. He spun around, and readiness to kill radiated from his mind and his body. Jode stood motionless, body and mind absolutely still. Kane's inner eyelids opened, changing the color of his eyes from violet to rain, a marvelous transparency wherein the shorter wavelengths of life turned lazily, emerald and blue and amethyst.

Sane.

"Your lias'tri?" asked Jode, the words a long sigh as he realized that whatever had looked out at him from Kane's eyes was no longer there.

"Alive. Hiding. From the likes of that." Kane's toe nudged the dead psi-hunter.

"Can I help?" asked Jode softly, afraid to touch Kane's mind. For only an instant the Jhoramon had touched what Kane had become. Jode would not willingly touch that aspect of Kane's mind again unless life itself depended on it. And even then, he would carefully consider the benefits of death.

"Take out your gun," said Kane, his voice harsh.

The weapon appeared in Jode's hands with a speed that had deflated more than one downside bandit. It was the swiftness that Jode had taught Kane and that Kane had learned so well. As he had learned other things. Deadly things.

"If Sharia dies," said Kane quietly, "kill me if you can."

Jode's face became expressionless, his eyes burning like black stars. "Why?"

"She's all that's keeping me from becoming . . . *that.*"

Jode glanced down at the dead Za'arain. "That looks like any other woman."

"Did I look like any other man when you called my name?"

Jode's only answer was a tiny motion of his middle finger that brought the weapon into firing mode. Kane smiled thinly.

"Tell Dani," continued Kane, "that if you die she's to get off Za'arain and beyond the reach of my mind instantly, even if it means killing every last member of the crew."

There was a pause. "It's done." Then, softly, "Why?"

"Za'arain has lost control over its own. What chance do you think the Joining would have if Kiri psi-hunters rode Dani out to the stars?"

A ripple of emotion coursed through Jode as he heard the Za'arain word *psi-hunter*. A word that in comspeech meant absolute and predatory evil. He made a curt gesture of agreement with his head. "I hope that your lias'tri lives. For all of us." Jode glanced around the expanse of whiteness broken only by the massive, elegant transformations of the Kiriy fountain. "Where is she?"

But Kane was already turning away, the civilized imperatives of his mind satisfied by the precautions he had taken against the siren call of savagery. He ran lightly yet powerfully toward the compound, through the sinuous hallways, choosing new directions without pausing, drawn irresistibly to Sharia. The gem turned and blazed against his chest. He was very close now, he was sure of it. Another turn, another twist, a long leap over jumbled bodies into the huge audience room of the Za'arain Kiriy.

Sharia lay unconscious, curled into an alabaster alcove like a baby in a womb. Her long, translucent silver hair rippled over her like water, concealing her body. Psi-hunters crouched near her. Kane wondered whether they were worshipping her or closing in for the kill, and then he realized it was both. The room was littered with dead Kiri hunters. As he raced soundlessly across the floor, he saw a hunter spring toward Sharia. The hunter's fist battered through the seething hair to her flesh. Even as her body quivered, timeshadow energies twisted, writhed, knotted. The psi-hunter fell to the resilient floor, as dead as the glass walls themselves.

One blow. One life.

The hunters howled and shifted. Kane's inner eyelids flicked down, transforming the room with hunter's light. Each shadow, each line, each particle of light and life was utterly separate, distinct. He leaped.

The first two hunters died without even knowing that Kane was in the room. The sound of neck bones breaking warned the remaining hunters. They closed into pack formation and turned toward Kane. The floor beneath his feet quaked and shattered. It did not affect him; he had jumped for the pack even as it turned toward him. Kiris scattered from his deadly presence like mist, but two more hunters died, broken by a Darien Kiri's five-fingered hands. Kane pivoted on the ball of his foot, graceful and deadly, his powerful arms reaching for more hunter lives.

As he turned, his body brushed against the seething cloud of Sharia's unbound hair. The pack howled in triumph: The trap had been sprung. Eagerly they waited for Kane to die as the other hunters had died. A tendril of Sharia's hair slid from Kane's fingertips to his cheek in a long, questing caress. Exquisite pleasure coursed through him as translucent strands combed his timeshdow, untangling and smoothing his torrential energies.

For the first time since he had landed on Za'arain, Kane was fully sane. And being sane, he realized what he had done. He, an exile, walked on Za'arain. He, a five, was touching a five. *And yet he lived.* The Eyes of Za'ar slept, all tabus suspended.

Blind, shaking, hardly able to believe that he was still alive, Kane sank to his knees beside the alcove as Sharia's hair flowed outward in healing welcome. Gently he lifted her unconscious body into his arms, cradling her against his greater strength as he had when she was a child long ago, before the Eyes of Za'ar had driven him into exile.

As one the psi-hunters sank to the floor, bowing their unprotected necks to Kane in a gesture of surrender that was as atavistic as hunter's light.

Kane did not notice. Sharia's presence was a slow, soundless expansion of light that promised to end a darkness as old as time. Like the predawn hush on a planet with only one sun and few stars, the sense of *imminence* was almost overwhelming. The promise of completion was devastating. Kane felt he was a man who had lived his lifetime caged and bound and blinded only to discover suddenly that freedom and movement and sight waited for him. All possibilities, all pleasures, all colors. Waiting. *Imminent.* He had only to know how to grasp the elusive silver energies.

Slowly the trembling left Kane's body. Elation sleeted through him. Alive! He was alive! He had broken both Great Tabus and survived. The Eyes were powerless against him. He could not even sense their radiance as he had in his memories of Za'arain. In the end, Za'arain's tabus had proved to be no different from those of other Joining cultures. What was prohibited on one planet might be celebrated on another and ignored on a third. Five touching five was not a guarantee of Za'ar death and cultural chaos. Five touching five was a healing light spreading through his darkness, awakening—

What? What was stirring, called by two fives touching?

The uneasy thought vanished as Sharia's eyes half-opened, violet and silver mixed, neither knowing nor unknowing, neither Darien nor atavism.

"Kane?"

With the whisper came a rush of emotion. Kane knew Sharia's joy at seeing him touch the edges of her deepest dreams; he felt his own warmth sweeping through her chilled body. And then he felt her shattering horror and denial. Five touching five.

"No—we can't—catastrophe!"

Sharia's eyes closed, shutting out time/now—shutting out him. Yet even as her Kiriy-compelled consciousness rejected Kane, Sharia's body shifted reflexively and she sighed against his chest, curling closer to him, sensing safety in his arms as surely as she had earlier known danger from the psi-pack. Her hair moved in light caress across his shoulders, his cheek, his mouth, then settled obediently in her lap. Uncovered, her luminous skin revealed bruises new and old, blood fresh and dried.

The tiny wounds called irresistibly to something deep within Kane. His lips and tongue moved softly over her, silently cherishing, remembering a time when neither blood nor violence had marred her flawless skin.

Lias'tri gems shimmered and blazed, colors incandescent with . . . *imminence.*

Kane did not see. He knew only the sweet weight of the five who curled trustingly against him, her hair shimmering with quiet life. He wanted to wake her, to know again the silver depths of her eyes where flashes of color turned like unexpected laughter. But he did not. He had felt the strength of the Za'ar imperatives driven deep into Sharia's mind.

DO NOT TOUCH HIM. EVER.

FIVE TOUCHING FIVE. CATASTROPHE.

Only time could weaken the hold of those words—time and the presence of the man Sharia had greeted with a joy that was even deeper than Kiriy warnings.

Kane would help Sharia to shake off the bleak imperative. He would take her to the Joining, let her see and think about its endless variations on the theme of human cultures. She had been alone in a Darien five's utter isolation for the last ten years. For her entire life she had lived and breathed and believed in Za'arain culture, Za'ar imperatives, the inevitability and rightness of Za'ar tabu.

Someday she would accept that his touch wasn't anathema. Someday. In some life. In some time—if not in this one, in time/now, then in some other. Having touched her, he knew that he could not live through all his lives and times without her.

"Captain. We have to go." Jode's voice was a blending of envy and triumph as he watched Kane's deadly hands move so gently over Sharia's body. The pilot blinked, blinded by the reflected light of lias'tri gems. "Dani says that the ground is unstable."

For a moment Jode thought that Kane had not heard. The Za'arain's dark head was bent over Sharia's. His lips brushed slowly over her closed eyes, then he looked up with a sadness that made Jode raise his hands in silent protest.

"She can't be dying," said Jode, the only thing he could think of that would bring such grief to Kane. "Look at the gems."

Kane did not need to look to know that no darkness moved in either gem. He felt the perfection of the untrammeled time-shadow energies in every atom of his body. With fingers that shook minutely, he smoothed the living beauty of Sharia's hair. Silently he prayed to gods he no longer believed in that she would not awaken until she was safe within a Wolfin cocoon. She had been through too much, seen too much, felt too much; and the Kiriy had sliced through her helpless mind with Za'ar imperatives. Knowing that Kane had touched her would be too much for Sharia to cope with right now. It could shatter her.

"She is alive," agreed Kane. Then, with soft finality, "And I am forbidden to her."

"But you're her lias'tri!" protested Jode.

"The word means little to me and nothing to her. We are mature fives. We are forbidden to each other. Za'ar imperative."

"I don't understand."

"You don't have to," Kane said curtly. "It's enough that I understand. We go to the ship. Now."

"What about them?" asked Jode, pointing to the Kiri pack that watched Kane and Sharia with violet eyes and obediently bowed bodies. "Aren't we taking them with us?"

"No. They saw two fives together." Kane's inner eyelids flicked down, making his eyes as violet as the psi-hunters'. "Listen to me, Jhoramon. If you tell Sharia that I touched her, you will finally find the release you seek."

Predatory death waited in Kane's violet eyes. Deeply civilized intelligence waited there, too. The combination was eerie, compelling. Jode's skin rippled in primal reflex. In that moment he understood why twelve Za'arain psi-hunters had bowed to Kane.

Without waiting for the Jhoramon's response, Kane rose and strode into the shattered hall, carrying Sharia in his arms. She shifted against him. Even unconscious, she held herself for his

greater ease. Her hair curled along his shoulders before falling
to pool quietly between her thighs.

People ahead. The Jhoramon's thought was a delicate mental
whisper that requested but did not require Kane's attention.

Kane did not ask if the people were hostile. He knew that a
five touching a five had no friends in these glass halls. *Tell
Dani to light up.*

She already has.

At the same instant both Kane and Jode leaped aside, warned
by the Jhoramon's questing psi. A Kiri hunter sprang through
an open arch and slammed against the other side of the hall,
missing her prey by less than a finger's width. She did not get
a second chance. Nearly-invisible slivers of metal poured from
the muzzle of Jode's weapon. The hunter convulsed and died,
teeth bared in a savage, unsatisfied snarl. Kane and Jode ran
down the rainbow corridor. Neither of them looked back. The
Joining had taught Kane that there were times when compassion
had the same survival value as a broken back.

I don't know how I let her get so close, apologized Jode.

*She was Darien, though not a five. We learn to shield before
we even have a name for what we're doing.*

They had come to another radiation of the network of corridors. Kane took the left opening in a single leap, running toward
the Kiriy sanctuary at the center of the compound where Dani
waited.

Behind us. Jode's clipped thought hesitated, then condensed
like ice. *Ahead of us, too. Does this corridor branch soon?*

No.

Jode waited, sensing Kane's mind working with the sweeping
power of a river in flood.

How many? demanded Kane.

There was a pause before Jode answered. *Too many. There
is something else, occasional flashes. They feel like that woman
did. I think some of them must be Dariens, if that matters.*

It matters, responded Kane grimly. *I think Dariens can force other minds to obey them. Perhaps that's how psi-packs are ruled.*

Perhaps? You think? Don't you know? Jode's exasperation was clear.

Kiris ignore their own minds. The Eyes were all the psi Za'arain needed. Or wanted.

Jode did not argue. Like Kane, the Jhoramon now understood Za'arain reluctance to pry beneath the civilized layers that had tamed the savage Kiri mind for a million years.

When Kane stopped suddenly, Jode was ready. He had set his teeth and maintained touch with the Za'arain's turbulent, untrained mind, knowing that an instant's hesitation could be fatal in the coming fight. Jode realized that Kane was staring through the radiant glass wall. The psi-master squinted, trying to see through the transparent wall with its shifting, fascinating colors. A startled sound escaped his lips. His black eyes narrowed as he waited for the colors to twist again. When they did, he saw the shape of a distant Wolfin lightship veiled in heavy layers of mist.

All we need is a door, thought Jode dryly, looking up and down the corridor. Not an opening in sight, and with every breath, hostile Za'arains were coming closer, sweeping the corridors for prey.

Guard me. I'll see if I can make a door. Kane's thought was oddly hesitant.

Jode measured the thick wall, understanding the Za'arain's lack of confidence. *My friend, even you aren't strong enough to batter down that wall.*

Kane did not hear. He was focused on the wall. His inner eyelids were down again, clarifying light and shadow alike. Timeshadow wakes beckoned. The wakes were strongest at floor level. Za'arains had walked this corridor every day for a million years, and with each footfall their timeshadows had left patterns of energy that a psi-hunter could read. The patterns remained throughout years and centuries, millennia and eons. There was no way of knowing how many wakes had thinned and faded into other dimensions. Nor did it matter. Kane knew that what remained could be manipulated.

And that was all he knew, residue of an instinct older than the compound's vitreous walls. The wearer of the Eyes trained some Kiris to use their innate skills; other Kiris were ignored. No one asked why. It was a Za'ar matter that only the Kiriy was able to understand. But there were no Eyes, now; no Kiriy to advise or withhold. There was simply anarchy and atavistic death gliding through Kiri corridors. Death, and a Darien five who was determined not to die.

Kane reached for the timeshadow wakes permeating the heavy wall. He did not feel Sharia's hair seethe outward, wrapping around his body like molten silver. He did not know that her eyes had opened, inner lids drawn down until her eyes were as violet as his. He only knew that the wakes answered his summons. Energy cascaded through him, a sad aching beauty, colored echoes of countless former lives. Kane kept drawing the energies toward himself, stretching them like a bridge between the *now* and the *then,* feeling the sadness and the beauty, the aching and the graceful lives. He called to the timeshadow wakes until they could stretch no further, energy pulled taut, linear time quivering.

And then he let it all go.

Glass burst outward like an explosion of crystal mist. Kane blinked, returning his eyes to their normal pale color. Sharia's eyes closed and did not open. Her hair was again curled around his shoulders and across her thighs in a translucent silver cloud. Through the cloud, lias'tri jewels burned with uncanny light.

Jode stood transfixed, too stunned by the backlash of psi energies to move.

Out!

Kane's curt command galvanized the Jhoramon. He leaped out into the white stone courtyard. As he hit his full running stride, cracks were radiating through the corridor ceiling, the floor, the remaining wall, visible evidence of the shock wave racing through the compound. Deadly shards of glass showered down to smash musically upon the floor. Screams echoed, telling of Kiris caught in the crystal death.

Kane's Za'arain laughter turned in Jode's mind like green lightning as they ran side by side toward the quivering ship. Jode smiled, knowing this Kane better than the one who had pulverized thick walls with a few moments of thought. On planets throughout the Joining, he and Kane had outrun, outmaneuvered and outfought more than one group of downside bandits. The fact that these particular bandits were near-mythical Za'arains simply made the process more amusing.

You're a renegade, thought Kane, but silent laughter spoiled the accusation.

No wonder we get along so well, retorted the Jhoramon. Then, urgently, *Dani says that the ground is coming apart beneath her.*

Keep going. I'll catch up.

Kane slid to a stop, pivoted, and measured the distance between himself and the Kiri pack. This time when he reached for timeshadow wakes he did not hesitate or wonder if instinct would achieve what his conscious mind had never tried. He swept up the wakes and quickly began knitting them into a trembling, multi-hued braid.

Jode skidded to a stop and spun around even as Kane turned to confront his fellow Kiris. All the Jhoramon saw was the flamelike seething of Sharia's shining transparent hair. He sensed a knife-edge of alien psi turning, poised. Jode cursed helplessly, remembering how long it had taken Kane to pull his psi-trick in the hall. Jode couldn't kill enough of the pack before it reached Kane and his lias'tri and pulled them down.

A layer of pavement burst apart beneath the psi-pack, white shards flying, slicing mercilessly through flesh. Kiri screams echoed through the stone dust drifting down. Pack members began staggering and crawling free of the wrecked pavement. Calmly Jode took up a marksman's stance and picked off survivors as they staggered out of the blinding white dust of the pack's destruction.

Get your lias'tri to the ship. The Jhoramon's thought was cool, clipped, as unflinching as the needles bursting from his weapon and bringing down psi-hunters with uncanny precision. *I'll come when I'm through.*

Kane hesitated, then curtly agreed. He turned and ran for Dani's familiar haven. As he did, he sensed Sharia at depths and in dimensions of his mind that only the Eyes had ever penetrated. It was a sensation like light quivering in darkness. Whispered promises. Levels unnamed and unknown, opening. Colors turning, condensing, questing. A hunger and a need as deep as time and as enigmatic as a Darien five's mind. Two fives. Touching.

The ship rose above networks of stabilizers which Dani had extruded in a pattern that looked random but was not. Beneath and through the satin pavement, timeshadow wakes rippled, disturbed by Kiri minds. Cool, dense mist from the fountain swept over Kane as the wind shifted. He wished that Jode were at his side, able to see through opaque water veils to the Kiri hunters who might lurk inside. Hungrily Kane wondered how the Jhoramon used his mind to find others. At that instant Kane decided that Jode was right: It was time and past time that Kane learned to use his mind.

The cocoon's scarlet shell glimmered in the mist. Kane bent and tucked Sharia into the supple folds. She responded as she had when he carried her, shifting and balancing to ease his handling of her weight; but her hair refused to let go of him. It curled around his neck, clung to his shoulders, wrapped around his hands as though to hold him close and share the beating of his pulse beneath his golden wrists. Gently Kane disentangled himself, savoring the smooth living beauty of Sharia's hair even as he tried to tuck it into the cocoon's protective interior.

Tendrils escaped, quested, found and then clung to Kane all over again. He smiled as he had not since the day of his exile.

Be still, little five, thought Kane gently. *I won't leave you alone again.*

As though Sharia understood, her hair slowly abandoned its restless seeking and coiled obediently across her hips.

Red shifted and shimmered, sealing itself seamlessly. Kane stepped away, releasing the machine to return to the ship. It took an act of will not to follow. He felt as though he were being stretched through dimensions of time as he had stretched timeshadow wakes. He was being pulled toward . . . *something*.

Five

Kane!

At Jode's mental cry, Kane tried to shake off the odd feeling of being caught between dimensions, helpless. Finally he succeeded, but it required an effort of will that would have shocked Jode if the Jhoramon had sensed it.

Sharia's on board. Kane's thought was clear, bleak.

Then might I suggest that we leave your charming planet? I'm out of ammunition. I'd hate to have more Za'arains show up and not be able to entertain them properly.

Dark, iridescent Kiri laughter flickered briefly in Jode's mind. *Can you see the ship?* asked Kane, knowing how easy it was to get lost in the fountain's shifting curtains of mist.

Can you? retorted Jode.

Yes.

Then go aboard. Dani will reel me in.

Kane ran toward the ship's looming silhouette as though an azir were pursuing him. Fleeing toward the ship helped to ease the feeling of being stretched between dimensions. Although still hot from her precipitous descent through Za'arain's thick skies, the ship was no longer incandescent: Boarding could be accomplished without benefit of cocoons. That being the case, Dani had thoughtfully extruded a personnel ramp for her missing captain and pilot—for her pilot, mainly; her Za'arain captain she would just as soon have left on his home planet. With equal foresight, Dani had pulled four of Kane's Xtian warriors from their cocoons and put them on guard. Their steel-scaled skins blended eerily with the shifting mist.

With a few long strides Kane gained the top of the ramp. He turned instantly, searching through mist for Jode's running figure. An Xtian's supple, claw-tipped finger touched Kane's skin, then pointed toward a dense swirl of water drops off to the left. Jode burst into sunlight, running with a Jhoramon's fluid grace.

In! Another pack is coming through the mist! warned Jode as he ran up the ramp.

Kane hissed a command in the sibilant language of Xt. As one, the four warriors turned and vanished inside the ship. Kane hurled Jode in after them and leaped through the closing slit himself.

Dani has to lift right now!

Even as Jode's mind called its warning, the ship shivered. Light and sound and force lashed out from her stern. The Xtians lay on the resilient floor and prepared to endure an uncocooned takeoff. With one arm wrapped around Jode's waist, supporting the psi-master, Kane staggered toward the control room. Leaning against the Za'arain's enormous strength, Jode moved grimly toward the center of the ship, wanting only to be with Dani during the dangerous instants of balancing forces in opposition to the planet's deep gravity well. Lifting off without a pilot was terribly risky, particularly when the ship's brain had been so recently tampered with.

In the control room the captain's cocoon was in its normal place, but it was already occupied by Sharia. The ship should have extruded another cocoon for Kane, but had not. He dragged Jode into the pilot's cocoon and unceremoniously stuffed him inside. Instantly Dani abandoned any pretense of finesse. She reached for the stars with a stunning torrent of power. Kane slipped to the floor as the Xtians had. The normally resilient surface seemed as unforgiving as stone. Kane's last thought before unconsciousness was that the Wolfin construct was enjoying her revenge on the Za'arain who had forcefully readjusted her comfortable view of time and reality.

Jode's mind sped through the ship, balancing the forces with a delicacy that even the most brilliant Wolfin engineers had not been able to build into a ship's brain. The first thing that the Jhoramon sensed was a certain indefinable aura of smugness. By the time he realized what Dani had done, it was too late. Kane was unconscious.

That was unnecessary, pointed out Jode curtly.

Though he sensed at some elusive level that Dani understood him in a way she never had before, she ignored him. Jode continued to use mindspeech anyway. It was a habit the psi-master had fallen into the first time he had realized that the Wolfin ship was almost alive. It had pleased him to talk to Dani even though she probably could not understand and certainly could not answer him.

Just how do you intend to get through that gold node without a Za'arain guide? asked Jode.

A distinct feeling of startlement coursed through the net of mindtouch joining Jhoramon psi-master and Wolfin construct.

Jode smiled. He had been right. Something had happened to Dani's level of awareness after Kane had taken apart and reconstructed her view of the universe. The ship was definitely . . . smarter. *Call it even, Dani. In every way that counts, he's stronger than you.*

There was a distinctly sulky silence emanating from the ship.

I mean it, Dani. Hear me?

Disgruntled agreement dragged through the mindlink.

And whatever you do, don't take out your pique on Kane's lias'tri. He'll take your so-called mind and turn it into a tiny cloud of stripped particles.

?

Oh yes he can, Dani. Depend on it.

!

Dani put both her Wolfin and her Za'arain aspects to work on constructing a new cocoon for Kane to sleep in. When Jode saw the scarlet tendrils seeping out of the floor and surrounding Kane, the Jhoramon smiled. Dani was indeed considerably brighter than she had been. The last time Kane and the ship had quarreled, Jode had had to start up the machinery in contention himself.

Jode's mind flowed into the ship's external sensors. No one was following. Nor were there energy patterns that suggested other lightships were anywhere near. His smile increased. Crooning a soft Jhoramon song, Jode programmed in a course change. They would take the distant green za'replacement rather than the nearby, deadly gold. There was no hurry, now.

Jode flicked a thought in the direction of Kane's cocoon, impatient for the Za'arain to awaken. There were questions to be answered about Za'arain, legends to understand or demolish. And what about the silver-haired woman whose eyes could turn as violet as Kane's at the descent of an eyelid? Was she as dangerous as he? How had she survived until Kane had found her backed into the alcove like a baby jhora in its natal shell? Why were two people who were so obviously *connected* to each other also forbidden to each other? Was that why Kane had gone into exile? What culture would be mad or cruel or stupid enough to forbid two fully mature lias'tris their inevitable and extraordinary commingling of minds and bodies?

Not by so much as a tingle did Kane's awareness suggest that he was coming out of his healing sleep. Jode thought pointedly and sarcastically about the shortcomings of a sulky Wolfin construct. Dani trembled in silent apology. She had not meant to hurt the powerful Za'arain. Not really. And she had not had time to build him a cocoon before fleeing the surface. Really. Not nearly enough time.

Jode had begun a cutting summary of Dani's subliminal excuses when he realized that Sharia's cocoon was opening.

A cloud of silver hair swept out and extended to its fullest length. Beneath the protective hair Sharia stirred restlessly, then froze. Memories of the last days of Za'arain ripped through her, making her hair seethe. She had been healing people, endless people, untangling timeshadows until her hair could barely lift. That was how the pack had caught her by the fountain. She had been too exhausted to run. And there had been nowhere to run even if she had been able. They had surrounded her, pulled her down. She had managed to break free once, twice, killing Kiris instead of healing; but she had been so tired.

Then the silver skies had been torn apart, thunder as though the world were ending. The pack had scattered, terrified. She had dragged herself back to the fractured walls and rooms of the Kiri compound. She had found an alcove, wedged herself in, and . . . That was all she remembered, except for a dream of exquisite beauty, a dream of healing and warmth, of combing through a man's torrential timeshadow energies, touching colors, touching him.

The sounds of a lightship flying through space penetrated Sharia's senses. She did not know what the sounds meant. She did know that she had never heard their like before. She sat up slowly and looked around. Her eyes went from silver to violet and back again as her inner lid flickered in a nervous reflex. She saw a sealed scarlet cocoon the color of the one that was even now sliding free of her body. A tendril of her hair hovered, then coiled outward to rest on the cocoon. The energies she sensed inside were familiar. Unconsciously she reached toward the sealed cocoon.

As Sharia leaned forward she spotted Jode sitting like an ebony statue in the pilot's slot. His couch had elevated and swiveled, forming a comfortable chair. He did not look very comfortable, however. He looked every bit as wary as the Za'arain woman rising naked out of the glittering red cocoon. With reflexive courtesy. Sharia held out her five-fingered hands in silent proclamation of Za'ar tabu.

"How do you feel?" asked Jode in comspeech.

Sharia flinched at the meaningless, oddly harsh-sounding words. She realized that the dark, slender man was expecting an answer. She made a gesture of Za'arain bafflement.

Delicately Jode attempted mindtouch. There was a fleeting sense of confusion and fear. Nothing more. Sharia was as closed to Jode as Kane had been for four years—until a lias'tri gem had torn apart his Za'arain control with the kind of pain no man should have to endure. *Dani. Get Merone in here now! Give me a sleep dart based on Kane's physiology. Half-strength. Six doses and a gun. Quickly!*

Other than a subtle whipping of her hair, Sharia didn't move. Jode did not look like a Kiri to her or feel like one at the edges of her mind, but so many things had changed that Sharia could not take courtesy, much less safety, for granted. Grimly she prepared to defend herself as she had against her psi-hunter cousins.

Dani, thought Jode harshly, sensing deadly possibilities suddenly bloom, *get ready to dump Kane out of that cocoon the instant I give the order.*

A definite feeling of assent flowed back through the mesh to Jode.

Sharia's hair seethed outward. She tilted her head as though listening for something.

"So you 'heard' me communicate with Dani," murmured Jode, surprised. Even Kane had never overheard ship-pilot communications. "Well, you don't respond to comspeech and I don't know Za'arain. How about Jhoramon?" asked Jode in that language. "Wolfin? S/kouran?"

Patiently, Jode went through the four languages he knew and fragments of the six others he could understand after a fashion. Sharia listened with equal patience, sensing that he was trying to communicate with her.

Many words and phrases sounded vaguely familiar to Sharia, for Za'arain's language was a template from which many others had sprung. But languages lived and changed even as cultures did. All that came through to Sharia was a sense of concern from the slender black man sitting so quietly in the alien chair.

"I don't understand your words," said Sharia clearly, "but I would feel better if I could see your hands. Are you a five or a six or a four?" *Are you tabu to me? Are you the timeshadow that I found living in the time/then of my mind? Are you the dream I touched while I was dreaming? Why aren't you Kane,*

*who would have come to me if he could? Do you know about
the Dust and the Eyes of Za'ar?*

The urgency of Sharia's questions penetrated the reflexive
levels of her mental control, allowing emotion, if not meaning,
to slip out. Jode's eyes widened as he sensed the sweep and
clarity of her mind, the hidden depths and silver heights.

Both Sharia and Jode turned toward the chevron-striped
woman who had just come into the control room. Her head was
bald but for very short black hair growing from the black stripes.
The alternating buff stripes were smooth. The pattern was repeated wherever flesh showed through clothing. Her body was
thin and wiry and tough.

"How are you feeling today, Merone?" asked Jode.

The question was not random or polite. Merone had a Wolfin
translator embedded in her brain. Like most things Wolfin, the
translator was both miracle and curse. It worked, but the cost
was extremely high. Most translator wearers were somewhat
insane in every language they knew. The more languages, the
greater the madness. Working for Kane, a trader in antiquities,
had exposed Merone in six years to more languages than most
Wolfin translators had to face in a lifetime.

"Adequate, pilot."

"Good. I'm afraid I have a new language for you."

Merone's yellow eyes closed and the blunt on her scalp
stirred.

"Sorry," sighed Jode.

"It is my life and my honor," returned Merone quietly.

Jode made a gesture of agreement. On Wolfin, Merone's family was praised and cherished for the accomplishments of their
translator-daughter. Unfortunately, those accomplishments
would also be the death of her.

Sharia sensed the woman's disturbed timeshadow, a massed
writhing of colors that made the Za'arain cringe with unbidden
sympathy. Of its own volition her translucent hair swept out,
quivering with the need to heal. Merone was out of reach,
though, leaving Sharia no choice but to endure the discomfort

of being near to one who needed her and yet not able to touch, to cure. It was a discomfort that she had never known until the Eyes of Za'ar had closed. The Eyes had kept Kiris sane in body and mind.

"Sharia."

Her head snapped back toward Jode at the sound of her own name.

"I'm sorry if I'm leaving out titles or honorifics," continued Jode in comspeech, "but the captain only thought-spoke of you as Sharia."

She blinked at the sound of her own name, but it was a normal blink only. Her eyes remained silver, translucent, calm.

"So far, so good," murmured Jode. "Now, to make you speak in your own language. Let's see . . . ah, this should do it." Very clearly, he spoke a single word. "Kane."

"Kane? Kanaen ZaDaraien/Kiri?" repeated Sharia eagerly. "Do you know him? Is he here? Can you take me to him? Does he know who stole the Eyes of Za'ar? What is the Dust?"

When the questions stopped, Jode carefully repeated Kane's full Za'arain name. Another spate of questions poured from Sharia's lips. Merone listened intently, mind and Wolfin construct laboring together to dismantle the new language into its inherent logic of construction and to understand the inevitable illogic caused by creative or careless usage throughout the language's history.

Abruptly Sharia fell silent. She watched pain and effort carve lines on Merone's oddly striped face. "I wish I could see your hands," murmured Sharia. "If you're a four or a six I could touch you. It would be just a breaking of custom, not tabu. I did it many times in the Kiri compound after the Eyes closed. I'm not absolutely forbidden to touch all people, just mature fives," she continued coaxingly. "Let me see your hands. I'm a five, but I won't hurt you. It will be uncomfortable or even painful for me, yes, but that is the nature of riding living timeshadows. So few are comfortable. Come, let me see your hands. Are you the one who lifted me out of the jaws of my psi-hunting cousins? Is that why your timeshadow is so tangled? Do you know my cousin Kane? Please. *Do you know him?*"

Sharia stopped talking when Merone drew a ragged breath and clutched her head. Timeshadow energies writhed. Sharia's hair seethed in quiet sympathy.

"Merone?" asked Jode softly.

"The language is old," she gasped. "Very old. Older than S/kouran. Older than Lakaranata . . ."

Jode came out of the pilot's seat and helped Merone over to a nearby chair. Sweating, shuddering, the Wolfin woman fought to assimilate the changes racing through her mind. At last she stiffened and pushed Jode away. Sharia saw five striped fingers outlined against Jode's black arm as Merone pulled herself to her feet. She walked toward Sharia, who held out her own five-fingered hands as a warning.

"No!" said Sharia urgently. "I am a five and so are you!"

Merone stopped, understanding the negative if not the context or meaning. "Talk," she said slowly, her tongue curling around Za'arain's liquid sounds. "You talk. I learn."

"Learn?" said Sharia, appalled. "Every five knows the Great Tabu!"

"Talk," urged Merone.

For a moment Sharia was too stunned to comply. "Where on Za'arain can I be that the Great Tabu isn't known?" She looked at Merone's yellow eyes but found nothing there except interest. Sharia shook her head as though coming out of a Darien dream.

"Talk," begged Merone. Until Sharia spoke at length, filling out the gaps in Merone's linguistic understanding, the Wolfin's mind would be an aching turmoil. "Please," she said, reaching for and finding a new word synthesized from Za'arain inevitabilities.

"Long ago, a million years or more," began Sharia, her voice calm as she recited what every Kiri child knew, "Za'arain was not civilized."

"Za'arain!" Merone's voice was almost a scream.

"Silence," snarled Jode in cold, precise Wolfin. "You are here to learn, not to teach!"

Merone bowed her head and listened—and learned.

Sharia, who had understood only the repetition of the name Za'arain, hesitated and then continued. "Psi-hunters roamed, using timeshadow wakes to track and manipulate their prey. We used our skills to destroy each other rather than to enjoy or build. And the fives were worst. They were the strongest, the most unusual in their strengths. The fives redeemed themselves when Za'ar gave the Eyes to one of them."

Sharia paused, caught by memories. The Origin of the Kiriy was her favorite of all the Za'arain histories she had been taught. "The first Kiriy was born the instant he held the Eyes over his own and survived," she continued in a low, musical voice. "He saw all the overlapping timeshadows, all the possibilities, all the lives and laughter and grief. He combed out the Kiris' tangled minds, choosing those colors and possibilities that led to creation rather than destruction, celebration rather than annihilation."

Silver hair lifted, then coiled delicately in Sharia's lap. When Merone said nothing, Sharia continued as though explaining simple facts to a backward child. "The Eyes lifted us from savagery. Cousin no longer stalked cousin. We learned to build rather than hunt. Working together, minds and bodies, Kiris created beauty where there had only been random death. Not all Kiris or Za'arains wanted this. Long ago, Za'ar took the discontented hunters out to the stars and left them to find their own creation or destruction. Nor were they or their offspring allowed to return, even if they ultimately learned to move among the stars. That was the second Great Tabu."

"What was the first?" asked Merone when it became apparent that Sharia was finished speaking.

"Five touching five." But in Sharia's mind a single name turned, hunger and tabu warring. *Kane.* Kane and the Dust and the Eyes of Za'ar.

"Talk." Then, reconsidering in light of the linguistic knowledge seeping into her seething Wolfin brain, Merone used the words of courtesy rather than demand. "Explain, please, the first Great Tabu."

"No mature five may touch a mature five," said Sharia, her voice resonant with patience.

"Five? What is five?"

Sharia's hair shivered with hidden life, silver disbelief. Wordlessly she held out her five-fingered hand.

Merone blinked, pulling a transparent membrane down over her eyes as though she were on Wolfin's dusty surface. For a Wolfin such blinking was a sign of contemplation or confusion, the two states of mind often the same. Merone looked at her own hand. Five fingers. "Am I five?"

"Of course!"

"But Kiri no," said Merone carefully, struggling to understand as the language began to coalesce in her mind. "I no even Za'arain."

Shock burst through Sharia. Her hair whipped out with a slight keening sound like a distant wind. Inner eyelids came down. In the sudden hunter's light, Merone's buff stripes stood out like V-shaped beacons beckoning to Kiri claws, Kiri teeth, Kiri savagery.

"Say something soothing and say it now!" ordered Jode, his fingers wrapped around the weapon Dani had discreetly delivered into the pocket of his couch.

The knowledge of imminent danger made Merone's mind work very swiftly. "I no hunter. I no prey. I Merone, from planet Wolfin. You safe—are safe," amended Merone hastily as knowledge came to her straining mind.

The hunter's eyelids withdrew, leaving Sharia's eyes like silver opals again, rich with colors and curiosity. Despite Za'arain's xenophobia, the Kiris were aware of other worlds, other cultures, other peoples living among the distant stars. Za'arain's children. "Wolfin," breathed Sharia. "What are you doing on Za'arain?" she asked quickly. "It is forbidden!"

"I am not on Za'arain," said Merone quietly, feeling a great sense of relief that the language had finally coalesced in her mind.

"I don't believe you."

"Why would I lie? You're on a Wolfin lightship. Look around you. Is this anything you knew on Za'arain?" asked Merone reasonably.

Sharia's hair writhed strand over strand, creating a subtle whispering sound. "Exile," she said in a strained voice.

"I don't know about exile," said Merone, trying to explain in a barely understood language that which she was not sure of herself in any language. Za'arain customs were nothing if not enigmatic. "The Captain must have decided that he wanted you. Does it matter? You are here."

"An exile," said Sharia, and the softness of her voice was terrible.

Panic raced through her on the clawed feet of irrational atavism. She forgot that the Kiriy was dead and the Eyes of Za'ar closed. She knew only that she was trapped once again, this time by strangers rather than by mad Kiri cousins. Her hair whipped out and her eyes went violet.

Now, Dani! screamed Jode's mind.

Afraid even to breathe, weapon ready, Jode waited for Kane's cocoon to split. The Jhoramon had no idea what dosage of sleeping drug a Za'arain could absorb without harm. He did not like to think what Kane would do if his lias'tri died.

Sharia turned and looked at Jode with violet eyes. The Wolfin woman was a five, and forbidden to touch even in deadly vengeance. But Jode was not. She could see his hand very clearly. Six fingers wrapped around an oddly-shaped white object. Slowly, silver hair seething, Sharia rose and walked toward Jode.

With equal slowness, the weapon in Jode's hand came up level with Sharia's breast.

Dani!

Six

The scarlet cocoon split. Dazed, Kane struggled into a sitting position, wondering why the ship had forced him to awaken before the healing process was finished.

"Kane!" Sharia's call came from both her lips and her mind.

For an instant she forgot Za'ar imperative and the dead Kiriy's urgent warning. She forgot that Kane was utterly forbidden to her. She remembered only the sweet hours and days, the years of companionship and laughter, silence and warmth, the intimacy he had not been afraid to give or receive. Her hair reached toward him, called by his pain and by her own need.

Then she remembered. It was not ten years ago. She was mature now, and five.

And so was he.

Sharia's hair jerked back and wrapped tightly around her head as though she still wore a five's hooded white robe. Yet she could not control the radiant delight she felt at seeing Kane again. Memories of him were all that had kept her sane during her isolation as a mature five. She laced her fingers together and held on to herself until she ached. Even then, the sharp temptation to touch him first appalled and then sickened her. She closed her eyes, hating herself for even thinking about breaking the Great Tabau, for doing anything that might disturb the boundaries of za'. She must always remember the Kiriy's warning: If she touched Kane, Za'arain would never live again.

Jode flinched and looked away, feeling Sharia's grief and determination break over him like a cold, heavy wave. Then her mind closed with a finality that was stunning. Jode opened his eyes in disbelief, expecting to see that Sharia had vanished from the ship as completely as she had vanished from his mind.

Kane did not have the blessed relief of being shut completely out of Sharia's mind. He sensed her emotions as clearly as though she had shouted each one. Though the memories of what he and she had once shared were like a core of light and color shimmering within the black years of her isolation, the thought of touching him now appalled her.

He had expected as much. That did not make his pain any less, or his anger.

Even so, he could not entirely contain his pleasure at seeing her again, alive and vital, her eyes as clear and silver as Za'arain's skies. He remembered the warmth of her body shifting against him as he ran to the ship, the feel of smooth skin beneath his hands, the softness and living beauty of her Darien hair curled around his shoulders. With a vicious curse, he shoved the memories down to the deepest levels of his mind. It would be a long time before he touched Sharia again. Perhaps never. But she was alive. He could talk with her, laugh with her, remember with her. That was enough.

It would have to be.

A paradoxical feeling of pain and loneliness and joy rose up through the levels of Sharia's mind. She thought that it was her own pain at first, her own joy, a mixture of emotions that scored her as surely as the Kiri psi-hunters had. Then she realized that the emotions were not hers. Not quite. The difference was subtle, yet as definite as the difference between time/now and the *now.*

Wearily Kane stood and stretched, then walked over and smiled down at Sharia. When he spoke, all the discipline learned under Za'arain tabus and in the harsh realities of the Joining made his voice warm and yet casual. "Hello, small five. I see that Jode got you off Za'arain in one piece."

Kane's gentle, teasing tone set Sharia at ease. She looked up at Kane's familiar eyes, silver with clear shards of blue and green turning in their depths. Her head tilted back on her neck as she returned his smile. Although she was far from short herself, Kane was very tall. She had forgotten how big Kane was. Bigger than any Kiri she had ever known.

Then the impact of Kane's words sank into Sharia. *Off Za'arain.* Her hair shivered but still remained tightly wrapped around her skull. "Then that alien five isn't lying?" asked Sharia softly. "I am an exile?"

Kane looked around, spotting Merone for the first time. He frowned, understanding the connotations that exile had for a Za'arain. The second Great Tabu. "The Eyes did not exile you."

"But I am not on Za'arain."

"No," conceded Kane. Then, calmly, "The Eyes of Za'ar are closed. The Za'arain you knew no longer lives. Would you rather have died with it?"

Sharia shuddered. Her eyes flashed violet for an instant before she sighed. She said nothing, but Kane heard her speak unknowingly in his mind.

It is worth exile to see again the Darien five who taught me how to laugh. But my people—did they have to die so that I could laugh again?

With an effort that left his muscles rigid, Kane prevented himself from gathering Sharia against his body and comforting her as he had so often in the past. Life could be very cruel for a small Darien five. No one knew that better than Kane. He had been drawn inevitably to Sharia even when she was a child. Together they had shared a companionship that custom and tabu denied them in the larger society. Now her grief and guilty joy at seeing him again were knives turning in him. His own emotions were no better. The uncivilized part of his mind counted Za'arain well lost if Sharia were again a part of his life.

But it was more than just Za'arain that would be lost. Without Za'arain, the Joining would go down into a long night of savagery. The Joining did not realize that, but Kane did, even as the Kiriy had. He had lived among the races and worlds of the Joining long enough to discover how much of the Joining's scientific and social expertise was actually an import carried in the minds of Za'arain exiles. Without Za'arain to act as a hidden, supportive framework, the Joining would fragment into competing, isolated planets unable to recover from the winnowing.

And even worse, if just one extraordinary four- or six-mind still lived among the ruins of Za'arain, psi-packs could be melded into a potent whole as had happened once before in Za'arain's long history. But the second time would be different. Without the Eyes to constrain Kiri atavism, psi-packs could pick the technological fruits of evolution and use them to go out to unlimited hunting among all the planets of the galaxy. Then would come a long night of savagery from which nothing might emerge but death.

"What happened to Za'arain?" Kane asked quietly, just one of the many questions crowding his mind.

Behind him he heard Merone murmur discreet translations to Jode. Kane considered telling them both to leave, to give two long-separated Za'arains the gift of private speech. He did not. Whatever took place between Kane and Sharia, the Joining and Za'arain, affected every living person.

"I don't know the beginning, only the end," said Sharia. "I led a five's life."

Kane's inner eyelids flickered down, causing a flash of violet that reflected the sudden rage turning in his gut at Sharia's simple statement: *I led a five's life.* Solitary confinement. No company but her own mind, her own memories and the knowledge that she would be the first Kiri offered to the Eyes of Za'ar when the present Kiriy died. If Sharia were still sane by then. Many fives went insane during the years of forced isolation. The thought of Sharia being shunned and caged for no better reason than an accident of birth sickened Kane. He had accepted it once, unthinkingly, just as he had accepted his own exile. He had been Za'arain, then.

He was no longer. Not in his conscious mind. He belonged to the Joining now. He had not known it until he had seen Za'arain and Sharia. He had had the varied planets to keep him sane in the isolation of exile, and the memories of a laughing Darien five who had not been afraid to touch him. And dreams, vivid dreams, dreams more real than the waking thoughts they replaced. He owed nothing to cruel Za'arain, everything to the Joining and the Darien five who stood before him, confused and courageous in her unexpected exile. He wondered how Sharia had remained sane, what her thoughts and dreams had been.

Surely she must remember something. Jode's thought was delicate, but persistent enough to capture a fragment of Kane's awareness. *Gossip or rumor or fragments overheard in the corridors. Something.*

Kane sighed, knowing Jode was right. "When did you leave your suite?" asked Kane gently.

It was a simple question, and of so few words, but it contained the breaking of every courtesy, every custom known to four and six and five.

"I had no choice." Sharia's voice was neutral but her hair twisted within its self-imposed restraints.

"I'm not condemning you for walking out of isolation," said Kane. His mind said more, much more; there was a desire to comfort and reassure her that was almost as soothing as a tangible caress. "You survived," he said huskily. "I ask nothing more of you than that. Sharia. Don't ask it of yourself."

Sharia bent her head. "I—thank you, Kanaen."

"There is nothing to thank me for. Za'arain no longer exists. You must realize what that means, small five." Then, hearing himself call her *five,* Kane winced. Tabu pervaded the very language of Za'arain. He would teach her comspeech, and quickly. Though Kane's voice was gentle when he spoke again, he could not conceal the emotional force behind the thought or his fierce hope that Sharia could learn to question Za'arain verities and evade Za'ar imperatives as he had done. "When you walked the corridors of the Kiriy compound, what did you see?"

"Death."

"Psi-hunter death?"

Sharia made a negative gesture with her hand. "Not at first. Disease."

"Fever, convulsions, wasting and then death?"

Sharia looked up quickly at Kane. "How did you know?"

"We've fought that disease for ten years."

"We?"

"The Joining. We have a vaccine now."

"We did not," said Sharia distantly, disturbed by the fact that Kane had placed himself with the races of the Joining rather than the people of Za'arain.

"I know. Za'arain accepted nothing from the Joining but the returning of the exile shuttle. Empty." Kane moved his shoulders in a rippling shrug. "Apparently one of the shuttles wasn't entirely empty. The virus of the winnowing came to Za'arain." He looked at Sharia, seeing her hair seethe with emotions and thoughts that he could sense but not separate into meaning. "The Eyes should have been able to control even the winnowing," he said quietly, statement and question in one.

"I think——" Sharia's voice squeezed into silence, then resumed more calmly. "I think that the Kiriy was among the first to sicken. I think that the Eyes helped her, but not enough. She could not ride her living timeshadow and cure herself."

"You could have," said Kane bluntly.

"I'm a five. And so was she. It was forbidden that we touch." Though Sharia said no more, the fact that Kane had even implied that there could be a valid reason for two fives touching sent waves of fear through her.

"So Za'arain died to keep a meaningless——" Kane bit off the rest of his words and shut down his angry mind with a finality that surpassed Sharia's. He had had more practice controlling his innermost thoughts than she had. "Za'arain died to keep Za'ar's Great Tabu." Kane shrugged again. "I hope it was worth the price."

Sharia's face showed her shock at the rage and contempt that had for an instant radiated from Kane. She said nothing, though. She had seen the flicker of violet across Kane's silver eyes, and knew that violence lurked in the atavistic depths of his Kiri mind as surely as it lurked in hers. "The Kiriy's death was not what brought chaos to Za'arain," she said in a neutral voice.

"Then what did?" snapped Kane, trying and failing to control his impatience. Deep inside himself he realized that his seeing Sharia within reach and yet not being able to touch her was an acid eroding his conscious control. He had not expected her presence to affect him like this, as though she were every promise ever made to him, every dream, every hope—*forbidden*. He sent calming thoughts through his mind, phrases triggering discipline that was the earliest part of his Darien education.

"The Eyes of Za'ar closed," said Sharia.

"How?" he demanded.

"I don't know. Before the Kiriy died she summoned me. She spoke . . . in my mind." Sharia shook her head, still hearing echoes of Za'ar imperatives, of the Kiriy's power, sinking through her unprotected mind. "She told me that I should call to you with my mind. She told me that if she lost her gamble, the Dust Raider would come and close the Eyes of Za'ar. Now I must find the Eyes and open them again." She made a helpless gesture. "The Eyes are not on Za'arain."

Kane said nothing, his mind racing at the implications of her words. Sharia had called to him with her mind . . . and he had heard her. It was her need that had driven him back to Za'arain.

"Did the Dust Raider steal the Eyes?" asked Jode, waiting impatiently while Merone translated.

"I don't know," said Sharia simply. "The Kiriy said only that raiders from the Dust might come and the Eyes might close. The Eyes did close, so the rest must have happened, too."

Kane tried to absorb what Sharia was saying. Dust raiders on Za'arain. The Eyes of Za'ar stolen.

"Ask her if anything else was taken," said Jode in comspeech.

Kane repeated the question before Merone could.

Sharia shrugged with the same fluid movement of her body that Kane had used. "I don't know. It doesn't matter. Nothing matters but finding the Eyes. Then I will take them up and either die or become Kiriy." She looked at Kane. "If I die of the Eyes, you must take them to Za'arain. There you will take them up and either live or die. Za'arain must have the Eyes. Without them, we are worse than dead. We are death incarnate, eaters of timeshadows in the *then* and the *now* and the *always.*"

Jode's body stilled as he heard the Joining's worst obscenities fall from the alien woman's beautiful lips. Sharia did not notice. She was looking at Kane as though he were the only thing in the universe that mattered.

"You'll help me find the Eyes, won't you, v'orri?"

The old nickname went through Kane like lightning. V'orri, the massive black feline that prowled Za'arain's stormy canyons. She had called him that one day when he had found her crying after a round of cruelty from her four and six cousins. He had gone after her tormentors, laid five-fingered hands upon them, and had ensured that they learned the meaning of a Darien's anger. But like the v'orri, Kane had been always gentle with his own kind. With Sharia.

"We must find the Eyes," she said softly. "Without them, Za'arain is lost."

Kane said nothing.

Jode did, using comspeech. He would have used mindspeech but Kane was too closed for even the most elementary mental link. "Does your lias'tri really think a ceremonial object can paste together the shards of a culture?"

"The Eyes of Za'ar are more than ceremony." Kane's words were clipped, angry. He had come to resent the power of the Eyes, but he did not underestimate it. "They are real in every dimension of energy, matter and time."

Jode's response was skeptical but discreet. "I realize that ritual objects can be a potent focus of disparate social forces—" he began formally.

Kane cut him off with a good deal less formality. "The wearer of the Eyes sees all the overlapping timeshadows, the *then* and the *now* and the *always*. The Kiriy sees everything!"

"Except a virus?" suggested the psi-master sardonically.

"The Kiriy might see and not act. Only the Kiriy knows what Za'ar choices and truths are revealed by the Eyes."

"Sounds like your average downside god—unpredictable and contradictory because we insist on omniscience to explain results that could also be explained by simple ignorance."

Kane was torn between anger and a wry approval of Jode's pragmatism. "Perhaps. And perhaps not. Only the Kiriy knows."

"Convenient," retorted Jode. "And again, typical of a downside god. Arbitrary, capricious, and unknowable."

"But not powerless," said Kane evenly. "You're a Jhoramon psi-master, one of the most powerful and skilled minds in the Joining. Could you have controlled even one of those psi-packs?"

Jode hesitated. "No. You did, though."

"One of them. For a time. The Kiriy controlled a planet full of them. All of the time. The only difference between me and any Kiriy is the Eyes of Za'ar."

Black eyes opened widely as Jode absorbed the implications of what Kane was saying. "Are you telling me that the Eyes are some sort of psi suppressor?"

"I don't know what they are. I only know what they do. They baffle the destructive Kiri urges and encourage the creative ones. Without the Eyes, Za'arain would never have risen from savagery. And," added Kane deliberately, "neither would the Joining. Not in the last million years. Maybe not even in the next."

"What are you saying?" whispered Jode.

"The Eyes gave exiles only their lives. The rest of what the exiles became they built from nothing with their own hands, evolving mentally and physically to meet the needs of their separate planets of exile. Only in the last few centuries have the cultures had the ability to reach toward one another. The Joining is a very fragile construct, built on the backs of Za'arain's children, made possible by the skills of recent Za'arain exiles. Without a steady stream of Za'arain scientists, Za'ara philosophy,

Darien curiosity and Kiri endurance, the Joining would not exist. There would only be a scattering of planetbound exile-descended cultures that believe the stars are painted on the inside of a black crystal bell."

Jode smiled at Kane's allusion to Jhoramon legend. "So?"

"So the Wolfin Taramemnone was Za'arain. An exile. She designed the quasi-life ship's brain that made the Joining possible."

Merone made a sound of protest. Both men ignored her.

"Explain," snapped Jode.

Kane's smile was Darien, lacking in comfort. "Taramemnone's father was exiled from Za'arain more than three hundred Wolfin years ago," continued Kane. "Her mother is the daughter of another exile. The schools Taramemnone went to and the mental training she underwent were designed on Za'arain to help potential future Kiriy control their minds. It had no effect on the number of Kiris the Eyes killed, so the schooling and the discipline were discontinued. By then, Taramemnone's father was in exile."

The Jhoramon's mouth opened slightly, then closed with a click. He very much wanted to ask why the Eyes killed Kiris—and why the Eyes were allowed to kill—but Kane's expression was not an invitation to open-ended discussions. "Q/larro?" asked Jode.

The name brought another Darien smile to Kane's lips. "S/kourat's greatest philosopher was born on Za'arain. He is a five, though not a Darien."

"And Colu?" asked Jode quietly, naming the Jhoramon who had developed the vaccine that finally had caged the winnowing.

"He is Darien, and a five. On Za'arain he would have been offered to the Eyes if they had killed Sharia. If he survived he would have been Kiriy."

"He was an exile?"

"Yes."

"No. He was born into my mother's family. He was her brother."

"Then your mother's parents were exiles," said Kane, looking at Jode with new interest. "That's the way we do it. Exiles foster other exiles. Discreetly. We take care of our own." He smiled slightly, a more gentle smile than before. "You're part Za'arain, my friend. I'm surprised this Wolfin ship doesn't give you a headache."

The Jhoramon barely heard Kane's light teasing. Jode was still caught in the moment of discovery about his parents. He thought quickly, remembering his own questions about the uncle who was both bigger and quicker than other Jhoramons of his generation. It had been his uncle who had taught Jode to accept his unusual mind, and to use it. It had been his uncle who had trained Jode to psi-master status. His uncle—who had died in the winnowing, raving in a language Jode had never heard before. "Who adopted you?" asked Jode finally.

"I was too old. I was exiled only ten Za'arain years ago—that's about twelve Joining years. Any exiled Darien would have taken me in if I'd wanted, though. All I had to do was ask."

Sharia leaned forward, fascinated by what she was hearing with the aid of Merone's quiet translation from comspeech into Za'arain. On Za'arain, the Joining had been little more than a vague collection of planets "out there." When the Kiriy had spoken of the Joining as Za'arain's child, Sharia had not understood what she meant. Sharia understood now.

"Why didn't you go to the other exiles?" she asked Kane. "Do they shun fives in the Joining?"

Jode gave her a grateful glance. He had been afraid to ask and risk the violent flash of Kane's anger.

Kane's glance lingered on Sharia's clear, black lias'tri crystal wherein a thousand colors shimmered and burned. He looked up to Sharia's eyes. They were more compelling to him than even the lias'tri gem.

"No. Fives are not shunned in the Joining. But I had my

memories and my dreams," said Kane quietly. "They were all that I needed of human warmth."

"And you had that," Jode added, looking at the lias'tri crystal flashing against Kane's golden brown skin.

Surprise showed on Kane's hard features. He touched the crystal consideringly, wondering about the nature of the gem he had worn for nine Za'arain years.

"A lias'tri stone is very good company," Jode said, his tone both sardonic and oddly yearning. "It allows you to dream. . . ."

Sharia's indrawn breath was loud in the silence. She glanced at Kane and then away, feeling almost guilty for her memories and dreams. There was no Za'ar imperative to rule her dreams; and she had dreamed of Kane, deep dreams that had kept her sane in her sensory isolation.

With a trembling hand Sharia shielded the jewel from Merone's curious glance. Sharia's nudity had not bothered her before this moment, but having strangers look at the dark crystal sent waves of unease through her. Abruptly she shook free her hair. In a long, shining motion, her hair whispered down to her feet, wrapping her and the lias'tri gem in translucent silver. It was as though she wore a waterfall instead of more common clothes. The flaring colors of the jewel glimmered through like a fire burning beneath a glacier.

Kane saw, and understood. *Dani.* Kane's curt thought brought the ship's attention fully to him.

?

The feeling of the ship's attention focused on Kane was extraordinary. He had never been quite so aware of Dani's multi-brained mind. *Ship's clothes for Sharia and me. Now.*

It was a standard request, phrased in the standard manner. Perhaps Kane's concern for Sharia had given the request an edge it would otherwise have lacked, but that did not explain Dani's reaction. Kane was surprised to sense a whiff of an apology from the ship for embarrassing the Za'arain woman. The only emotions Dani had displayed before the gold za'replacement were of the most primitive sort—anger, blunt humor, fear.

To apologize for a minor oversight to human comfort was entirely new. Startled, Kane glanced toward Jode.

"Don't look at me," said the psi-master sardonically. "I'm not the one who took Dani's tiny little mind and stretched it in new directions and dimensions."

"I simply pointed out some of the inevitable ramifications of multi-faceted time," Kane muttered.

Merone winced and looked away. Nonlinear time was the penultimate Wolfin obscenity. The ultimate obscenity was one who had intercourse with timeshadows. A Za'arain.

"Is that all you did?" said Jode to Kane, sarcasm curling like a whip through the Jhoramon's supple voice. "To Dani, a few moments in a Za'arain's mind was on a par with breaking through to another universe."

"Does that mean she'll be easier for me to get along with?" asked Kane without real hope.

"I doubt it."

"If Dani gives Sharia a hard time—" began Kane.

Jode interrupted, knowing what was coming. "I've already explained to Dani that if she gave your lias'tri any problems, you would turn her Wolfin mind into a tiny cloud of stripped electrons in terminal orbit around the nearest black hole." Jode's smile was a thin crescent of serrated gold. "Did I leave anything out?"

"Did Dani believe you?" retorted Kane.

"Yes."

"Then you didn't leave anything out."

Ship's clothes—very sumptuous ship's clothes—appeared in Kane's and Sharia's cocoons. The clothes had a satin glow. Kane's were the exact color of his hair. Sharia's were the color of hers. Delicate traceries of colors moved within the fabric like shattered rainbows within Za'arain eyes.

"Looks like an apology to me," observed Jode. "Dani outdid herself. You could go to a Joining century feast."

"Is she apologizing for dumping me out of my cocoon before I was healed?"

As Merone translated, Sharia turned toward Kane with a hungry speed that made her hair whisper outward. She had sensed his pain as though it were her own; yet to have him admit injury was like having him ask to have his timeshadow ridden. Silver tendrils rippled toward him in the instant before Sharia's conscious mind reacted in horror. She could not touch him no matter how her mind and body hungered for him. Too much would be lost if five touched five. Za'arain. The Joining. Za' itself. Her hair whipped around her own head so tightly that she ached.

"Forgive me," said Sharia hoarsely. She looked at her own bare feet, for she was too ashamed to meet Kane's eyes. "I—I haven't been myself since the Eyes closed. To have injury or illness near and not be able to heal it is . . . painful. Especially yours, v'orri," she added, whispering, not knowing what her honesty did to Kane.

"We aren't on Za'arain, Sharia." Kane's voice was calm and oddly coaxing despite the flash of violet that had shuttered his eyes at her revulsion to the thought of touching him. "Customs are different in the Joining."

"Do mature fives touch mature fives?" she asked, her voice scathing and miserable at the same time.

"Yes."

"I don't believe you," Sharia whispered, shaking.

"Merone." Kane's clipped voice brought the Wolfin woman to his side in an instant. "Hold out your hand."

A tiger-striped hand was extended. Five fingers, clearly. Unmistakably. Kane's five-fingered hand closed around the Wolfin's hand. Sharia shuddered and looked away. Sweat bathed her luminous skin as she bit down on her own knuckles in an attempt to control the fear rising in her throat.

"The Eyes of Za'ar are closed," said Kane harshly. "There are no more Za'ar tabus."

No! screamed Sharia's mind.

Yes! countered Kane forcefully. His eyes flashed to violet. He did not stop to question the fury that Sharia's revulsion caused in him. He only knew that her rejection of even the thought of touching him enraged him as nothing ever had. He dragged Merone forward and held their joined hands under Sharia's nose. *Open your eyes!* The mental command was a feral snarl fully suited to Kane's suddenly violet eyes.

No! Don't make me! Please. Don't. V'orri. . . .

In the instant before she fainted rather than confront Kane's demands, Sharia's tangled, searing emotions poured through him, telling him what he already knew, what a surge of atavism had made him forget. Sharia had been torn away from her planet, her culture, her people, and now the one person who had ever returned her love was tearing apart her very mind.

Kane dropped Merone's hand and caught Sharia as she fainted, lifting her into his arms while he cursed himself in the molten phrases of Za'arain rage.

Jode gestured curtly to Merone. "You will say nothing of this to anyone. Go."

Merone turned and walked out of the control room with relief in every line of her body.

"I hope you're calling yourself every obscenity known to the Joining and Za'arain," said Jode after a moment of watching Sharia lying limply against Kane's much more powerful body. The Jhoramon's voice was rich with contempt. "Your lias'tri isn't a Wolfin construct to be dragged screaming into new universes at your godlike pleasure. Give her time. How long were you in exile before you could touch a five-fingered being?"

"Today," said Kane hoarsely. "Sharia. She was the first."

"By the Stone Gods!" shouted Jode, suddenly furious. "It took you twelve Joining years to overcome a tabu and you expect Sharia to overcome it in twelve minutes? You don't deserve that stone you're wearing!"

"I know." Gently Kane lowered Sharia into a cocoon, then knelt beside her with bowed head. "What's happening to me, Jhoramon?" asked Kane raggedly. "I've never been cruel to her before. Not to her. Not in all the years of our isolation. She is my life and she doesn't even know it. She is horrified at the thought of touching me even to heal me. What's wrong with me?"

"It's not you," sighed Jode, touching Kane's mind with a comforting, wordless tendril of thought. Jode understood more than the Za'arain about the nature of lias'tri and rejection and rage. At least Kane's lias'tri was alive. Given time, they would find their way through the tangle of manmade obstructions to the universal currents of life and need and beauty beneath. "It's just that you're a five," continued the psi-master. "Nothing personal at all. You must know that, Kane. If you had any other number of fingers, Sharia would have wrapped that beautiful, deadly hair around you and never let go."

The image made Kane shudder with a deep hunger that he could not have concealed from Jode if he had wanted to.

"Yes, exactly," said Jode swiftly. "You're beginning to understand something of what lias'tri is." The Jhoramon's voice was both calm and very said. "Did you know that the word lias'tri translates into comspeech as *hunger?* Body, mind, soul, all that you are. *Hunger.* It's the same for her, and it's terrifying her because she still believes in her childhood tabus."

Kane said nothing, merely watched Sharia's still body lying within the scarlet cocoon. His eyes were haunted by memories.

Jode sighed and stroked Kane's shoulder lightly with a six-fingered hand, understanding finally why his friend of four years had always retreated from human touch. Za'arain custom and tabu had hobbled an exile to the Joining. "Give her time, Kane. Tearing at her is like tearing at yourself. She's an intelligent being. After she's been out in the Joining for a while, she'll realize that Za'arain is just another planet, one among many. Its tabus are no more or less sacred than any other planet's."

"Do you really believe that?" asked Kane wearily. He touched Sharia's mouth with a gentle fingertip. Though she was unconscious, the deepest levels of her responded and a silver wisp of hair settled around his finger. The tiny caress made every muscle in Kane's body tighten.

"Yes," said Jode. "I believe that." He sensed the unease turning deep within Kane's odd Za'arain mind. "Don't you?"

"You've never seen the Eyes of Za'ar."

"Anything that can be stolen by a Dustman isn't a manifestation of the *All,*" snapped Jode.

Kane smiled bleakly. "A comforting thought, Jhoramon. I'll cling to it like my timeshadow clings to me."

In silence Jode watched Kane dress Sharia's unresisting body and then, slowly, permit the cocoon to seal around her. Because Kane had not closed his mind down again, the Jhoramon also felt the instant of startling agony that came when Kane no longer touched Sharia. The psi-master frowned and moved uneasily. There was a depth of need between the two Za'arains that was . . . too great. Perhaps it was simply that lias'tri was different between Za'arains. Perhaps it was that lias'tri had been denied too long, like a vast river dammed until the massed weight of too many seasons' water had burst out and swept down to the consummation of the sea, destroying everything in the way.

Troubled, Jode said nothing. He stood motionlessly but for his hand stroking his own dimmed lias'tri crystal.

Kane stood and pulled on his own clothes. The rich fabric murmured over his skin like translucent Darien hair. He turned away from Sharia's cocoon and faced Jode. "Get us to Jhora the fastest possible way."

"Why?" asked Jode, surprised out of his preoccupation.

"What single thing does every Dustman hunger for?"

"Ancient artifacts," said the Jhoramon quickly. It was common knowledge that among the Joining traders that the people of the Dust sifted ancient ruins, hoping to find the technological secrets of races and civilizations long dead. There was something about the Dust—or the people who were drawn to live there—that made Dustmen obsessed with ancient knowledge, ancient power.

"And what Joining planet has the greatest wealth of those artifacts?"

"Jhora." Jode hesitated. "But the winnowing killed so many of the wind traders."

"It's our best hope. We don't have time to sift the Joining for artifacts. Even as we talk, Za'arain is sliding deeper into atavism. If it goes too far, even the Eyes may not be able to bring it back." Kane made an abrupt gesture. He did not want to hear his worst fears spoken aloud. "We don't have enough money to buy information on Doursone, much less the Eyes themselves. With wind-trader artifacts, though, we can play upon Dust obsessions to get information about the Eyes."

Jode looked skeptical. "If the Eyes are a tenth what you say they are, whoever has them will hide them very well."

"No matter how carefully hidden, the Eyes will attract attention. Especially among recent Za'arain exiles. Our minds are . . . sensitized . . . to the Eyes. Even though I was far away, I sensed *something* when the Eyes closed." Kane shook himself, remembering the sudden leap and clarity of his thoughts, as though a gentle yet muffling veil had been removed. "First Jhora," he said firmly, "then Doursone."

"That pit," sighed Jode.

"Of course. Exactly the place a Dust raider would sell the Eyes of Za'ar." *Or wear them and die.* Kane said nothing aloud, however; he did not even want to confront the thought of someone taking up the Eyes and dying. Sharia dying. And most especially he did not want to confront the thought of what might happen if someone took up the Eyes and lived. Someone who had not been Kiriy trained, Kiriy chosen. Someone who might have nothing better to do with the Eyes than indulge the Dust's obsession with psi power. It was unthinkable that the Eyes of Za'ar would permit themselves to be so abused.

Yet he was thinking just that.

"We have to do it, Jode," said Kane. "And we have to do it quickly!"

The nearest sensible za'replacement was weeks distant. Jode hesitated. "Gold node?"

"Yes. Dani will handle it this time," said Kane, emphasizing the word time with cold certainty. *Hear me, Dani? If you don't handle it, I'll just have to teach you a few more things about reality.*

The threat-promise quivered through Dani. Before Jode could act, she reversed course and raced back toward the deadly gold node on full emergency power. Jode said nothing, for Kane was watching him with predatory violet eyes.

Seven

With wide silver eyes, Sharia watched images of the crew assemble in the lightcube that Dani had created in the control room. In their various quarters the crew saw smaller cubes that showed the control room. What they saw made uneasiness race through the ship. There was a stranger standing just beyond arm's reach of their captain. Nor were they comforted when Dani extruded a command chair for the woman to sit in, a simple act that proclaimed Sharia's status.

The crew was accustomed to the myriad human variations of the Joining, yet no one had seen Sharia's like outside of childhood myths. Her skin was softly luminous, brushed with silver. Her eyes were uncanny, both clear and glinting with color, as though silver opals had been set at an angle to the arching lines of her face. Her hair was a translucent, braided silver mass piled above her forehead. Light moved through her hair as though it were alive.

Kane began to speak. Only then did the crew look away from the woman. Uneasiness moved over their faces, an uneasiness that had begun with the silver woman and had redoubled as they looked at their captain. Kane understood the crew's instinctive response. He stood before them subtly changed: The dye had been stripped from his hair. His hair was still black, but it was translucent now. Light rippled deep within the thick, hand-length strands as in a finely polished gem. Freed of the dye, Kane's hair was oddly alive.

The Xtian warriors were the first to trace the source of their captain's changed appearance. They realized that Kane, like the silver woman, was Za'arain. They realized, and waited calmly—for they were Xtians, and Kane's.

Sharia watched the images of the assembled crew in the lightcube. The variety of shades and shapes of humanity did not surprise Sharia. Za'arains came in all colors, all shapes, all varieties. Any of the crew, even the subtly scaled Xtians, could have passed for native somewhere on Za'arain; under the guidance of the Eyes, Za'arains had explored and exploited the totality of their genetic heritage for the last million years. What did surprise Sharia were the subtle signs of former disease and imperfectly healed injuries that she saw among the crew. Such things simply did not exist on Za'arain.

Or *had* not. They existed now.

Eyes closed, Sharia fought to control the fear that crawled over her skin every time she thought of living in a place and a time unprotected by the Eyes of Za'ar. Being a Darien five on Za'arain had not always been pleasing or even pleasant—but it had been certain. She had known what each day would bring. Isolation. She had dreamed, days and nights mingling, true memory joined with thoughts of what might have been had Kane or she not been fives. The dreams had been vital, alive, as though she lived in another dimension, knew Kane in another time.

At first she had worried about going insane in her isolation and oddly real dreams. Then she had stopped worrying: If the world of her dreams were insane, then so be it. To live alone without dreams was another name for death. If she were to serve her people by taking up the eyes of Za'ar, she had to be alive. It was for the Eyes to judge whether she were sane.

Kane's voice drifted through Sharia's thoughts. She turned and looked at him with lambent silver eyes. To actually see him again was a miracle she still had difficulty assimilating. So much had happened, so quickly, so terribly: death and change, reunion and fear, joy and tabu, exile and Kane. She had dreamed many times, all times, and her dreams had been of seeing him again. She had a Darien's innate hunger for simple touch, for the warm glide of flesh over flesh, for the sweetness of another's breath flowing over her lips. She also had a Darien five's inculcated shrinking from physical touch.

Yet she hungered for Kane as she had never thought to hunger for anything, even life itself. And she dreamed.

None of it showed on the outside. A lifetime of Darien-five discipline was reflected in Sharia's utterly serene exterior. Her hair was so still that it ached with the ferocity of her restraint. Even so, she had noticed that the dark, slender man next to Kane watched her with a compassion that was almost tangible. She wanted to ask Jode why he hurt for her, but she could not do that without acknowledging that she hurt.

Besides, it was not a conversation Sharia cared to have by means of a Wolfin interpreter who looked at her as though she were hell incarnate.

Grimly Sharia decided to double the amount of time she had spent with the comspeech learning tapes. The language was not wholly alien; it was rooted in Za'arain complexities. Common speech was just that—common. It was a yeasty melange of Joining cultures, and it changed as the Joining itself changed. Comspeech was as intimately connected to the Joining as a timeshadow was to the life it sprang from. There was an innocence and power to comspeech's evolving meanings that fascinated Sharia almost as much as riding a living timeshadow.

Sharia tilted her head toward Kane. Eyes closed, she let her mind drift into its most receptive mode. When Kane spoke in comspeech, it was easy for her to understand the language. It was as though the rhythms and timbre of his voice made meaning inevitable. Like the sacred fountain, Kane's voice compelled and caressed her. She could listen to it endlessly, intuiting that which was never quite put into words.

". . . adjustments to the ship's brain which will permit us to use za'replacements that aren't available to other traders," continued Kane, easing up to one of the purposes of his speech.

Then, calmly, he told them what they did not want to hear. "The last replacement we came through was a gold."

Sharia watched and listened to the disbelief that bubbled up from the crew's images. She frowned and searched her mind for comspeech understanding. *Za'* was simple enough. It was the Za'arain verbal symbol for any nonlinear manifestation of time. The word replacement— Her thoughts scattered as Kane moved suddenly, impatiently, making light ripple through his Darien hair and smooth ship-created clothing.

"Silence!" he said curtly, a command that froze the crew. "Impossible is just another word for something you haven't done yet," he snapped, irritated by the crew's reluctance to accept a thing that had already occurred. "The first time in the gold node nearly finished us. That's the one you remember, if you remember anything. The second time Dani simply dumped speed. It was no worse than a red. The next time might be even easier. Dani is learning," he added dryly.

It was the first time Kane had used in public the name that the crew called the ship in secret—Dani, a demon out of Wolfin mythology. Kane measured the surprise on faces looking back at him out of the lightcube Dani had suspended at eye level in the control room. The fact that their aloof captain knew their secrets had surprised the crew. Kane smiled thinly. It would be the first—and least—of the surprises that he would deliver to them today.

"There are a few other things you should know," continued Kane, his eyes hard as they searched the assembled faces of the crew. "While you slept within Dani's tender cocoons, we landed on Za'arain."

The shock was too great for words. A collective grunt arose from the crew, as though a body blow had been delivered simultaneously to each member. Myth or reality, Za'arain was a terrible thing for Joining mortals to confront.

"The woman beside me is Za'arain."

Another low sound came from the crew. As one, people turned and stared at Sharia's image staring back at them.

"And I am Za'arain."

Silence, absolute and unbroken.

Kane met the massed stares of his crew with outward calm. He had known that he could not conceal Sharia's heritage; he would not have contaminated her Darien hair with dye even if she would have permitted him to do so. And after having removed the dye from his own hair, he had realized how much the dye had blinded his Darien senses. He had shut down his own mind, tried to stifle all that was Za'arain within himself. It had been necessary for his survival. The time cycle had changed, however. Yesterday's Za'arain necessities were nothing in today's Joining where the Eyes no longer ruled.

"Each of you has your own myths, your own demons, your own gods," continued Kane calmly. "So does Za'arain. We aren't gods. We aren't demons. We're simply human. Like you. Like your brothers and sisters, your mates and friends, your parents. Your ancestors. We are one and the same. The blood of Za'arain flows in every race of the Joining."

They did not believe him. It was there in their faces, their fears.

Silently Kane held his hand out to Jode, palm up. *Your knife,* thought Kane, and his mindspeech was as calm as his voice had been. *Cut me. Now.*

"We bleed as other men do," said Kane, his voice soft and deep. "We are human."

Jode's hesitation showed only in his mind. His hand moved swiftly. A line of bright scarlet welled from Kane's left arm.

Sharia's breath hissed out. A line of bright scarlet welled from her left arm. Reflexive]y she tried to heal herself. She could not. The injury was not hers. It was Kane's. Her hair seethed beneath her restraints, seeking to heal him, to touch him. She fought herself with the strength of panic. *She must not touch him!*

Kane heard her small cry, felt her turning deeply within his mind. He spun around, saw the red welling from Sharia's arm, and swore in the twisting phrases of Za'arain.

Jode understood what was happening before Kane did. He had heard of lias'tris whose minds were joined so closely that to bruise one was to bruise the other, but never before had he seen it so graphically displayed. The crew did not know of the lias'tri gems, however. The crew saw only evidence of gods or devils in the twin, simultaneous wounds.

Quickly Jode reached into Rae's loose black shirt and yanked out the lias'tri stone. Colors blazed in the cabin as the gem swung from Jode's clenched hand.

"The woman is his lias'tri," said Jode incisively. He glanced at Sharia, knowing that she did not understand comspeech but hoping that she would somehow understand what had happened. She surprised him by pulling her stone out of concealment beneath her shimmering silver robe, holding it out as he held out Kane's. "See?" continued Jode. "There's nothing evil here, and nothing divine. Simply lias'tri."

A long sigh escaped from the crew. Lias'tri was, if not common, at least not alien.

A chime called attention to Kane's command chair. A slot opened and closed, leaving behind a clear tube of medicine that was precisely formulated to Kane's physiological specifications. Jode snatched up the tube and spread its contents over Kane's bleeding arm. Within moments the cut began to heal.

So did Sharia's.

The crew shifted, murmured among its members, and accepted what had happened. Jode and Kane breathed a collective, discreet sigh of relief.

Next time you want to make a dramatic gesture, thought Jode, *warn me.*

I didn't know what would happen.

Obviously.

Jode's sarcasm echoed in Kane's mind. Kane stifled a scathing retort and turned to Sharia. "Are you all right?" he asked in soft Za'arain.

"I—I couldn't heal myself," she whispered. Though tightly

restrained, her hair writhed, twisting light into supple shapes. "Why couldn't I heal myself?"

"It wasn't your wound," said Kane simply.

"But it was. I hurt. I bled."

"My hurt. My blood."

Sharia watched Kane with dazed silver eyes, trying to understand. "Lias'tri?" she asked, the word unfamiliar on her tongue. "Is that—what does it mean?"

"Hunger," said Kane, his voice flat.

Sharia did not ask for any further explanation. She did not need one. Hunger. And Za'ar imperative screaming *catastrophe*. Her fingers trembled as she concealed the fiery stone within her clothes. With a feeling of sickness and shame, she looked away from Kane's eyes. Lias'tri.

Hunger.

Kane's anger and regret burned as brightly as fire for an instant. Then he turned away and faced his crew again almost gratefully, for their lack of understanding did not tear at his soul. "As all of you share in the profits, it's only fair to tell you that I'm breaking our trading schedule. S/kourat won't be our next stop. Jhora will. Then Doursone."

The crew shifted and murmured. Few but raiders traded on Doursone. Though technically part of the Joining, Doursone's grubby soul belonged to the Dust.

Kane hesitated, then decided to tell less than the full truth. "Something of Za'arain's has been stolen. I'm going to buy or steal it back. If I'm successful, each of you will become wealthy beyond your secret dreams. If I fail," Kane shrugged, "then your profits will be zero and I will be dead."

There was an instant of shock rippling through the images of the crew. People moved restively, then leaned closer, eager to hear more. They had followed Kane into some unholy, savage places; as a result they were unusually wealthy for their class and time. Kane was one of the richest traders of the Joining. His uncanny ability to separate rare archaeological artifacts from masterful frauds had made his name synonymous with success. The crew would not willingly separate from a captain such as Kane.

Even if he were that creature out of myth and nightmare—a Za'arain.

"In three days we'll be on Jhora's moon. Anyone who wants to opt out of ship's contract will be released there without prejudice. Your profits, of course, will leave with you. If I survive I'll return to Jhora as soon as I can and pick up anyone who wants to sign on again. Questions?"

There might have been, but no one was brave enough to ask any at that moment. The crew was too busy absorbing a reality that had shifted beneath their feet without warning, as though the ship were a planet subject to devastating, unpredictable quakes.

"Good," said Kane briskly. *Dani, shut down the cubes.*

Before Kane's thought had ended, the lightcubes vanished.

Sharia blinked, startled. Though lightcubes were common on Za'arain, she had rarely used them. She preferred her own memories/dreams to the bright entertainment and shallow communication offered by the cubes. Somehow the cubes had only underlined rather than alleviated the grim restrictions of Za'ar tabu.

Abruptly Sharia realized that Kane had said nothing to the crew about her being tabu to five-fingered beings. In fact, in the twenty-seven hours she had been aboard the ship, there had been no attempt to shut her away from Merone or Jode or anyone else. Even Kane. Especially Kane. She had been given a small cabin near his; she had tried to stay there in a Darien five's required isolation. Kane had not permitted it. Yet it could be so painful for her to be out among others. She was a timeshadow rider and a five. She looked at her damning hands, then clenched them and buried them in the loose pockets of her clothing.

"Kane?"

Though Sharia's voice was soft and she would not meet his

eyes, the sound of his name spoken with Za'arain music was enough to make heat dance beneath Kane's dark gold skin.

"Yes, small fi—Sharia?"

"You didn't tell the crew that I'm tabu."

"This isn't Za'arain."

"For me, Za'ar tabu knows no limit," she said quietly.

"Perhaps. Perhaps not."

"Kane, the Kiriy warned me. About you. About us. Touching. She—"

"Listen to me," said Kane, the underlying metal of command back in his voice as it had been when he talked to the crew. "The Eyes have closed. I will not cage you in the name of a time and a way of life that is dead. Nor will I permit you to cage yourself. Did you listen to what I told the crew?"

"Yes," said Sharia, her voice still soft, her eyes still refusing to meet the dark demand in his.

"Za'arain exiles have gone out to the stars for a million years," said Kane coolly. "Some of them have been fives. Some of them must have survived to maturity. If they did, they undoubtedly touched others. Did the worlds of the Joining come to an end at that moment? Did catastrophe strike even one world? Did the two fives who touched die the final or even the simple death?" Kane waited, but Sharia said nothing, did nothing, not even lifting her clear eyes to his. "Look at me," he said, his voice harsh. "In a million years, doesn't it seem likely that somewhere, somewhen, fives touched fives? Answer me, Darien cousin."

Sharia shuddered. "I don't know," she said in a strained voice. "I only know that the Kiriy's dying words were . . . Za'ar imperative."

"Count the fingers on my Xtians," said Kane grimly, cutting across words he did not want to hear, needing more from her than words. Much more. Lias'tri. *Hunger.* "They are fives. And they touch each other—frequently and with the greatest of pleasure. They are symbionts. They are fives. They are very much alive in this and every time." Kane took a deep breath and said what he hoped was—what simply had to be—a lie. "Za'ar tabus have no real force off Za'arain. In time you'll realize that, but not if you hide in your room. You must come out of that Za'arain shell and look, really look, at the worlds and peoples of the Joining. It won't be easy. It wasn't for me. But you've had less conditioning than I had. I was thirty-five when I was exiled from Za'arain. You're barely twenty-five. Don't hide, cousin. Learn to live as others live. Freely. Touching."

"I wasn't hiding." Sharia's head came up proudly. Her eyes were the brilliant color of fog just before the sun burns through. "Not in the way you think. I'm a living timeshadow rider. Do you know what that means?"

"Yes." Kane's voice softened. remembering many things, but most of all the incredible pleasure that had come to him when her Darien hair had wrapped around him, gently combing his seething timeshadow. Even when she was unconscious, her gift was potent. The thought of holding her conscious in the same way made him want to— Abruptly, Kane schooled his mind. It would be a long time before Sharia touched him in the way he wanted to be touched. A very long time. Thinking about it would only make it seem longer. "Yes," he said again, his voice flat, "I know what you are."

"Do you? Do you know that it is very painful for me to touch a living person?"

Kane's clear silver eyes opened wide. "What? How would you know? You've never touched anyone."

Shame took the luster from Sharia's skin. Her hands clenched together, fingers intertwined. "After I came out of my suite, I—there were other people. Kiris. I *tried* to warn them. *I held out my hands.*"

She looked at Kane in mute pleading, asking that he understand that she had not willingly or easily broken the tabus of courtesy and custom. Kane fought with his desire to gather Sharia in his arms and comfort her as he had so many times in the past. But she had been younger then, a very small five. She was small no longer.

"I know you wouldn't have willingly broken courtesy," said Kane, his voice gentle. "Don't judge yourself too harshly, sv'arri."

Sharia heard the affection and respect implicit in the word sv'arri. "I used to be 'small five,' " she said. "What have I done to become the storm walker's mate?"

"You survived." And only Kane knew just what she had survived, psi-pack closing, silver hair writhing.

"You also survived," she said, her voice barely a whisper. "Help me. v'orri."

Storm walker. V'orri and sv'arri. Mates.

Kane did not know whether the words came from Sharia's mind or his own. He did know that he was grateful for every bit of the Darien discipline he had ever achieved. It was all that kept him from touching Sharia, shocking her into a revulsion that would lacerate both of them.

"How can I help?" he asked simply.

"If I touch people who have wounded timeshadows, I can't help healing them. On Za'arain, a woman brushed against me in the hall. She was ill, injured, all but mad." Sharia's hands clenched. "I couldn't help myself. I touched her, rode her living timeshadow. It was horrible, like molten glass pouring through me, but I couldn't stop until her timeshadow was whole. It happened again and again with other Kiris. Some were not so painful; others were worse. Do you understand? With or without Za'ar tabu, I can't bear the agony of human touch!"

Kane closed his eyes, fearing that he understood all too well. *Like molten glass pouring through her.*

"Yes," he said bleakly. "I understand." Kane's eyes opened more dark than silver. He understood too much. He understood that if he touched Sharia when she was conscious, it might destroy her. He could fight tabus, even Za'ar tabus, Za'ar imperatives. He could not fight timeshadow realities. "I understand more than you know. I'll tell the crew that you're not to be touched."

Sharia sensed sadness condensing around Kane, twilight

draining colors into onrushing night, a night that knew neither color nor light nor the possibility of dawn. "Kane? Would it be better if I stayed in my room?"

His hard Za'arain mouth almost smiled. It was not a gentle gesture. "I don't know. Would it?" Kane measured Sharia's bewilderment in the soft line of her lips. For an instant rage turned in him. Psi-hunter eyelids descended, violet warning. Then control came again. Whatever had happened was not Sharia's fault. She could no more help what she was than he could help wanting her. "Don't lock yourself away. You've spent your life in a cage. You're free." He laughed curtly. "Odd how confining freedom can be, isn't it?"

"Kane," said Sharia, her voice strained, "I don't understand."

"Be grateful," snarled Kane. "I wish to Za'ar that I didn't!"

"What have I done?" she cried. "Do you hate me because I broke tabu? I touched no fives! I was the only five still living on all of Za'arain! I didn't break the Great Tabu!" She searched Kane's expression, but neither saw nor sensed a lessening of the rage burning deep within him. "Don't you believe me?" she whispered.

Kane's hand balled into a large fist as his eyes went violet. "I wouldn't care if you touched every five ever born. Including me! Most especially me!"

Sharia's eyes widened even as the thought of touching Kane made her hair shift and quiver, twisting light into shapes of desire. With a low sound she jammed her knuckles against her teeth and bit down, using pain to deflect her undisciplined thoughts.

"Don't look so horrified," said Kane wearily. "I won't touch you." He closed his eyes and gathered what was left of his discipline. When his eyes opened again they were both silver and dark, clear and flat. When he spoke it was in the lucid, unemotional tones of Kiri courtesy. "The ship routine is quite simple. The chimes—"

"I've memorized them," Sharia said, her voice strained. She felt Kane retreating from her, sliding away, twilight into endless night. *Courtesy? With me, his image?* Anguish was like lightning scoring through her. *Can't we even talk to one another as we once did? Did I survive the psi-hunters only to lose even my deepest dreams?*

Kane continued as though he had not heard Sharia's silent mental cry. He had no choice. There was nothing else he could do that would not hurt her more. Za'ar had had the last word after all, all tabus intact.

"Your emergency and normal stations are the same," continued Kane calmly, "—next to mine. When Dani turns on the sonics, get to your station as fast as possible." Kane indicated the command chair that Dani had positioned next to his. "That will change to meet the needs of your body and the requirements of safety. When the cocoon comes out, don't fight it. If you fight, Dani will drug you and roll you up tight rather than leave you unprotected during a violent za'replacement. Your ship duties are simple: Learn comspeech and the history of the Joining. You may eat alone or with the crew, whichever you prefer."

"What about you?"

"I eat alone."

Sharia looked down. "May I eat with—" She sensed as much as saw the sudden tension of Kane's body. "No, I'll eat alone," she said quickly, her voice too ragged to conform to courtesy. "I'm used to it."

Tension rippled through Kane as he fought against his deepest impulses. He did not want to hurt her. He did not trust himself not to touch her. Lias'tri. *Hunger.* He wondered if she felt it, too.

Then he realized that he did not want to know. If he found out that she hungered in as many ways and times as he did, even his Darien-five discipline would not hold. He did not understand what lias'tri was. He was afraid that it was older than Kiri atavism and deeper than time. If that were true, then he had no weapon to combat it.

And he needed to combat lias'tri. Anything that powerful also had to be deadly in the wrong circumstances. Unfortunately, he could not even begin to guess what those circumstances might be—which meant that the two of them had to be separated as soon as possible.

"As soon as you learn comspeech," continued Kane grimly, "we'll find a planet and a profession that suit you. Not that you have to work. I—any Za'arain—-would be more than pleased to give the Kiriy's niece a secure life."

Sharia's silent protest went through Kane like a knife. He knew that she had expected to stay with him, to laugh with him, to know again the warm companionship of her memories. But that was not possible. Kane could not spend an indefinite time close to her and not touch her. The sooner she was off the ship and out of his sight, the better it would be for both of them.

"What about the Eyes of Za'ar?" asked Sharia finally. Her voice was like her eyes, shattered silver, as she watched the dark stranger who stood in front of her where she had expected to find the gentle five of her memories.

"I'll find them," said Kane, his voice neutral, civil. "For the Joining, not for Za'arain. Does that satisfy your wants?"

Kane's thin smile made Sharia want to hide.

"You're the only one I ever wanted to be with," she whispered, "and you don't want to be with me. On the whole, I prefer isolation." Before Kane could speak, she added calmly, "It doesn't matter, v'orri. I'll probably die among the billion timeshadows of the Eyes."

No!

Though it had been thought only, Kane saw Sharia flinch. Her eyes widened into blank silver pools of shock.

"Yes," Sharia said finally, her voice unnaturally calm. "I am Darien and five. There is no other place for me, is there." It was a statement, not a question.

But her silent questions quivered in Kane's mind. *Why isn't my place with you? What have I done to make you turn your back on me?*

Kane could have answered those questions in the same silent manner that they had been asked, but to do so would have been to raise more questions, unanswerable questions, and questions whose answers would destroy her, victim of a dying Kiriy's mad imperative.

"Sv'arri," said Kane, his voice supple and caressing once again, "I would die the final death rather than hurt you. No matter what happens, you must believe that."

Kane sensed the rush of emotion that swept over Sharia as clearly as though it had been his own. And perhaps it was. Perhaps there was no difference. A single knife. Twin wounds. Lias'tri.

Hunger.

Eight

Sharia disengaged the teacher with the mental flick that Jode had taught her. Instantly the multi-leveled murmurings of com-speech and Joining history stopped. She stretched and watched the glittering tendrils of the teacher retract into the wall. The machine fascinated her, for it was unlike anything she had known on Za'arain. On Za'arain, the Eyes were the only teacher of fives. But this was not Za'arain. The Wolfin machine was a delicate, very useful shortcut for traders who had to know the basics of many planets and cultures.

Smiling, she remembered what was "known" about Za'arain. It was as unlikely a combination of myth and madness as she had ever encountered. Then her smile faded as she remembered that some of what she had learned was true. Psi-hunters existed. They were as deadly as anything in the known universe. Timeshadow riders—which the Joining either refused to ac-knowledge or confused with psis—could bring ecstasy or ag-ony, life or death, depending on the skill and the intention of the rider. Za'arains lived longer than the Joining norm of four hundred years; they weren't immortal, though. They bled and died just as any Fourth Evolution race.

Wolfin teaching machine and reality agreed on one thing, however. If Za'arain existed, it was forbidden to the Joining.

The other things that Sharia had learned caromed around in her mind like a tumble of jhoras trying to find a place in the sun. So many words, so many cultures, endless rules, myriad tabus. The only consistency was the lack of rationality. Marriage

between fraternal cousins was forbidden on one world and required on the next. On some worlds mottled skin was desired;
on others it was abhorred. The same with furred or unfurred
races. On yet other worlds, the precise hue of the skin rather
than its covering was all important. On one planet only men
held power; on another, only women; on a third, only men-
women pairings.

That was not the end of conflicting customs. It was not even
a tenuous beginning. It was as though there were nothing better
for human intelligence to do than create rules and requisites out
of the infinite variety of possible human experiences. There
were no logical explanations for the torrent of customs and
tabus. Only four-fingered people could rule on Zartag. On Megot, four-fingered people were slaves. The same held true for
five- and six-fingered beings; each had a planet of elevation or
scorn. But most of the Joining planets did not count digits—or
if they counted, the results were not codified into law or custom.

Was Za'arain no different in its tabus? Was the Kiriy wrong
in her fierce, dying command? Could five touch five without
catastrophe? Could she touch Kane?

The thought had come to Sharia the first time she had put
on the teacher and begun to realize the enormous variety of
human customs and laws. No matter how hard she fought
against it, the question kept returning to her mind—had she
spent a lifetime in isolation for no better reason than humanity's
inexplicable need to make distinctions where there were no
meaningful differences? The question repeated itself with each
new fact about the Joining, each new discovery, each new realization that the only absolute in human customs was that there
were no absolutes.

The conclusion ripped through a lifetime of Sharia's certainties, expanding through her mind like a shock wave, leaving
everything in its wake changed. She was too intelligent, too
much used to living in her own mind to hide from the ramifications of what she was learning. Tabus were relative. It was
that simple. And that shattering.

Like the Eyes of Za'ar closing.

Sharia lay on the bed and shuddered with the force of the conflicting certainties warring within her. For a moment she could not help wishing that she were back in the serenity of a five's isolation. So many changes had come to her. So quickly. Every truth overturned, every expectation mocked. And through it all, the recent Za'ar imperative chaining her mind. She wanted to scream *Enough! I can't take any more!* She wanted to turn away and pull the black of space around her and hide.

But there was no place to hide. The Darien part of her mind held her ruthlessly, forcing her to see, to learn, to change. The need for change was an urgency driving her in every level of her awareness. Even her timeshadow quivered with urgency. She had to change as the circumstances changed; she had to accept the unacceptable; she had to believe the unbelievable; she had to—what? What inexplicable revelation was she rushing toward? What was driving her as surely as a psi-pack keening on her heels?

Danger.

Sharia froze, sensing personal threat as surely as she sensed her own living timeshadow. She did not know the nature of what stalked her or how to combat it; she did know that her only weapon was movement, change, knowledge. She had to learn. She had to use her mind for something more than dreaming and regrets. She had to be as strong as the day ten years ago when she had sat in isolation and known that Kane would never again laugh with her. The choice then had been the same as now—ride the life that time/now had given to her, or fall off and die.

Ten years ago, part of her had thought that death or madness would be preferable to a life of isolation. The ruthless Darien part of her had refused to surrender. Denied external stimulation, her Darien mind had turned its questing, curious awareness inward. For a year she had sat wearing two gems, one light and one dark, and she had remembered in extraordinary detail the world that was now denied to her. The world that was Kane. She had lived in time/then, memories permeating everything that she was or would be, memories nearly alive, memories more real than a time/now of isolation.

At the end of that year she had taken off the silver brilliance of one stone, stared deeply into its uncanny fire, so much brighter than it had been, almost alive. She had held the stone cupped in her palm for a time that knew no measure. Then she had sent the stone out to the unknown, glittering stars. To Kane.

A month later, her memories had begun to change. More vivid, more vital, more alive.

And then she had dreamed deep dreams, visions of the *then* and the *now,* Kane a fire and a light burning up through her timeshadow, warming her. She had survived the isolation that had killed or driven mad so many Darien fives. Time had pooled around her soundlessly as she waited, wearing a gem that grew brighter with each day, each dream.

She had survived Za'arain's inflexible law by accepting it in her own way. She had slid through the cracks in time, running like sacred water through Za'ar's ageless restrictions. Today she would do the same. She would adapt to the Joining's chaotic freedom. She would learn what she could and slide through the cracks in what she could not accept.

She would survive because she must. On that at least, her Darien mind and the dying Kiriy's Za'ar imperative agreed.

Grimly Sharia sent out a mental command for the teacher to return. Just as the clear tendrils began to settle around her head, chimes quivered through the ship. The chimes were very low, sensed as much as heard. Not a full emergency but certainly an alert.

Even as Sharia sat up, the teacher whipped back into the wall. The corridor door hissed open an instant before she would have run into it. The narrow passageway contained a few hurrying crew members. Reflexively Sharia hesitated at the presence of others. Then new knowledge took over and she walked quickly toward the control cabin. She broke neither courtesy nor tabu nor Za'ar imperative by mingling with other people. She simply had to be careful not to touch them. Especially the five-fingered ones.

The Eyes of Za'ar might have closed, but the Kiriy's warning was clear. Despite Sharia's ruthless mind pointing out the illogic of clinging to old truths in a new reality, Sharia was careful not to touch crew members whom she knew to be fives. She, after all, was Za'arain. Literally, of Za'ar. The surface of her Kiri conditioning had been cracked by the necessities of survival, but the hard shell of that conditioning was still largely intact and heavily reinforced by her last audience with the Kiriy. It would take more than the teacher's subliminal seductions to change that. It would take time and repeated experiences as well as the urgency to change that was consuming her.

Chimes came again. Deep chimes. Last warning.

Sharia began to run, wondering what had gone wrong. Normally the ship gave everyone more than enough time to reach emergency stations. Suddenly a side door hissed open and someone hurtled out into the hall. There was no time to avoid a collision. Sharia braced herself for the pouring agony of touching someone's living timeshadow. In the instant before collision, she knew a flash of horror—the crewman was an Xtian.

A five.

There was a tangle of limbs, a feeling of almost metallic coolness as Sharia's hands closed around the Xtian's thick forearms, and a slamming fall that would have broken bones but for the Xtian's incredible quickness. He yanked Sharia onto his chest and took the brunt of their combined fall with his muscular back. The Xtian's timeshadow rippled and flowed around her like a multi-colored, irresistible cloud. With a reflex far deeper than Kiri conditioning or Kiriy command, Sharia's hair flowed out and surrounded him. She rode the man's timeshadow, combing out the knots and tangles she found, widening constricted currents, narrowing others where the colors had become too pale.

Within moments the Xtian felt physically more whole than he ever had in his memory. His eyes widened into green pools of surprise as Sharia's hair released him and coiled tightly around her head once again.

"Forgive me," said Sharia in shaking comspeech. She was surprised that she could speak at all. She had expected agony when she touched anyone, much less a five. She had felt only the odd texture of Xtian skin and the man's concern that she not be injured in the fall.

As the meaning of Sharia's words penetrated the Xtian's blinding sense of well-being, he shook himself like a jhora coming out of the rain. "Forgive you?" he said incredulously. "I knocked you off your feet and then you—what did you do to me?"

"I rode your—" Abruptly Sharia realized that if she finished the sentence, she would be uttering comspeech obscenities that would shock even an Xtian. The myriad conflicting customs and beliefs of the Joining whirled through her mind. She felt amusement flicker at this final, bizarre manifestation of human irrationality. "I, ah, healed you."

"I wasn't sick."

"Not in time/now," explained Sharia. "Old injuries."

Green eyes widened even more. The Xtian stared at her, then shot back the loose sleeve of his shirt. The powerful, vaguely scaled arm beneath was free of any sign of injury. He stared up at Sharia again with a combination of curiosity and something close to fear. "My scar," he said flatly. "It's gone."

"Of course." Sharia eased away from further contact with the Xtian, hardly knowing what she was saying. Amusement had evaporated in the hot seething of her mind as she tried to absorb the ramifications of the last few moments. She had touched a five and lived. There had been no agony, not even a little lash of it. Nor had Za'ar raked her timeshadow with the black claws of *forever.* Za' remained whole, untouched.

"But it's gone!" repeated the man, his voice rising. "The scar is gone!"

Sharia dragged her mind back to the Xtian. Suddenly she realized that she might have deprived him of something important. At least, the teacher had indicated that some cultures indulged in ritual scarring as a rite of passage into wealth or power or fertility.

"Did you value it?" she asked carefully.

The Xtian looked stunned. "What?"

"The scar. Did you value it?"

The man swore rather violently in the sinuous, sibilant phrases of his native tongue. Then he added in comspeech, "No."

Sharia sighed. "Good. I could give it back to you but it would hurt just as much as it did when you got it the first time. Besides, the scar was interfering with the full use of your wrist."

The man blinked, then began laughing. The whispery, breathy sound was oddly appealing, as was the knowledge that the Xtian warrior met the inexplicable the same way she did, with laughter. Sharia smiled in return, realizing that it had been a long time since she had simply smiled spontaneously at someone. What she did not realize was that her smile transformed her, giving her a beauty that transcended cultural prejudices.

The Xtian's smile revealed deeply serrated teeth. It was a very respectful, very male smile of appreciation. "This has been worth whatever punishment the captain gives me."

"Punishment? Why?"

"I touched you. He forbade it."

"It was an accident," said Sharia quickly. "I won't say anything about it."

"He'll know anyway."

"How?"

"He is Kane," said the Xtian simply. "And you are sses-Kane."

Sharia blinked. "What?"

"His mate."

"But—"

A sweet, mellow chime murmured through the ship, overriding Sharia's explanation.

The Xtian stood with a thick yet oddly graceful movement. "Whatever the alarm was, it's past. Are you all right?"

"Yes."

"Then it's back to work." The Xtian held out his hand and pulled Sharia to her feet. Then he swore. "Sorry," he mumbled in comspeech as she reflexively flattened against the wall to avoid his touch. "I forgot."

"It's all right," she said suddenly. And maybe it really was. Her hair had not even quivered at the brush of his flesh against hers. The Xtian's timeshadow held no allure for her now. There was no healing left to be done. "I'm just not used to being touched by anyone."

There was a moment of startled reassessment on the Xtian's part. "Then you can't be sses-Kane!" he pronounced. He smiled again, watching her with speculative jewel-green eyes. "Thank you, zas-Sharia." The smile faded as he looked at her. "It isn't good to go without touching," he said softly. "Especially for a woman whose hair smells and feels like Xt's spring sun. I am Szarth. If you would like to be touched, ask for me."

Before Sharia could reply, the Xtian vanished through the same opening in the wall where he had first appeared. She stared at the wall for a moment, thoroughly bemused. Then she laughed softly, meeting the inexplicable in the manner of all sane Fourth Evolution races. She smelled a wisp of her hair, looked at her five-fingered hands and laughed again. Still smiling, she walked back to her cabin and the seductive, merciless teacher.

In the control room a lightcube winked out. Jode turned toward Kane, whose expression was enough to give even a brace of armed Xtians pause.

"Satisfied?" asked Jode sardonically.

"If your little experiment had hurt her," retorted Kane, "I would have taken you and Dani's tiny little mind and—"

"Spare me the details. Dani is quivering enough as it is."

Kane sighed and ran his fingers through his thick, restless hair. He felt the ship's uneasiness as much as Jode did. Only a

Jhoramon psi-master could have persuaded her to set up Sharia like that without Kane's permission. "How did you know that touching the Xtian wouldn't hurt her?" asked Kane finally.

"Xtians are psi-null. It's the psi, not the flesh, that hurts her."

Kane's thought came too quickly for him to conceal it from Jode. *Then I'll never be able to touch her!*

"Don't be ridiculous," snapped the Jhoramon, his mind smarting from the force of Kane's undisciplined cry. "She's your lias'tri."

"I'm hardly psi-null," said Kane coldly. "I'll hurt her."

Jode ran his palm over his hairless skull in a Jhoramon gesture that meant he was puzzled, exasperated and amused all at once. In silence he studied the ship displays on the control panels, trying to control his absurd impulse to laugh. After a moment he took a breath, turned, and gave the powerful, volatile Za'arain a long look.

"Are you listening?" asked Jode quietly. "Or would you like me to stuff it into your mind, too?"

"I'm listening," said Kane grudgingly, scowling.

"If you and Sharia weren't mentally and physically compatible down to the bottom of your bizarre Za'arain souls," snapped Jode, "those lias'tri crystals would have killed you years ago."

Kane turned on Jode with a swiftness that could only be equaled by an Xtian warrior. "What are you taking about?" he demanded.

"Lias'tri. But you're not listening."

Kane opened his lips in a snarl. For an instant his eyes showed violet. Then he subsided with an effort that left his muscles rigid. "I'm listening." He hesitated, then added in the forced tones of courtesy, "I'm sorry, pilot. Lately it's all I can do to keep from killing something. Anything. I don't know what's wrong."

Compassion shone out of Jode's dark eyes. He gave Kane a gentle mental touch. *Lias'tri. Hunger.* "That's why I forced the issue," said Jode, abandoning mindtouch with Kane because it was like thrusting his hand into lava. "Sharia has been in her cabin for five days, never leaving, letting the teacher pour a lifetime of experience and philosophies into her. Anyone else would have gone insane under that kind of forced learning."

"She's Darien, and five."

"Someday you must tell me what that means."

Kane's smile was feral. "It means that she will survive. That's what Dariens are best at. Surviving. Most of the Kiriys of Za'arian have been Dariens. Three of the last four have been Darien fives."

What Kane did not say was that the Eyes killed a hundred Darien Kiris to get to the one who did survive. The thought of Sharia facing those kinds of odds made rage uncurl deep in his body and his mind. So he did not think. He focused all of his awareness on Jode's words. He listened.

"The teacher indicates that Sharia is an apt pupil." Jode's smile was sardonic. "Not surprising. Survivors are those who learn the first time, and quickly. She's asking questions, drawing conclusions, thinking. A lot of that." Jode smiled absently. "Your lias'tri has a fine, deep, quick mind. Unlike you, she uses it. She's learning in a few days what it took you years to realize. The Joining is not Za'arain."

Kane laughed harshly but he said nothing.

"She has a greater incentive to learn than you," admitted Jode, smiling. Then the smile faded. "She doesn't know why, but she knows that she will have to overcome her ingrained revulsion against touching a five. She knows that her sanity and very probably her life depends on it." He hesitated, then shrugged. There was no point in withholding the truth. "And so does yours."

"What?"

"Lias'tri," said Jode simply. "That's why you're within a heartbeat of killing rage every moment you are awake. That's why your dreams are raging, hungry, wild. Circumstances have kept you separate from her for years. Then you are suddenly together. Everything that you have damned up, everything that you both are, is demanding that you live as you were meant to live. Together. Touching. Mind and body and timeshadow," said Jode, using the comspeech word despite its obscene connotations. "Dreams are no longer enough to survive on. Lias'tri will know itself whole . . . or it will destroy itself."

Kane shuddered at the certainty and compassion in Jode's voice. "How long?"

Again, the Jhoramon hesitated. Again, he decided that the truth was more valuable than any evasion. "I don't know. How long can you hold onto your control? How long can she keep that hungry, healing hair under wraps?"

The shudder that went through Kane this time had nothing to do with Jode's words, everything to do with memories of Sharia's hair moving over him in a living caress. He wrenched his mind away from memories' dangerous temptations.

"How long will it take her to overcome a lifetime of conditioning?" continued Jode. "And it must be overcome completely. If she is unwilling at any level, you'll destroy instead of create each other."

"How much time?" asked Kane tightly, remembering the instant on Za'arain when he had sensed the Za'ar imperative ruling Sharia's mind.

The Jhoramon's compassion lapped over Kane like a warm breath. "She's learning very quickly. Remember her smile? She didn't find Szarath repulsive, despite his five-fingered hands."

Jealousy went like black lightning through Kane's mind. Jode winced but said nothing. Thwarted lias'tris were not known for their rationality. Their rage, however, was legend. Za'arains, too, were legendary in their rage.

"I am a Za'arain, a Kiri, a Darien, a five," said Kane, his voice bleak, his inner eyelids flickering down, changing everything he saw. "She may be able to exempt an alien from Za'ar tabu. She won't exempt me. Not easily. And certainly not quickly. The last act of the Eyes of Za'ar was to specifically renew the tabu against me in Sharia's mind. Somehow the dying Kiriy knew—" Rage swept up, closing Kane's throat against all but feral sounds.

Jode saw the violet-eyed Kiri sitting in the captain's chair and held his breath. Slowly, keeping his mind carefully blank, Jode's fingers curled around the potent soporific he had concealed within his pocket. The drug would not hurt Kane, but it would surely put him down. Jode did not want to use it. He wanted Kane to control himself. Drugs only worked on the surface of the mind; lias'tri went all the way through to the soul.

What is the most beautiful thing you have ever known? asked Jode softly, his mindtouch deft despite the molten agony spreading through him from contact with even the surface of Kane's awareness.

Immediately a picture came to Kane's mind: Sharia asleep in his arms, curled trustingly against him, her lips smiling though tears still glittered in her smoky eyelashes. He had made her laugh despite her anger and shame at her cousins' taunts. He had soothed her until she slept. Then he had stood and carried her to her bed. When he would have walked away, her hair had whispered out to him, surrounding him in a silver cloud. It was the first time that her hair had lifted for anything but the healing that came so potently to her. Torn between the beauty of her touch and the knowledge that soon she would be tabu to him, he had lain beside her, held her, known the glory of her Darien hair clinging to him. She had been on the breakpoint of womanhood, too young to realize what she was doing. He had known that, and had taken from her only a single kiss, a man's kiss for a woman he desired. She had responded with a beauty that had transformed him. He had felt her flow through him, felt himself answer, felt her wild silver hair caressing him as their flesh and timeshadows reached hungrily for that which waited.

And then they both had known the brush of the Kiriy's iridescent, implacable mind. Compassion had poured through them, a sad understanding that was like night descending. In the wake of darkness came a sleep that had not ended until Kane awoke on a shuttle headed for Za'arain's inner moon. Exiled. Sharia had awakened in her suite knowing the icy sheath of a lifetime's isolation stretching before her.

Jode sighed and withdrew from Kane's mind, disturbed by the memories they had shared. Kane knew little about lias'tri. Jode was discovering how little he knew about Za'arain.

Kane's shared memory of the Kiriy's incredible mind sent prickles of awe through Jode. A mind like that could be anything, do anything, know anything. A god. A god ruling a planet. No. A god ruling many planets. The Joining. A million-year reign, Kiriy after Kiriy taking up the Eyes, stepping into godhood. Knowing.

Jode's whole being prickled with uneasy, unwanted intuition: that kind of omniscience would destroy him. The Kiriy *knew*. And the Kiriy had gently, ruthlessly, separated two people who were lias'tri. At best the Kiriy had doomed Kane and Sharia to a lifetime of soul-deep loneliness; at worst, to a destructive madness. It had not been done through ignorance or cruelty. But why, then?

What had the Kiriy known? Why had the caress of Sharia's hair signaled the beginning of exile and isolation?

And why had the Kiriy wept even as she divided lias'tri in two?

A light blinking on the console finally pulled the psi-master out of his grim thoughts. He realized that Dani had been seeking his attention for several minutes. He glanced at Kane. The Za'arain was still lost among his own thoughts, but his eyes were no longer violet. In that much, at least, Jode had succeeded in putting off the explosion by forcing Kane to think of beauty instead of violence.

What is it, Dani? asked Jode.

A lightcube appeared. Inside were pictures of various crew members packing their few belongings.

And? pressed Jode, wondering why Dani had bothered to show him what he already knew——that several people had decided to get off at Jhora. Jode smiled grimly. He did not envy them. Jhora had been one of the first planets to be struck by the winnowing. His own people were still trying to crawl out from under that catastrophe.

Jhora had never been one of the most sophisticated planets in the Joining. Now it was almost primitive. Lightships rarely came, for there was nothing to trade. The soft-furred, singing jhoras had been susceptible to the winnowing; and the khera wine so favored by wealthy Wolfins had not been made for five years following the onset of the disease. Nor had wind traders gone into the wastes to look for the ancient, eerie artifacts that the autumn winds revealed beneath moving mountains of sand.

The jhora population was slowly coming back. Within a few months, the first of the post-winnowing wine would be ready. No doubt the brave or desperate among the wind traders were already preparing to go out to the sand mountains. The Joining traders who could afford to buy jhoras or khera wine or the jumbled fragments of a long-dead race would become very wealthy indeed. In a way, Kane was doing the crew a favor by dropping them off on Jhora. All they would have to do would be to survive in surroundings that were considerably more primitive than Dani's bright body provided for them. But then, traders were good at surviving. They had to be.

?

Jode gathered his thoughts with a sigh. Dani was not capable of following complex associations. She would not understand what thoughts the picture of the men getting ready to leave had triggered in his mind.

What did you want me to see, Dani?

The lightcube changed. He saw Szarth laughing with a slender crewman from Jiddir. It was Ine, Kane's master trader. The Jiddirit was packing to leave. For a moment Ine stopped, a startled expression on his face. Then he looked at Szarth's unmarked arm again.

So Szarth is showing off his healed arm. So what?

!

Jode sighed. *Keep trying, Dani.*

In the lightcube Szarth walked out of the room——and out of sight——with an Xtian's lithe stride. Ine remained behind, a thoughtful look on his face. Abruptly he left the room. The cube winked out, then reformed around a view of another cabin. Ine was there, with two other Jiddirits. They began to speak. No words came out of the cube.

Sound, Dani. I can't hear them.

!!

Jode leaned forward, watching the Jiddirits' animated faces. They were arguing among themselves. No sound came, though. *What's wrong? Why can't you give me sound?* asked Jode of the ship.

The view in the cube shifted until a single portion was lit. That portion expanded, revealing an oddly shaped apparatus no larger than Jode's hand. A Jiddirit sound absorber.

I see it, Dani. Thank you.

Frowning, Jode leaned back in his chair. Jiddirits were a clannish sort, holding themselves to be better than others. They were also first-class traders with a visceral understanding of any opponent's weakness and how to exploit that weakness. It did not surprise Jode that they had opted out of the search for the Eyes of Za'ar. Nor did it surprise him that Ine used a sound absorber to baffle the possibility of eavesdroppers.

What surprised him was that Dani had eavesdropped in the first place. She had never done that before unless specifically ordered to for the purposes of a crew assembly or a conference among personnel. Why had she done it now? And why had she chosen to call it to his attention?

Dani.

?

I don't know why you spied on the Jiddirits. I do know that Kane would be furious if he knew.

?

Jode grimaced. How could he explain the concept of privacy to a Wolfin construct that had been forcibly educated by an impatient Za'arain?

Would you like me to try? Kane's thought was a razor-thrust of anger. He did not wait for Jode's response. *Dani—*began

Kane, his mind closing over the ship's brain centers like cold tentacles, squeezing.

The ship whimpered and shut down. Indicators went wild.

Get out of her mind! ordered Jode. *Now!*

But Kane did not retreat fast enough for the psi-master. Jode took a terrible risk and forcibly ended the contact without waiting for Kane to agree.

Psi-darkness closed around Kane, a soft thickness like fog. Instinctively he struggled against it.

Gently, murmured Jode in Kane's mind. *I won't hurt you.*

Kane stopped fighting. A distinct feeling of relief spread through his mind. Jode's relief. Through Jode, Kane sensed the ship coming to life around them again. With a sigh, Jode released Kane's awareness from bondage.

"You're too strong, Za'arain," said Jode, apology and explanation at once. He grimaced and rubbed his head against echoes of pain lancing through his brain. "Dani's not like you or Sharia. Dani will break if she's forced to learn too much too soon, and she's just bright enough to know it. Dani was afraid that you were going to teach her something else she didn't want to know and then she would go crazy."

With a searing curse, Kane closed his eyes and mind with a finality that needed no words. He waited in brooding silence, watching Jode's dark Jhoramon face as he calmed the silly, frightened Wolfin. It did not take too long. Like a child, Dani could be coaxed and flattered and crowded into obedience. Unlike a child, she held the life of the crew in her immaterial hands.

Grimly Kane wished he had never taught Dani to view events through just a few of time's many filters.

"Well?" he asked curtly when Jode finally stretched and sat up.

The Jhoramon muttered a succinct curse, then shrugged. "I've promised to protect her from you, and she's promised not to do anything that isn't within her preexisting program——except when it comes to gold nodes. Then she'll use whatever you taught her that changed a machine into a child."

"Will she keep her promise?"

"Most of the time," retorted Jode sardonically. "As for the rest, she'll just try not to get caught."

"I think I'd better rearrange her tiny little mind again. We can live without gold za'replacements."

Jode hesitated, then shrugged. "I can't stop you. I can point out that if Dani guesses what you're up to, she'll go crazy and we'll be as dead as rocks orbiting a burnt-out sun." Then, sarcasm rippling in every word, "How deft and subtle are you feeling today, Za'arain?"

For an instant the violet eyes of death stared at Jode. The Jhoramon psi-master waited with the calmness of one who truly did not fear dying. Kane's outer eyelids closed. When they opened, his eyes were normal again, silver and darkness turning.

"I don't have much time, do I?" asked Kane softly.

Jode did not answer. He did not have to. He had seen the future in a Kiri psi-hunter's eyes.

Nine

The debris-strewn shuttle station on Jhora's inner moon was abandoned; a machine beamed comspeech messages across the empty, fused landing surfaces and into the darkness of space beyond. Dani's exterior sensors picked up the words and relayed them to the command cabin where Kane and Jode listened with equal intensity. Sharia frowned, understanding the words but not their import.

"Well, at least they're giving us a choice," said Jode, leaning back. "Wait twelve days, for a shuttle or take the risk of going downside on our own."

"Downside," said Kane immediately. "We can't wait."

Jode did not bother to disagree. The two days since Dani had panicked at the touch of Kane's angry mind had been excruciating. Kane's tension was a living thing; it prowled through Jode's mind like an azir on razor claws. He closed his eyes and rubbed the hinge points of his jaw. Lightning strokes of pain bolted through him—Kane's agony, inadvertently shared. Jode had felt nothing like it since his lias'tri had died nine years ago.

Kane looked over at Jode and realized what was happening. With a soundless curse Kane began ordering his mind, using the discipline that Jode had taught him in the last two days. It was an elusive discipline, acceptance rather than ignorance or knowledge. Rage denied is rage increased. Rage described is rage strengthened. Rage accepted is . . . not rage.

After a moment, Kane succeeded in accepting. He felt a sudden loosening of the coils of his mind. There was an almost dizzying sense of freedom and lightness. He sighed and rolled his head on the bunched muscles of his neck, encouraging his body to relax as his mind had.

You learn quickly, Za'arain. Thank the gods!

It won't last.

Then you will find acceptance again, and then again, until it is as much a part of you as those frightening Kiri eyes.

Kane smiled oddly. He looked over at Sharia and realized that she had been watching him with an intensity that made her hair shiver. "I'm all right, sv'arri."

It was a lie, and they both knew it. Neither said anything. Sharia's temper was as uncertain as Kane's. She showed it differently, though. For the first time since the onset of fertility, she was wearing her hair bound by more than her own will. She did not trust herself not to touch Kane with just one silky, conveniently forgotten tendril. She had dreamed of doing just that, dreamed of it so vividly that she had awakened sweating, terrified, horrified. She had lain awake and tried to reason herself out of her fear. She had told herself that Za'ar tabu meant nothing off Za'arain. She had told herself that five touching five did not mean Za'ar death and catastrophe. She had told herself that there was no difference between Szarth and Kane, both fives. She had told herself that it did not matter that one was Xtian and one Za'arain. A five was a five. She had touched a mature five and survived, the Great Tabu broken. She had told herself that she was free, that the Kiriy had died insane as she poured herself into the *then* and the *now* and the *always* in a futile attempt to change the circumstances of time/now. She had told herself that the Kiriy's cold, implacable warning against touching Kane was as meaningless as the thunder of the sacred fountain.

And then Sharia had gotten out of bed and bound her untrustworthy hair with the long silver chains and tiny silver bells that Szarth had given her in thanks for his healed arm. The chains were still there, woven through soft strands, silver on

silver, Darien hair bound and yet shimmering, alive with light
and music.

No matter what she told herself, she feared touching Kane
as she had never feared anything, even the Eyes. And she wanted
to touch him as she had never wanted anything, even life itself.

Sharia closed her eyes and looked away from Kane. His
timeshadow seethed and beckoned endlessly, tormenting her
with the knowledge of tangles forming, strangling him slowly,
so slowly. She could heal him. All she had to do was release
her hair from its chiming silver bondage, let soft tendrils caress
Kane as she had so long ago, just before the Kiriy in her
unfathomable wisdom had exiled Kane.

Yes, Sharia could heal Kane. But deep inside her mind she
was afraid that if she touched Kane they both would die in the
now and the *then* and the *always.*

Was that what the Kiriy had murmured to her just before the
Eyes had taken consciousness and replaced it with sleep? Was
that why the Kiriy had wept as she died, pouring away this life,
every life, ensuring that she would never again be born?

Was that why Sharia herself wept now, deep in her mind,
darkness shivering through all the colors of lias'tri?

"Tell Dani to take us down now." Kane's voice was curt, raw,
showing the strain from having Sharia's thoughts inadvertently
mingling with his own.

*Psi-master, can you teach Sharia to wrap her mind as tightly
as her hair? Knowing she wants me, knowing how much . . .*

The Jhoramon clenched his hands at Kane's agonized request.
*I'll try. She doesn't know about mindspeech, though. There's no
word for it in Za'arain, according to Merone.*

Kane's laughter was a cold darkness slicing through Jode's
mind. *Yes, there is. Kiri. Communication. And the Kiriy is the
One Who Communicates. Teach Sharia not to communicate so
clearly to me! If you don't, I'll have to try to do it myself. And
I'm afraid, Jhoramon. I'm afraid that the temptation to touch
her mind is every bit as overwhelming and potentially more
destructive than the temptation to touch her body.*

What makes you think that? retorted Jode angrily, suddenly disgusted with all things Za'arain. *More Za'ar legends?*

All legends have some truth somewhere in time, thought Kane, his mind cold and clear to its farthest depths. *Maybe Za'ar truth lies in the future. Maybe Sharia and I will be that truth.*

You're not making sense.

With an incredibly swift, feral movement, Kane turned and looked at Jode with psi-hunter eyes.

Jode's hands clenched into fists. Using every bit of his discipline he pulled his awareness away from Kane's far stronger, untrained mind. "I'll do what I can," said the psi-master curtly.

The descent to Jhora's surface was accomplished in silence. The downside port city of Ramhos showed signs of disrepair both subtle and obvious. It was night but only scattered lights burned. Shuttles that had not been abandoned in orbit were lined up haphazardly along gloomy causeways. Equipment lay abandoned on landing strips and launch pads. Piloted by Jode, Dani picked her way down with a delicacy that few ships could have achieved. But then, few ships had known the harsh instruction of a Darien five and the affectionate tutelage of a Jhoramon psi-master. Dani settled onto the cracked synstone surface without a single jar. Chimes rippled through the ship, telling the crew that the landing was a secure one.

"Find out if anyone is home, pilot," said Kane. Then, *Nice job, Dani.*

A distinct sense of pleasure washed over the edges of Kane's mind as Dani understood the compliment. Kane sat up as his cocoon peeled away, letting him feel the slightly heavier pull of Jhora's gravity. Sharia emerged from her cocoon at the same time. Jode was already free.

Jhora's dry air circulated through the control cabin, bringing scents and hints of an alien world. Sharia looked at the downside displays with enigmatic silver eyes. Opaque greenstone buildings radiated out from the port. Their geometries were blunt, their profiles low, their windows faceted. The air and the architecture and the planet itself were unlike anything Sharia had ever known.

"It's real," Kane said in quiet comspeech, watching Sharia's eyes and remembering his own awe the first time he had physically felt the alien reality of a Joining world. "The air is dry. Much drier than Za'arain. There aren't very many native flowers in this sector, except for the khera vines. When they bloom the wind turns pale rose with pollen and the air smells like rain."

"Blue," breathed Sharia.

"What?"

"Blue. The sky. Not silver at all."

"No," said Kane gently, realizing how such a simple thing, just one among the Joining's endless variations, could overwhelm. Tangerine seas and golden rains, skies where lightning was an incandescent purple and thunder crushed the air until perfume bled down to wash the earth with scents unimagined on Za'arain. Places of scarlet clouds and black crystal mountains where diamond insects swarmed, their myriad wings flashing in the lavender light. And there was more, so much more, an infinite universe swirling beyond Za'arain, inviting them to taste and to know whatever they had the courage to accept.

Without realizing it Kane spoke directly into Sharia's mind. *I wish we had more time, sv'arri. There are so many things I want to show you.*

Sharia's eyes widened until they were oval pools shimmering in her pale face. "You spoke," she breathed. "In my mind. Like the Kiriy."

Kane began to deny it, then shrugged. "Yes."

"How?"

"Psi."

The comspeech word made Sharia frown. She searched her mind for similar Za'arain words. "Kiri?" she murmured in Za'arain.

"Perhaps. Darien Kiri, surely."

"Can I?"

"Yes."

"Have I?" asked Sharia suddenly.

"Yes."

"When?"

"In your fear. In your . . . hunger."

"I'm sorry," she whispered. "I didn't know." But her mind shuddered at the ramifications of the unexpected unheard-of intimacy. *Was that like two fives touching? Was it tabu? Had she endangered or revolted Kane with her ignorance of her mind mingling with his?*

No. Kane's thought was hard and bright, a lightning stroke amid the turmoil of Sharia's thoughts. "This is not Za'arain," he said aloud. "And even if it were," he added deliberately, "there is nothing you could do that would revolt me. *Nothing.* Someday I hope you will be able to say the same to me."

Sharia's hands clenched one around the other as her hair seethed, making silver bells shiver and cry. "Can mindspeech be controlled?"

"Yes."

"How?" she asked starkly.

"Jode will teach you while I select trade goods."

"Why can't you teach me?" asked Sharia, uneasy at the thought of such intimacy with anyone but Kane.

Kane's laughter was as much a warning as his violet eyes. It was his only answer. It was enough. His mind had touched Sharia's as he laughed and his hunger burned through every bit of her. Her throat closed around a cry that was a terrible mixture of withdrawal and desire, as though two people lived within her, two people fighting to the death.

"Now do you understand?" asked Kane, his voice as bleak as his psi-hunter eyes. "I'm not the one who is revolted. You are."

"Kane—" she began helplessly, wanting to explain that it was not he who revolted her. *Za'ar imperative. A dying Kiriy's final act.*

"I know," said Kane. "Too bad that knowing doesn't change anything."

Kane walked out of the cabin, down the spiral corridor and out onto the dry face of Jhora. The Jiddirits who were leaving waited for him in the midst of the Xtians who always guarded Kane when he left the ship. Merone waited, silent as always, more than a score of languages locked within her half-mad mind. A native Jhoramon gestured toward the greenstone trading city where little but the wind moved. Szarth stepped forward and began speaking in the sibilant language of Xt, a language Kane had learned three years ago, when he had been imprisoned with Szarth and his four companion-symbionts.

"We're the first lightship in months. And we're in luck," added Szarth, his green eyes narrowed in an Xtian's odd smile. "The autumn winds came early this year. The first of the wind traders are already back in the city. We'll have our pick of the old things."

"Good. Doursone is always avid for wind-trader artifacts. What about the wine?"

Szarth's pale red tongue touched his lips delicately. "Ready and waiting."

"Jhoras?"

The Xtian's steel-tinted hands moved in an ambiguous gesture. "She says yes," he muttered, indicating the native woman with a flick of green eyes, "but her body says no."

"Let's hope her body lies."

Szarth's eyes narrowed in silent laughter. He knew as well as Kane that lips lied much more often than body language did.

Sharia and Jode walked down the ship's ramp just as Szarth and Kane followed the native woman into one of the green-stone buildings.

"Where are they going?" Sharia asked Jode.

"The trading circle. Dani has already announced what we have to sell and has recorded what others want to buy," explained Jode. "When there's a match, she records that and sends out an invitation to trade. Whoever wants to accept takes a chair in the circle. At least," he added, "that's how it used to work. Since the winnowing, a lot of customs have changed."

Sharia looked doubtfully around the almost-deserted landing area and the greenstone buildings beyond. "I guess there aren't many traders."

"Not any more. It was different before the winnowing. Then Joining lightships gleamed on the aprons like raindrops on khera vines." Jode's voice was calm but the lines of his face were grim. "It will be like that again, unless Kane is right."

"What do you mean?"

"Kane says that without Za'arain, the Joining will die. Za'arain's exiles have brought to the Joining all the skills that keep us alive and intact as a culture." Jode looked sharply at Sharia. "How many exiles are there, anyway?"

"I don't know. It is a Kiriy thing. Only the Kiriy knows who should stay and who should not."

"Why would a planet exile such brilliant scientists and philosophers and poets and engineers and—" Jode made an abrupt gesture. "All the skills needed to build and sustain civilization. It doesn't make sense."

"There is a difference between Kiri knowledge and the wisdom of the Kiriy," said Sharia, closing her eyes as she remembered her early training as a Kiri and a Darien. "Kiri knowledge is individual, reflecting the drives of a single, unique mind. Kiriy knowledge is collective; it reflects the imperatives of our civilization. What benefits the Kiri does not necessarily benefit Za'arain. Kiriy knowledge is the wisdom of stability rather than the unpredictability of creation. That's why so many Dariens end up exiled. We don't have predictable minds."

"That's an understatement," said Jode sardonically. "Kane's mind is enough to send a psi-master into catatonic shock."

"He doesn't mean to hurt anyone," Sharia said in quick defense.

Jode's retort was mental and searing. He was careful to make sure that it went no further than his own mind, though. He had no desire to argue with another Darien five whose eyes could go violet between one instant and the next. Having experienced unleashed psi-hunters on Za'arain, Jode was in no hurry to know them again.

"How long will the trading take?" asked Sharia, wanting to talk about something that would take her thoughts from Kane and the hunger that grew inside her, the hunger that was devouring Za'arain learning and Kiriy imperative, devouring her. Lias'tri, as dangerous as a Kiri psi-pack.

"How long is time?" shrugged Jode.

It was meant as a rhetorical question. On Za'arain, however, time was anything but rhetorical. Sharia started to answer Jode before she realized just how different their views of time were. Comspeech had no words to describe the many facets of time.

In silence Jode led Sharia toward the trading circle. By the time they arrived, Kane was seated. Ine, Kane's master trader, stood at his shoulder. Ine's knowledge of Joining markets and Fourth Evolution races knew no peer. Merone stood at Kane's other shoulder, ready to translate if comspeech proved inadequate to the traders' needs. In the brilliantly clothed gathering of traders, Kane's black, subtly iridescent tunic and pants were like pools of moonless night.

"Once the trading begins, say nothing," murmured Jode. "Jhoramon customs are different from Za'arain. And keep that hair under wraps!"

Sharia's hands went to her head, smoothing restless tendrils back beneath the cool strands of tiny silver bells. "I'm sorry," she said, embarrassed by her lack of control. "It wasn't this difficult on Za'arain. There are so many tangled timeshadows here." And there was Kane, a torrential invitation that she could not accept and could not ignore.

Tactfully Jode said nothing, despite the use of the comspeech word timeshadows. What was obscenity in the Joining was the quintessence of beauty on Za'arain.

Without speaking, Jode and Sharia watched Kane run the khera wine samples through a pocket analyzer and then across a much more sensitive instrument, his own palate. He declined two lots of wine, accepted a third without question and began to bargain in earnest over the fourth and fifth. Ine bent over Kane's ear from time to time, murmuring words that went no further than his captain. Kane deferred to Ine's judgment, buying both remaining lots of wine despite their high price.

When a tumble of jhoras was brought to the circle, Sharia made a soft sound of sympathy. Their tiny, tangled timeshadows haunted her. The animals themselves were a muddy orange, their fur ragged, their wasted bodies no larger than her palm. They were unnaturally passive. Their pelts should have been as lively and bright as flame. They were not. Dull, almost coarse, the pelts were an accurate reflection of the animals' lack of health. Normally the jhoras would have been seething with movement and small melodies and pure notes of harmony. The only sound that came from these animals was a sour, uncertain humming that grated on the nerves of anyone who could hear.

Kane grimaced and waved away the sick jhoras without a second look.

No! cried Sharia silently, urgently, not knowing if Kane would hear. *Bring them to me, v'orri! Let me comb their sad timeshadows!*

Kane's body stiffened in the instant before he controlled his reaction to Sharia's untrained mental scream. *Gently,* he returned, damping down on the contact in ways that he had learned by observing Jode. Unlike the psi-master, Kane was not skilled. He was powerful, though, and managed to thin contact to a tolerable level. *You don't have to yell at me,* Kane added whimsically, pleased that there was finally something he could give to Sharia that she would not cringe from. *I'll buy every little beastie on the planet if that's what you want.*

With the thought came a mental picture of Sharia buried beneath a wave of jhoras, the jhoras of Kane's memories, song and softness and seething life, fully living up to their group designation—a tumble of jhoras. Sharia laughed softly at the image, all but feeling the tiny hand-paws tickling her skin and the incredible smoothness of jhora fur sliding over her.

Kane gestured to Ine. The Jiddirit bent over, argued softly

against the purchase, then gave in. A price was quickly reached. The Jhoramon trader scooped up the jhoras and put them back into a large basket which he pushed across the table to Kane. Immediately Sharia started forward to claim the suffering animals. Jode's hand closed around her wrist, chaining her to his side.

Wait.

Jode's neutral mental command startled Sharia, but it was his touch that stunned her. She felt prickles of awareness and near-pain chase over her nerves. It was not like touching her Kiri cousins. Not quite. But there was a similarity that made her deeply uneasy. She sensed the psi-master's aching timeshadow, ecstasy and grief and regret; yet it was all at a great distance. He neither overwhelmed nor compelled nor hurt her. She knew that he felt constant anguish, that his timeshadow was distorted by it, but she was not forced by touch to share that anguish or to heal him.

I'm a trained psi. Your cousins were not. Jode released her wrist as Kane stood. *Go.* Then, with a curl of power that surprised her, he added, *But whatever you do, don't say anything, especially the word timeshadow!*

Sharia hurried forward to where Kane waited. He held his hand out to her. On his palm lay a baby jhora that was too sick even to fear being removed from its customary tumble. She hesitated, not wanting to brush accidentally against Kane's forbidden skin. Abruptly Kane's eyes went violet. He snarled a few words in Xtian. Szarth leaped forward. He took the basket and the jhora and offered both to Sharia.

Kane . . . cried Sharia silently; sensing his rage and his pain at her rejection.

Nothing answered her cry, not even a silent Kiri snarl. Kane was closed to her. She stretched out her hand to Kane and started to say something despite Jode's injunction against speech. Hastily, Szarth put the sick jhora in her outstretched hand, trying to prevent her from saying anything.

All thought of speech fled as the animal's wounded timeshadow flickered into physical contact with Sharia. Uttering a soundless cry of compassion she released a tendril of hair from its bonds. Hands cupped around the tiny jhora, she stroked it with her breath and caressed it with her hair. She rode the jhora's timeshadow so delicately that the animal quivered with delight. The baby was very easy to heal. It had not lived long enough in linear time to have a timeshadow knotted deeply in time/then. The source of the jhora's disease was easily found and defeated, time/then flowing through Darien awareness, time/then untangled and reaching cleanly toward time/now, Darien hair caressing and then retreating back beneath silver bells.

As the tendril of Sharia's hair withdrew, it revealed a jhora burning like flame upon her palm. The jhora blinked golden eyes and sang a single pure note of joy that burned as brightly as the lustrous pelt.

The jhora's clear song brought every Jhoramon trader inside and outside the circle to his feet. Sharia did not notice. She sank down onto the greenstone floor and held out her hands for the basket. As Szarth put it into her lap, she shook her hair free of all restraint. Bells chimed sweetly, then slid to the floor in glittering strands of silver. Unbound Darien hair swirled around the basket, concealing it beneath a shifting, translucent cloud.

Kane walked forward, drawn inevitably by Sharia's seething hair. It took all his Kiri discipline and his Darien strength not to steal just one small touch of translucent hair over his timeshadow or his skin. He closed his eyes, hoping that if he could not see he would not hunger quite so intensely.

It did not help. Not really. He sensed the surge and fire of Sharia's timeshadow as though it were an ancient artifact brought to his hand. Although her timeshadow was vibrantly alive, it was not closed to him in the way other living timeshadows were. He felt the rich strength of her energy, saw the infinite variety of its streaming colors, sensed the condensation of shadows and gaps in the recent past. He knew that he had caused the radiating network of darkness and the breaks, that he could heal them if Sharia would let him. It would be so simple. Five touching five.

With a wrench Kane disciplined his treacherous thoughts just as his hand would have buried itself in seething silver strands. He stepped back, turned away, and stood so that he had an unobstructed view of a gleaming greenstone wall. He heard the sudden, sweet harmonies of a healthy tumble and the sighing, hissing surprise of the watching Jhoramons. He waited until Sharia had had enough time to wrap her seductive, forbidden hair beneath Xtian silver again. Only then did he turn around.

Sharia sat with a tumble of jhoras singing in her lap. Baby jhoras played in her hands, clung to the iridescent silver folds of her clothing and nibbled teasingly along her ears. She laughed softly, delighted by the tiny, bright flames of their timeshadows flickering through hers. She stroked their meltingly soft pelts until the animals quivered and sang in rills of pleasure. When she hummed to them in return, they sang paeans of praise and joy. She turned toward Kane with an incandescent smile.

Thank you, v'orri. Once again you've brought me laughter.

This time there was no need for Kane to damp the intensity of Sharia's mindspeech. She had learned very quickly, knowing almost intuitively what brought pleasure or pain to him. Her words sang as perfectly in his mind as did the healthy jhoras playing over her like tongues of fire. Kane had no words to give to her. He simply smiled as she had, neither knowing nor caring that the people watching were shocked by the unexpected beauty of the smiling Za'arains.

Reluctantly, Kane turned back to the trading circle. He saw the Jhoramons standing six deep, staring at the woman who had made dying jhoras into healthy animals. A dozen Jiddirits had appeared, Ine's clansmen who lived and worked in Jhora's premier trading city while their cousin traveled to the stars in search of more trade. Despite everyone's clear and overwhelming interest in Sharia, no one spoke. It was forbidden for anyone within or without the trading circle to speak unless that person was actively involved in buying trade items. At this point Kane was the only person actively buying. It was for him to speak, and for him to choose the topic of speech. He had no intention of discussing Sharia, who was Za'arain and rode living timeshadows. He gestured to Ine.

"Wind traders," said Kane quietly.

It was all that he needed to say. Ine motioned toward a group of Jhoramons wearing the supple leather clothes and gauze face masks of wind traders. A woman stepped forward. Behind her came three others bearing boxes of carefully wrapped artifacts. All of the traders were gaunt, scarred, and obviously on the ragged edge of collapse. In the best of times, stealing artifacts from the wind-driven mountains of sand was a dangerous profession that could be pursued only by the most healthy, and then only for a few years. Since the winnowing, wind trading had become a synonym for suicide.

Kane sat again in the trading circle. Though he made no outward sign, Sharia looked up sharply, sensing that he was gathering himself for something. Something which at best was unpleasant and at worst could be excruciating. Frowning, Sharia stood up again. Jhoras clung to her easily, their tiny, retractable needle-claws buried in the silver of her clothes. Absently she eased the claws free and returned the animals to their basket. She gave Jode a quick, questioning look before she focused her attention entirely on Kane.

The psi-master watched Sharia uneasily. Unlike her, he knew what was coming. What he did not know was how Sharia would react to it.

Remember, Jode cautioned, *whatever happens, don't say anything.*

Sharia turned and looked at him with hammered silver eyes. *What will happen?* Though quietly spoken in his mind, her words carried more of a demand than a request.

He's going to read the artifacts, explained Jode. *Some of them won't bother him much. Others will be painful.*

Read?

Learn from them. Know them.

How?

Dryly, Jode responded, *I was hoping you could tell me. He simply holds onto the things, sweats, hurts, and learns.*

Sharia's uneasiness went through the psi-master's mind like a cold wind. *Timeshadows.*

The objects are dead. Kane told me that only living things have timeshadows.

The artifacts must have been touched by living beings, replied Sharia calmly. *Owned. Life leaves a mark, a wake, on everything it touches. The more often touched, the deeper the wake. I can only ride—read—living timeshadows, life still connected to time/now and the* now. *Kane can only ride the wakes of the dead, connected to time/then and the* then.

No wonder he hurts. Jode's emotions were as grim as his words were simple. *Pawing through the massed deaths of the past must be a miserable thing. By the savage gods, what an awful psi gift to have! It's a miracle he can learn anything at all.*

He is Darien, and five, responded Sharia with unthinking pride in Kane. *His timeshadow is a torrent of power and beauty. If any Za'arain ever born can untangle the knotted timeshadows of the past, it is Kanaen ZaDarien/Kiri.*

Jode stared at her. *And you untangle the timeshadows of the present. Two halves of a whole. Your minds were shaped for each other. Literally. That, too, is part of the meaning of lias'tri.*

Jode sensed both the flinching away and the hunger that his words called out of Sharia. He was appalled to discover how deeply ingrained the withdrawal was. Judging from Kane's example, Za'arains might have known little or nothing about the uses of psi, but they were very good at conditioning minds. Lias'tri was one of the most tenacious forces known to man, yet Za'arain conditioning had managed to stalemate it.

Why?

Five touching five is the Za'arain ideograph for catastrophe. Startled by Sharia's mindspeech, Jode realized that he had not closed his mind well enough to keep the untrained, powerful Za'arain from knowing his thoughts. She learned as Kane learned, with terrifying speed.

How?

Kiri is the Za'arain word for communication. Sharia's unwanted, unexpected explanation was both delicate and relentless. *Darien is the word for dimensions, manifestations, all the patterns of time. Sharia is the word for rider of living timeshadows, and you are very much alive, Jode. Mindtouch is just that. A touching.*

Is there a Za'arain word for rude? asked the psi-master coldly.

With his words came an exact transmission of the feelings of nakedness and anger that were evoked by invasive mindtouch. Despite his status as psi-master, Sharia and Kane made Jode feel like a child. The worst of it was that they did not mean to. If they had been arrogant in their power, Jode could have brought them to their knees with a few savage psi tricks he had learned. But the Za'arains were not arrogant. They were simply, incredibly, powerful.

Sharia's sudden feeling of shame washed over Jode. She withdrew from mindtouch as best she could, using Kane's recent withdrawal from her as a pattern to follow. It was not quite good enough. Her embarrassment and confusion still resonated quietly through Jode, making him feel ashamed of his own response to Za'arain psi gifts. Feeling ashamed, of course, just made him more angry. For the first time since his lias'tri had died, the Jhoramon slipped the leash on his own self-control. It was a small lapse, but it allowed him to slide into Sharia's mind like a knife into flesh.

Take your thoughts—so—and tighten your control—here. Got that? snarled Jode within Sharia's mind. *Good. Now tighter. Tighter! Control your mind the same way you control your damned Za'arain hair.*

Sharia flinched and paled under Jode's brutal instruction. Pain ripped through her, but in its wake came knowledge. The pattern that he had shown her was not difficult, merely unexpected. It involved stifling an awareness of the *now* that was basic to Za'arain minds. Once the *now* was stifled, though, other patterns emerged, other possibilities.

Teach that little trick to your lias'tri, ordered Jode coldly. *It will make life easier for all of us!*

Jode opened his eyes again—and saw himself watched by the atavistic psi-hunter who lived within Kane. At that instant Jode remembered that whatever pain he had inflicted on Sharia had been felt by Kane. Jode might hurt Kane with impunity, but the psi-master knew with cold certainty that Kane's forgiveness did not extend to anyone who hurt his lias'tri.

In a fluid surge of power Kane came to his feet. His violet eyes were fixed on Jode with predatory intent.

Ten

Sharia realized what had happened almost as quickly as Jode did. She remembered how Kane had always tried to stand between her and whatever caused her pain. She remembered his swift punishments of her cruel Kiri cousins. And she remembered the violet eyes of the psi-packs spreading death through the glass corridors of the Kiriy compound, atavism overwhelming rational thought. Swiftly she stepped between Jode and Kane.

The pain was necessary, v'orri.

Sharia's words murmured soothingly in Kane's mind. He paused in his stalking and watched the unflinching Jhoramon with psi-hunter eyes.

He did it in anger, snarled Kane.

The anger was necessary, too, countered Sharia calmly. *If he hadn't lost control, he wouldn't have gone deep enough into my mind to teach me.*

Both Kane and Sharia felt the mental flash of Jode's surprise. Sharia's words were true, but the psi-master had not known it until that moment. His realization that Sharia knew instinctively what even his Jhoramon training had overlooked was as disturbing to Jode as the moment when he had understood precisely how powerful the Za'arains were.

Kane's agreement was reluctant, for atavism still seethed. He blinked several times before violet was replaced by silver. Fortunately he was in the position of being able to speak aloud without being thrown out of the trading circle. It was fortunate because Kane did not trust himself to use mindspeech with Jode. It would be too easy to hurt him, and too tempting.

"Next time, Jhoramon, don't enjoy causing her pain."

Jode's answer was a silent wash of shame and an anger that was not directed at either Za'arain. A single word burned among the three of them: *lias'tri*. Only Jode knew whether it was explanation or apology or warning.

Silently, Sharia combed the most elusive of the jhoras from her clothes and hair, putting the last of the clinging tumble back into its deep basket. Kane watched each movement, listened hungrily to each puffing note of jhora music. Atavistic rage seeped from him, giving him back complete control.

Kane turned and sat down. At his gesture, an artifact was unwrapped and presented to him. The object was so oddly shaped that it was impossible to tell whether it was intact or broken or merely part of a larger whole. It was also impossible to know what purpose it might have served. Even before he touched the artifact, Kane knew that it was old, very old, deeply rooted in linear time and thick with timeshadow wakes. If he had wanted to, he could have called the wakes, braided them, and shattered the artifact into dust. Learning from the wakes was more difficult. For that he had to touch, to comprehend, to become a part of all the myriad former lives and deaths.

Only Sharia sensed Kane's inner shrinking as he held his hand out to the artifact's many-leveled, elegantly formed spiral. Kane's reluctance reminded her of her own reflexive flinching away from touch, any touch—from living timeshadows overlapping in unwanted intimacy. She wondered if Kane would know an agony similar to hers when she had healed her Kiri cousins.

Kane's hand touched the smooth metal curves. Pain sliced through Sharia, making her sway. Kane was better prepared for the riot of conflicting sensations, the timeshadow wakes calling out to him, demanding that he instantly and completely see-hear-know-taste-remember-*be* each of the echoes of former lives. Even as chaos assaulted him, Kane loosed his mind. His timeshadow shivered and twisted violently, sleeting through each of the wakes, absorbing them, knowing them. With the burst of agony came memories/images.

Skies of metallic gold by day and a night without stars. A metal city growing according to unexpected rhythms, unspoken needs. A Fourth Evolution city older than Darien or Kiri, a city from Cycles before Za'arain, unknown and unnamed. Lives heaped and spilling over, timeshadow wakes rippling and pooling, calling to him. So many had died. So many had lived again. So many. . . .

Kane's grip on the object shifted. His dark gold fingers loosened as the first onslaught of chaotic need passed. He had absorbed the worst of it. Now he could move delicately among the wakes like a man walking through the bright dead leaves of winter, picking and choosing among the possibilities swirling around his feet.

Music. Slow and stately, infused with ceremony. Fingers tracing the spiral design again and again. With each complete tracing came new understanding. Reverence. Eternity. Infinity. Exaltation. Peace.

Sighing, Kane released the artifact. He looked at it with new eyes, seeing the beauty of past ages beneath the ruined, pitted surface of time/now.

Ine bent over and set the object to Kane's right, reading Kane's acceptance of the artifact's veracity in his strained face. Without pausing, Ine picked up the next unwrapped offering of the wind traders. This artifact could have been a natural crystal but for the almost-invisible etchings running across each teal-blue plane.

Unhesitantly Kane's fingers closed around the palm-sized crystal. There was no overwhelming assault of past lives and imperatives. There was simply *laughter, wonder, a child's joy slowly transformed into adult pleasure.* Kane smiled and looked at the crystalline bauble that had no greater purpose than to bring pleasure from the sheer purity of its color shining up through the graceful, alien ideographs covering each facet. Gently he set the crystal next to the religious artifact's broken spiral.

The third object was a cluster of odd angles and mixed metal-crystal surfaces. Obviously broken, the artifact suggested nothing of its origins. As Kane reached toward it, Sharia took in a swift, silent breath. She understood now that touching ancient things was as difficult for Kane as touching living beings was for her. Kane's fingers brushed over the object, hesitated, then returned for a firm grasp. She sensed his powerful mind searching and finding—nothing.

Not quite nothing. There was a thin shimmer of timeshadows attached to still-living beings. Echoes of the living wind traders who had found the artifact in Jhora's lethal sands. Beneath those echoes was silence, emptiness, stillness. Either the object was machine-made and had never been touched by life other than that of the wind traders, or the metal-crystal construct was a fake made by desperate traders. Whether the latter or the former, Kane would not buy the artifact. He took nothing to which he could not assign a name and place and time. That was what had made him wealthy in such a short time as a trader. If anyone bought one of Kane's ancient objects, that person would be certain that he was buying old truth rather than new, carefully wrought lies.

Saying nothing, Kane set the suspect artifact to his left, separating it from the crystal and the spiral. Movement rippled through the wind traders, though no one said a word. To be refused by Kane was to find no market at all, anywhere. Except on Doursone, perhaps, and Doursone was as dangerous as it was distant.

Sharia stood quietly, watching Kane with haunted eyes as he reached for yet another artifact. There was the instant of touch, a lightning slash of agony that made her sway, and a terrible sense of drowning in conflicting energies. Then came the slow moments of learning, of knowing.

The pattern was repeated again and again—five objects, ten, twenty—and Sharia sensed Kane's strength pouring out into time/then as surely as though it were her own. She sensed the chill seeping into his mind, Darien warning of the unbalanced *now,* of energy bleeding from time/now into time/then. She saw the cold sweat gleaming on his skin as he coped with artifacts that once had been used to exploit the *other.*

Jode watched Kane occasionally, but most of the Jhoramon's attention was for Sharia. He did not need psi to see the moment of decision reflected in her expression. His hand shot out and wrapped around her wrist.

Don't interfere, ordered Jode neutrally, careful not to make mindspeech painful for Sharia.

He shouldn't—began Sharia.

He must.

Why? she demanded.

Doursone is the nexus between planets of the Dust and the Joining. The raiders were from the Dust. They trade exclusively for ancient artifacts such as those found on Jhora and a few other Joining planets. If you hope to find the Eyes of Za'ar, you must have something to trade for information, something extremely valuable. For people of the Dust, that means ancient artifacts. Jode hesitated, then gave the mental equivalent of a shrug. *We were lucky to be the first traders here. Kane will judge artifacts until there aren't any left or until he can't endure any more pain. If you value Za'arain, don't interfere.*

Sharia watched Kane with eyes the color of Za'arain winter. She did not speak. Nor did she share her thoughts with Jode. The Jhoramon was grateful. He doubted that he would have enjoyed knowing precisely what she felt as she watched her lias'tri pour himself into a task that drained him as surely as though he had opened one of his veins and allowed blood to pool on the greenstone floor.

With a good salesman's flair for the dramatic, the wind traders had saved their most unusual artifact for last. Either a long necklace or a hip belt, the object was set with gemstones unlike anything Kane had ever seen. Vivid green with sunbursts of incandescent silver, the jewels were as brilliant as though they had just been cut. Time had not pitted their polished surfaces, nor had it dimmed the glow of the hammered platinum links strung between the gems.

Kane's strong hand closed around the links. Though his expression did not change, Sharia went to her knees. Her silent scream made Jode stagger. Sweat ran from Kane's gold fingers onto a silver-green gem. The salty drops slid off, leaving the jewel as brilliant as before. Links and facets cut into Kane's palm but he did not notice. Even Sharia's mental scream was distant to him, attenuated by the driving force of the quasi-life he held in the palm of his hand.

For the jewels were alive. It was not the life of the First Evolution, the living crystals whose resonances could be both extraordinarily beautiful and utterly lethal to the softer bodies of the Fourth Evolution races. If the gems had been First Evolution, Kane would have been spared the agony that clawed through his mind. But the stones had just enough of the aspect of the *then* to be accessible to Kane. The jewels were rather like Wolfin ships—intelligent, quasi-living constructs. Machines. Kane could not fathom their purpose. From the powerful interplay of timeshadow wake energies surrounding them, however, he could guess that the gems had been worn only by one person from birth to death. Then the necklace had been put aside until that person was born again, and the proof of that rebirth would be the ability to wear the silver-green jewels.

Gratefully Kane released his grip on the alien gems. They were waiting to bathe once again in the radiance of a timeshadow that was not his. They had been waiting for eons. While not deadly to him, the gems were distinctly hostile. No one of any psi-sensitivity would be able to wear them for more than a few moments unless that person, too, had been haunting the long reaches of time in hope of finding the missing aspect of his or her mind that the gems embodied.

Kane gestured for the Jiddirit to take the odd artifact. Ine picked it up and put it next to the other objects without showing any sign of discomfort. Kane smiled grimly. He had always suspected that Ine was psi-null. Now he was sure of it.

Behind Kane, Jode stood close to Sharia, supporting her unobtrusively while she recovered from the effects of sharing Kane's handling of the alien jewelry. The chill of her skin startled Jode. He looked at Kane with increased worry; the psimaster knew that Sharia was an accurate indicator of Kane's state of health.

He's all right. Sharia's thought was barely a whisper. *Tired. Just tired. So much time, linear and* other. *So many wakes.*

With a weariness that he had difficulty concealing, Kane leaned back in the trading chair and listened to Ine earn his five percent of the cargo. Normally Ine would have had to wait until the objects were sold to claim his fee. Because the Jiddirit was staying on Jhora, however, Kane had agreed to pay him immediately—though on the basis of the purchase price rather than the sale price.

Ine proceeded briskly, offering a price that would allow the wind traders to pay their expenses and not much else. The traders countered with a much higher price. Kane listened impassively, though he was surprised by the sum the wind traders were demanding. It was far higher than usual, probably because of the silver-green gems.

Kane let the words flow by him. He lacked Ine's enthusiasm for bargaining, and his skill. Ine knew as well as Kane that there was a limited amount of money in the ship's coffers. The normal trading patterns had been disrupted by the emergency trip to Za'arain. The ship's hold was filled with trade goods destined for the special desires of Jiddirit and Megat and S/koura. Some of the cargo could be traded here on Jhora. Some was simply not saleable except on the planet for which it had been intended. It was up to Ine to get the Jhoramons to take things that they did not particularly want instead of the currency they needed to buy medicines from the Megat ships that would come eventually.

Comspeech offers and counteroffers came quickly, and futilely.

The wind traders were sticking by their unreasonably high price for the artifacts. Though Kane's face gave away nothing, he began to get uneasy. He needed every one of those ancient things for Doursone. The Dust raiders who had come to Za'arain had not taken the Eyes accidentally. He doubted that they would be for sale—unless the thieves had discovered that without a Kiriy's unusual mind the Eyes were just two rather large violet psi-stones set in a double band of silver metal. Valuable, yes, in the way that all old things were valuable; but the Eyes of Za'ar were not the sole force behind Za'arain's greatness. Kiri minds were also necessary.

It would take time for the raiders to discover their mistake, however. Time that Za'arain could not afford. If the Eyes of Za'ar were not for sale, Kane knew he would have to steal them. In order to steal them, he had to first find out who held them. And information was expensive on Doursone. Unless he sold the ship itself, he simply did not have the wealth to pry information out of Doursone. Only the artifacts could do that.

Ine cursed quietly in his own language, but not quietly enough. Kane heard. What he did not understand, Merone translated for him. She spoke so softly that only her captain could hear. Ine turned toward Kane.

"We are having a problem in communication," said Ine formally.

Kane gestured curtly toward Merone. She stepped forward and addressed the Jhoramon wind traders in their own language. They answered quickly, concisely.

Jode cursed in the privacy of his mind. The solution the Jhoramons offered to the impasse was perfect for the needs of both parties involved. He doubted that Kane would agree to it, however. The wind traders all had some degree of psi; it was how they sensed the presence of artifacts beneath Jhoramon's lavender sands. For Sharia to heal the psi-gifted wind traders would be painful at best. At worst, it would be impossible.

Yet it was the only way of obtaining the ancient artifacts. The wind traders were adamant in that.

Can you heal people even when it causes you pain? asked Jode quickly.

Yes. No more, just a single word and a psychic withdrawal that went to the bottom of Sharia's mind.

They want to trade those artifacts for the healing of their clan, continued Jode.

How many people?

Hundreds.

Sharia made no response. None was needed. They might as well have asked her to move a sand mountain one handful at a time. It could be done, but it was doubtful that she would survive doing it.

"No," said Kane curtly, sitting up suddenly as Merone's soft translations penetrated his daze of fatigue. Rejection radiated from his mind and body. "She's not a machine. Healing on that scale is impossible."

Merone relayed Kane's objection, listened, and said, "They don't expect it to be done in a day. They'll give her as long as she needs, up to the beginning of the next wind season."

"We can't wait around for fifteen months," snarled Kane. "No."

Sharia leaped forward unconsciously, trying to listen in Kane's mind without using the intimacy of mindtouch. It was not possible. She turned toward Jode. He was listening intently, ignoring her. With an impatient movement of her head, she turned back to Kane.

"They ask that you leave her here until the healing is complete," said Merone in her husky Wolfin voice.

Kane's only answer was a measuring, violet stare. Merone shifted uneasily, sensing danger as clearly as she sensed the sunlight radiating through the building's thin windows. Hastily she turned back to the wind traders. Before she could open her mouth to speak, they made a counteroffer. They, too, had read the violence of Kane's negative in his predatory silence and changed eyes.

What are they saying? demanded Sharia of Jode when she could stand the waiting no longer.

They're arguing over you.

Jode's succinct summary did not tell Sharia anything that she did not already know. Her lips flattened into a thin, impatient line as she listened to quick exchanges in a language she did not understand.

How many can you heal without hurting yourself? Jode asked Sharia, using an absolutely neutral mental voice.

I'll do whatever I must for the Eyes.

That doesn't answer my question.

Doesn't it? retorted Sharia. *Think about it, psi-master. Like Kane, I'm Darien and five.*

Can you heal ten at once? Thirty? Fifty?

Yes.

Have you ever healed that many at once before?

I don't know.

How can you not know? demanded Jode harshly, his frustration ringing in Sharia's mind.

Sharia's answer was a torrential sequence of memories taken from her last days on Za'arain, when she had been sucked into an orgy of healing without beginning or end, only knotted, screaming timeshadows tangling around her as she lived through each person's memories of Za'arain's fall, an endless period of violence while the *now* broke around her, until the Kiri psi-pack had come and hunted her into an alcove and her hair seethed around her body in a lethal silver cloud.

Jode asked no more questions. He wanted no more of Sharia's answers. The raw violence of what she had lived through was like an open sore in his mind. He wondered how much worse it had to be for her, a woman who had never known anything but Za'arain courtesy and the isolation of a Darien five. When Jode spoke in Sharia's mind again, it was with gentleness and respect. He did not know any other being who could have survived all that Sharia had survived in the last weeks and still have remained sane.

Kane is refusing to let you heal at all, summarized Jode. *Is there a reason for his refusal that I don't understand?*

He knows that healing them will hurt me.

Will it kill you?

No.

Maim you?

No.

Will it do any lasting damage to your mind or body?

No.

There are seventeen of the wind trader clan present. How long would it take for you to heal them?

One hour. Several. Maybe more. I'm sorry, Sharia added quickly, sensing Jode's frustration. *I just don't know. I don't have any awareness of the linear aspect of time while I'm riding timeshadows.*

Absently Jode brushed his palm down the length of Sharia's arm. Affection and apology radiated from his touch. She smiled at him almost shyly, still unused to being touched. It was pleasing to her, though. Very pleasing. Kiris were born to communicate, and tactile sensation was one of the most basic yet most complex forms of communication known to Za'arain. Hesitantly, Sharia returned Jode's touch, using just a fingertip. She sensed the psi-master's surprise and then his pleasure at her overture.

It's a good thing that I trust you, Jhoramon. Kane's thought was cool and deadly, though it was a mere flicker of his attention. The bargaining was not going well.

Jode winced. Once Kane and his lias'tri got past their Za'arain conditioning and were united, Kane would not be a violently jealous man. Until then, he would be as uncertain as a star burning toward nova.

"No." Kane's flat response to the wind trader's latest offer needed no translation by Merone.

The wind traders conferred among themselves and then repeated their offer. Jode sensed Kane's refusal even before Merone had finished translating.

Quickly, urged Jode, pulling Sharia forward with a hand around her wrist. *He's not being rational. They're offering to settle for ten healthy clan members. They'll go no lower, and we must have those artifacts.*

Sharia shook her head, making silver bells chime sweetly. Her hair flowed outward like a sentient, wind-driven cloud. Silver chains and bells slid from her hair to Kane's shoulder as she passed by him. Because he could not touch her, his hands clenched around the fine, silky chains and softly crying bells. Pleasure shimmered through him, the clean joy of holding something that was warm with her warmth.

When Sharia's hair licked out over the first startled wind trader, Kane closed his eyes and brought the fine Xtian silver to his lips. He did not want to see the moment when her hands would touch alien flesh. He felt the endless, searing instant when Za'arain and Jhoramon timeshadows overlapped. Dimly he sensed Sharia sliding away, riding the timeshadow dawn into time/then, unknotting, combing, healing, and finally riding upward into time/now.

Her hair swept back, revealing a wind trader who was almost a stranger to his clanmates. He looked decades younger, all sand burns gone, all broken bones knitted perfectly, breathing easily with lungs no longer clogged by sand, all residue of the deadly winnowing combed from his timeshadow and his flesh. He peeled back the veil that had covered his wind-scarred face and laughed the laugh of the newly born.

The other traders crowded closer in a thoughtless rush. Kane surged out of his chair and vaulted over the trading table with a single powerful motion. Instantly the other people backed away from Sharia. Grimly, Kane nodded. He gestured toward the nearest wind trader. The woman did not wait for a second invitation. She walked to Sharia and stood within the seething alien hair. Kane clenched his jaw against the agony tearing through him. The woman's timeshadow was raw, raging, as potent and unforgiving as a river of lava. It was too late, though. Sharia had already merged with the violent, incandescent energy, riding it with a courage and skill that Kane could only admire.

Silently Kane endured, as Sharia had endured his own sliding among inimical timeshadow wakes. Trader after trader came to her, stood within her translucent Darien hair, felt the odd heat of her hands searching over their bodies, and walked away reborn to greater strength than they had ever dreamed of having, timeshadow and body and mind fully integrated utterly balanced. Even the Jhoramon edict against speaking on the trading floor could not completely stifle the murmurs of disbelief and awe that rippled through the onlookers.

Kane barely noticed. He was fighting for self-control as he had never had to fight in his life. Every cell of his body screamed that he was risking Sharia's life in pursuit of the Eyes, Eyes that he hated as much as he respected. The Eyes had exiled him, dividing him from the only person he had ever cared about. For her, he had come back to Za'arain in defiance of the Eyes, risked Za'ar death, had won—and even now the Eyes stood between him and what he wanted. How much worse would it be when the Eyes of Za'ar were within his grasp? How could he allow Sharia to take them up and either die or be driven insane?

And how could he not?

He could not doom Za'arain and the Joining to violence and savagery that might know no end, to Kiri psi-packs roaming first the planet and then the galaxy, Kiri psi-packs whose atavistic minds were not entirely limited to time/then. He was Kiri, yet when his inner eyelids flickered down, he did not lose everything of time/now. Atavistic did not mean stupid. It simply meant savage on a scale unknown to the Joining. And power. A power undiminished by civilized considerations. Voracious, ravenous, cunning.

If it took the Eyes of Za'ar to control the Kiris, then he must find the Eyes of Za'ar.

Even at the cost of Sharia's life? Kane asked himself, the words like cold Kiri psi-hunters sliding into his guts, tearing him apart. *Feel it. Feel her life draining away. Feel it and know that you could have prevented it. And did not. Did. Not. You're killing her!*

Jode clenched his fists until he ached. With every bit of his skill and power, he grappled with the wild storm of Kane's emotions. Finally the psi-master was able to speak deeply, urgently in Kane's mind, words and emotions reassuring the Za'arain that his lias'tri was not dying.

Look at your stone, Kane! Look at your stone!

Unnoticed, Kane pulled out his lias'tri gem and cupped it between his palms. Light blazed and licked over the surface of his hands, colors pooling impossibly, thick with radiance and life. Whatever the cost of healing in the temporary pain of time/now, Sharia was not injuring herself in the *now* or the *always*.

At least, not yet. The danger in time/now waited for her as surely as it had lurked among the artifacts of time/then for him. No one's energy was infinite. Darien fives were strong but they were not gods. They could break and die as surely and as finally as a Wolfin or a Jhoramon. Sharia could no more heal every person's time/then and time/now than she could live in the shifting, featureless *always*.

Kane sat and watched his lias'tri gem reflect the racing colors of Sharia's timeshadow. He lost count of the trader who came to her. He lost count of linear time. Mesmerized, he watched the flux and scintillation of Sharia's life in the gem held between his hands.

And then everything changed. Colors drained and dimmed. Darkness shattered through the stone. Too many timeshadows. Too many psi-aware, untrained minds. Too much draining out of her into them. Too much.

Stop her! cried Jode in Kane's mind. *If I touch her now she'll just try to heal me too. That will kill her. I can't be healed. I'm joined to death in ways neither one of you can comprehend. Lias'tri.*

Yet Kane could no more touch Sharia than Jode could. Kane,

too, required healing. If he dragged Sharia away from one wind trader, it would only be to suck her into a far more powerful timeshadow than any she had yet ridden. Suddenly Kane remembered how Jode had stifled Kane's mind, forcing it to turn back upon itself, wrapping it in gently muffling negatives.

Jode followed Kane's thought as though it were his own.

I'm not powerful enough to do that to Sharia without hurting her. Not when she's using every level of her mind like she is now, responded Jode quickly. *Take your awareness like so*—the psi-master touched Kane's mind in swift demonstration—*Now throw it . . . yes!—curl around her mind. Gently. Gently! You're like a falling mountain. Better. Yes . . . yes . . . that's it! Now— very, very gently—never mind. I'll do it myself. You've done the hard part.*

Jode squeezed Sharia's awareness with consummate skill, shutting down the free flowing of her mental energies deftly as she herself could shut down or open timeshadow energies.

Sharia shuddered and awoke from the dangerous daze of endless healing. She looked around with nearly blind silver eyes. She blinked several times, violet and silver alternating until all levels of her mind were assured of her safety. Then she closed her eyes and sank wearily onto the hard stone floor.

With an immense effort Kane forced himself not to go to her, to lift her and carry her back to the ship as he had on Za'arain. It would be safe for him to touch her now; her mind was under control. But now he could not touch her without calling forth all the conflict of the Za'ar imperative. She would know he had touched her. At some level she would know; and it would tear her apart.

Wearily Kane looked away from her. Seventeen wind traders stood tall and powerful in front of him. Seventeen, when the bargain had only called for ten. It was too late to do anything about that, now. It had been too late the instant Sharia's seeking, time-combing Darien hair had been loosed among the wounded, tangled wind traders.

"The bargain is complete," said Kane in comspeech, ritual words to mark the end of his interest in doing business.

The wind traders hesitated, conferred among themselves, spoke into a Wolfin transmitter and then stood quietly. Kane was forced to wait as well. Until the wind clan accepted the bargain, the trading was not over. From the back of the room came a voice calling out in Jhoramon demanding that people give way. Kane turned and watched seven Jhoramons press through the crowd. None of the Jhoramons were of the wind clan, though each carried one of the leather boxes wind traders used to hold artifacts. One by one the boxes were put in front of Kane.

"We are the last of the wind trader clan," said one of the women Sharia had healed. "There can be no repayment to equal the future that your woman gave us. All that we have is yours."

Kane looked into the woman's proud blue eyes for a long moment before he gestured to Ine. Too quietly for the woman to hear, Kane instructed Ine to transfer two-thirds of the ship's currency to the wind clan's account. It was not a tenth of the price the contents of the boxes should bring, but it would ensure that the wind clan could buy the tools and equipment they needed to survive. Ine argued softly against the unsolicited payment, saying that it was unnecessary, that the wind traders had named the bargain. If they wished to be sentimental, that was their problem, not Kane's. Kane cut off the argument with a curt gesture and a blunt command.

"Do it."

The Jiddirit shrugged and turned away, his brown fingers dancing over the subtle rises and indentations of his fist-sized recorder. A blue light glowed, signifying that the transaction had been registered.

"It's done," sighed Ine, offended to the depths of his shrewd Jiddirit soul by the unnecessary expenditure.

Kane turned back to the waiting wind trader. "The bargain is complete," repeated Kane.

"The bargain is complete," she agreed.

With surprising quickness Ine bent over Sharia, pulled her to her feet and turned to face Kane. Against the Jiddirit's brown hand, the pearl glow of a Wolfin energy weapon was startlingly clear. The muzzle was pointed toward Kane, but it would take only a tiny movement to bring the weapon to bear on Sharia.

"Now," said Ine clearly, "our bargaining begins."

Eleven

Kane felt savagery wake and prowl deep within his Kiri mind. He fought the atavistic rage; right now it was as dangerous to Sharia as the Wolfin gun lying next to her neck. His uncanny senses picked up the movement of Jiddirits behind him. He did not need to turn around to know that more weapons had been drawn.

"You've been valuable to me, Ine," said Kane, keeping his voice casual despite the flickering of his inner eyelids, dark silver to violet and then to dark silver again. "If you think you deserve more than the five percent we agreed upon, I'm willing to bargain."

Ine made a Jiddirit gesture that conveyed inevitability. "Of course you are. Unfortunately, you have nothing that I want except her."

Sharia stood very still. She knew that she was in no real danger. Not yet. Not until Kane refused whatever bargain Ine offered. And Kane would refuse it. She knew that as surely as she knew that Kiri rage was swelling beneath Kane's calmness. She could do nothing, though, for Ine's weapon could not fail to kill Kane at this range. Nor would there be any help from the Jhoramons. Ine's shipmates and downside friends had fanned out facing the crowd, weapons drawn.

Don't move, Jode cautioned, linking minds with both Sharia and Kane. *Ine's too close to miss.*

I know.

Sharia's thought was the same as Kane's. Acceptance—and

4 BESTSELLING HISTORICAL ROMANCES BY YOUR FAVORITE AUTHORS CAN BE YOURS, FREE!

Kensington Choice, our newest book club now brings you historical romances by your favorite bestselling authors including Janelle Taylor, Shannon Drake, Rosanne Bittner, Jo Beverley, and Georgina Gentry, just to name a few! Each book is filled with passion, adventure and the excitement of bygone times!

To introduce you to this great new club which is part of Zebra Home Subscription Service, we'd like to send you your first 4 bestselling historical romances, absolutely free! And once you get these 4 free books to savor at home, we'll rush you the next 4 brand-new books at the lowest prices available, as soon as they are published.

The way the club works is that after your initial FREE shipment, you will get our 4 newest bestselling historical romances delivered to your

doorstep each month at the preferred subscriber's rate of only $4.20 per book, a savings of up to $7.16 per month (since these titles sell in bookstores for $4.99-$5.99)! All books are sent on a 10-day free examination basis and there is no minimum number of books to buy. (A postage and handling charge of $1.50 is added to each shipment.) Plus as a regular subscriber, you'll receive our FREE monthly newsletter, *Zebra/Pinnacle Romance News*, which features author profiles, contests, subscriber benefits, book previews and more!

So start today by returning the FREE BOOK CERTIFICATE provided. We'll send you 4 FREE BOOKS with no further obligation: A FREE gift offering you hours of reading pleasure with no obligation...how can you lose?

*We have 4 FREE BOOKS for you
as your introduction to
KENSINGTON CHOICE!
To get your FREE BOOKS, worth
up to $23.96, mail the card below.*

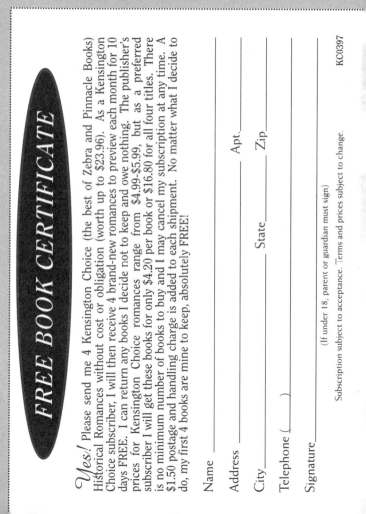

FREE BOOK CERTIFICATE

Yes! Please send me 4 Kensington Choice (the best of Zebra and Pinnacle Books) Historical Romances without cost or obligation (worth up to $23.96). As a Kensington Choice subscriber, I will then receive 4 brand-new romances to preview each month for 10 days FREE. I can return any books I decide not to keep and owe nothing. The publisher's prices for Kensington Choice romances range from $4.99-$5.99, but as a preferred subscriber I will get these books for only $4.20 per book or $16.80 for all four titles. There is no minimum number of books to buy and I may cancel my subscription at any time. A $1.50 postage and handling charge is added to each shipment. No matter what I decide to do, my first 4 books are mine to keep, absolutely FREE!

Name _____

Address _____ Apt. _____

City _____ State _____ Zip _____

Telephone ( ) _____

Signature _____
(If under 18, parent or guardian must sign)

Subscription subject to acceptance. Terms and prices subject to change.   KC0397

4 FREE
Historical
Romances
are waiting
for you to
claim them!

(worth up to
$23.96)

See details
inside....

KENSINGTON CHOICE
Zebra Home Subscription Service, Inc.
120 Brighton Road
P.O.Box 5214
Clifton, NJ 07015-5214

beneath that acceptance a feral desire to kill. Kane waited motionlessly. With predatory patience he thought of nothing at all while he watched for just one instant of his prey's inattention.

"There's always a bargain to be struck," said Kane, quoting an ancient Jiddirit maxim. "Is it health you want?"

"Yes."

"Then she'll heal you. But not this instant. She's much too tired. You wouldn't poison the well you hope to drink from, would you?"

Kane. Jode's thought was swift, calm. *I'm closer to Ine than you. I'll take him down and then help you with the rest.*

There was a flash of agreement so savage, so eager, that Jode winced.

"I'm not going to poison anything," said Ine. "I'm simply taking my five percent of the last bargain struck. I'll keep your healer here on Jhora with me and my men. This isn't a healthy planet since the winnowing. When you return—if you return— from your unprofitable quest, I'll give her back to you. Untouched, Captain. That, too, is part of the bargain."

"Let me think," Kane said quietly.

Ine tipped his head in a gesture of agreement.

Kiri eyelids came down, stayed down. Jhora transformed with psi-hunter light. The timeshadow wakes were not nearly so thick here as on Za'arain. There was no million-year history, no thickly massed lives and deaths waiting to be called by a Kiri who was also a Darien five. But many had died in Jhora's winnowing, and each death had freed a timeshadow wake for a psi-hunter to use. Kane called to those wakes as he had on Za'arain. They answered, but slowly, slowly. It was as though he had attempted to call down the moon's untouched brilliance and pool it in his cupped hands.

There were not enough wakes beneath Ine's feet. Kane reached more widely, calling to wakes throughout the room. He plaited the dimensional energies with agonizing slowness, wondering why they seemed so elusive, so reluctant. Finally he stretched the wakes, pulling them, calling to them with every bit of his power.

Jode sensed Kane straining toward something, saw the bottomless violence in his Kiri eyes and knew what to expect. Soon, somewhere, the floor would move. In that moment Jode would leap for Ine. A single blow was all that was necessary. Just one.

The trading floor shivered and shattered beneath everyone's feet, deflecting Ine's aim. But not enough. Not quite. Bright death poured from the muzzle of Ine's gun as Jode's long, lean leg lashed out. The blow missed being deadly because the footing was unstable. Ine went down, though, and stayed there. Sharia screamed Kane's name as she spun away clutching her side. She turned toward Kane screaming, and her Darien hair swept out in a violent silver cloud.

In the grip of Kiri rage, Kane had barely felt the moment when deadly energy sliced into his side. He had already been turning, reaching, his powerful body intent on death. As he leaped toward Ine's friends, the floor shuddered again. He went through five of the Jiddirits in a deadly golden blur, tearing them from life with savage finality before the terrible wound in his side brought him down even as he was reaching for another man.

The remaining Jiddirits would have killed Kane but for the sudden onslaught of wind traders. With the disciplined rush of clansmen who hunted sand dragons for sport, the wind traders disarmed the Jiddirits and their downside Jhoramon supporters.

The fight had lasted only a few seconds, not even long enough for Sharia to reach Kane. The last of her screams still echoed in the huge room as she clawed her way across the greenstone floor toward Kane's motionless body. Blood poured from her, turning her clothes the color of rust. Her blood, but not her wound—Kane's wound, and Kane's blood flowing, blood pooling brightly on the floor beneath him.

Jode reached down to help Sharia, then saw her violet eyes and remembered dead men littering the floor of a shattered glass room on Za'arain. He flinched away the instant before her hair would have touched him. The reflexive action saved his life. Sharia was in the grip of atavistic rage and lias'tri fury. She would have killed anything that came between her and Kane's dying, writhing timeshadow.

With a final wrenching effort, Sharia dragged herself to Kane. Her hair flowed out, concealing both of them in translucent silver. Inside that rippling cloud her hands thrust into Kane's shorter, darker hair, seeking the warmth beneath its translucent thickness as though she could stem the outpouring life with touch alone.

Suddenly Sharia felt strength sweep through her, strength leaping into time/now from the *then* and the *now*, strength pouring into her from every point of physical contact between her body and Kane's. Sharia did not ask where that strength came from; she simply took it ruthlessly, filling herself with it. Then she dove into the torrential violence of Kane's timeshadow, riding it down into the recent past, pouring her own energy into the cold black gap that marked the instant when Ine's weapon had torn through Kane's living flesh.

The force of the energy Sharia had called went through her like a shock wave, answering her instinctive requirements. Flesh and timeshadow knit together, balancing each other, currents of color and warmth overwhelming the blackness that had radiated up from the instant of injury. Kane healed, and yet still the energy welled up from the points where Sharia's hands touched him, where her legs twined with his, where her cheek lay against his chest, energy welling out from the *then* and the *now*.

Smiling, Sharia let Kane's Darien hair run between her fingers as smoothly as warm, scented water. His timeshadow shimmered and flexed like wind-driven flames, wrapping around her with sweet, hungry fingers. His presence poured through her and hers through him. She felt him stir, awakening from unconsciousness. Her smile was as caressing as her hair. Her sensitive lips moved over his, drinking the warmth and life that radiated from him. Abruptly the reality of what she was doing broke over her in a chilling wave. Five touching five. Za'ar tabu. A dying Kiriy's imperative.

Energy arced suddenly, borne on the rising wave of Kane's consciousness. Energy straining to be released. Energy of the *then* reaching toward the *now*. If that gap were bridged, the result would be catastrophe.

Sharia's eyes opened no longer violet, but knowledge was a shadow turning within their silver depths. The vise of Kiri conditioning and Za'ar imperative returned, constricting her. With a silent cry of rebellion and regret, she let Kane's hair slide from between her pale fingers and rolled aside until she no longer touched him.

Suddenly cold, alone as he had never been, Kane awoke completely. He reached automatically for the warmth and pouring life that had touched him so recently. A tendril of Sharia's hair met his hand in bittersweet caress. Then she wrapped her vital silver hair around her head so tightly that her lips thinned with pain. The temptation to know again Kane's exquisite, torrential presence made her shudder and cry out silently. Conditioning closed around her in a rush, supporting her in her weakness. It was cold comfort for what she had lost; but comfort nonetheless.

Kane caught Sharia's fleeting thought/memory. He understood only that she had healed him—and that she had then withdrawn as finally as though they had never known one another, never laughed, never touched. He tasted the acrid instant of her terror and the bitter moment of her acceptance. All that kept him from grabbing her in anger and demanding her warmth was that there had been no hint of the horror that had so enraged him before. She had not shrunk from him. She had shrunk from . . . what?

Catastrophe. Her thought was barely a whisper in his mind.

A myth! retorted Kane impatiently. *Two fives touching aren't—*

The icy clarity of Jode's mindspeech intervened, cutting off

Kane's thought. *Argue later. We have more urgent problems now than Za'arain word games.*

A low sound rippled through the watching people as Kane and Sharia rose to their feet unaided. It was astonishing enough that they both were alive. The fact that neither one showed any sign of injury, not even so much as a bloodstained tunic, made the crowd cry out in denial of what they were seeing. Only the wind traders stood without retreating, their broad, hard feet planted firmly on the shattered greenstone floor. People who hunted ghost relics in the shifting lair of sand dragons had learned long ago to control their fears.

Kane's eyes went from the wind clan to Ine, who stood quietly within Jode's grasp. For an instant Kane's eyes were violet promises of death. Sanity returned with the next breath.

"You didn't kill him," said Kane flatly to Jode.

"He's the best trader in the Joining," said Jode.

Kane's flat, tarnished silver eyes measured the Jiddirit. "Yes, but he needs educating about the nature of timesha—healing."

Jode shrugged. "So educate him. Be quick about it, though. When word of Sharia's healing ability gets out, we'll be mobbed. As Ine said, Jhora hasn't been a healthy place since the winnowing."

Kane turned toward Sharia. He expected to find her exhausted. She was not. She was luminous with light and life. The energies she had called to heal him had healed her as well.

I'm sorry to ask this of you, Kane murmured regretfully in Sharia's mind, *but it's the only way I can protect you. They must know that even if I'm dead, you aren't an object to be traded from hand to hand.*

What do you want me to do?

Ride Ine's timeshadow. Not to heal, but to teach. Don't kill him if you can help it. And if you can't help it—Kane's smile was hard, feral, like his suddenly violet eyes—*well, that too is a kind of lesson.*

I can't do anything but heal.

Kane realized then that Sharia had no memories of the time

when she had killed psi-hunters with a single deadly touch of her hair. He did not want to tell her.

Sharia listened to her own words echoing in her mind, and realized that she was wrong. She could untangle or she could knot. She could comb together into smoothness or she could tear apart into ragged shreds. She could expand or she could constrict the colors. She could heal or she could kill. The realization was both bitter and . . . sweet.

Sharia turned toward the man who had tried to murder Kane. Her eyes were violet and her hair was a silver fire.

Control her, Kane! urged Jode frantically.

Dark Kiri laughter turned deep within the psi-master's mind. He did not know whether it was Sharia's or Kane's laughter. Jode did know that it was like a slash of ice against the warmth of his life.

"Let go of him, Jhoramon."

Though Sharia's eyes were violet Za'arain atavism, her words were Joining comspeech. That alone was enough to shock Kane back from the edge of savagery. Psi-hunter and Joining combined. Za'arain's worst nightmare was standing before him, embodied in the woman he loved.

Sv'arri . . . !

Slowly, Sharia turned toward Kane. "He tried to kill you," she said in husky Za'arain. "You are mine, v'orri, and he tried to kill you. We are one."

Kane's eyes blazed at Sharia's words, echoes of Za'arain marriage rituals and Kiri rage vibrating in her voice. She might not touch him, but she was his.

"You are mine, and he would have taken you," said Kane, the Za'arain words he used both musical and savage. "We are one. I will kill him."

"No! Not with psi-hunter eyes! The atavism is too hard to control!"

"And you, my silver Darien, what color are your eyes?" asked Kane softly.

Sharia looked and saw herself reflected in Kane's violet eyes.

She closed her own eyes once, twice, but still the room remained bathed in eerie hunter light. Timeshadows twisted and rippled and called to her, hundreds of timeshadows dancing like rainbow flames streaming out from time/now into the *now*, energy reaching, flowing back to time/then and into the *then*. She realized at that moment that the ability to heal or destroy came from the same source, identical energies. Only the result was different. Her eyes opened slowly, rational and violet at once, atavism and discipline united. It was a volatile mix, difficult to control; but she would not have to control it for long.

Translucent hair seethed gently, waiting for Darien command. "Do you want Ine dead or merely educated?" asked Sharia calmly in Za'arain.

Kane watched her for a long moment before he smiled, his own atavism and discipline combined as equally as hers. "Educated, and educated in a way that will also put the fear of Za'ar into his followers."

Sharia's smile was both beautiful and chilling. As she approached Ine, he understood the ice, if not the beauty.

"Let go of him, Jode," she said softly in comspeech. "Your presence won't stop me and might cost Ine his life. Not to mention a certain amount of your own . . . discomfort."

Jode muttered a Jhoramon obscenity and stepped away from Ine. "He really is a good trader." Jode observed coolly. "And by the customs of Jiddir, what he did wasn't treachery."

"I'll remember that," promised Sharia. "Just as he will remember this."

Sharia's hair lifted in a disciplined surge of silver that concealed Ine behind a shifting, translucent veil. Long tendrils combed Ine's timeshadow, learning its currents and colors, its gaps and its darknesses. Without her self-discipline, her Darien gift would have compelled her to heal him or her Kiri atavism would have compelled her to kill him. The two competing urges united in uneasy partnership, held by the bonds of a five's acceptance of the continuum between healing and killing.

Delicately, Sharia rode Ine's shivering timeshadow. It would have been so easy to kill or heal him. A single knotting of the thick current of his life or a single combing out of the tangled shadows. Instead, she combed the shadows into rather than out of his timeshadow, pulling the moments of sickness or injury further back into Ine's time/then and letting the dark ramifications radiate upward into his time/now. Not too far back, for the result would be unpredictable and almost certainly deadly. Then she followed the bright scarlet river of his life-force back to the moment of its condensation from the *always* into time/then. Gently, gently, she eased the moment further back into time/then, watching darkness condense throughout the rippling colors as she aged the life-force, dimming its power as linear time always dimmed life.

Translucent hair whispered into stillness, revealing Ine. A low, horrified sound rose from the watching people. The Jiddirit who had moments ago stood before them in his bursting prime was now shrunken, twisted, wasted, a man on the last downward years of a long and unhealthy life. He would have fallen but for Sharia's support.

Kane looked at the shaken people who had watched Ine's unwilling metamorphosis. When Kane spoke, his deep voice carried to every angle of the room. "Remember this when you're tempted to force a healer's touch. What she gives she can also take away."

No one moved or spoke. Kane measured the silence with grim satisfaction. He turned back to Sharia. Only she knew the regret in his mind for what he had asked her to do.

May I heal him? she asked quietly in Kane's mind. Then, quickly, *I'll leave Ine like this if I must, but I'd rather kill him. He earned death, not torture.*

Kane looked at the distorted, disoriented remnant of one of the best traders in the Joining. "Whatever you like, sv'arri," he said in Za'arain. "We've made our point."

Silver seethed outward, surrounding the shrunken man. Sharia rode the attenuated timeshadow easily, skillfully, pulling his life forward into time/now, combing out darkness. She healed him completely, leaving him stronger than before. Her hair swept back, wrapping around her head in a sinuous crown. Ine stood before her, erect again, vibrant with life.

There was only one difference to mark his second transformation. On the back of his right hand was a bright Za'arain ideograph.

Sharia touched the silver design that was now as much a part of Ine as his brown Jiddirit flesh. "That will burn every day of your long life, Ine," said Sharia in comspeech. "It is the Za'arain ideograph for catastrophe. Remember it, and me."

Ine flexed his hand. Slowly he went down on one knee in a Jiddirit gesture of acceptance. After a few moments he stood again and turned toward Kane, waiting for whatever his captain might do.

"You're free," said Kane, his voice neutral. Then his eyelids descended in a flash of violet. "Don't mistake Za'arain compassion for weakness, Jiddirit. Next time will be worse for you, and there will be no mercy. No death. Life everlasting, and every instant of it will be agony."

Ine looked at the silver brand on his flesh. Though it was cool to his touch, heat radiated from the mark, burning him. He knelt once more, this time in front of Kane. "I've learned, Captain. Your woman is yours. For that, there can be no bargaining. Will you let me serve you again?"

"I said I'd come back for you. If I survive. I keep my bargains."

"Take me with you as you did before. I can help you find the Eyes."

"How?" asked Kane, focusing his mind instead of his rage on the man kneeling before him.

"I have spies among the Dust raiders."

For a long moment Kane watched Ine with unblinking silver eyes. "All right." Then, softly. "For your sake I hope you have a long memory. The lesson won't be repeated."

"I accept, Za'arain," said Ine in his native language. He stood swiftly and walked from the trading room without a backward look.

Jode watched Ine's retreat with dark, speculative eyes. "He's rather like having an azir for a pet," observed Jode in comspeech. "Quick, intelligent and deadly. But not to you. Not anymore."

"I wish I were as confident as you," said Kane dryly, turning to look at the Jiddirits and Jhoramons still held by the wind traders.

"You should be confident," said Jode. "He accepted the bargain in the speech of Jiddirit. If he goes back on it, he'll be killed by his own men."

Kane looked startled. "Does that mean I can trust his men, too?"

"So long as they're with Ine, yes."

Kane tilted his head thoughtfully and watched the captive Jiddirits with flat silver eyes. Then he addressed the wind traders in comspeech: "Let the Jiddirits go, unless you want them for yourselves."

Wind trader hands lifted, releasing the wiry brown men.

"Take your choice," said Kane to the Jiddirits. "Jhora or the ship."

"The ship."

"Load up the trade goods," said Kane.

As one, the Jiddirits grabbed boxes and hurried to follow Ine from the greenstone building.

"Do you want these?" a wind trader asked Kane, gesturing toward Ine's downside friends.

"Not particularly."

The man's smile flashed startlingly against his dark face. He gestured with a leather-clad hand. The wind traders withdrew, taking the downsiders with them. For a moment Kane wondered what would happen to the luckless Jhoramons. His curiosity did not last long; whatever their fate, the Jhoramons had known the risks before they took up positions in the game.

Jode made a curt gesture that suggested Kane start for the

ship immediately. They divided the remaining boxes and walked quickly toward the downside landing area. Merone moved with them like a well-trained shadow. Sharia led the way, carrying a basket full of bright jhoras. The natives they met between the trading building and the ship looked at her, then looked at her again. More downsiders began to appear. Carried by Jhora's restless wind, phrases in several languages floated across the synstone roads toward the group of off-worlders.

They want her. Jode's thought to Kane was cool, precise.

Did they think Ine was a fluke? retorted Kane, his thought rich with disgust at human stupidity.

They don't know about Ine. They know about the jhoras, though. A few even know about the wind traders.

If rumors of Sharia's potential deadliness had not caught up with rumors of her healing abilities, the Jhoramons looking at her so covetously would believe that nothing stood between them and eternal health except a few off-worlders heavily burdened with wind trader artifacts. If the natives were armed, the contest would be brutally uneven until Sharia came within touching distance of her would-be abductors. Kane did not want that to happen. He been mortally wounded once today; he had no desire to repeat the experience. Next time Sharia might not be able to overcome her own sympathetic agony in time to heal him.

Or next time the shot might be instantly fatal.

Kane measured the distance between Sharia and the ship, and Sharia and the natives. A Za'arain curse sizzled in his mind— and in Jode's.

Dani tells me that there are a lot of downsiders gathering around the ship, offered Jode, his mindspeech unemotional.

Tell her to light up.

There was a pause. Then, *She's hot and getting hotter.*

Kane turned toward Merone. "We're in trouble."

The Wolfin woman's striped face turned toward Kane. She nodded once in the comspeech gesture of understanding. "I'm armed."

"Draw your weapon on my command."

"Yes, Captain."

Sharia looked from one to the other, then to the empty syn-stone streets. Only they were not empty any longer. Natives had gathered, trickling out of doorways by twos and threes and fives. A murmur of sound arose from them, words without meaning, a sound of hunger. They had been ill since the winnowing and now a miracle of healing stood within their midst. If word of healing's other, deadly, side had gone out among the greenstone buildings, no one was heeding it.

Can Dani send out the Xtians? asked Kane, curious about the ship's new abilities. Sounding alarms and getting ready for a hot takeoff was standard Wolfin programming. Alerting individual crew members to needs outside the ship was not.

She's thinking about it. Jode's response had equal amounts of surprise and amusement in it. *While she thinks, can you do your stone-shattering trick?* he continued calmly, measuring the odds as Kane had measured them. Too many natives, and the ship was too far away.

It would take too long to break the ground, responded Kane.

Not if Sharia were touching you.

Kane threw a dark silver glance at the Jhoramon walking quickly beside him. *What do you mean?*

Don't be more stupid than Za'ar made you, snarled Jode in Kane's mind. *When lias'tris touch they become much more than either one alone. All their former lives and knowledge are there for the taking—all their skills, their powers, everything. Why do you think you were so deadly on Za'arain?*

A million years of timeshadow wakes, retorted Kane succinctly.

Really? Then why couldn't you use those wakes easily before you were holding Sharia? Remember? prodded Jode, his mind-speech like chips of razor ice. *You worked like a kax beast and not much happened. But when you were carrying Sharia and her hair flowed over you, you all but pulled the city apart!*

The natives seethed restlessly, like water in a geyser feeling the first pressure of superheated steam rushing up from below.

"Weapons," said Kane calmly, drawing his own as Jode and Merone drew theirs. "Jode, take the rear. Merone, watch the group on the left." He hesitated, then added quietly, "Sharia, walk beside me. I may need you."

"I don't have a weapon," she said.

He laughed roughly. "Don't you? Loose your hair, sv'arri." *It might touch you!*

Sharia's mindspeech was multi-leveled, complex, conveying background thoughts and extrapolations, emotions and the pervasive yearning that tore at her with every heartbeat. But amid all the conflicting thoughts and emotions, there was nothing of revulsion due to Kiri conditioning. There was an uneasiness that was just short of unbridled fear, an uneasiness based upon recent experience rather than past teachings. Two fives touching. The *then* and the *now* surging up, meeting, overlapping. Catastrophe.

The echoes of Sharia's thoughts resonated in Kane's mind, telling him the source of her fear—experience, not conditioning. Unconsciously he increased the pace of his stride, closing in on the ship as quickly as he could without bringing out the natives' hunting instincts by running. He started to ask questions in Sharia's mind before he realized that she had shrunk from even that tenuous touch.

"Listen," he said urgently. "Even if you're right—and I'm not sure you are!—you controlled the za' factors long enough to heal me."

He sensed her reluctant agreement.

"If I'm wounded again, you'll be compelled to heal me again," continued Kane relentlessly. "You won't have any choice." Though he said nothing, the comspeech word *lias 'tri* quivered in his mind, and hers. Even if she could overcome her Darien compulsion to heal, there was this other, totally unknown force yet to deal with.

"Yes," said Sharia her eyes silver, deep, "I know."

"Wouldn't it be better to touch me before you're compelled, while you're still in control?"

Kane sensed her surprise and then the quick, deep considerations of her mind.

"How long?" she asked tightly.

"Just long enough to make the streets shatter."

Sharia remembered the greenstone building where the floor had shifted subtly and broken beneath the Jiddirits' feet. She remembered feeling Kane's mind stretching, straining, long minutes of reaching for something just beyond his grasp. "Too long," she whispered.

"It won't take that long if you're touching me," Kane reassured her quickly. "At least, that's what Jode believes. Lias'tri. We're more powerful together. Much more powerful."

The crowd of Jhoramons moved closer by increments. Kane watched them with eyes gone suddenly violet. Kiri eyes. Timeshadow wakes beckoned like ghosts, static pastel shadows of the pouring energies he had known on Za'arain. He reached for the wakes, knowing as he did that they were too elusive, subtly removed, as though he tried to touch them through a wall of glass and time a hundred feet thick.

Sharia sensed Kane's urgency and his frustration. She looked at the downsiders with experienced eyes. She had seen people like this before, on Za'arain, when a million years of culture had been coming apart around her, civilization going down before an onslaught of undifferentiated animal need. The time to act was now, instantly, before the natives had a chance to organize their hunger into a concerted attack.

Before they had a chance to use their weapons on Kane, destroying him beyond her ability to heal.

Kiri eyelids flickered down, transforming the world. The Xtian silver Sharia had woven back into her hair trembled and chimed and dropped into the basket of jhoras she carried in her hands. The small sound was the only warning Kane had. A cloud of translucent hair floated up as Sharia stepped closer to him. Silky tendrils caressed his shoulders, his jaw, his lips, then flowed over his arms like molten sleeves. Deliberately she put her hand in his.

Timeshadow wakes leaped into multi-colored clarity. Thick, taut with energy, wakes twisted and shimmered up from the streets and the buildings like streamers of immaterial, rainbow wildfire. So many people had died in the winnowing. So recently. Their wakes were turgid with energy just short of the full power of living timeshadows. Kane laughed unconsciously, chillingly, and he summoned the thickly layered wakes. They came to him as to a master long missed, curling around him, braiding, stretching—time stretching and then suddenly released.

Around Kane's small group the synstone streets heaved and exploded into millions of razor shards.

Shock waves of time and sound broke over the stunned downsiders. Jode and Merone stood as transfixed as any native, their eyes reflecting the translucent silver storm of Sharia's hair and Kane's feral laughter ringing in their ears. Stone dust lifted chokingly on Jhora's uncertain winds. Sharia and Kane did not notice. They felt nothing but the utter rightness of their flesh touching, timeshadows overlapping, colors coruscating as time shivered and . . . changed. Fierce elation nipped through both their minds. Lias'tri gems blazed blindingly, equally, promising an incredible consummation of all possibilities that had ever been, a promise held deep within za' and space and the heat of two Darien bodies anchored richly in the sensuality of time/now.

The *then* and the *now* and the *always* reached hungrily for undifferentiated unity, all dimensions flowing one into the other.

Catastrophe.

Sharia shuddered and forced her hair to leave the torrential perfection of Kane's timeshadow and her hand to withdraw from the sweet warmth of his fingers laced through hers. She did not know that she cried out at the parting as though it were her skin being peeled from her living body rather than her hand from his. The temptation to touch him again made her shudder and bite her lip until blood flowed. She stood apart from Kane, watching him with wild silver eyes.

"Now do you understand?" she whispered.

He understood, for there was blood on his lip as well. Her wound, his blood, za' factors swirling hungrily. He understood, and he hated every split instant of that understanding.

"Get moving," said Jode roughly, shaking Kane. The Za'arain's grief and rebellion scored across the psi-master's mind. "Move quickly or you won't live to find out what a fool you're being!"

With a snarl Kane turned and ran through crushed synstone streets. He did not notice the disoriented, frightened downsider, he shoved aside; neither did the woman who ran beside him, her Darien hair tightly bound, her eyes violet, her mind closed.

Yet even as they fled for their lives through the broken streets, the two Za'arains were careful not to touch one another. They had learned that Za'ar tabu had a terrifying basis in reality. The Eyes might have closed in time/now, but Za'ar knowledge, Za'ar retribution, did not depend on linear time.

Lias'tri wrapped around them, potentially more deadly than the Eyes of Za'ar.

Twelve

Doursone was seven za'replacements from Jhora. During the trip Sharia and Kane were careful to avoid all but the most necessary conversation. Jode watched them for two days, unwillingly sharing their deep longings and deeper fears. Finally he lost his temper.

"Captain," said the psi-master harshly, "if you and Sharia don't stop circling each other like hungry scorals at mating time, you're going to have to find yourself a new pilot on Doursone. Surely two adult, intelligent, Fourth Evolution people can overcome a ridiculous downside tabu!"

Sharia and Kane exchanged a long look. They had done that a lot lately, one looking at the other and then looking away hurriedly when the glance was returned. Each time it had been harder to look away. Now it was becoming all but impossible.

"It's not that simple," said Kane bleakly.

Jode's answer was wordless, savage and obscene. Then, more calmly, he said aloud, "Why not?"

It was Sharia who answered. Her voice was tight, vibrating with leashed emotions. "We could—and have—overcome Kiri conditioning, Kiriy warning, Za'ar imperative. What we can't do is overcome the za' reality tabu is rooted in."

"I suppose that should mean something to me," said Jode impatiently. "It doesn't."

Sharia's eyes closed. They were still silver when they opened, to Jode's hidden relief. As much as the two Za'arains irritated him with their blind subservience to childhood training, he had no desire to face them when they watched him out of violet eyes.

"I don't know if we can explain it to you," said Kane quietly, sensing that Sharia's emotions were too uncertain for her to speak at that moment. "Comspeech has only one word for time."

"What does that have to do with two foolish lias'tris?" snapped Jode.

Kane blinked but his eyes, too, remained dark silver. "I don't know," he said evenly. "It has everything to do with Za'ar tabu, though."

Both Za'arains felt the sudden heat of Jode's impatience. They also felt the equally powerful reigning-in of his emotions.

"I'm listening," said the Jhoramon coolly. Then, with a sarcasm that made them flinch, he added, "Please tell me something worth hearing."

Sharia looked at Kane. He looked away from her with an effort that made Jode's hands clench.

"Talk to me, Captain," commanded Jode.

"The energy of life is unique in its relationship to time and is also extremely tenacious," said Kane in a clipped voice. "Life's energy permeates everything it touches. Stones, earth, furniture, jewelry—even time itself. Especially time. The resonances of that energy comprise what we call a timeshadow wake. Everything that has ever lived has left a wake in some aspect of time."

Jode grunted, a sound that neither agreed nor disagreed.

"So long as that wake is still connected to a living timeshadow," continued Kane, "I can only sense the fact of the wake's presence. I can't learn from the wake or manipulate it, because my Darien gift is to comprehend the *then*, not the *now*, and living timeshadows are connected to the *now* as well as to the linear aspect of time we call time/now. Timeshadow wakes are connected to the *then*, which is why I can use them."

Jode started to ask a question but decided against it. Kane had warned him that comspeech was inadequate to the task of explaining Za'arain reality. Intuition and intelligence, however, had been known to overcome the limitations of language. The psimaster listened intently, trying to understand the inexplicable.

"Sharia's Darien gift is to comprehend the *now* of living timeshadows," said Kane. He tried, but could not prevent the instant of emotion that came to him when he remembered the beauty of his timeshadow caressed by her shimmering hair. He heard Sharia's sudden intake of breath and knew that she had sensed his memory, shared it, added her own to it. It was as though each time they touched, the levels of their communication increased and the complexity expanded. Even though each was trying not to infringe upon the other's mind, the connections remained inviolate, a subtle sharing that was both a warning against and a siren call toward greater intimacy.

Grimly Kane focused again on the reason Sharia should never touch him again. "She rides living timeshadows in both linear time/now and the *now,* which is why she can heal in linear time/then—if she's careful. Very careful. All life is rooted in and stretched between the *then* and the *now.* It's part of life's symbiotic relationship with some aspects of time. The older you are, the more deeply you become rooted in the *then.* When the balance shifts too heavily, the timeshadow loses its grip on the *now* and you die. If she rides a timeshadow too far down, or is careless, she'll fall off in the *then* and die."

Kane said nothing more. He waited as though he had said enough.

"Even if every word you say is true," said Jode carefully, "what does that have to do with Za'ar tabu?"

Kane closed his eyes. Jode felt the lash of Za'arain frustration.

"Let me, v'orri," Sharia said in a soft voice. She focused her transparent silver eyes on Jode. "On Za'arain, nearly everyone is born with some type of psi gift. The Kiris have the most powerful abilities. That's how they are recognized as members of the Kiri clan. Most Kiris are born to other Kiris. Not all, though." She shrugged, dismissing the random mutations that occurred. "There are many families within the Kiris. One of those families is called Darien. Kane's father was Darien. Kane is Darien. My mother was Darien, and she passed the peculiar Darien gift on to me."

"Timeshadows," said Jode, remembering what Sharia had told him before about the Darien gift.

"Yes. And their wakes." Sharia waited, then sighed. Jode still did not understand. "Throughout Za'arain, most people have four- or six-fingered hands. There is no difference in psi gifts between them. Fives used to be rare. Extremely rare. And extremely powerful in the expression of the Kiri gifts. Mature fives were forbidden to each other by the Eyes of Za'ar."

Unwillingly, Sharia looked at Kane. He was watching her with hungry eyes. For a timeless instant she shared her own hunger with him, watching him. Then she forced herself to look back at the slender black man who was watching her with an uneasy mixture of compassion and anger.

"It was not a difficult tabu to keep," continued Sharia, her voice husky. "Fives came only once in three or four hundred years. The chance of mature fives touching was minimal. But in the last thousand years, more fives were born, many more. Several dozen in each generation. Nearly all were born to the Darien family. In the last generation, hundreds were born. Most were exiled, for there was little chance that the present Kiriy would die."

"Why did that matter?" asked Jode.

"Fives have been Kiriys far more often than fours or sixes," explained Sharia. "It's a matter of power, the power to survive the first searing touch of the Eyes."

Jode had more questions but he doubted that the answers would help him right now. He listened, his black eyes narrow and intent.

"Of the hundreds of fives born in my generation," Sharia continued softly, relentlessly, "I am the only timeshadow rider. Of those hundreds of fives, only Kane and I survived the crumbling of Za'arain that came when the Eyes closed."

"Go on," Jode murmured, fascinated by the glimpse of Za'arain history.

"Don't you see?" whispered Sharia bleakly. "Kane and I are Kiri, Darien and five. He can manipulate wakes in the *then* and in time/now. I can manipulate timeshadows in the *now* and in time/then."

"Precisely," Jode said, odd triumph rippling in his voice. "That's what I've been trying to tell you. You're two halves of a whole. Perfect complementary minds and talents. A fit in all times and lives. Lias'tri."

"You don't understand," said Kane roughly.

"Don't I?" Jode's tone was sardonic. "I think you're the one who doesn't understand."

"When Sharia and I touch, the linear aspect of time begins to . . . dissolve. The *then* and the *now* and the *always* reach toward each other. The longer we touch, the closer linear time comes to dissolving." Kane waited but saw no understanding reflected on Jode's dark face. "Fourth Evolution life is an aspect of time," said Kane suddenly, savagely. "Linear time. Without linear time, our life isn't possible. Without life, there is no linear time as we know it. Without linear time, there is nothing but a state of all/time, every/time, no/time. Chaos. Catastrophe. Or, as we say on Za'arain—*two fives touching.*"

Jode looked from Sharia to Kane and back again. He was convinced that they believed every word Kane had spoken. They believed that if they touched too long they would die. And that something more, something worse would happen. They were too intelligent to view their own personal deaths as a cosmic catastrophe. There was something else riding both of them, a conviction that their deaths would only be the opening flourish in an event more deadly than any Joining-born man could comprehend.

The ship chimed, warning of the sixth za'replacement on the route to Doursone.

"I'll think about what you've said," sighed Jode. "While I think, I want you to consider this: psi gifts, no matter how bizarre or powerful, can be disciplined. If you can control your minds, you can control your heritage. Kiri, Darien, five, all of it. And then you may touch each other and know a heritage that transcends Kiri, Darien and five. Lias'tri."

What Jode did not say, what he would not say until he better understood Za'arain manipulations of time, was that people who were lias'tris not only could touch, they *must*. It was as inevitable as life itself. Or death.

During the four days between the sixth and seventh za'replacement nodes, Jode worked with first Kane and then Sharia, teaching them the most basic forms of mental control. They learned with a speed that startled the Jhoramon psi-master. The benefits were immediately apparent. No longer did their thoughts echo through Jode's. No more did shadows of despair and rage flicker like violet lightning in the depths of Jode's mind. By the time Dani was ready to hurl the ship and crew into Doursone's blue-green node, Sharia was able to control her own mind to the point that she could heal the crew one at a time, easily, holding most of her timeshadow aloof from theirs. Their small aches and major scars were combed out of their time/then; leaving their time/now a smoothly flowing richness of unimpeded life.

There were three exceptions to her healing. Kane, of course, was one. She did not touch him. Merone was another. Sharia could heal the Wolfin woman's time/now, but access to her time/then was blocked by the Wolfin construct within Merone's brain. The translator device was quasi-life, and as such was unavailable to Sharia's gifts. In fact, even with the more disciplined mental rapport she had learned from Jode, she found psychic intercourse with Merone to be an aching experience in dissonance and draining energies. Sharia had to be satisfied with simply soothing the woman's troubled timeshadow, a temporary succoring at best.

Jode was Sharia's third failure. She had tried to heal him despite his protests. She had discovered that his timeshadow was expressed in all the colors of darkness, reflecting a yearning toward the *then* that was incurable. Mind and body, Jode was connected with death through dimensions of time and reality unnamed and unknown by the Joining. Even the language of Za'arain lacked the words to describe the dark, rich shimmering of Jode's timeshadow, life and death mingling impossibly.

In the end Sharia accepted the Jhoramon psi-master as he was: darkly burning, sardonic, gentle and skilled.

The crew members each brought to Sharia something of their own in thanks for their healed time/now. She wore Challilian perfumes, rare as a triple eclipse, that had been compounded of the essences of flowers that grew on only one tiny island out of all the land of all the planets in the galaxy. When she walked, each step sang sweetly with Xt's silver and crystal bells. Whether she was awake or asleep, jhoras wove wild, improbable harmonies around the Xtian bells.

And each scent, each pure sound, each brush of mind against mind, was like a knife going into Kane and turning deeply. It was no better for Sharia. At some unknowable level, through dimensions unknown and unnamed by Za'arain or Joining, she and he were connected. The knives that turned in him also turned in her. Separately, they drove themselves to learn whatever Jode could teach them of controlling their minds, hoping that the psi-master was right in his belief that once they controlled themselves there would be no danger in touching each other.

They feared Jode was wrong, however. That fear was a darkness between them, driving them to learn until Jode refused to teach any more.

"There will be enough time after Doursone," said Jode impatiently. "You're both at the edge of your control. Your eyes are violet more often than not. If you don't let your minds rest you won't be any good to anyone."

Sharia started to protest.

"No!" snapped Jode. "Look at Kane. Instead of sleeping he's been going through boxes of those vicious wind trader artifacts so that we can trade them on Doursone. He's exhausted now. He'll be azir bait if he doesn't get some rest in his cocoon. Or doesn't Doursone matter anymore? Have you decided to give up on finding the Eyes?"

Both Za'arains were too tired to conceal their shock at Jode's taunting words.

Suddenly the Jhoramon looked inexpressibly weary. "I thought so. Though, it might be better for both of you if you concentrated on your own problems and let Za'arain choke on its own improbabilities."

"And the Joining?" said Kane, kneading his neck with a long five-fingered hand. "Should we let the Joining choke on its own inadequacies while an unleashed Za'arain preys on the dying worlds?"

Jode's eyes closed and then opened, dark and bleak as a winter midnight. Yet when he spoke, his voice was deceptively mild. "I have children on Jhora and Wolfin. I'd feel better knowing that their children won't die at the hands of technologically sophisticated Za'arain psi-hunters."

Chimes came, warning of the last za'replacement.

Sharia was grateful when Dani closed the cocoons over the three people in the control room. She needed to know that soon there would be more space between her and Kane than the ship's spiral walls. She needed to know that there was a sky and a sun and a land that turned beneath the stars. Kane was all around her in the ship. She sensed his timeshadow wake in everything she touched, in the very air she breathed. No other wakes were accessible to her. Only his.

She knew it had to be the same for him. She had seen him pick up a strand of her Xtian bells, hold it, *know* it as he had known ancient artifacts. Only she was living. Her wake should not be accessible to him. But it was. No matter what they learned from Jode, no matter how hard they fought not to overlap, they continued to expand into each other in dimensions neither could describe or control.

Dani popped out of the za'replacement at greatly diminished speed. Only under the driving mind of her captain would she submit to flaring down a planet's gravity well under full power, and Kane was not requiring that right now. Sedately, Dani aligned herself with the trade beacon and slid down the well with a nice calculation that sent a distinct feeling of smugness radiating throughout the ship. Though she had not appreciated the learning, she definitely enjoyed the results of the Za'arain equations Kane had forced into her unwilling mind.

Acting on Jode's orders, Dani kept Sharia's cocoon closed even after the ship was downside. A mild soporific permeated the cocoon, giving Sharia the sleep that her restless mind had denied her. As she slept, the transparent leads of a teacher snaked out. When she awoke, she knew as much about Doursone as the ship's answer cube did. She also knew that Kane and most of the crew had already taken up a trading station at the Desheel, a downside gathering place where anything could be bought and sold. Or stolen.

Szarth waited at the bottom of the ship's narrow personnel ramp. He was fully armed. For an Xtian, that meant an impressive array of weaponry.

"Welcome to Doursone, cesspool of the Joining and jewel of the Dust," said Szarth, smiling up at the silver woman whose healing touch was an endless miracle to him. "Come. The captain said you needed to feel a planet beneath you again."

Sharia had not told Kane of her restlessness. She had hardly admitted it to herself. In silence she let Szarth lead her into Beoy, Doursone's capital city. As she walked, she saw nothing to make her disagree with Szarth's assessment of Doursone's fecal nature. Like most planets with an easy, nearby za'replacement node, Doursone was a grim and nearly barren world. Convenience of access had outweighed the manifest drawbacks of the planet's natural environment, however. It was the only planet within seven safe za'replacements of the Joining and eight za'replacements of the Dust. As such, Doursone had begun as a pirate port and had progressed to the kind of entrenched viciousness that came only from a civilization based on unbridled greed.

The cities and occasional mineral outcroppings gave contrast to the pitted blue-black of the planet's natural surface. In deference to Doursone's endless scouring winds, the buildings were made of the same grey synstone as the streets. There was little natural atmosphere, but huge machines sunk beneath each city compensated for the lack. These machines ate whatever was fed them, manipulating the raw input with streamers of plasma as hot as stars, and giving back oxygen, water and a handful of heavy elements.

Though vast amounts of money poured through Doursone's ugly port cities, most Doursonians were poor, hungry and ridden by disease. Everything, including the air they breathed, was purchased. Those who could not pay either died or sold themselves as "colonists," slaves to the Dust. Doursone did not care what happened to its population, so long as the air tax was paid on the living and the export tax was paid on colonists. The average citizen of Doursone was a three-dimensional testament to the tenacity of life in the face of brutal odds.

Doursone's streets were as clean as Dani's exhaust tubes. Scavengers kept the cities spotless, for the voracious machines beneath the cities required constant feeding, and air tax could be paid in refuse as well as in more standard coin. Sometimes people came under the heading of refuse. As long as the scavengers were not caught in outright murder, little was said. Few people who could afford a choice lived on Doursone. The result was as grim a population as could be found on any civilized planet in the Joining.

Sharia felt Doursone's thin, sour breath in her lungs, saw greed and viciousness and despair walking Doursone's streets with her and was sickened to the bottom of her mind. Szarth walked next to her with weapon drawn. The Wolfin gun had only one purpose: the swift and irrevocable destruction of oxygen-burning life. It was a type of weapon that was forbidden on every planet in the Joining but one—Doursone. Five other Xtians fanned through the streets around Sharia and Szarth, making it clear that the price of taking the silver-haired alien woman was more than she would be worth on any planet in the Joining or the Dust. As

Doursonians were nothing if not pragmatic, Sharia was as safe as though she were still on board ship.

Yet she felt uneasy. Her senses told her that she was being watched. Kiri eyelids flickered several times and then stayed down. Hunter light did not enhance Doursone's minimal attractions. It showed timeshadows very well, though. The shadows were as attenuated as the people except, for one timeshadow that burned with the pure colors of a rainbow. Energy streamed outward from it in time/now and time/then, the *now* and the *then*. Energy was a burning nimbus licking outward into dimensions that Sharia had only sensed before. But there was darkness, too, black ice radiating through every aspect of time and za', emptiness growing as she watched.

Sharia blinked and looked around with silver eyes, trying to see who was so ill, wondering if she would be permitted to heal. Because she wanted, and needed, to heal. There was something in the wounded timeshadow that was irresistible to her. Its complexity was teasing, unique, its colors iridescent despite the spreading blackness. Yet as she looked she saw only Doursonians slinking by with downcast eyes. Nowhere did she see someone huddled against a building, waiting to die. And it was death that the person waited for, of that Sharia had no doubt.

She stopped and stared into every shadow and right-angled doorway along the left side of the street. Her silver eyes saw nothing but normal light, normal shadow. Yet something living was there. It had to be. With a sound of impatience she crossed the street on the narrow bridge provided for pedestrians. Szarth made no objection. Kane had told the Xtian to protect Sharia, not to lead her by the hand.

The sense of being watched increased as Sharia approached a wide walkway between two residential buildings. Despite its inviting width, no downsiders used the walkway. Perhaps it was the deep pool of shadow between the buildings that put off the natives. Or perhaps it was the odd quality of the shadow itself. Part of it . . . rippled.

Kiri eyelids flashed down. A potent timeshadow blazed forth

where nothing had been an instant before. The energy was so great that it concealed the shape of flesh beneath. The blackness radiating throughout the timeshadow was also great, and it concealed nothing, certainly not the death that was draining all the colors of life into darkness.

"Sharia," began Szarth, looking around nervously. "I don't like this place."

Sharia's only answer was to move closer to the shadow.

Szarth stared intently at the pooled darkness. He saw nothing, nothing at all. Yet there was something there—every bit of his warrior's instincts told him so. Every nerve in his body screamed in full battle alert. There was no reason for this walkway to be deserted—unless others had sensed something as he did now.

There was something here, something inimical to life.

Then from the corner of his eye Szarth caught the ghostly rippling of the shadow pool and saw Sharia bending down. "Sharia!" he screamed. *"No!* That's an azir!"

Sharia heard as though at a great distance, but it was too late. The azir's wounded timeshadow was irresistible to her. Xtian bells chimed as Sharia's hair slid free of restraints. Translucent hair swept forward like wind-driven silver flames as she went to her knees in front of the pooled, shimmering darkness and gathered the azir to herself.

It was the most curious timeshadow she had ever ridden. So little of it existed in time/now, so much in the *now* and the *then* and the *always.* Perhaps even in the *other.* Yes, surely she was touching the *other.* She had never touched that aspect of time, had never known it in the way a Darien knew timeshadows or their wakes. Even for a Za'arain, the other was more an intellectual construct than a tangible reality.

There was a loneliness in the wounded timeshadow that was as deep as the past, as wide as the present, as long as the future. The hunger could have been predatory, would have been deadly, had Sharia not been a Darien and a five. The condensed presence of time did not annihilate her. Without hesitation she poured her energy into the torn timeshadow, healing gaps be-

tween life's grip on the *then* and the *now,* thickening attenuated
streamers of color, riding the rejuvenated timeshadow until life's
energy flowed heavily between them/then and time/now.

Even when life seethed thickly, a delicately iridescent pattern
of black remained behind. It was woven inextricably into the
living timeshadow, an aspect of the *other* that could not be
combed from the azir's flaring energies. The black network was
a completion of rather than an intrusion into the azir's timeshadow. The azir was an offshoot of the Fifth Evolution, ex-
pressing itself and its life-force in dimensions and aspects of
time that were not available to other evolutions of life.

After a final, wondering caress over the astonishing timeshadow, Sharia sighed and let her hair sweep away to curl softly
down her back. Sitting in front of her was a magnificent beast
the color of clear ice. The azir's eyes were a slice of eternity,
black and bottomless. Like Darien hair, the animal itself had
an odd quality of translucence. Smooth, very short fur molded
the muscular body. The azir's muzzle was blunt yet graceful.
Its teeth and retractable claws were the same pellucid black as
its eyes. Iridescent, transparent, enigmatic in its length and
structure, the azir's ruff circled the base of its skull and ran
down its long back to its tailless rump. The ruff shifted and
shivered as though independently alive, tasting and testing energies in this and other dimensions. With lithe strength the azir
rose to stand on four legs, leveling its blackly gleaming eyes
on the kneeling Za'arain.

Sharia became aware of Szarth's hissing phrases pouring over
her in a scalding stream. She did not need a Wolfin translator
to tell her that Szarth was both furious and frightened. She
turned and smiled up at the Xtian.

"Don't worry," she murmured dreamily, her eyes very silver
in the radiant aftermath of riding the azir's curious timeshadow.
"It won't hurt me. It was unhappy. Now it isn't."

The azir watched Szarth with obsidian eyes. The transparent,
almost fluid fringe lifted and searched the length of Xtian without touching him. It assessed the man's body, energies and emo-

tions with an azir's sweeping skill. Then it turned back to Sharia, knowing that Szarth represented no danger to the woman.

Absently, Sharia reached out and stroked the beast's powerful body. The silky water-clear ruff curled over her hand. It was impossible to tell where the ruff ended—if it ended at all. Odd energies shivered pleasantly through her. "And don't you worry," she said soothingly to the azir. "Szarth won't hurt you."

The hissing laughter of Xt had never sounded so harsh. "As if I could!"

Startled, Sharia shifted her gaze from the fascinating translucence of the azir's body. She looked at Szarth, an unasked question in her silver eyes.

"You really don't know, do you?" asked Szarth.

"But you'll tell me, won't you?" Sharia asked with a resigned smile.

The Xtian did not smile in return. "Azirs can't be killed," said Szarth bluntly. His eyes were very green, very feral. "As far as I know, the beasts never die."

Sharia shrugged off the awe that underlay the Xtian's fear of the azir. "Descendants of the Fifth Evolution are different, but I'm sure they die in some dimensions, some times."

"Maybe. But let me tell you this, healer. I could point my gun at this azir and fire until I died of old age. The beast would not die. It would not even be wounded. It could kill me, though. In an instant. It could kill me now and forever. Azir bait is never born again. That's what azir means. Soul-eater."

Sharia's Kiri eyelids snapped down. The azir's timeshadow blazed. She turned toward Szarth. His timeshadow rippled with life and color. Nowhere did the azir's timeshadow overlap with the Xtian's or with her own. If the beast were a timeshadow predator, it was not preying upon them. She opened her eyes and saw the azir's bottomless black glance fixed on her with the patience of time itself. Her hand lifted until her fingers could tangle in the oddly cool, wonderfully silky ruff. An equally cool, silky black tongue swept over her skin, tasting her delicately, stroking her.

"It won't hurt us," said Sharia, her voice certain.

"Not you," agreed Szarth. Then, sighing, "And not me so long as I don't hurt you."

He spoke into the tiny Wolfin transceiver that was part of his weapon harness. The other Xtians slowly closed in from their guard positions. Their movements were reluctant, wary.

"Get it over with," said Szarth curtly, gesturing his fellow symbionts forward.

One by one the Xtians lined up for the azir's inspection. Each time the beast turned its head, muscles rippled sleekly beneath short, icy fur. When the azir was satisfied, it returned its space-black gaze to Sharia.

"Go guard Kane in the Desheel," said Szarth to the other warriors. His hissing laughter filled the walkway. "We sure as death don't need you here anymore!"

Sharia watched as the Xtians walked quietly into Doursone's gathering twilight. "Why don't we need them?" she asked when she could no longer see the warriors.

"Azir," hissed Szarth.

"Is that an answer or a curse?"

The warrior smiled and held his hand out to pull Sharia to her feet. "Both." The smile vanished, leaving his concern visible. "No sane person will hurt an azir's companion. The azir would eat the killer, body and soul."

"Am I an azir's companion?" asked Sharia, amusement and currents of disbelief rippling in her voice.

"You touched the beast and lived. By definition, that makes you its companion."

"Then you touch it. It won't hurt you."

"I know. It won't hurt anything so long as you're its companion. Unless you're threatened. Then it's sudden death on four feet."

"Then touch it. It was very lonely," she added, half serious, half challenging. "It could use more than one companion."

Szarth's smile showed every sharp angle of his teeth. He looked at the azir. The azir looked at him. Szarth sighed and held out his hand to the ice-clear coat of the beast. The azir . . . dissolved. Szarth's hand touched . . . nothing. The Xtian straightened and turned toward Sharia with another sharp smile.

"Only companions touch azirs," said Szarth softly. "One companion. One azir."

Shaken, Sharia watched the azir condense again. It looked at her with eyes as deep as time. A cool, translucent black tongue licked out soothingly. Sharia sighed and let her fingers find the fascinating textures and energies of the azir's ruff.

"All right, companion," she murmured. "Let's take a look at the city."

Sharia walked out into Beoy again, an Xtian warrior on her right hand and a translucent soul-eater gliding silently at her heels.

Thirteen

Kane sensed the presence of Xtians at his back before he turned and confronted them. "Sharia?" he asked, giving her name the sibilant emphasis of an Xtian name.

"Safe," hissed an Xtian.

The single word told Kane all that he thought he needed to know. He was relieved. The Desheel was no place to be with only a handful of crew for protection. Though Merone could eavesdrop in many languages, that was no guarantee of safety. The place was rife with unknown languages. Merone had had to learn a new language for the first group of people who had approached his trading table. Fortunately the language had been so recently evolved from S/kouran that it was little more than a dialect. Learning it had not unsettled the fragile balance of Merone's mind.

The Xtians needed no instructions. They moved unobtrusively through the crowded room, taking up positions where they could watch both their captain and each other. A surprise attack might overwhelm one of them, but no more. The rest would be in a position to unite and burn their way through to Kane, cutting a swath of destruction that would be enough to discourage further attacks.

Ine glanced up in time to catch the last fading gleam of Xtian skin. He sighed in quiet relief. The odds were now in Kane's favor, and the inhabitants of Doursone were pragmatic to the last breath. Ine's brown eyes searched the avaricious crowd that had gathered in front of Kane's table. Even as Ine watched, men and women melted away. The people who remained were interested in buying and trading, not in killing and stealing.

A woman stepped forward. She was very tall, as thin as a shadow, and had the faded orange skin that could have come from Megot or Norlyken. Ine prayed that it was the former. That language Merone knew. Comspeech was common only in the Joining. Technically, Doursone was part of the Joining; in reality, Doursone was a law unto its own mercenary self.

"Comspeech?" asked Ine carefully.

The woman hesitated.

"Do you speak comspeech?" repeated Ine.

"Sha mesarol," murmured the woman.

Inwardly, Ine winced and motioned toward Merone.

The Wolfin woman stepped forward. She tried several languages, each one related to Megot's tongue but separated by time and za'replacements. Eventually, through a combination of body language and words, Merone got her point across. The orange woman began to talk freely, eagerly, giving Merone the words and structure she needed to learn the new language.

Kane watched and hoped that this would not be the language that sent Merone into insanity. Translators were so fragile, yet he had never needed Merone more than he did now, on Doursone, where fringe languages and Dust languages evolved at incredible speeds. Without Merone he had little chance of tracing the Eyes of Za'ar. There were just too many languages and too little time.

And there was the enigma of the Eyes themselves. They had not killed the Dust raider who stole them. Why? Had someone been born off Za'arain who could control the Eyes? Had an exile returned, evading the Eyes long enough to steal them? Was that what Sharia had meant when she had whispered in his mind about the dead Kiriy's other half, the forbidden soul, exiled? Were they all doomed to drown beneath an onslaught of atavism?

Merone's words blended with Kane's thoughts, bringing him back to an awareness of the Desheel's grimy ambience.

". . . drowned city where ancient jewels sing."

Ine made no attempt to hide his lack of interest in Dust legends. "Does she have some of those jewels to show us?" he retorted.

"Yes."

Abruptly Ine's eyes became hooded. "Trade or purchase?"

"Trade. The wind artifacts."

Ine grunted and rocked back on his chair, pretending to consider the woman's offer. The hammered metal of his chair made a tortured sound as he slammed all three supports into contact with the pitted floor. After four endless hours in this stinking cave someone finally had something that might be worth trading. Of course, she might be lying. Perhaps he should dismiss her and see who was sent next. By her clothes, she was merely the slave of some Dust world colonist.

Kane did not sense the specific thoughts Ine had. He did sense that the trader was ambivalent about the items being presented for trade. *Don't send her away. We haven't time for finesse.*

Ine stiffened as he heard Kane's voice speaking softly in his own mind. Ine might have anticipated it from the Jhoramon psi-master, but not from Kane, who had never given any indication of being a psi. Caught in the grip of disbelief, Ine started to look over his shoulder.

Don't turn around. Am I hurting you? The last question was almost an afterthought. Even though Kane was barely establishing contact at the most shallow level, it was possible that Ine could not take mindspeech as well as Jode could. Ine, after all, had proved that he had no psi by handling the jeweled wind artifact without discomfort.

Ine made a gesture with his left hand, a comspeech negative reinforced by conscious thought. Kane was not hurting him.

Good. Now bargain, trader. When she shows the jewels, bring them to me. If they aren't what I'm looking for, buy them at a high but not a ridiculous price. We want to appear hungry but

*not stupid. If I want the jewels, be prepared to get them by trade
if you can and force if you can't. Understood?*

Ine's right hand moved slightly even as his mind agreed. He
understood.

*If you have any suggestions for a faster way to get to the
Eyes of Za'ar, tell me.*

At a distance Kane sensed the Jiddirit's quick mind turning
over possibilities. Kane could have bored in and examined each
possibility with him, but saw no need. If Jode said Ine could
be trusted to treat Kane's interests as his own, then there was
no need to crowd the master trader too hard.

Urgency was suddenly riding Kane, though. An urgentcy like
the time when Za'arain had been crumbling around Sharia and
she had called to him.

Ine's left hand moved in a small negative. He had no suggestions to offer his captain. Kane's plan was shrewd, so long as
the Eyes of Za'ar—not a low price for random Dust gems—was
the ultimate goal. Ine leaned back casually and gestured to
Merone. The Wolfin woman stepped forward, her buff stripes
gleaming in the Desheel's grimy light. Speaking softly, her face
lined with the pain of yet another language, Merone opened the
trading.

"We would see the jewels."

The thin Dust slave withdrew a packet from within her loose
brown robe. She spilled the contents onto the black, soft fabric
Ine had used to cover the trading table. The gems varied in size
from no larger than a fingertip to as big as man's palm. When
light touched their facets, an eerie keening rose from the jewels.

Kane sensed Ine's flash of interest, though the Jiddirit was
far too astute a trader to show it to the Dust woman. Ine turned
and looked questioningly at Kane. The woman was visibly nervous now that the gems were out in the open. If Ine brought
the jewels to Kane, she might think that they were being stolen
and panic.

You're right, Kane thought quietly. *It would be better if I
came to you.*

Kane straightened and walked toward the trading table with a lazy stride. Only one of the jewels was big enough to be an Eye. It was not an Eye, though. Its polished surface was faceted, but it did not divide light into all visible colors. Kane blinked, bringing down Kiri eyelids. The stone shimmered faintly as tenuous streamers of energy lifted from its surface. It was alive as all First Evolution creatures were alive—ambiguously. It was a life that Kane could not comprehend.

Several of the remaining gems showed similar living time-shadow sheens. He gathered those gems into his hands, wondering as he often had if the Eyes were the product of the First Evolution or the constructs of other evolutions. The Fifth Evolution was the most likely origin of the Eyes, for it was that evolution which had opened up time to the colonization of life the way the Fourth Evolution had opened up space.

The living jewels lay quietly in Kane's large hands. If the gems had thoughts and desires, they were not available to Kane. They would not have been available to Sharia, either. The only thing the First and Fourth Evolutions had in common was life itself, the ability to interact with and leave a wake upon time.

Kane set aside the living crystals and focused on the remaining stones. In the sudden violet light of hunter's eyes, the gems clearly displayed the unmoving colors of timeshadow wakes whose originators had died. He picked up the jewels singly. Though they resonated with the music of the First Evolution's singing jewels, the gems he held one after the other had no songs of their own. Once they had been worn against living flesh, Fourth Evolution flesh. But it had been long, long ago, on a world known only to the Dust.

Gently, Kane put down the last jewel. *They aren't the Eyes,* he told Ine silently.

Ine acknowledged with a small movement of his right hand. He turned to Merone and opened the bargaining for the purchase of the stones, which Kane did not really want. But if other jewels were to be brought to them, jewels that might be the

Eyes of Za'ar, then Kane's trader had to be seen buying gems at a good price.

The bargain was quickly struck. Two small wind artifacts in exchange for the gems. It should have been only one artifact, and even that would have been generous. Ine's inner displeasure at appearing to be an easy bargainer was hidden from all but Kane.

Think of it as a lure, and the Dust raider who stole the Eyes as a fat, smart scoral, offered Kane soothingly to his master trader.

Ine's answer was an incoherent mental snarl. He gestured curtly, signifying that he was ready to trade again. There was a concerted rush to stand on the trading line. The lure had certainly been effective; up until now, trading had been desultory at best. After a brisk shoving match, one man managed to toe the trading mark and stay there. He bristled with weapons like an Xtian warrior, but it was not the weapons that had gained him the trading mark: He was nearly as big as Kane and quite willing to use his muscle on smaller people. The Dustman was such a mixture of races that Ine could not even begin to guess at his origins. He was dressed in the sturdy, ragged clothes of an independent colonist. To Ine's immense relief, the man spoke a recently evolved dialect of comspeech which Merone could learn almost painlessly.

Kane listened while another Dust legend unfurled. This time it was not a world where drowned cities sang. It was a planet of ice and darkness circling a guttering sun. Once there had been cities on that planet, and life. Now there were only ruins and gems that called out to men's minds. Psi-stones.

Only long practice at concealing his emotions allowed Kane to keep his sudden, intense interest hidden. According to Za'arain history, the Eyes of Za'ar had been found by a Kiri who could not resist them. He had died in their taking. After him others had died, many others, compelled by the Eyes but unable to control them. Finally a Kiri had touched the Eyes of Za'ar, held them, worn them. The first Kiriy of Za'arain—the

first ruler of a million-year reign. Or the first one ruled by the
Eyes. Kane had never been sure who was ruled and who was
ruler. Perhaps there was no difference. Perhaps the Kiriy and
the Eyes had been one.

With violet eyes Kane watched the Dustman open a small
chest woven of pale plastic insulation strips. He tipped the chest
and let stones as big as a woman's fist roll out onto the soft
black fabric covering the table. A murmur of appreciation rippled over the room at the jewels' fire and brilliance. Kane did
not hear. Nor did he see the beauty of the stones in time/now.
His Kiri eyes were drinking in the radiant timeshadow wakes
that wove through the gems, time/then and the *then* as clear to
him as time/now was to the other people in the room. The gems
had richly layered timeshadow wakes, and something else,
something living.

Kane realized that, like Dani, the stones were both living and
nonliving, constructs of an advanced evolution.

And they were calling to him.

As Kane reached for them, Jode's voice spoke harshly in his
mind.

No. They could be dangerous.

Users rather than used? asked Kane, his fingers hovering
over the biggest of the three stones.

Exactly.

Just what did you think the Eyes were? retorted Kane. *Bau-
bles for a child?*

Jode's answer was a bleak curse and withdrawal.

The psi-master's warning had not been in vain, however.
Kane's hand moved from the biggest stone to the smallest. The
jewel flared brilliantly the instant it came into contact with his
flesh. People stepped back hurriedly. Kane didn't notice. He
was learning the gem's history in a single torrential instant.
Sweat gathered and ran down his powerful body as the gem's
timeshadow wakes revealed themselves, psi-master wakes pouring one after the other, energy focused in the gem and then
released elsewhere, elsewhen. Sometimes the stone had been

used to create, sometimes to destroy. In all times it had grown stronger, more potent; it subtly used its various masters as it was itself being used, a symbiosis of time and psi energy that only a Darien five might comprehend.

The gem reached out into time/now, feeding on Kane's sweeping timeshadow.

Instinctively Kane slid among the gem's timeshadow wakes, reinforcing aspects of the *then* by pinching off the static streamers of color reaching into time/now. Slowly, gently, Kane dominated the gem without destroying it. When he was finished, his timeshadow was safe from the stone's innocent piracy. Should he desire it, the gem was available for his use, capable of enhancing his manipulations of time/then and the *then*.

Kane let the sparkling, flashing jewel roll from his hand to the table. The Dustman drew in a quick breath—he had expected Kane to be unable to release the stone once he had held it. The Dustman had expected an easy, coerced sale at a very high price. The smile Kane gave to the Dustman was thin and feral. The man shifted uneasily. Kane's long fingers brushed quickly over the remaining two jewels. Again the wakes called out to him, but he was ready this time. He escaped easily.

The stones were not the Eyes of Za'ar. They could have been, however, given a million years of Za'arain Kiriy manipulations.

If he found the Eyes, Sharia would be the first one to touch them, chosen for that ambiguous honor by the Kiriy herself before she had died. With a chilling feeling of unease, Kane turned his mind from the thought of Sharia touching the Eyes of Za'ar. There was no other way, no help for it, nothing but the hope that the last Kiriy had sensed in Sharia something that might subdue the Eyes before they killed her. That kind of hope was not enough for Kane, though. He would take what time and space and fate brought him. Sharia might learn something useful from the Dustman's remaining unbridled psi-stones, something that might save her life.

Buy them.

Ine's face showed no outer indication that he had received

Kane's blunt command. Expressionless. the Jiddirit opened the trading. As he talked, an Xtian eased through the crowd and came to stand by Kane's side.

"I overheard two men talking in some kind of comspeech," hissed the Xtian in his native tongue. "I didn't get all of it, but enough. This Dustman usually sells over in a pit called the Jorke. Some other big Dustman has a fixed trading table there. He also has a standing order for psi-stones. Big ones. He particularly wants matched pairs."

Tightness raced through Kane. "Did he have any color preferences?" whispered Kane in Xtian.

"Violet."

Jode's head snapped up at the instant of unleashed hunter response that ripped through Kane's control. But his mind was as closed as an unliving stone; the psi-master found out nothing as he probed. He had taught Kane well.

"See if you can find out who the psi-stone buyer is," Kane hissed. "Don't reveal our interest though."

The Xtian melted back into shadows and the indecipherable conversations of the Dust. Kane spoke silently in Ine's mind.

Have your spies reported yet?

Ine's left hand twitched and showed two fingers even as Kane sensed the negative answer forming in the Jiddirit's psi-null mind.

There's another gem buyer in Doursone. He's looking for large psi-stones in matched pairs. Violet.

Ine's interest flared as Kane's had. Kane smiled. In some ways the Jiddirit was as predatory as any Kiri ever born.

Are your spies familiar with a pit called the Jorke?

Again, Ine's right hand moved slightly.

That's where the man has a permanent trading table. We go there tonight.

Ine's right hand twitched.

Merone bent over and murmured translations. Ine looked bored. The big Dustman looked uncomfortable. His chance for an easy, stone-coerced sale was gone. Ine laughed insultingly and countered the Dustman's offer with one a tenth as large. Merone relayed. Kane watched, trying not to display his impatience. Even now the Eyes might be in this room, carried by a psi-null raider immune to their siren call.

Suddenly the big Dustman reached out as though to return the gems to their plastic casket. Ine's hands shot out and gathered in the stones, signifying acceptance of the Dustman's most recent offer. With a feeling of hidden anger, Ine watched one large and one minor wind artifact vanish into the Dustman's pack.

The next three traders were a disappointment. The jewels they brought were inferior grades and colors that even a child might have shrugged at. The gems were neither First nor Fifth Evolution nor ancient artifacts with thickly layered timeshadow wakes. At best, the stones were lures for fools.

Ine wanted to dismiss the traders as he would have dismissed blood-sucking insects, but was afraid to anger Kane.

I said we should look eager, not stupid, retorted Kane dryly. *Tell those junkmen to take a gold za'replacement into the nearest sun.*

With clear pleasure Ine did just that. It did not discourage the remaining traders. If anything, it encouraged them. Another shoving match ensued and was not resolved until a man withdrew, bleeding. The woman who came to the trading mark adjusted her razor-tipped gloves, looked around with challenging pale eyes, and spilled the contents of a skin bag onto the trading table.

Jewels coruscated across velvet. Kane's Kiri eyelids flicked down, measuring the age and/or awareness of the gems. Not one timeshadow flickered. Not one wake sent static streamers into time/now. The gems were either just mined or just created. Kane told Ine as much in a single swift moment of mindspeech. The trader gave the woman a cold glance, then closed his eyes and put his hands over his ears, shutting out all possibility of argument in a gesture of refusal that needed no translation. The woman gathered up her dubious gems and vanished into the crowd. Men and women fought for footing along the trading line.

Suddenly an icy pain shot through Kane. Even as his hand went to the hidden lias'tri stone, he knew that Sharia was in deadly danger.

"You said she was safe!" he shouted in Xtian, turning furiously on the closest warrior.

If Kane's harsh voice did not warn the Desheel's patrons, the sudden electric tension in his big body did. Black, translucent hair shivered and trembled as though in a wind. Deadly Kiri eyes measured the crowd in a single, assessing glance. Even as Kane leaped forward people scrambled and clawed to get away from the violet-eyed alien. Jode and the rest of the crew followed in their captain's wake, finding easy passage through the Desheel's stunned patrons. None of the crew asked questions. Only the psi-master knew what was wrong. The slicing instant of Kane's mindtouch had told Jode that Sharia was in danger.

Running at full speed Kane burst out into Doursone's cold, empty night. He quickly outpaced the Xtians, despite their long-legged strides. Frantically the Xtian second-in-command triggered his transceiver and called Szarth. The thin sound of Szarth's scalding curses pouring from the transceiver button did nothing to reassure the Xtians of Sharia's safety. Grimly they ran as fast as they could, listening to Szarth's directions.

Kane did not need the directions. He knew where Sharia was as surely as if he himself were standing there. And in some unnamed way, he was. He could almost see the buildings surrounding Sharia, almost smell the coarse odor of sweetmeats and Doursone cabbage wine, almost feel the cold synstone against his knees and the slat-thin bodies of Beoy's poorer citizens as they pressed around Sharia in waves, lapping over her like an endless hungry tide.

As he turned a corner, a timeshadow seemed to burst into being in front of him, blazing through the massed, all-but-lifeless timeshadows of Beoy's hopeless denizens. Sharia. Radiant, seething, incredibly alive despite the icy shards of black spreading through the pouring colors of her life. The dense, bottomless needs of Doursone's hopeless people had thrown Sharia into a healing frenzy that was literally draining her life away into the massed hunger of those in need.

Kane plunged into the crowd, throwing people ruthlessly aside as he reached for Sharia, determined to free her physically from Doursone's killing demands. He did not even notice the ice-clear azir gliding toward him from the other side of the crowd.

"No, Captain!" Even as Szarth shouted, he leaped and kicked high, knocking Kane away from Sharia.

Kane staggered back and turned on Szarth with violet eyes. Then the shock of being attacked by his own Xtian warrior penetrated even Kane's atavistic Kiri mind. He brought himself under control and confronted Szarth with a civilized mind and a psi-hunter's deadly eyes. Kane's hand was wrapped around a Wolfin gun.

"Explain."

"She's an azir's companion," said Szarth, speaking clearly, knowing he would not get a second chance to live. "If you prevent her from doing what she wants, the azir will kill you."

Before the last words were out of Szarth's mouth, Kane's eyes had focused on the azir gliding toward him. In the same instant the crowd swayed and shifted, releasing someone newly healed, replacing him with someone else who was desperate for the miraculous touch of the alien woman.

"But she's dying," said Kane tightly, turning slowly, bringing the gun to bear on the azir.

"No!" Szarth's agony was clear. He prepared to attack Kane, certain that the Za'arain would kill him this time. "You can't kill an azir!"

"I can try."

Szarth leaped. Kane twisted, sloughing off the attack with a lithe movement of his shoulders. Szarth went crashing into the side of a building. Before the Xtian could recover, Kane turned his weapon on the azir and held down the firing stud.

Deadly, coherent energy poured out soundlessly. The azir stood and watched with space-black eyes. Pure green light lanced into the translucent body . . . and vanished. As though the azir were a hole in space and time, it absorbed the lethal emerald light. There was no change in the azir's stance, no marring of the perfect muscular body. The azir glided forward, its enigmatic, transparent ruff shivering and swaying, black eyes focused on Kane.

Kane swore in the savage, twisting phrases of Za'arain and threw aside the useless weapon. Kiri eyelids snapped down. With a savage cry Kane leaped, his bare hands reaching for the azir's smooth throat.

Fourteen

There was an instant of terrible shock, a feeling of black ice exploding through Kane's body and timeshadow. As though at a distance he heard himself scream, heard Sharia echo that scream in a terrible duet of fear and pain. Stunned, reeling, Kane forced his long fingers to close around the azir's throat. He felt the silky texture of the beast's transparent ruff as it washed over his tunic, felt the cool tendrils slide over his skin and the warm lias'tri stone. Clear, sentient black eyes looked deeply into Kiri violet.

The azir dissolved.

Kane looked at his empty hands in utter disbelief. Translucent, perfect, patient, the soul-eater reformed at Kane's heel. When Kane moved toward Sharia the beast paced beside him, offering no further resistance. Kane did not stop to ask why the azir had changed its mind. He simply ripped through the crowd around Sharia. The azir moved like a translucent shadow beside Kane, touching people lightly with its ruff, teaching them . . . something. Wherever the azir touched, people withdrew, their eyes wide with horror.

Within moments the crowd vanished back into the cracks and crevices of Beoy. Alone, untouched, Sharia swayed to her feet, her Darien hair a seething silver cloud around her. She did not know where she was. She did know that for an instant agony had exploded through Kane, tearing her from the timeshadow she had ridden. Suddenly Sharia's legs gave way. Kane caught her an instant before she would have struck the cold pavement.

A feeling of intense well-being swept through Kane as his hands caught Sharia. As though Kiri eyelids had descended to reveal yet another reality, the world seemed to leap into diamond focus. Colors were brighter, more intense, more distinct. The difference between light and dark was an endless spectrum of possibilities rather than a simple division between bright and shadow. The sunshine scent of Sharia's living Darien hair as it settled around him was a soothing caress filling his senses. He felt the textures of her skin and clothes with a vivid discrimination that was utterly compelling. There was the supple warmth of living flesh and the slightly rough coolness of her tunic, the resilience of muscle moving beneath smooth skin and the silky touch of her pulse beating beneath his fingertip. Her breath was a transparent warmth bathing him, beckoning him to other sweet warmths, other womanly textures.

Power flowed out of Kane into his lias'tri, a bright flow of substance replacing what Sharia had lost when she had poured herself into the energy sink of cultural despair. His heightened awareness sensed his timeshadow reaching, stretching, links forming to the *then* and the *now,* energy shifting and pouring. He was not healing her, not quite. He did not ride her suddenly radiant timeshadow, nor did he comb the tangled darkness from her flaring colors. He simply gave her the strength to heal herself, gave until he felt her timeshadow shimmer and tremble, overflowing with life.

Sharia's eyes opened, violet and silver in an equal and incredible mixture. She was not surprised to find Kane holding her in his arms. She had dreamed this before, had experienced this instant as surely as she knew her own heartbeat, her own rippling timeshadow. Languidly, lulled by the unreality of the moment, she smiled up at him. *You feel like my dreams of you, sv'arri. Hot. Powerful. Perfect. Do you taste like my dreams, too?*

Her thought caressed Kane as surely as her translucent silver hair combing through his living timeshadow and her five-fingered hands threading deeply into his black Darien hair.

Slowly he lowered his head until his lips could brush over hers. He meant it to be for only an instant, a glancing caress. But the instant passed and he was still touching her. Timeshadows overlapped hesitantly, then with greater certainty, twining sweetly as each color sought its complement. Reality expanded in a silent, sentient explosion. Then she was tasting him and he was tasting her, their mouths joined in a wild pleasure that each had known once before, on Za'arain. Five touching five.

And then the Kiriy had exiled him.

Catastrophe.

The knowledge of what they were doing battled against the inevitability of their mutual need. Desperately each fought to control the yearning, consuming power of their timeshadows and flesh reaching out, catching, holding. The torrential, tantalizing rightness of each completing the other was a siren call that became more irresistible with each sweet instant.

Twin-voiced, the azir howled an eerie duet of time and life. The higher voice shivered through all dimensions in fierce celebration, mocking distinctions among the *then* and the *now* and the *always*. The lower voice understood that death was the price of such unity. Only life differentiated among colors and tastes and scents and textures. Only life moved among the unnamed interfaces between time and matter. Only life understood death.

Both lure and warning, the azir's song trembled in the Za'arains' minds. At the same instant Kane and Sharia released one another, knowing that if they did not move quickly they would never move at all. Trembling, eyes closed, minds held so tightly that they twisted in futile protest, Kane and Sharia stood with their backs to one another while the azir wept for them in harmonies and dimensions impossible to man.

With each breath the Za'arains took, their lias'tri crystals shifted and blazed with redoubled power. No longer were they dependent on reflection and refraction of existing illumination for their glory. The stones scintillated with shared life, each facet a separate statement of dimensions touched, possibilities to be consummated. White-hot hunger swept over both Za'arains, an incandescent punishment worse than either had known before.

Kane clenched his teeth against a primal scream of agony and despair. He felt as though every nerve in his mind were being dragged through a burning sieve. He knew that Sharia felt the same, their heartbeats and pain as much in harmony as the azir's twin voices.

Dimly Kane heard Jode give curt orders to return to the ship immediately. When the Jhoramon's hand closed over Kane's arm, leading him forward, he moved in a daze. As though at a distance he saw himself and Sharia walking slowly toward the ship. The azir walked between them, its shoulder brushing Kane's knee and its ruff curled tenderly around Sharia's hand, guiding her as Jode guided Kane. The ship welcomed them with a soothing murmur. Separated only by the azir, Kane and Sharia walked slowly to the control room.

Dani. Jode's thought was like a whip bringing the ship to attention. *Remember those blue-green seeds we picked up on Megot?*

There was no sense of questioning in the ship's tenuous awareness. She remembered.

Grind them up with some of the Jhoramon wine. Eight seeds in Kane's bulb. Five in Sharia's. Understand?

A clear feeling of agreement pressed against Jode's awareness. Dani was below the threshold of intellect required for precise mindspeech, but her focused emotions were easy to pick up.

Good. Quickly, now. I want it down their throats before they start asking inconvenient questions.

Jode pressed gently against Kane. The big Za'arain sat in the captain's chair. The azir nudged Sharia into her chair. Jode eyed the azir with a mixture of disbelief, uneasiness and admiration. In the artificial light of the cabin, the creature's short fur shone like a clear glacier under moonlight. Whatever its origins or nature, the azir was a handsome beast. And smart. Frighteningly so.

"Do you use comspeech?" asked Jode whimsically.

The soul-eater watched him with eyes as bottomless as night, and as transparent.

Mindspeech?

The azir smiled. It approached Jode, ruff erect, quivering with unasked questions. Silky, cool, the transparent tendrils stroked over Jode's black skin. From an immense distance, Jode sensed . . . something. A song sung in darkness and silence. Energy rippling, a black iridescence that whispered of power. A cold, deep wind blowing back from the end of time.

The azir's ruff slid down to curl around the beast's muscular neck. Jode shivered and looked away from the soul-eater's uncanny eyes as Dani chimed sweetly, calling his attention to her. The compartment on the side of Jode's chair slid open to reveal two bulbs of wine mixed with ground seeds. Jode took the bulb marked with the captain's insignia.

Drink.

Jode's simple, calm command slid between Kane's pain and his confusion. He squeezed the contents of the bulb into his mouth, swallowing several times. Almost immediately a feeling of tranquility spread through him. Though he still hungered for lias'tri completion with an intensity that was agonizing, he no longer felt as though his mind was being ripped from time/now with each heartbeat, each breath. With a long, shuddering sigh, Kane released the terrible grip he had taken on time/now.

Sharia moaned softly.

The azir's ruff lifted, trembling and iridescent. Black eyes shifted from Jode to Kane. Jode's hand closed around the second bulb. He looked at the soul-eater. Little was known about the creatures except that they defended their companions with lethal efficiency.

"Give the drink to Sharia," said Kane hoarsely, letting relief wash through him in waves. "She needs it as much as I do."

Jode picked up the bulb and turned toward Sharia. The ice-colored beast flowed to its feet. "What about the azir?" asked Jode. "Is it yours or hers?"

"Hers."

Jode grimaced. He had suspected as much. Kane had not been out of his sight long enough to have tamed an azir. Or vice versa. Jode took one step toward Sharia. The azir waited, motionless.

Kane looked at Sharia. Her eyes were closed, her skin drawn tautly over the delicate bones of her face. Her hair lay in silver profusion across the scarlet fabric of the chair. He looked at her luminous skin and graceful body, and remembered the incredible leaping clarity of reality when he had held her. Kane's expression changed from relief to a hunger as deep as the azir's eyes.

"I'll give her the wine," said Kane, his voice husky. "The azir trusts me."

"I don't." Jode's voice was curt. "Stay away from Sharia, Kane. Do you hear me? Don't touch her!"

Kane looked at Jode, shocked. The psi-master sounded like a Kiriy quoting Za'ar tabu.

Sharia whimpered, feeling the lash of Kane's savage, rebellious mind deep within her own.

With courage an Xtian would have admired, Jode took the three steps that put him next to Sharia. The azir faded in front of him, then condensed again near Sharia's hand.

Drink.

With Jode's silent command came a wash of compassion and affection. Despite the danger she represented to every psi within reach, Jode cared for Sharia as he had never thought to care for another woman after his lias'tri died.

Sharia drank. The potent seeds spread through her body and mind, divorcing her gently from the raging hunger that was consuming her will to remain separate from Kane. The feeling of relief was enormous as the psychoactive seeds sent their calming benediction throughout her troubled mind. She knew she still hungered, knew that the reprieve was temporary; the reprieve was very real nonetheless. She sighed and let her knotted muscles begin to relax.

The azir rested its graceful muzzle in her lap and closed its black eyes. Jode looked from the deadly, near-mythical beast to the woman whose silver hair could heal or kill with equal ease.

"How did the azir find you?" said Jode quietly.

Sharia's eyes opened. Silver turned in their depths, as did shards of Kiri violet. "It was hurting. Dying, I think."

"I didn't know anything could kill them."

"All living things die, Jode. Somewhere. Somewhen." Sharia sighed. "It has an incredible timeshadow," she said softly. "So many dimensions, so many colors. Like Kane and I when we touch. . . ."

Jode drew in his breath swiftly. Kane heard the betraying sound, as did Sharia.

"What is it?" she asked, feeling Jode's uneasiness despite the calming drug he had given to her.

"Later. First I have to know more about the azir."

"There's nothing to tell. I rode its timeshadow, combed its colors, touched its lacework of glittering darkness. . . ." Sharia's voice died. Slowly she smoothed her fingers into the azir's iridescent ruff. The animal rumbled a bass chord of pleasure as their timeshadows mingled.

"You healed it." Jode's voice was careful, neutral.

"Not like I'd heal a Fourth Evolution person," said Sharia. "The azir wasn't ill. Not really."

"What was wrong with it?"

Sharia hesitated, searching for a word in comspeech or Za'arain. There was none. "Loneliness," she said finally. "For the azir, emotions are as real and as tangible as the fingers on our hands."

"Loneliness," said Jode, keeping the disbelief from his voice.

"Not loneliness as we know it," corrected Sharia. "Not really. To the azir, loneliness is a way of bleeding to death physically. Maybe it was the azir's first excursion into our dimension. Maybe it was stretched too fine between the *other* and time/now. I helped it, because I'm deeply rooted in the *now.*" Sharia sighed and shook her silver hair until its long strands caressed the azir's strong body. "I can't explain what I did, I only know that it worked."

"Too well," muttered Jode.

Kane caught the fear beneath Jode's words. So did Sharia. She turned quickly, facing the Jhoramon.

"What's wrong?" she asked tightly.

"Not yet." Jode's expression, like his voice, was implacable. "When did you notice that the azir was a psi?"

Sharia's surprise was clear in her face and in the brush of her mind. "It is?"

Jode hesitated. A curious expression transformed his dark face, as though he could not decide whether to believe Sharia's words. He sensed Kane's mental probe. The psi-master deflected it after a brief skirmish, grateful that he had taken the precaution of heavily blunting Kane's mind.

You have to trust me in this.

Jode's thought was as neutral as distilled water. No hint of emotion spilled over to tell Kane what was driving his friend. Reluctantly, Kane allowed the drugged wine to lull him again.

All right. But if you hurt her. . . . Kane did not finish the thought. He did not have to. The white-hot promise of lias'tri retribution burned just beneath the calming drug.

Jode watched Sharia with his eyes and his mind. No matter how carefully and deeply he probed her drugged mind, he sensed nothing but truth. She had not sensed the azir to be a creature of psi.

"I believe the azir is a renegade psi," said Jode. His voice was calm but tension curled tangibly around him.

Sharia looked confused. Jode glanced from her to Kane. Equal confusion.

"My sweet, shivering Jhoramon gods," said Jode in disbelief. "Neither one of you knows what I'm talking about."

"Er, no," admitted Sharia.

"Yet you both have powerful psi," exclaimed Jode. "The planet of Za'arain itself must have been crawling with psi! The Kiri psi-packs and the Eyes of Za'ar. Are you saying that in all your history you've never encountered a renegade, wildfire psi?"

Sharia made a helpless gesture.

"Describe it," said Kane in a clipped voice. He had been drugged, but he was Darien and five, more powerful than Jode knew or Kane would admit. He had not sensed the possibilities of his own power until his timeshadow had begun to mingle with Sharia's. The thought of what a complete mingling would mean was a fire raging in the depths of him.

"A renegade psi is a mind that is both catalyst and tyrant," explained Jode. "It can sweep up all other psi-minds it touches. After a certain point it can suck up even minds that are psi-null. With each mind comes greater strength, greater reach, more minds captured. It twists the minds into new shapes, new dimensions, new possibilities. It sweeps out to the limits of its power and then it . . . burns. Wildfire psi. They all burn—the minds. The lucky ones die. A few survive, the way moss survives. Dumbly."

Sharia and Kane exchanged a long look.

"How long does the process take?" asked Sharia quietly.

"What?"

"From the moment of inception to the burning. How long?"

"It depends on the renegade," said Jode. "Some manage to control their greed for new minds for many years. Some burn out the first time they realize what they're capable of and act on it." He waited, but neither Za'arain spoke. "Why?" asked Jode finally.

"By your definition, the Kiriy of Za'arain is a renegade psi," Kane said in a calm, weary voice. "The Eyes of Za'ar are both catalyst and judge."

"I don't understand." Jode's voice was quiet and yet very hard. He would understand if he had to ask questions until time itself froze solid.

"On Za'arain, the Kiriy controls the expression of psi." Sharia's words were calm, precise. Only Kane understood the fear and despair beneath her gentle voice. "It isn't greed that drives the Kiriy, but necessity. With the Eyes, Za'arains can control themselves. Without them, we are at the mercy of what you call a renegade psi."

"What do you call it?"

"Darien five."

The soft words seemed to explode in the Jhoramon's mind. For a moment the psi-master was stunned. He left Sharia's statement go through him like a shock wave, rearranging reality in its wake.

"I'm not sure I understand," Jode said, his dark eyes looking from Kane to Sharia. "Neither one of you felt like a renegade psi, much less a wildfire psi until the azir came along."

"What do you mean, 'felt'?" asked Kane.

"It's hard to explain," said Jode, smoothing his palm over his naked scalp. "When lias'tris touch, there's a heightened sense of reality. Everything is much more clear."

Kane's eyes showed violet and then tarnished silver as he remembered. "Yes. Go on."

"What I sensed was like that, only much more intense—an incredible increase in the reach of the mind and the senses. Do you understand what I mean?"

"All places, all times, all possibilities," said Sharia softly. "All of them. Ours."

Jode winced at the yearning threaded through Sharia's words. "That's what a renegade psi wants. All of it. To get it, the psi will burn out every mind within reach. Wildfire psi."

"Five touching five." Kane's voice was empty, as empty as his eyes. His mind and emotions were not empty. They surged at the point of explosion. "Catastrophe."

"Superstition," said Jode, but his voice said that he was afraid that he was lying. "It was the azir. Soul-eater."

Jode. Sharia's mental touch was sure and swift despite the drugs she had been given. Her hair seethed out over the azir as she deliberately mingled their timeshadows. *What do you sense now?*

The psi-master concentrated, reaching out to the Za'arain-azir pair. No matter how carefully he probed, he sensed nothing of the immense, sweeping power that he had sensed once before. Sadly he withdrew. He answered Sharia's question verbally because even the lightest touch of his mind on Sharia's made her grief and hunger vibrate through him. She was lias'tri. Her completion waited in a man who was forbidden to her.

"I sense nothing," sighed Jode. "Just you and a cold wind out of time."

"The azir," said Kane.

"Yes." Jode shook his head as though to clear his brain. "Then what was it I sensed before?" he asked, half afraid that he already knew the answer.

"Tell us about lias'tri," Kane said. "What is it besides *hunger?*"

"Completion," said Jode simply.

Kane could not conceal his hunger and regret that lias'tri completion was denied to him. Nor could Sharia conceal the depth and power of her agreement with him.

"Yes," Kane said, his voice harsh, "but why? Why Sharia? Why me?"

"All your other lives together," said Jode, his voice rich with his own memories, his own regrets. He looked down at the gems blazing visibly beneath the Za'arains' clothes. "Many, many lives. I've never seen so vibrant a bond. I've never heard of one." He looked up at Kane. How did you meet Sharia?"

"I heard that another Darien five had been born. I knew the isolation that would be her life. After the six-year mark, when babies are brought out of the nursery, I came to her."

"Who told you?"

"About her isolation?" asked Kane. "No one had to. It was mine, too, Darien and five."

"No. Who told you that Sharia had been born?"

Kane opened his mouth as though to speak. No words came out.

Jode made a gesture of agreement. "Yes. As I feared. No one had to tell you. You simply knew. If Sharia had been born first she would have known when you were born. Lias'tri. You are bound to each other in ways you haven't even begun to realize. I didn't know that my Chayly had been born. We didn't meet until we literally bumped into each other during the Wind Festival. When we touched, we . . . *knew.* Lias'tri was very strong in us." Jode was silent for a long moment, then he continued, "If five touching five isn't permitted, why were you allowed to be with Sharia?"

"Mature fives are prohibited," said Sharia. "Men are considered mature at their thirty-year mark. Women are considered mature at the onset of fertility."

"How is that determined?"

"The Kiriy knows," she said simply. "Kane was exiled when I was fifteen."

Jode did not want to ask the next question, did not want to hear the answer he feared; but there was no choice. "Did you touch each other as a man and a woman before Kane was exiled?"

"Just one kiss." Hunger and regret resonated through Sharia's words.

"When?"

"Just before Kane was exiled."

"Did you know then that he would be exiled?"

"No."

Jode looked at Kane. "Did you know?"

"No. If I had . . ." He shrugged.

"If you had . . . ?" asked Sharia softly, watching him with eyes that were violet and silver at once.

"I would have stolen you."

The shudder of Sharia's response told Kane more than words could have. At that instant the cost of controlling himself seemed much more than it could possibly be worth. With a small cry, Sharia looked away, knowing what Kane felt because it was in her, too—a fire burning from the *then* to the *now.*

Jode spoke quickly, trying to defuse the coiled sensuality that threatened to break through both drugs and Kiri training. "Most psi gifts only come into full potency with physical maturity.

When Kane and you touched that last time, you must have been mature or nearly so. The Kiriy must have sensed your minds joining and known—" Abruptly Jode stopped speaking.

"Known what?" demanded Kane.

Jode hesitated and then made a gesture that was composed of equal parts of anger and regret. "That together, you and Sharia are an incredibly powerful, wholly uncontrolled, wildfire psi."

"But—" Sharia's voice broke, then reformed. "We don't want other minds, other lives," she said, her voice soft, certain. "All we want is to touch, to let our timeshadows and minds and bodies know each other deeply."

"Uncontrollably," said Jode. Then he swore terribly in his own language, switching to comspeech only when he ran out of Jhoramon curses. "If the Eyes of Za'ar are powerful enough to control psi-packs, why in all the names of all the gods didn't the Kiriy use the Eyes to teach you to control your minds!"

"She didn't have to, Kane said in a clipped voice. "She simply exiled me, as so many other fives have been exiled throughout Za'ar's reign."

"Or perhaps," said Sharia, "it's simply that we can't be controlled short of death. Sometimes, two fives touching can disturb za' itself. Two fives who were also lias'tri. Kane. Me. I—I don't think my like has been born before on Za'arain," she said slowly, remembering resonances and shadings of the Kiriy's dying communication. "It's the same for Kane. Together, we're much more than either one alone."

Jode swore wearily. "So the Kiriy did what had been done in the past—she exported Za'arain's problems to the Joining rather than solving them on Za'arain."

"Only half of its problems," said Kane. "The Kiriy kept the other half at home. Like Sharia. And it worked, Jode. It worked for a long, long time. There have been no wildfire psis on Za'arain."

Jode looked skeptical. "Any planet as rife with psi as Za'arain is, must also be rife with the ramifications of psi. Wildfire and renegades are just two of the most dangerous problems."

"Not with the Eyes." Sharia's voice was calm, certain. "The Eyes . . . judged. Those whom the Eyes rejected, died. Za'arain survived. A million years."

"And how many lias'tris were divided?" asked Jode softly. "How many—"

Abruptly Jode stopped speaking as he controlled his anger at a culture whose only solution to lias'tri problems was to condemn the partners to a refined torture of mind and body that was limited only by the endurance and life-spans of the lias'tris involved. He wanted to ask how many lias'tris had gone mad, like desert animals staked out by a well on a steel leash until they died raving, knowing that water was just beyond the reach of their quivering muzzles. But he could not ask that question, for Kane and Sharia did not know yet that lias'tri would not be denied short of death.

And even that was only a truce, a dimensional pause between lives.

"How many lias'tris did the Kiriy deny? How many suffered as you and Kane suffer?"

Sharia's smile was sad and swift. "I think—hope—the problem of very powerful lias'tris is new. Kane and I are . . . different. Za'arains are still evolving. Kiri, then Darien, then five." She looked at Jode. "Despite what you believe, the Kiriy isn't capricious or cruel. Though Za'arain doesn't have lias'tri stones, we have men and women who have loved from the *then* to the *now*. The Eyes didn't reject their joined minds, their shared lives. The Kiriy's greatest strength came from them. Together those couples were far, far stronger than they were apart."

Jode sank into his chair and let it flow soothingly around him. "Then why didn't she help you instead of exiling your other half? She must have known what an empty life she was dooming you to."

"The Eyes had aged her. I think she knew that within a few years I would either be Kiriy or dead. And then—how could I miss a completion I'd never known?" asked Sharia, her hand wrapped around the burning jewel beneath her robes. "Kane," she breathed, her voice too soft for him to hear.

But he did. He heard his name as though she had whispered it against his lips.

"The Kiriy did what she had to, did what had always been done," said Sharia, her tone bleak with the knowledge of the Kiri-trained, the Darien-disciplined. "She protected Za'arain and the Joining by separating two fives. Two halves of an overwhelming, destructive whole."

"Shari—" The word was more a groan than a name, for Kane did not want to hear his greatest fear spoken aloud by the woman he must have and could not touch. "Don't."

"But it's true. Together, we're destructive. We don't want to be. We just want—" Sharia clenched her hands, driving fingernails into flesh until blood welled up.

"Don't, sv'arri," murmured Kane, holding his hands out to her. Blood stood redly across his palms.

Jode swore in phrases as black as the azir's eyes.

"If your Kiriy wanted you separated, she should have forbidden you that stone," said Jode, indicating the glittering jewel Sharia wore. He looked at Kane. "Where did you find them?"

"A cave on Xt. Not a cave, really. A building buried by sediments and time. Older than Za'ar." Kane's eyes closed as he remembered the thickly layered timeshadow wakes that had drenched the building in static streamers of color. "The jewels looked identical until I touched them. Then one shone dark and one light. Both were clear, though. Both were alive with fire and memories and . . . possibilities. I wore both for a time, then I sent them to her."

"Why?" asked Jode softly.

"I don't know. I simply had to."

Jode turned to Sharia. "Why did you keep one jewel and send the other back to Kane?"

"I don't know. Somehow I sensed . . ." Sharia closed her eyes. "It was all I could send of me, all I could keep of him."

The psi-master let out a long, harsh breath. "Do you know what would have happened if you had kept both stones or sent both back?" he asked Sharia.

"No."

"Kane would have died."

Sharia's luminous skin seemed to fade to transparency with the shock of Jode's words.

"When he touched those stones," explained Jode, "Kane keyed them to his own mind, his own deepest desire. You. If he hadn't loved you, if hatred had been his deepest desire, you would have been the one to die. Like any other force, lias'tri is neutral. The uses to which it is put are not."

"Like time," murmured Sharia.

"And psi, and gravity, and fire and life itself—all neutral, until they're used by intelligent beings. Then," shrugged Jode, "those forces can be anything from pure good to absolute evil."

The azir stretched and yawned delicately, revealing translucent black teeth and tongue.

"And the azir," added Sharia wryly. "Another force."

"Soul-eater." Jode shrugged again. "Companion and protector." He looked at Sharia. "Why didn't the Kiriy take away your lias'tri stone?"

"Why should she?"

"She wanted to separate you and Kane. The instant he put on the stone you sent him, you were connected again."

Sharia's mouth turned down in a sad smile. "That explains it, then," she murmured.

"Explains what?" asked Kane.

"I woke up one morning and the necklace was gone."

"What did you do?"

"I don't remember. I was eaten up by fever. When at last the fever broke I was wearing the necklace again."

"Why didn't you heal yourself?" Kane asked, uneasiness running over his skin like a tumble of jhoras.

Sharia looked at her hands, then at Kane's tarnished silver

eyes. "I didn't want to," she said simply. "I was lonely, v'orri. Death looked very good to me."

Kane moved as though he would go to her, comfort her. Then he remembered that he could not touch her. His hands clenched on the arms of his chair.

"She gave it back to you," said Jode, watching Sharia fight to keep from going to Kane, touching him. They all knew she could not do that. Each time they touched it would be more difficult to stop. Each time they touched they went deeper into each other, knew more, wanted more, became more powerful came closer to the instant of wildfire psi.

"Who?" asked Sharia, forcing herself to focus on Jode.

"The Kiriy. She took the lias'tri stone, but then realized that without it you had no reason to live, and she needed you to live." Jode sighed. "You and Kane must have shared many lives for the bonds to be that strong when you were so young. Lives without number, without end. No wonder you two are so powerful together."

Perplexed, Kane and Sharia looked at each other. Intellectually they knew that they must have shared lives before time/now. It was the only explanation of their instant, enduring, consuming attraction for each other. But though they accepted the fact of other shared lives, neither had access to the memories.

Nor did they want access. Dealing with time/now was difficult enough. And they suspected that if they knew what they were missing—really knew—even Kiri training and Darien discipline would not hold them apart. Then they would touch, minds and timeshadows and bodies intertwined, time collapsing until there was only the imploding *other.*

That could not be allowed to happen. They could not touch.

Jode sensed their mutual thoughts, mutual conclusion. He wished it were as simple as two people deciding not to become one. But Jode knew it was not. The psi-master knew one more thing about lias'tri that he had not told them: Lias'tris *had* to touch. Fighting that simple fact was like fighting gravity without the aid of a Wolfin ship—futile at best; lethal at worst. You could resist and resist and resist, but you could not win.

"I think," said Jode quietly, "that you should be very careful not to touch each other. At all. I'll help you as much as I can, teach you what I know about baffling and controlling your minds."

"Jode." Kane's voice was quiet, calm, hard.

"Yes, Captain?"

"It won't work. Not for long."

"It doesn't have to work forever," said Jode. "Just until we find the Eyes of Za'ar."

"What good will that do?"

"If those ruthless stones controlled a planet full of psis, they should be able to control two half-trained lias'tris," the psi-master snarled.

"Or kill one of them," said Sharia calmly. "Me."

Jode closed his eyes and said nothing. There was nothing he could say.

Fifteen

Sharia murmured a Za'arain prayer for the dying. Then she looked at Jode with psi-hunter eyes. Her words were com-speech, precise and very civilized, atavism and time/now united.

"Then the Kiriy wasn't insane," she said. "The Eyes were stolen by or for a Za'arain exile."

"Who?"

Sharia hesitated, remembering the words of the dying Kiriy, words whose meaning had been overshadowed by the Za'ar imperative she had driven into Sharia's unwilling mind.

"A man the Kiriy called her lost soul, her tabu soul." Sharia closed her eyes, remembering more, understanding too much. "Lias'tri," she whispered. "She called him the forbidden half of the Kiriy of Za'arain." Her eyes opened, silver and violet, searching Jode's dark face. "What would a thwarted lias'tri do after nearly four centuries of *hunger?*"

"Whatever he had to in order to get his other half," said Jode grimly. "What I can't understand is why the Kiriy exiled her own soul."

"He was five. So was she. And," added Sharia, "she had the Eyes. All the billions of cascading timeshadows. She had never touched the man she exiled. She didn't know. She believed the Eyes were enough."

Without thinking, Sharia looked toward Kane. Just as quickly she looked away. She had touched him. She knew that nothing would ever be enough. Except Kane.

Jode's voice was like a whip driving Sharia back from her

hunger. "The Kiriy—" snapped Jode. "Was she a powerful psi? As powerful as you?"

"In her own way, yes," said Sharia. "Very powerful. Easily as powerful as I. And when she wore the Eyes, she was Za'ar, the massed minds of the Kiri."

"Her lias'tri would be equally powerful, given the Eyes and other minds," said Jode flatly. "If he's trafficking in psi-stones. he could have become as good at manipulating reality as your Kiriy. He would lust after psi power in order to fill the emptiness of lias'tri thwarted. He would be ruthless. Insane."

Sharia made a broken sound and bowed her head. "That must be what the Kiriy meant," she whispered.

"What?" said Jode, his voice harsh.

"She said that she sent the other half of herself into the Dust and it returned changed. Diseased. Somehow he brought the winnowing to Za'arain."

"As the Kiris died, the Kiriy would lose power," Jode said quietly. "Then the exile might be able to take the Eyes from the Kiriy. Even so, he must have been afraid to return to Za'arain as long as the Eyes were open, so he hired a Dust raider to steal the Eyes for him."

"But the disease killed his own lias'tri!" objected Kane.

"He probably assumed that the Eyes would make her immune," said Jode. "In any case, he isn't rational. Lias'tri will be united, or it will destroy the life holding it in search of other lives, other times, when lias'tri might be whole. Lias'tri is patient."

"The Kiriy died the final death," said Sharia hoarsely. "I felt it. She called the name of her lost soul and deliberately bled herself into the spaces between time. She will never be born again."

Jode's breath sucked in. "You come from a very courageous race. The Kiriy must have known that was the only way to defeat lias'tri." He closed his eyes and murmured a few words in Jhoramon. "So now the Eyes are in the hands of a man as powerful as the Kiriy was brave."

"No," said Kane certainly.

The word was exactly echoed by Sharia's voice.

"How can you be sure?" snapped Jode.

"The Eyes aren't open," Kane said. "Even many za'replacements away from Za'arain, I knew when the Eyes closed. I'll know when they open again."

"Yes," said Sharia simply.

Jode sat without moving except for the tip of one finger circling the textured surface of his chair. All right," he said after a moment. "The Dust raiders' ships are much slower than Dani on full emergency power, especially with the shortcuts we've been taking through rough nodes. We must have beaten the Dust ship back to Doursone. But not by much," he added grimly.

"Is the Dustman waiting in the Jorke for his raider to return?" asked Sharia. "And when Ine's men started asking for violet psi-stones, the raider killed them?"

"You're sure you would know if the Eyes were in use?" countered Jode. He flinched immediately under the double mental *yes* he received. "Then we go to the Jorke," said Jode, turning toward the viewcube where the image of Ine waited patiently.

"If we're going to the Jorke, you'll need Merone," said Ine. "My spies here spoke eight languages and fourteen dialects among them. They used every last one of them and wished they'd had a hundred more." Ine hesitated, then made another fluid gesture. "Whoever killed my spies took their most recent trading cubes. I have the rest. I'm still going through them. There are six dialects and three languages that I've never heard before. These were hidden recordings. There was no translation included. My spies knew about Merone. They hoped that she would be able to make sense out of the recordings. Maybe she can," shrugged the Jiddirit. "Maybe then we can avoid whatever mistakes killed my spies. If Merone can still learn languages, that is."

Kane frowned. "Is Merone in one of her mad phases?"

Ine made an ambivalent gesture. "She was singing in the hall a moment ago."

Dani. Get Szarth. Kane's mental command was swift and clean despite the drug still circulating in his system.

The Xtian's image glowed forth from a second cube.

"Bring Merone to me," said Kane. "Gently. But bring her."

Szarth hissed a brief agreement. The viewcube winked out.

"Bring your spy cubes to me," Kane said, turning to Ine's image.

The Jiddirit bowed. His viewcube vanished.

"Are you strong enough to soothe her?" asked Kane quietly, watching Sharia, knowing that so long as the Wolfin machine lived within Merone's brain, true healing was impossible. Quasi-life was beyond Sharia's ability to deal with successfully.

"Of course I'm strong enough to help Merone. After you healed me in the streets, I felt—"

"I didn't heal you," interrupted Kane. "I—shared with you."

"Shared? It was more than that, v'orri. I took more than I gave."

"Never," said Kane softly, remembering the exquisite, coursing pleasure of holding Sharia alive and vibrant in his arms.

Jode looked away from them and hoped that Szarth brought Merone on the run. The tension in the cabin was strong enough to magnetize steel.

Merone walked in humming, gently mad, hiding among the multiple, sometimes-conflicting realities of her many languages. Szarth guided her with unobtrusive touches. Kane tilted his head toward Sharia. The Xtian nudged Merone within reach of the rippling silver hair. Xtian bells chimed and slid down into Sharia's waiting hands. Kane stiffened against the discomfort that suddenly lanced through him as Sharia rode the Wolfin's troubled timeshadow, combing out the most recent knots. Both Za'arains knew that the knots would reform again, soon, more tightly. Sharia was treating symptoms, not cause. Kane might have been able to treat the cause—the unbalanced, quasi-living machine—but as long as it was embedded in a living brain, the Wolfin construct was out of his reach, too tangled in Merone's living timeshadow to be accessible to a wake rider.

Like Sharia, like Merone, Kane clenched his teeth and endured what he could not change.

The humming stopped. Merone blinked and looked around as though waking from a long sleep. The last translucent tendril of Darien hair fell away. Merone made a startled sound. Fear bleached both the dark and the light stripes of her skin.

"I did it again, didn't I?" she whispered. "So soon. The attacks are coming much faster."

Kane said nothing. He did not want to open his mouth, to speak, to ask Merone to learn more languages and drive herself mad again, perhaps irrevocably this time.

Ine walked in, a box of teacher cubes in his hand. Silently Merone went to him and took the box. She knew her duty as a Wolfin translator. Kane made a movement as though to take back the cubes.

No. It's the only way. Jode's thought was both compassionate and unflinching.

Kane did not answer. In silence he watched the Wolfin woman accept the hair-fine net of leads from Ine, position them on her head, and then connect the master lead to the first cube. Random sounds came from her lips, either words or fragments or pleas. Sharia started to go to Merone. Jode moved to intervene, his hand reaching quickly for her wrist. The azir hummed a twin-voiced warning—nothing got between an azir's companion and that companion's desire. Jode snatched back his hand as though he had thrust it into fire.

Sv'arri. Don't.

Kane's thought stopped Sharia as though she had walked into a synstone wall. She looked at him for a long moment and then returned to her couch. Merone never noticed. The cubes and their languages utterly compelled her. She went through three cubes with a speed that worried Kane. He said nothing, though. They had to have the information in those cubes.

Trembling, Merone put back the third cube and dragged the linkage net from her head. Her eyes were glazed, unseeing. Six more cubes waited in the box.

Sharia came quickly to her feet. This time no one stopped her. She stood next to Merone, caressing her with soothing silver hair and luminous hands. After a few minutes Merone stopped shuddering.

"Thank you," Merone said, her voice harsh. "I'm all right now. I just need . . . rest. A few minutes."

It was a lie, and at least three people in the cabin knew it. No one protested. There were times when a lie was more useful than the truth. The truth was that Merone was poised on the brittle edge of a madness that was beyond even a Darien timeshadow rider's ability to combat. With each new language learned, the balance between the quasi-living construct and the living mind became more precarious. It was a limiting factor known to all Wolfins and to those who became an extension of their constructs. No matter how clever the Wolfin scientists might be, they refused to admit that life and time were symbiotic. Without that understanding, any balance achieved between life and construct was only temporary. It was just a matter of time before Merone went crazy. How much time depended on her resilience and the number of languages she was forced to learn. Most Wolfin translators knew only twenty. Merone knew twice that.

Merone's distress made Sharia's hair quiver with the need to heal. Sharia physically grabbed the silver mass and held it against her body. Szarth approached. Chains of Xtian bells dangled musically from his hands. Swiftly Sharia bound her rebellious hair.

"Did you learn anything about the Eyes of Za'ar?" asked Kane.

Absently, Merone rubbed her palms over the alternating textures of skin and fur on her arms. "There's a Dustman. A trader. A raider." She moved her hands jerkily. "In the Dust, one is the same as the other. He specialized in gems. They say he could tell whether a gem was ancient or newly mined, First or Fifth, living or construct or dead."

Timeshadow rider, Wake rider.

The thought was neither Sharia's nor Kane's. It was theirs, spoken in the deepest part of their minds, They said nothing aloud, but their eyes went violent in a single flicker of Kiri eyelids.

"Which type of gems did he prefer?" asked Kane softly.

"Either ancient constructs or Fifth Evolution." Merone frowned. "The cubes weren't clear. I don't think that there is a difference."

Time.

Again the thought was theirs. Constructs were not living, not quite. The *now* was beyond their reach. Fifth Evolution minds, like that of the azir, were somehow part of the *other* as well as the *now* of Fourth Evolution. But that was Za'arain knowledge. Merone was Wolfin, and more than half mad.

"Go on," said Kane, his voice gentle despite the cruel violet of his eyes.

"The trader's name is SaDyne."

ZaDyneen. Kiri, Darien and five. Close cousin to the dead Kiriy. Brother to Kane's father. Exiled long, long ago, the hour after she took up the Eyes and survived. That was when she knew. Lias'tri. The boundaries of za' overwhelmed. Catastrophe.

Some of the knowledge was Kane's, some was Sharia's, some of it came from lives in time/then. All of it was theirs, though, time sliding elusively from one life to the next.

Jode looked from one Za'arain to the other. He sensed their odd communication but it was so deeply held that it was far beyond his skill to tap. Though they were apart, not touching, their lias'tri stones blazed and shimmered more brightly than Jode's ever had, even when he had held his lias'tri and they had known one another in every way a man and a woman could. The radiance of the Za'arains' stones was frightening. They should not be that bright. Ever. It was as though every life, every mind, everything that the two Za'arains had ever shared throughout time lived now within the stones. Waiting to be tapped. Growing with each shared breath, each echoed heartbeat. Burning.

Uncontrolled.

"The raider has a room at the Jorke," continued Merone, unaware of the currents of psi coiling throughout the cabin. "Ine's men approached him. They asked about psi-stones. Matched psi-stones. They offered a ship's ransom if he had just what they wanted."

"And?" prompted Kane.

Merone sang broken phrases to herself. Xtian bells shivered in odd harmony. Soothing Darien hair combed through Merone's troubled time/now. She sighed and trembled and ran smooth palms over her arms. Only Kane and Sharia suspected that Merone deeply resented the healing. For Merone there was relief in madness, in finally letting the languages own her, letting them pour like molten glass through her mind, cauterizing all fear and hope and pain.

Even Merone did not realize how deeply she longed for insanity. Part of her thought she wanted to be sane. The rest of her wanted mindlessness with a savagery that equaled a Kiri psi-pack on the hunt.

"I—that's all." Merone's honey-colored claws slipped in and out of their sheaths with each shallow breath she took. For a civilized Wolfin there was no greater sign of distress. Razor-edges glinted in the cabin light. "They never spoke to SaDyne directly," she said, her voice tight—too tight, warning echo of a mind stretched too far between sanity and madness. "He always sent one of his men. And each time, the man spoke a different language. There are six more. New languages. One for each cube."

Merone looked at her amber claws for a long moment, then visibly willed them back into their sheaths. Her hands trembled as she fitted the linkage net back over her head.

Kane, we can't let—

Sharia's thought was never finished. With a feral sound Merone leaped for Sharia. Wolfin claws flashed. Kane was out of his chair with incredible speed, his eyes violet with rage and fear as he realized that he could not reach Sharia in time.

The azir struck. The *other* condensed. Time/now stopped.

Merone's body wavered as though it were suddenly seen through a thick layer of transparent ice. The view shivered, shifted. The Wolfin woman's scream was oddly distant, wrapped in layers of distance—or time. The scream stopped. The eerie distortion fell away.

In the sudden silence, the sound of Merone's clothes whispering to the floor seemed very loud. There was a slight metallic ping, then the rustle of something rolling across the floor. The azir stepped back, glowing with translucent colors. It ran its ruff caressingly over Sharia's hand, as though reassuring itself that she was unharmed.

Kane watched, and knew that their best hope of finding the Eyes of Za'ar had just been killed. Without a translator he could search for the Eyes as fruitlessly as a blind man searching for moonrise.

Kane bent and scooped the glittering crystal-metal construct from the floor. The slim Wolfin machine shimmered in his palm, refracting light in tiny shards of brilliance. For all its slender lines and slight curves, the translator was unreasonably heavy, its molecules both heavy and densely packed. One end of the tiny, slim spiral had a point so fine that it was invisible. The ability to understand languages was impregnated in the machine. All the enigmatic words and phrases, plus the capacity to learn even more. All there within his grasp.

What the machine lacked was a Fourth Evolution brain to activate it.

"The azir took only her body," said Jode. "Nothing else. Not her mind. Not even her clothes."

"A simple death in time/now," agreed Kane, his voice raw. Later he would regret the loss of the troubled life they had known as Merone. Now it was all he could do to combat his anger and fear. He gave the azir a hot, violet glance. Serene black eyes looked back at him.

"We should all die so cleanly," Jode said, envy clear in his voice.

"Is that what she wanted?" asked Sharia, shuddering, her timeshadow writhing with the unexpected resonances of azir time and Wolfin death.

The azir nuzzled Za'arain fingertips, then tasted them with a translucent black tongue.

"Of course," said Jode, his tone impatient. "She's wanted death since her sixteenth language. She was Wolfin, though. She knew her duty to her people." Suddenly he leaned forward, catching the glint of light from Kane's palm. "Be careful, Captain! That's her translator. If it pierces your flesh it will go right to your brain and then you'll be as crazy or as dead as Merone. Destroy it!"

Kane looked at the tiny construct with Kiri eyes. Merone's timeshadow wake was bright, vivid, still faintly quivering with the shock waves of death in time/now. Slowly, delicately, Kane searched among the barely moving colors. It was painstaking but quite uncomplicated to sort out the wake of former life from the continuing distortions of quasi-life. The tangled energies of the construct fairly shouted their dissonance to Kane's mind.

Gently Kane insinuated his timeshadow into the construct. The puzzle of its disharmonies intrigued him. There was no reason for them to exist, no intrinsic necessity for the dynamic imbalance built into the machine. It was simply that, like Dani, the Wolfin construct had been designed and grown with a complete disregard for any but the linear aspect of time. Unlike Dani, however, the construct had neither the intelligence nor the desire to fight back when Kane sought to balance Wolfin construct with Za'arain reality. Rearranging the translator's references was a slow, tedious, but essentially simple operation.

And very, very draining. Kane was sweating heavily and trembling with a combination of physical and mental fatigue by the time he had finished educating the quasi-life that permeated the energy field of the Wolfin machine. Finally, the intricate, densely packed molecules and elusive energies of the construct were balanced in the *now* and the *then*. The construct would no longer resonate with destructive dissonances, driving its Fourth Evolution wearer insane. The changes were not permanent, however. Like all life the construct would change through linear time.

"If the translator were bigger," murmured Kane, "it would be able to hold a hundred languages."

"If it were bigger," retorted Jode, "it would kill whoever wore it even faster than it drove them mad."

"No," said Kane, feeling the unreasonable weight of the tiny machine resting on his palm. "Now that its energies are balanced, it could be twice as big as this. In fact, if this translator were bigger it would stay balanced longer." Delicately he ran his fingertips down the shining, spiral length of the construct. "But it will have to do as it is. We don't have enough time to find and negotiate for another Wolfin translator."

With no more warning than that, Kane reversed the construct and rammed its deadly, invisible point into the pulse beating at his throat. With every heartbeat the construct dissolved more thoroughly inside him, dispersing through Kane's blood only to reform deep within his brain.

Swearing bitterly, Jode pulled Kane toward his cocoon. The azir did not interfere. Like Sharia, it sensed quite clearly that Jode was concerned with furthering Kane's life rather than delivering his death.

"In," said Jode curtly, trying to maneuver the much larger Za'arain toward the captain's couch.

"I'm all right," Kane responded, his words slightly slurred as the alien molecules began to sweep through his blood. "I balanced the machine."

Mentally Jode called Kane a fool in every language he knew. Aloud he said, "You could balance that Wolfin disaster from here until the universe froze solid and it wouldn't help your body absorb the shock of the construct's presence!"

"I—" Kane's tongue thickened and his heart raced violently.

Coherent thought ended as Kane's physiology exploded into total rebellion at the alien presence coursing through it. Between one second and the next, Kane's body produced an overwhelming chemical storm in an attempt to reject the Wolfin molecules. Fluids suddenly pooled, restricting the movements of his heart, his lungs. Kiri eyelids flickered down but there was nothing to see except the red-shot midnight breaking over him.

Sharia—I—! Kane's mental cry ended as he fell unconscious to the floor.

"Get Sharia to her couch," snarled Jode to Szarth, knowing without looking that Sharia's body was undergoing the same convulsive rejection that Kane's was. *Dani, cocoons!*

Szarth had already leaped forward, catching Sharia before she touched the floor. He swung her into her unfurled cocoon with a single easy motion. Then he went and helped Jode with Kane's slack weight. Together they heaved their captain into his cocoon's scarlet embrace. The azir watched, ruff erect, quivering, tasting every emotion in the cabin. It knew its companion was in deadly danger. It also knew that the people in the cabin were as protective of the Za'arains as the azir itself was.

The cocoons closed over their unconscious occupants. Within moments Jode realized that the cocoons weren't enough. Nor would he stand and watch while two people died for no better reason than the probability that Za'ar tabu had a dangerous basis in reality.

Jode grabbed Sharia's cocoon. *Dani. Release the couch.* When Sharia's cocoon was positioned next to Kane's, Jode gave the ship curt instructions.

Combine the cocoons until Kane and Sharia touch each other. Then get ready to fill the cocoons with sleep gas and separate them when I give the order. Instantly. Gas and separate. Understand?

Dani's assent reassured Jode. He stepped away from the couches, letting the cocoons flow together. He did not notice the azir dissolve and reform around his feet with each step he took. Nor did he notice the sudden, electric attention of the beast when Sharia and Kane touched within their joined cocoons and their timeshadows overlapped.

Sharia did not awaken. Not quite. Kiri eyes looked at Kane

in the reflected blaze of lias'tri crystals. With an instinct born of other times other lives, Sharia fitted herself against Kane's tortured body, increasing the overlap of flesh and timeshadows. Instantly she was sucked into the cataract of his timeshadow energies. Like a fragile, iridescent bubble she rode the wild torrents of his strength, learning the depths and colors of his mind.

At first there was little Sharia could do but survive. In his fight for life in time/now, Kane had ripped through the normal barriers separating this life from other lives, other times. His timeshadow radiated in all directions, drew energy from unnamed dimensions and violently sought purchase for itself in time/now. Life. There were no rhythms to him, no long currents of color and purpose, nothing for a timeshadow rider to grasp and follow back toward time/then, toward the moment when disaster had struck. And with every instant passing from time/now into time/then the chaos of his timeshadow increased, threatening to kill both of them.

Sharia caught a single strand of color, a single powerful surge, and rode it back. The color exploded and vanished, leaving her spinning, imploding, utterly disoriented. Her own timeshadow flared desperately, reaching for and finding purchase once more in time/now. When she was in control of herself again, her hands instinctively tore at Kane's tunic and her own as she sought a greater contact with his flesh, which was solidly rooted in time/now.

Suddenly lias'tri crystals rolled free of cloth, were pressed between Za'arain flesh, and burst into impossible brilliance. Light and life and time burned through Sharia in a single searing instant. Other lives. Other times. Her own. His. Theirs. She could sense beyond the chaos of his timeshadow in time/now to the branching, twining, potent currents of life coursing through him, through her, through all the aspects of time both named and unnamed. Power such as she had never known poured through her, skills and responses from their other lives, new aspects of time and possibilities she could barely understand.

Sharia flowed into Kane's timeshadow, immersing herself in his agony and power. She both sought and attracted his chaotic energies, combed darkness from his torrential colors, and then braided forces as though she were a wake rider until she had a stable current reaching out and back into time/then. She rode the current down, balancing on conflicting, explosive energies with a skill unknown to Kiri, Darien or five, a consummation of other lives, other times.

The moment of destruction was not hard to find. It was an explosion of darkness through the sweeping streamers of color and energy that was Kane's timeshadow. Like a black sunburst, the moment radiated through his timeshadow, trying to divide it from the life of time/now. With all of Kane's time/then and time/now grasped within her seething Darien hair, the only limitation to Sharia's healing abilities was her own strength. When that began to fail she reached ruthlessly back into other times, other lives, other energies.

She was answered by an explosion of power that nearly destroyed her. It was like grabbing a sun when she had been expecting a candle. Stunned, her mind spun aimlessly, all but torn from its purchase within time/now. Only her Kiri heritage saved her, the cunning and stamina of a race that had survived its own violent beginnings by learning to defend itself in unusual ways— and times. With a reflex as old as hunter's light, she deflected the unexpected energy, scattering it into the *then* and the *now,* shedding it like a jhora shedding water drops from its golden fur.

And like water on jhora fur, some small amount of energy remained with Sharia. She used it to complete her untangling and combing of Kane's timeshadow. She rode him swiftly, surely, and with each split instant of contact came greater knowing, greater certainty, as though it were her own currents rather than his she rode. With dreamlike ease she spread through him, discovering him and herself. Branching, intricate, potent, compelling beyond anything she had ever known, the reality of Kane called to her.

She rode his life-force backward and forward along linear time, healing and enjoying him. She let herself ride further into his time/then, beyond the rapidly healing moment of Wolfin implant, past the agony of finding her hunted on Za'arain, past the oddly dimmed colors of the years when he had held so much of himself aloof from life, stifling his own heritage.

And then she discovered just where the missing radiance, missing resonance, missing power, had gone during the dim years of lias'tri separation. His timeshadow branched and . . . vanished. No, not quite vanished. It simply became translucent and then transparent. The timeshadow did not disappear, however. It remained like a window into another aspect of time, an aspect of the *other* that had no Za'arain word to describe it.

Fascinated, Sharia let Darien hair caress the transparent yet potent energies. They whispered seductively to her, radiating from Kane's time/then into . . . when? She followed, drawn irresistibly. Slowly the transparency thickened, shimmered, took on colors and currents, a network of possibilities slowly condensing once again into a living timeshadow.

Her own timeshadow.

Though separated by space and linear time, at some point in time/then Sharia's timeshadow and Kane's had joined. Somehow they had reached through an unknown dimension and met, twining, draining off life energies from linear time to support their mesh in unknown kinds of time.

Sharia hesitated, disturbed that something had been bleeding her energies and his without their knowledge. She rode the transparent currents with a delicacy that would have been impossible to her just yesterday, rode them with skills learned in many other times/then. Gradually she realized that the currents were not bleeding her timeshadow or Kane's, but were adding to them. Without that infusion both she and Kane would have wasted away by increments, consumed by a sickness that had neither name nor cure. Without that transparent bridge between them, she and he would have died—for before Kane's exile, their timeshadows had been as deeply rooted in each other as life was in linear time.

And even when Sharia was wrapped wholly within her own timeshadow on a ride back into time/now, still she sensed the connection with Kane. It was both with her in time/then and reaching back toward her from time/now, knitting them together in dimensions both known and unknown. She passed through the dim years of being separate from him in her own time/then and saw the pouring radiance of time/now sweeping toward her.

Instinctively Sharia knew that the explosion of colors had occurred at the moment when Kane had come to her in the shattered glass rooms of the Kiriy compound and had touched her. Mature five touching mature five. In that instant their timeshadows had flowed back together in time/now with a force that reverberated back to time/then. No longer divided by space, rapidly devouring their division by linear time, she and Kane were radiating through each other like sunrise through night, illuminating a dawn of awareness such as neither had ever experienced before. With each new touch, each lingering instant of five touching five, he and she twined more inextricably.

Time/now and time/then and timeshadows permeating, rooting, becoming . . . what? What waited for two fives touching?

It was so easy, so right, like the heat of his body next to hers, the taste of him in her mouth, the radiance of him wholly healed and awakening in her mind. Trembling silver hair combed the last shards of darkness from his timeshadow even as her luminous five-fingered hands smoothed over his hard body. Nothing had ever felt half so compelling to her as his flesh, the scent of him as close as her own skin, his heat a hunger and a burning that she had never known before. She felt him slide through her living timeshadow wake, riding it with skills she had taught him unknowingly. Long, five-fingered hands caressed her, learning her warmth and textures. The exquisite pleasure of his touch rippled through her time/now to time/then, making her body and her timeshadow shiver like a crystal bell perfectly struck.

There was no hesitation in the arms that closed around Sharia, nothing weak about the male body moving over hers. Kane was wholly healed, alive as he had only been alive once before in his life—when he had kissed her on Za'arain and sealed his own doom as an exile. But here there was no Kiriy, no Eyes of Za'ar to separate five from five; there was only the hot, sweet instant of time/now and a hunger that knew no bounds.

Time/then and time/now lapped together, Za'arain timeshadows mixing inextricably as Kane and Sharia unknowingly sought to wipe out the divisions of the past in a single impossible instant. Their timeshadows and bodies intertwined, moving as one, time flowing in all directions and dimensions toward a consummation in the *always* and the *other* that was both unity and death.

Lias'tri stones blazed so brightly that the scarlet cocoon was bleached to transparency.

Now, Dani! NOW!

At Jode's command the ship drenched the doubled cocoon with a potent soporific gas. Sharia fought the drug's effect wildly, yearning toward Kane with every bit of her strength, trying to rip through time itself to be with him. He fought as she did, using skills he had not known he had, skills that had come to him in the timeless instant when she had ridden his dying timeshadow. Together they reached backward and outward through all the dimensions of time that they had shared in all of their lives, seeking the power to overcome this drugged moment of time/now. For an instant they touched all the aspects of time, sent their hunger and their demand reverberating through the *always*.

But their strengths were too new to them, the sleep gas too overwhelming. Everything they sought slid away from them, stranding them in time/now.

With a mental cry that sent Jode to his knees, Kane and Sharia sank into unconsciousness.

Sixteen

Szarth watched the azir warily; the azir watched Jode with unblinking attention; Jode watched the two scarlet cocoons. They were separate again, opaque, lying at opposite sides of the cabin from each other.

"Is it going to attack?" hissed the Xtian, eyeing the ice-pale translucence of the beast.

"I don't think so." Jode's voice was distant, thinned by emotion and the backlash of the Za'arains' agonized psychic cry when they had lost their hold on one another.

"Why not?"

Sadness and regret washed over Jode, memories of his own loss, his lias'tri dead, never to be reborn into this time/now. He knew what the Za'arains were suffering. Even worse, he knew what they had yet to endure. "Neither Kane nor Sharia knew that I was the one who separated them. The azir knows that I want only life for both of them." He shrugged. "There is nothing for the soul-eater to attack."

"What if they wake up mad at you?"

"Then I'll die."

"Maybe you should take a walk on Doursone," suggested the Xtian.

"Do you really think a small bit of space and time would fool an azir?" asked Jode sardonically.

Szarth hissed and said nothing more. They both knew that if an azir wanted someone, there was not enough space or time in the universe in which to escape. Like a two-dimensional creature trying to hide from a three-dimensional predator, people were at a lethal disadvantage when it came to eluding azirs.

"What do we do?" asked Szarth.

"Wait."

The azir lay in the center of the cabin, equally distant between the two cocoons. That fact made Jode deeply uneasy. Sharia was the beast's companion. It should have chosen to lie next to her—unless lias'tri was progressing to its enigmatic conclusion: two halves joining into a whole such as the Joining had never seen, Fourth Evolution timeshadow riders seeking a dimensional unity that only Fifth Evolution creatures knew. What would it be like to live among all times, all places, all dimensions, the universe blossoming around you like an immense glittering flower? What joys would be discovered . . . and what dangers would follow upon the joys?

For nothing came without cost, and of all those "nothings," time was by far the most expensive.

The thought of another dimension of unknown dangers was even more unnerving to Jode than waiting to discover if he would be as lucky as Merone had been, and die only a simple death by azir. "What happened to Sharia while we were in the Desheel?" asked the psi-master quickly.

"She started healing people and couldn't stop. I tried to stop her but the azir wouldn't let me." Szarth frowned, causing sinuous lines to form over his face. "I don't understand why the beast stopped me. I wanted only what was best for her."

"But *she* wanted to heal. Azirs won't prevent their companions from killing themselves. After all, what is simple death to a soul-eater?" asked Jode grimly. "Azirs will kill anyone who tries to harm their companions or prevent them from doing as they please." He paused. "What made Sharia stop healing? Did she finally faint?"

"No. Kane waded in and started throwing people in all directions until he got to Sharia."

"The soul-eater didn't object?" asked Jode softly.

"No." Szarth's skin creased even more deeply with his frown.

"The azir ran its ruff over Kane and then stood back." The Xtian's clear green eyes searched Jode's as though Szarth was looking for answers within the Jhoramon's dark glance. "In fact," said Szarth slowly, remembering, "I think the creature even helped the captain clear out the crowd. It went through people like clear lighting. Didn't hurt them. Just terrified them."

Jode looked at the azir. The azir looked back. "It stopped you from helping/thwarting Sharia, but it didn't stop Kane," murmured the psi-master absently, thinking hard.

Szarth hissed Xtian agreement.

Jode said nothing more. The implications of the azir's actions made multiple icy claws scrabble over his nerve endings. In silence he waited for the Za'arains to awake.

He did not wait long. Not nearly as long as he had expected. Apparently their bodies were stronger than they had been. Or perhaps it was simply that Sharia's silver hair had combed the drug from her timeshadow as though sleep were a disease.

Sharia and Kane awoke as one. As one, their memories burst over them. Translator and rejection, danger and timeshadow riding and . . . touching. Five touching five. Fragments of the very recent time/then, hot and sweet and wild. For a searing moment they allowed the memories, savored the heat and sweetness, admitted to themselves and each other that neither wanted more from this or any other time than to touch again, flowing together, twining and burning in a unity that was both more compelling and more dangerous than anything they had ever known.

And then, together, they realized that they could not touch again or they would die the final death, drowned in all the pouring dimensions of time.

But they would touch again. It was as deep and inevitable as linear time and life intertwining.

The azir rose to its translucent feet. Twin-voiced harmonies poured from its throat as though melancholy resonated endlessly through all aspects of time, pleasure and grief blending in an eerie beauty never meant for human ears. Jode would have wept but he had no tears left from the years after his Chayly had died. Szarth did, however. His supple face shone with re-flected sadness.

"Make it stop," hissed Szarth, hands over his ears, face twisted with a grief he had never known before and never wanted to know again.

Jode simply clenched his jaw and endured, realizing that nothing could stop the azir but its companion. Or companions. There was always that possibility, said the scrabble of icy claws over Jode's nerves.

The cocoons opened in the same instant.

Sharia and Kane sat up, letting the scarlet wombs retract into the couches. Though dimmed, their lias'tri gems were still in-candescent with colors. For one long moment the Za'arains looked at each other while the azir wept in scales and dimen-sions unknown to man. Then Sharia looked away. Her silver hair flowed toward the soul-eater in silent invitation. The beast dissolved and reformed within the cloud of her compassionate Darien hair. The terrible, beautiful keening ended.

Szarth and Jode took deep, shaking breaths and stood up straight again.

"I'm sorry," said Kane. The words were husky, oddly reso-nant, as though somewhere within his body lurked an azir's second voice. He looked at Jode and tried to explain what had happened, what was still happening, what could not be allowed to happen. But there were no words in any language Kane knew—and he knew many languages now.

"You can't help it," the psi-master said, weariness and regret quivering through his voice.

"But we must," Sharia said. "The Kiriy was right. There was a reason for Za'ar tabu. Each time we touch, it becomes harder to control ourselves, harder not to touch again." Her voice was flat, defeated.

"Compulsion is another name for lias'tri," said Jode. "That is, if you consider breathing to be a compulsion," he muttered to himself.

"What?" asked Kane.

"Nothing." The Jhoramon turned away. He picked up the information cubes that Merone had dropped when the azir had—what had the azir done to her? Jode shrugged off the thought impatiently. It did not matter now. All that mattered was finding the Eyes of Za'ar as soon as possible. The Za'arains were strong, stronger than any people the psi-master had ever known. But they were not gods. They were simply a man and a woman caught in a horrible trap. "Did the Wolfin construct survive having Sharia ride your timeshadow?" Jode asked.

The blunt comspeech made both Kane and Szarth flinch. Sharia had not been among the peoples of the Joining long enough to realize that there was no more obscene phrase in comspeech than timeshadow riding. She looked curiously at Jode, sensing the uneasy mixture of anger and compassion that seethed within him. She said nothing, however. She was beginning to understand how much the psi-master had lost when his lias'tri died, stranding him in the desolate confinements of linear time.

Kane sighed. "The translator survived."

Jode looked at the unread cubes in his hand and described obscene possibilities in the sliding consonants of Jhoramon.

"I've never tried it that way," said Kane, smiling slightly, understanding every hot word of Jode's vocabulary. "An intriguing possibility—if my toenails would just grow long enough."

Jode smiled unwillingly. "Your command of Jhora's language is impressive. I'll have to watch my tongue."

"That, too, is an intriguing possibility," Kane said sardonically. Then, with a speed that made Jode blink, Kane swept the cubes from the Jhoramon's black palm. "Mine, I believe," said Kane.

Sharia saw her lias'tri fit the silver leads to his own head. Though she said nothing aloud, her objection to and understanding of Kane's actions spoke as deeply within his mind as his own thoughts.

Jode looked at Sharia. *Shield yourself if you can.* The psi-master's thought was both compassionate and as hard as the stone flashing between her breasts. *You must learn how to protect yourself or you won't be worth a handful of warm spit to him when he needs you. And he'll need you, woman. When he rammed that Wolfin construct into his throat he wrote his own death warrant.*

The thought would have been cruel but for the bottomless well of the Jhoramon's understanding. If anyone in the Joining knew what it cost the Za'arains to remain separate, it was Jode.

"Wait," whispered Sharia as Kane moved to activate the first cube.

Her voice was too soft for Kane to hear. But he did. He looked at her curiously.

Help me not to be so deep within you, she explained, withdrawing from mental contact even as the thought formed.

They worked together using what Jode had taught them and what they had learned about themselves in the tumult of desire and timeshadow riding. Gently they discovered the filaments of awareness, the currents of energy joining them through unknown dimensions of zä'. Every time Kane and Sharia had touched since Za'arain had deepened and increased the connecting network, making of it a shimmering, strengthening web which could not be destroyed short of Za'ar death.

Though Sharia could not end her commingling with Kane, she could evade it for a while; her mind could retreat along every path she and Kane had discovered linking themselves together. But even that simple nondestructive act was agonizing, like having skin torn from their living bodies. As they worked to separate themselves, the azir's uncanny voices screamed for the anguish of companions caught within linear time.

After they had done all they could to separate themselves, Sharia wept soundlessly within a cloud of lashing silver hair. She had not known how deeply, how subtly, she and Kane had been joined. She had never felt so alone, even on the morning she had awakened and found Kane exiled. She knew that he had to feel the same. Instantly she rejected the thought, for if she permitted herself to dwell upon it she would rush to him along all the myriad pathways and links she had just discovered. She could not do that. She had to be apart from him in case she was needed to untangle his timeshadow after he absorbed the new languages in the cubes.

And deep within Sharia was the hope that Kane would need her, that she would have to come to him once more in a cloud of hungry, healing Darien hair. Then she could fit herself to him again, taste again the male textures of his passion, know again the searing possibilities of being a woman in the arms of a man who suited her perfectly, body and mind and time without beginning or ending.

She looked up and saw Kane watching her with eyes that were both silver and violet. The small sound she made was lost within the silky wildness of her hair. She glanced hurriedly around, wondering what had happened to the chiming bells and fine chains she had used to bind her hair before she had ridden Kane's timeshadow.

Szarth reached into a pocket of his tunic. Crystal and silver bells chimed as he held out to her the chains she had lost. As always, he had retrieved the jewelry when her hair had escaped its delicate Xtian bonds.

"Thank you," Sharia whispered raggedly. She fumbled with the chains, her hands clumsy, her eyes empty.

Szarth did not need to be a Jhoramon psi-master to recognize the face of a woman who was suffering. As though she were one of his own symbionts, Szarth folded Sharia into his scaled arms and rocked her, murmuring sibilant reassurances. At first the unexpected comfort shocked Sharia; on Za'arain, no one had ever touched her but Kane. Yet she did not struggle against Szarth's touch, for the Xtian's compassion was as clear to her as the deep green color of his eyes.

Kane's eyes went Kiri violet for a second before he closed them and looked away, not wanting to deny Sharia any possible source of comfort. Deliberately, he activated the first cube, eager to lose his mind in something other than the picture of Sharia being held gently by the Xtian warrior.

Kane felt a moment of spinning vertigo shot through with impossible noise, a thousand thousand sounds screaming for his attention. He did not know what he had expected the translator to draw from the cube, but he knew that it was not this. Grimly he reached into the boundless chaotic babble with his mind, knowing that there had to be meaning in at least some of the noise. It took quite a while to find the meaning, though. Like any new skill, learning to use the Wolfin translator took practice. Most Wolfins trained for years with constructs of greater and greater complexity before subjecting themselves to the reality of a translator.

Kane, however, was Kiri, Darien and five. Time was . . . *available* . . . to him. He learned with uncanny speed in time/now. And he learned well, tapping potentials within the Za'arain-adjusted translator and cube that the Wolfins had never suspected. Within instants of separating the first words from the chaotic violence of sound, phrases came to him, then whole sentences, paragraphs bursting with meaning, a linguistic complexity that was stunning in its beauty and nearly infinite in its possibilities.

And then the vision came, whole blocks of time/then condensing out of the words. The images glowed translucently in Kane's mind, azir pure, hints of rainbow timeshadows giving color to the recreated reality. As though in a dream, Kane knew that he was both within and removed from the room where he watched/listened to two men talk in an anonymous language of the Dust.

"Did they have names, these men who described the Eyes of Za'ar?"

The man asking the question was tall and lithe, with the body of someone who had been born to strength. His hair was concealed beneath a cloth of gold. His eyes were violet, gleaming with the cold clarity of Kiri heritage. Five-fingered hands were by his side, relaxed, deadly in their power and quickness.

SaDyne. ZaDyneen.

"No names. One was Jiddirit, I think. Small. Dark. Quick.

Neither one was new to the Desheel or to Doursone. They've been here a long time, buying and selling and trading things."

"What did you tell them?"

"That I was always ready to earn a ship's ransom for a simple trade."

"They described the jewels as violet, bigger than one of their clenched fists?"

"Yes."

In the silence that followed, Kane memorized what he could see of the translucent room. Curved walls rather crudely made. A startlingly beautiful mineral specimen set on a table that could have graced the Kiriy's own rooms. A tapestry woven by and from living plants, Second Evolution life twining in patterns meaningless and yet compelling to man. A nest of tiny First Evolution crystals singing softly among themselves, their facets and crystal lattices as flawless as their alien harmonies. The blue and violet flash of stones ringing SaDyne's forehead like a brilliant crown.

Other sounds filtered through the room, familiar sounds: the multilingual curses of men gambling and shouting and shoving for space on the trading mark. Faint odors of stale food and aphrodisiac smoke, Jhora's winter wine and garbage stacked somewhere beyond the walls waiting for the licensed scavengers to descend. SaDyne's room could have been above either the Desheel or the Jorke or the Crux. Any of the three casinos-trading centers could have yielded the odors and sounds that the cube had captured.

And then SaDyne's voice, as cold as his violet eyes: *"When did you set up your next meet with them?"*

"Tonight."

"Bring them here. Leave them to me. And then never speak of this again."

The Dustman left.

Kane expected the images to stop. They did not. Apparently Ine's spies had followed SaDyne's man and then had managed to implant their eavesdropping equipment in such a way as to have access to SaDyne's room itself. Other men came and went, speaking in familiar languages of unfamiliar things.

When the first cube was exhausted, Kane activated another cube without pause. Another new language sleeted through him, another intoxicating universe of possibilities, reality viewed through yet another cultural filter. The Eyes of Za'ar were not mentioned again.

Slavery was. SaDyne was the ruler of a large Dust empire based on a planet riddled with long-dead, deeply buried cities. He dug among them in search of psi-stones and ancient artifacts used to expand the reach of the individual mind. Wolfin machines could have been used for excavation but they were too expensive, too difficult to acquire, and the psis who could run them made intractable slaves. Psi-null people were neither expensive, difficult to acquire, nor intractable.

As the cubes and languages came and went from Kane's hands; he learned that the artifacts SaDyne's slaves dug out of the nameless planet's past were often deadly. But then, so were the Eyes of Za'ar. A man who had been raised on Za'arain in the knowledge that one day he might die reaching for the Eyes would not shrink from handling lesser artifacts, lesser psi-stones. Instead, SaDyne pursued them with a purpose and ruthlessness that had become legend among Dustmen. He gathered psi-stones to his hand like a black hole gathering light; nothing escaped from him. Some stones he bent to his purpose. Others crumbled to dust beneath his demands.

It was the same with the people who came to SaDyne. Some he used, others he destroyed, their minds forced to bend or break beneath the weight of Za'arain imperative. Kane learned of minds captive while SaDyne in concert with his lethal alien stones tried to plunder the energies of time/then in order to control time/now, watched minds dying while SaDyne tried to understand the baffling, overlapping, torrential energies of the *always* and the *other*.

SaDyne was obsessed with time as only a thwarted lias'tri who was also Za'arain could be.

The last cube came into Kane's hand. Without hesitation he brought the leads to his skull, not even hearing Jode's muffled command that he rest. Sharia's concern was like a silver flame burning beneath the translucent scenes recreated by the cube. Sharia could have stopped Kane, but she did not. Despite the consuming languages falling one upon the other, she sensed no lines of blackness to indicate life being torn from time.

Kane blinked. Behind his violet eyes SaDyne's room condensed. A woman entered, her skin the color of rust and dark eyes that had seen too much. She began to speak. Chaos burst over Kane again. Again he reached into the babble, pulled out sounds and phrases, built them into words and meanings, a language resonating. He learned with a speed that would have shocked the designers of the Wolfin translator. But unlike them, Kane was not limited to time/now. All of the energies the cube had innocently absorbed were available to him—including the elusive, tenacious energies of za'.

Chaos condensed into a clear voice speaking of betrayal and loss:

"Your psi tricks won't work on me, SaDyne. There's too much mixed blood in me. My ship is protecting me. If she detects any variation in my mental energies she'll melt the Jorke right through to Doursone's core."

SaDyne's eyes were violet cold as a winter dawn. The stones on his forehead glowed like a row of atavistic Kiri eyes. *"I should have broken you years ago, before you could afford a Wolfin ship."*

The woman shrugged. *"Then I wouldn't have been much use to you, would I? What do you want this time?"*

SaDyne's smile was even colder than his eyes. *"I have a raid in mind."*

"Tell me something new," she said sardonically.

"The Eyes of Za'ar."

The woman's breath came in with a soft sound. *"You've found them?"*

"I never lost them. I just had to wait until the winnowing finally found its way to Za'arain."

"Then the Eyes are still on Za'arain?"

"Yes. Bring them to me."

"No." The woman's voice was calm and very certain. *"No one survives a landing on Za'arain."*

"You will. The winnowing has weakened them."

"No."

"Yes."

The woman winced at the harshness of SaDyne's determination. *"No. Not at any price."*

"Your family will regret hearing that," said SaDyne smoothly, turning away. *"When I'm through with them, I'll send you what remains."*

The woman's eyes became even more bleak. *"Give me the coordinates to Za'arain."*

SaDyne tossed her a small cube. She caught it with the reflexes of a top raider pilot. He waited for a moment, then tossed an oddly woven metal-plastic box toward her.

"Take a psi-null with you. Have him put the Eyes in this." SaDyne paused while his violet eyes weighed the woman. *"Don't let the Eyes tempt you. If you touch them you will die."*

"Touch them? Never! I'd sooner be slave to you than to the timeshadow riders of Za'arain."

SaDyne's laughter was as predatory as his eyes, but he said nothing about being Za'arain and a wake rider. Some things even the Dust would not tolerate. The reality of Za'arain was one of them.

"If I die on Za'arain, my family will be free of you and your shetadyn psi-stones. Agreed?" asked the woman.

"Agreed. Bring the Eyes to the Jorke. Someone will wait at my table for the first five days of the Broken Star month. After that"—he smiled slightly—*"I'd better have the Eyes or proof of your death on Za'arain."*

The translucent scene faded into the original scene, beginning another cycle. Kane had no need to experience the cube again.

He pulled the leads through his living Darien hair and focused on Sharia's silver-violet eyes for a timeless instant before turning to Jode. "When is the month of the Broken Star?" asked Kane, his voice harsh.

It was Szarth who answered. "Now."

"What day of the month is this?" demanded Kane.

"The fifth. Nearly the sixth. They change days at twilight on Doursone. That's about an hour from now."

Violet eyes flared. Kane's hair shifted and quivered suddenly, as though testing the currents of time stretched between time/then and time/now. Crystal bells shivered as Sharia's hair stirred in response, combing energies as though she could comb back the too-fast passage of time. But she could not. She was not a product of the Fifth Evolution, able to move among all the slipfaces of time and still keep mind and life intact.

"Did the teacher give you Jorke's location?" asked Kane. The words were clipped, rapid, like darts pouring from the muzzle of a gun.

"Yes."

"Get the other warriors. Be on the ramp, fully armed, in three minutes."

Szarth left on the run even as Jode was telling Dani to turn out the other Xtians.

"Light up Dani," said Kane to Jode. "Keep her that way. Tell her that on my command she's to take the closest gold node out of here."

"That node is way down in Doursone's gravity well," said the pilot. *A killer,* added Jode silently.

"Do it."

Jode did not object again. There was no silver or blue left in Kane's eyes, nothing but deadly violet.

Dani quivered to life.

"Stay with the ship," said Kane, heading for the cabin door.

"No."

Kane's head snapped around at Jode's negative.

"You're more powerful but I'm far better trained," said Jode calmly. "If you're going to tangle with psi, you'll need me."

Silver flickered within Kiri violet. "I don't want you to die for a Za'arain problem."

"As you pointed out, there's no difference between Za'arain and the Joining. I'm going."

Kane smiled grimly. "I'll be glad to have you." He turned to Sharia. "Stay—"

"No. I'm going with you, v'orri."

The azir condensed between them, smiling its translucent smile. The beast howled softly, twin-voiced, anger and determination in perfect harmony.

"The soul-eater would be very useful in discouraging attacks," said Jode neutrally. *And where Sharia goes, the azir goes. Not to mention the fact that you're a very large target, my Za'arain friend. You really didn't expect to go into danger without your lias'tri healer, did you?*

With a snarl Kane accepted what he could not change. Together the three people ran for the personnel ramp.

The ice-pale azir wove between the two Za'arains, keening savage triumph with both its voices. Shards of color and light flashed from lias'tri crystals as the beast touched first Kane and then Sharia, subtly weaving them together again, using dimensions neither Za'arain had ever known. The azir knew what its companions wanted deep within their odd Fourth Evolution minds.

And what azir companions wanted, they got. With each instant of linear time, each Za'arain heartbeat, lias'tri crystals glowed brighter, harder, hotter, lias'tri burning toward unity through all the facets of time.

Seventeen

The Jorke was a seething stew of Dust despair and Joining ambitions. There was no more space at any of the tables, no more standing room in the spectator circles, no more places to wait behind any of the trading lines. The light inside the room went from pale green to an emerald so dark it was almost black. It was S/kouran light, but if any S/kourans were present, they were not obvious. Nothing other than the mixed, ragged races of the Dust was visible. The only clean surfaces in the room were the small crystal faces of First Evolution life-forms embedded in the Jorke's synstone walls. The crystals hummed softly among themselves, vibrating with alien dreams, inhuman patience.

Silence rippled out from a verdant curve of the room as person after person registered the azirs presence. The soul-eater tipped back its oddly graceful muzzle, sang in twin-voiced harmony and waited. The lithic races imprisoned in the Jorke's walls blazed once and then were silent; not so much as a murmur of sound lifted from their tiny, flawless faces. Quietly, urgently, the Jorke's habitués jostled each other in an attempt to determine if the soul-eater had a companion—and if so, who was the person so dubiously blessed.

The azir stood squarely between Kane and Sharia.

No one wanted to test which of the aliens belonged to the soul-eater. With a rustling sigh the mixed races of the Jorke marked off the two aliens as exempt from the normal lawlessness of Doursone. Many of the people closest to the door started to ease out into Beoy's sour streets. The azir dissolved and re-formed across the doorway. The people withdrew instantly. The azir returned to its post between Kane and Sharia. The Jorke's denizens realized that the soul-eater did not want anyone to leave. Cursing in a hundred tongues, the people of the Jorke returned to their murderous games of chance and trade.

They know azirs in the Dust, Jode observed sardonically. *Just as wind traders occasionally know azirs among the moving sand mountains.*

Kane did not answer. He walked forward, slowly weaving himself into the crowd, absorbing words and languages old and new, searching for SaDyne and the Eyes of Za'ar.

It's the leakage of za' in Doursone that attracts azirs, Sharia whispered in Jode's mind. *Azirs are creatures of time. All of time.*

Then why didn't you have them on Za'arain? asked Jode, remembering Kane's lack of belief in the reality of azirs. *Your people are obsessed with time.*

On Za'arain the Eyes restrained most manifestations of za'. Not like here or among the wind traders. Some of the ancient artifacts the wind people and the Dust trade in overlap into the za'. That's why the wind artifacts were so difficult for Kane to touch. They took from him and did not give back. The wind traders, too. They die young for Jhoramons, don't they?

Jode's agreement was a grim curiosity about the nature of ancient wind artifacts and za'. Sharia could give him no answers beyond what she had already told him: In other, earlier cycles, some Fourth Evolution races had reached beyond the restrictions of linear time. The ramifications of that outreach pervaded some of the artifacts that remained from those lost cultures. In some places and times, azirs were associated with those artifacts and races, those leakages of za'.

When the psi-master would have silently pursued the topic, he realized that Sharia was no longer paying attention to him. Her whole mind was focused on the large Za'arain who prowled through the Jorke as gracefully as the azir that kept forming and reforming between the two lias'tris.

Kane sifted through the large room, listening intently. Half of the Xtians followed him discreetly, as did the unpredictable, translucent azir. Kane did not notice. His mind was alive with languages. He knew nearly seventy now, and with each new language he learned more about the nature of culture and life and time. Alien languages dissolved into him and reformed as curious knowledge, new sensations, unusual thoughts. Learning became easier with each breath, languages raining down on him, sinking into him.

He listened with an intensity that no one except Sharia understood, for she was listening with him. Unknowingly she rode his living timeshadow with extraordinary deftness, combing the physical strain of forced, rapid learning from him. Her presence was like a transparent shadow of light surrounding him, a timeshadow echo expressed through dimensions of time only an azir knew.

Then a name burst upon Kane, a muttered conversation in a language that condensed in his mind even as he reached for it.

"—been here for the last five days."

"Who?"

"The devil SaDyne. He's not here anymore."

"His raider must have come back."

"Wonder if she was successful?"

"If she wasn't, she's dead."

Kane's heart raced as a chemical storm overtook his body, jolting him with adrenaline and fear and rage. SaDyne's raider had come. SaDyne had gone. Kane was too late. The Eyes of Za'ar had come to Doursone, to Beoy, to the Jorke; and Kane had not been quick enough to keep them from SaDyne's hands.

You can't be sure. Sharia's words were a soothing murmur in his mind.

His answering rage prowled with unsheathed claws through the mindlink. He turned to one of the men who had been speaking about SaDyne.

"Where is SaDyne now?" asked Kane, his eyes violet.

The man hesitated. He looked from Kane's savage eyes to the azir condensing nearby. The man answered quickly, words tumbling over each other in his eagerness not to bring down the wrath of a soul-eater's companion.

"He went up with his raider," said the Dustman.

"Up?" snarled Kane.

The man jerked his chin toward a shaft leading to the Jorke's upper stories. "The top. He owns it."

Even as Kane spun toward the shaft, a hammer blow of psi sent him to his knees. Linear time shifted, yielded, as the *then* and the *now* licked out. Za' time sliced through Fourth Evolution minds, Fourth Evolution bodies. Life-forms that had never been meant to live among the elusive surfaces of za' found themselves adrift, in pain, screaming their bafflement and agony.

The azir's howl was visible, a black, iridescent outpouring shot through with all the colors of time. Its body thickened, becoming more opaque and yet more brilliant with each instant. Instinctively Sharia and Kane flowed together along the very mental network they had so recently abandoned. Their Darien hair fanned out wildly, seeking familiar currents of time, combing time/now and time/then from the chaos of za'. The linear time of Fourth Evolution reality struggled to condense around the two Za'arains.

Suddenly the deadly outpouring of za' stopped as completely as though it had never existed. There was an instant of dazed silence. Then panic broke out. The Jorke exploded into a melee of Fourth Evolution life trying to flee the site of a nearly fatal encounter with the *other*. No longer did anyone worry about offending the azir's companion; they simply fought their way to the Jorke's exit with the mindless determination of people caught in the grip of terror.

Sharia's hair spread out in a wild silver cloud as she tried to protect both herself and Jode from the mob. People shrieked and threw themselves aside as her no-longer-gentle hair raked through living timeshadows. For every person who struggled to avoid her, three more were hurled forward by their panicked friends. Jode fought to protect Sharia and himself, using every deadly move he had learned among the planets of the Joining. But he was only one and the mob was hundreds. It was the same for Kane, overwhelmed by numbers.

Pale, translucent light filled the Jorke. Icy light. Azir light. Time . . . changed. Icy light expanded throughout the room, bathing everyone in a radiance from other times, other realities.

The odd, sourceless light faded, freeing the Jorke from the azir's grip. Clothes whispered to the floor, clothes no longer inhabited by anything at all. The soul-eater had not taken everyone. Not quite. Only those people who had threatened or stood between Sharia and Kane were gone. The survivors looked around mutely, chilled by azir light, too numb to feel anything, even panic. Slowly, the people of the Dust sifted out of the room, giving Kane and Sharia a very wide berth.

Sharia turned to Jode. She touched him with a questing tendril of hair, riding his timeshadow very lightly, going no further back into his time/then than the first outbreak of fighting in the Jorke. The Jhoramon's injuries were minor, for he had stood next to her, within the shadow of the azir's instant protection. The Xtians had not been so fortunate. She went quickly to the gathered warriors. Bruised, bloody, they were kneeling around one of their own. Sensing her presence they pulled back, allowing her to see who lay unmoving on the floor.

"Szarth!"

Sharia's hair swept over Szarth in a translucent silver storm that swept through his dying timeshadow. She rode his writhing currents of life silently, desperately, trying to comb the darkness from his rapidly fading colors. No matter what she did, he kept slipping further into time/then, retreating before her, sliding through pathways of life and time that a living timeshadow rider could neither understand nor manipulate.

A wake rider could, though. Kane understood time/then and the *then*. Kane knew Sharia's need, knew her difficulty, knew what she had to do. He met her deep within Szarth's dying timeshadow, where time/then became the *then* in which no Fourth person could survive. Kane told Sharia where the *then* would intrude, helped her to balance on the slowing currents of life, gave her his understanding of timeshadow wakes so that she could anticipate and defeat the quiet condensation of death. She did not ride a dead timeshadow's static wake—not quite. He did not ride a living timeshadow's rippling currents—not quite. They overlapped, though, pervading each other in ways and times that neither could name.

And the azir watched, glistening with pleasure, radiant with the growing, incandescent blaze of lias'tri stones.

Grimly, not knowing whether it would be the last thing he would ever do, Jode snatched Kane back from physical contact with Sharia's hair. The azir spun and watched the Jhoramon with bottomless eyes. Kane cried out in anguish, a cry reinforced by Sharia. Azir light bloomed around Jode. He waited to die, sensing it would be the final death, for the soul-eater had no mercy left in its icy body.

No!

The thought was Kane's, Sharia's, theirs, a single voice calling off the azir. Jode heard the unity of their minds, felt it sing to him on all the levels of his own mind. promising him . . . everything. All times, all places, all sensations, a siren song that could not be denied. The psi-master shuddered violently as he twisted away from the incendiary psi-contact. He knew even as he fought and dodged that lias'tri would go to completion very soon no matter how Kane and Sharia struggled against it. Then would come a time of wildfire psi, psi burning out of control—

—through all the layers of time. Yes, we know. Better than you, psi-master. We know. All the energies of past lives, our lives, all psi lives, all the vast reach of za'. Everything. Forever. There is no end to the possibilities. Or to the destruction. The Kiri was right. We should not touch.

And we must.

Jode staggered and caught himself as he was released from the Za'arains' compelling mindspeech. They were controlled again, overlapping only in dimensions the azir ruled. They sensed those dimensions but could do nothing about them without rending their own living timeshadows from linear time, killing themselves. They would not do that yet. Not while there was still hope of finding the Eyes, mastering them, mastering themselves, dragging Za'arain and the Joining back from the endless night of barbarism and psi-hunter bloodlust.

Szarth awoke in a swirl of silver hair and Za'arain despair. He blinked slowly. He had never expected to wake in this life again. He caught a translucent strand of Sharia's hair between his fingers and hissed a prayer to his own steel-scaled gods. Then he looked around at the stunned symbionts who had sensed his death as surely as he had.

"Being dead isn't bad," Szarth assured them sibilantly, "but I'd rather be alive."

They laughed a bit wildly and touched him as though he were newly born. He returned their touches, laughing. He came to his feet in a controlled rush and was swallowed up in the welcoming hugs of his symbionts.

Kane and Sharia watched with an envy that made their eyes violet. As one they turned away and began walking quickly toward the shaft that led to the Jorke's upper levels. Jode and the azir followed.

What happened? What panicked everyone? asked Jode, speaking in both of their minds at once.

Kane's response was clipped: *The Eyes.*

They're here?

They're on Doursone. Or they were. And they aren't controlled.

How do you know? demanded Jode.

It was Sharia who answered as they stepped into the shaft and were whisked upward. *Without a Kiriy to control the Eyes, za' leaks out.*

Was it always like that?

Both Za'arains paused, searching their individual memories and their much more far-reaching, subtle shared memories. A vast glittering universe of experience was available to them. They dared not tap it. Jode's question was answered, though, as inevitably as if they had asked it of themselves.

No. In the beginning, the Eyes weren't as powerful. With each Kiriy, each mind, each reaching into all the aspects of time, the Eyes . . . changed. There will come a time when only Darien fives can control them. Or the Eyes will be destroyed. That, too, is waiting among the possibilities of time.

What shut down the Eyes this time? pressed Jode. *SaDyne?*
No. It was nonliving.
What?

Kane's mind raced, trying to find analogies to explain Za'arain intuition to a Jhoramon pragmatist. *Something nonliving absorbed the stone's emanations. Remember the wind trader artifact I bought three years ago, the one that nearly killed me?*

Too well, responded Jode grimly.

Whatever shut down the Eyes was like that. A psi-sponge. Like the plasteel strips the traders use to carry unbridled psi-stones.

The shaft deposited them briskly at the top level of the Jorke. Jode psi-searched quickly but found no one. Before Kane could move, the azir flowed forward. Lethal light blazed forth, charring the floor beneath the azir's feet. The soul-eater stood calmly, soaking up the deadly trap until hidden circuits fused and the attack stopped. A supple, translucent black tongue flicked out as though tasting the air. The azir continued to stand motionless, blocking the door, absorbing unseen radiation that was even more lethal to Fourth Evolution life than the coherent light had been.

Useful beast, thought Jode grudgingly.

Kiri laughter turned deep within the psi-master's mind. The azir looked back at Jode before it moved slowly ahead of the three people, quartering each room for dangers only an azir could sense or see or combat. There were more traps, lethal traps. The soul-eater tripped each one; and each time, distant, twin-voiced laughter glittered within the others' minds. The azir was enjoying its stroll through SaDyne's lethal rooms.

Jode flinched as minute darts flashed through the soul-eater. Its musical laughter rippled through his mind again. "Do you suppose that tickles the beast?" he asked Kane in a voice rich with disgust.

The soul-eater smiled.

The psi-master shut up.

The azir continued padding through empty rooms as though looking for something. Or as though it knew that its companions were looking for something. The four of them searched but found nothing that could have been the Eyes of Za'ar, whether muffled or not. Kane went through the rooms again, touching objects that had belonged to SaDyne.

"He's still alive," said Kane.

"How do you know?" asked Jode.

"His timeshadow is still alive. And," continued Kane, looking at Sharia, "he's not wearing the Eyes."

Jode watched relief break over Sharia's face, sensed it spreading through him like a benediction. "What were you afraid of?" he asked curiously. "Do you really want to be the Kiriy of Za'arain?"

I want nothing but what I can't have: Kane. Yet all Sharia said aloud was, "SaDyne has been collecting psi-stones since the day of his exile. And artifacts, too, things that overlap into the other, I was afraid that he might have found a way to enhance his own mind in order to control the Eyes."

"How do you know so much about SaDyne?" asked Jode quietly, afraid that he knew the answer but wanting to hear it just the same.

"Kane told me after he read the cubes."

"When did he tell you?"

Sharia said nothing. Surprise pooled visibly in her clear Za'arain eyes as she realized that Kane had not told her anything, not really. She had simply absorbed it from him during the timeless instant when he and she had ridden both Szarth's condensing wake and living timeshadow.

"I thought you had withdrawn from each other," said Jode softly.

"We did," Sharia said. "The za' leaked. To stop it, we had to work together."

As we worked together over Szarth, timeshadow and wake rider as one. Learning. All those past lives. All those past skills. And the future, too. The always *of all our lives. It's there, too, waiting for us in lias'tri completion. And the za' also waits, overwhelming, death in all dimensions and times, a nonexistence that reaches back into the* then *to deny life in every time.*

But none of their deeply held interior communication leaked to Jode, for they were connected one to the other in ways that even a Jhoramon psi-master could not imagine.

"Can you separate yourselves again?" asked Jode quietly. "If you can, you must. For yourselves. For Za'arain. For the Joining. Be separate until the Eyes can teach you how to control what lias'tri will inevitably bring to you." Though they did not respond either verbally or mentally, Jode sensed the depth of their rebellion, and he saw the lightning stroke of their matched stones. "I know what I'm asking of you," he continued softly. "It's a kind of death. The kind I've lived with since Chayly died. But your taste of death is only temporary. You will be reunited in the Eyes. . . ."

Pain twisted both Za'arains' features as they tried to retreat along all the seductive pathways joining mind with mind. Jode hesitated only long enough to cast an enigmatic, almost hopeful glance at the azir. The soul-eater did not notice or did not care when Jode slipped into linkage with the two struggling Za'arains.

Like this, whispered the psi-master in their minds, knowing what he had to do if they were to survive—for he had done it to himself in order to survive, done it because Chayly had asked him not to die. He had known that he could not come to her in another life if he sought a selfish death in this one. So he had survived.

Deftly Jode blocked a current of hungry, unwitting communication between the two lias'tris. He had been born with a gift for facilitating communication among psis; that same gift could also be used to baffle linkage. Yet he was all but overwhelmed by the richness and complexity of the network joining Sharia and Kane. And the subtlety. For every current of psi he managed to deflect, he uncovered four more. Even more startling, the tendrils of thought and currents of communication seemed to form out of nowhere, intertwine, then vanish. Yet the intercommunication remained. He could sense the power of the linkage. It might not have existed in any way—or time—that he understood, but it did exist, potently.

The azir watched, radiating icy unease as its companions twisted in pain and effort. It mewed softly, musically, and its eyes measured Jode's timeshadow hungrily. The soul-eater did nothing, though, for neither Sharia nor Kane was fighting against Jode. They were fighting against themselves, cutting themselves off from the very energies that infused them with life. The azir keened in eerie harmonies that warned of danger. While the soul-eater itself could not experience death in linear time, it knew that its companions could. It also knew that they did not want to abandon the existence within linear time that was the Fourth Evolution's gift to intelligent life. Given that, it was the azir's duty to warn its companions of just how close to the boundary of linear time they were drifting as they closed off current after current of energy and communication.

Jode stopped abruptly, sensing danger to Sharia and Kane in the soul-eater's beautiful cry. Gently he disengaged himself from their separated minds. They were not completely separate—that would be impossible short of death in linear time, and probably separation would not occur even then—but they had pulled back from each other, delaying the inevitable, incendiary moment when lias'tri would no longer be denied. Jode looked at Sharia and saw that her skin was no longer luminous and her eyes were shades of silver and darkness. It was no better with Kane. The lias'tri stones glowed with a sullenness that the psi-master had never seen. He swore violently, excoriating himself and the necessity of what he had done. He felt as though he had murdered his two friends.

"Just for a little while longer," Jode said quickly. "Just until we find the Eyes."

Kane and Sharia did not look at each other. They could not. They could only try to absorb the burning agony that was their minds.

"Trade the artifacts—for information—about SaDyne." Kane's words were harsh, his breathing ragged, as though he had run across the face of Doursone without a breathing pack. "Find him."

Jode felt Kane and Sharia sliding away from mindtouch, shutting down through all the levels of their individual and joined minds, suspending themselves in a place where agony became merely pain. It was a technique that the psi-master had learned from his uncle on Jhoramon; now Jode realized that it was a Za'arain technique that Dariens used to survive the often-conflicting demands of their culture and their biological heritage.

With a slicing command, Jode alerted Dani to turn out Ine. While Kane and Sharia walked in a daze to the downshaft, Dani galvanized Ine. He met them at the front of the Jorke with one of the ship's small, downside transports. Silently the master trader watched while Jode guided both Za'arains into the vehicle. Separately. He placed them so that they would not touch even if they sprawled into total unconsciousness. The azir watched and murmured uneasy harmonies. Then he appeared between the two Za'arains, a living sculpture condensed out of time.

"What happened?" demanded Ine. "I thought the azir would protect them."

"It can't protect them from themselves," said Jode curtly. "Find out where SaDyne is. Use the wind artifacts. Don't bargain—just find out. We need time more than we need anything else. We have to find SaDyne. Now!"

Ine looked at Kane. Kane did not look back. His eyes were

both dazed and feral, shards of violet burning beneath the harsh control he had imposed on himself, a control that was just short of unconsciousness. Ine made a weary gesture of agreement as he turned away and went to scour Beoy's streets for word of SaDyne.

Jode took the Za'arains back to the ship. No one spoke. There was nothing to say. Jode glanced uneasily at the lias'tri stones seething silently. Their colors were oddly skewed, less intense yet very clear. It was as though azir light veiled everything. The alien clarity of the stones did not change even when both Kane and Sharia were within the soothing embrace of the command couches. Jode watched the stones burn beneath their ship's clothes, above them, through them, the lias'tri light a ghostly, incandescent promise of other dimensions, other realities, the *other,* lapping over into linear time.

Had lias'tri always been like that, a force equal to time? Or was it simply that these two lias'tris were powerful psis with their race's unique ability to comprehend more than linear time?

No answer came to Jode. Nothing but fear. He knew that he had to keep Kane and Sharia separate. He did not want to have to kill them in order to thwart their immense, incendiary mental powers. He did not want to be azir bait, to know the last death, no rebirth ever within the radiance of Chayly's mind and body. He would rather die of incendiary psi as the Za'arains drew every psi within reach into their searing, lethal mindlink.

Within reach.

What was their reach? A ship? A planet? Three planets? The Dust? The Joining? All of it?

And time. Linear time. Was it a boundary? Or had the synergy of Za'arain's unique gene pool and the unbridled Eyes of Za'ar made of the Za'arains something more than Fourth people? Were they evolving even now toward the Fifth? Or were they something new? Kiri, Darien, five—were they the seeds of the Sixth Evolution?

Perhaps. And perhaps they simply were the destruction of the Fourth.

Azir music sifted through the Jhoramon's mind, sinking down to his core, a soul-eater singing of time without end, of lives that were both gems on an endless golden chain and the chain itself, of Fourth Evolution emotions such as love and friendship and regret, sorrow and despair, betrayal and hatred and love, always love. Jode's love for Kane, and Kane's for Jode. Jode's love for Sharia and her love for him. An azir's timeless love for his companions.

And lias'tri, stronger than everything, even time and life. Lias'tri, a manifestation of time and life intertwined. A force like gravity. A force that compelled minds the way gravity compelled matter—but more beautifully, more perfectly, more inexplicably, because time was also an aspect of mind.

Could Jode kill that if he must?

Could anyone?

Eighteen

The last pure notes of azir harmony shivered over Jode, making him want to scream and laugh and weep at the sheer beauty of the soul-eater's twin voices. Silence came in a soft rush. Only then did Jode realize that Ine was sitting in front of him, had been sitting in front of him for a long time, and that Dani was whimpering softly in his mind. The ship was afraid for him. She had learned enough about time from her Za'arain god to also learn about love. She had enough intelligence to imagine a time without Jode, and the thought frightened her. He tried to soothe her. He could not. He had no truth to soften the reality of time and life, loss and love.

"SaDyne?" asked Jode hoarsely, his voice rough from lack of use and the constriction in his throat caused by Dani's fear and the azir's trembling song.

Ine flinched and glanced up. "Pilot?" he asked, his voice nearly as hoarse as Jode's had been. "Are you back?"

"Was I gone?"

"The soul-eater was watching you." Ine made a gesture of warding off. "You glowed, pilot. Like ice."

Jode looked at his own black hand. Nothing different. His mind, though. Yes, that was different. He knew more about time and life and lias'tri than he wanted to. Especially time. The dimensions of time his Za'arain friends talked so easily about seemed real now, the *then* and the *now*, the *always* and the *other*. Very real. Like life and intelligence and lias'tri. Inevitable.

"Am I glowing now?" asked the psi-master softly.

"No."

Jode looked over at the two Za'arains. They were reclining on scarlet couches, their eyes closed. They were not asleep. At the limits of his awareness he sensed them, a distant hum of time and lias'tri, life draining from time/now into dimensions Jode did not know or want to know. Was pain also a facet of time? Was that where the Za'arains lived now, trapped by imperatives that could not be reconciled within linear time?

"Tell me about SaDyne," said Jode, his voice harsh.

Ine looked for a long moment at the azir. It looked back with black, patient eyes. The Jiddirit shuddered and looked at Jode. The Jhoramon looked back with black, patient eyes. Ine would have run then, but he had made a bargain in his own language with Kane; and Jode was Kane's second-in-command.

"SaDyne has been known on Doursone for hundreds of years," said Ine quickly.

"Then he shouldn't be hard to find."

Ine made a despairing sound. "That's just it! No one has ever seen him outside the Jorke. No one! And his rooms are empty now, all traps sprung.

Jode remembered the azir bathed in deadly radiation. Had the rooms above the Jorke contained the life accumulations of SaDyne? Had SaDyne lived there and nowhere else, a Za'arain god exiled to a single suite of rooms?

Impossible. Not only had the man himself been missing, there had not been one single ancient artifact in any of the rooms. Yet SaDyne had been collecting just such artifacts for hundreds of years.

For an eerie moment Jode did not know whether the thought was his own or Kane's or Sharia's or some alien permutation of the three. He looked quickly at the Za'arains. They had not moved. Nor had their eyes opened. Yet they were . . . present. Aware. Watching and listening with that part of their minds which had not shut down, could not shut down, short of death.

"He must come and go in disguise," said Jode curtly, looking back to Ine.

"Of course," snapped Ine. "But no one knows what that disguise is."

"Then look harder!"

Ine laughed humorlessly. "Use your finely trained mind, Jhoramon. Do you think that I can discover in six hours what the pirates of the Dust haven't been able to discover in hundreds of years?"

His raider. Ask about her.

The thought was Kane's, definitely, but there also was a haunting sense of Sharia just beneath. The thought was very tenuous, like a faint mental whisper. Apparently Kane was too involved with controlling his own mind and the imperatives of lias'tri to spare the effort to communicate directly with Ine's psi-null mind. Jode, however—Jhoramon psi-master and friend—was easy to communicate with.

"What about SaDyne's Dust raider?" asked Jode.

"Rizah of Skire."

"Keep talking."

"She's Jhoramon, or was," continued Ine. "Her parents were wind traders. She opted out before the winnowing. Like you, she's a psi-master with a Wolfin ship."

At any other time that bit of information would have caught Jode's interest. At this instant, though, it was just so many words standing between him and his goals: SaDyne and the Eyes of Za'ar; the survival of his friends; the rebirth of Za'arain and the continued life of the Joining.

"Go on," demanded Jode.

Ine made a vague gesture. Rizah was seen going up to SaDyne's room just before we came to the Jorke. Neither she nor SaDyne came back down. Or if they did, no one recognized them."

"Find her."

"Oh, I've found her—for what good it will do us. She's wrapped in her psi, and dying. SaDyne killed her family and poured their ashes into her hands. Then he tried to kill her with psi. Something went wrong. There was panic. SaDyne went one way and she went the other."

"Bring her here."

"She doesn't want to come. If I force her, Dani had better be prepared for the fight of her life. Wolfin ship against Wolfin ship, psi-master against psi-master. They're already placing bets on it at the Jorke. The money's with Rizah. She defied SaDyne and survived. No one else has. But she won't live for long. He did something to her mind. It's like she's bleeding to death inside."

Jode sensed communication flowing too deeply for him to tap. The azir whined softly, protest and sadness intermingled. Sharia blinked and looked around for an instant as though orienting herself. Her eyes fastened on Ine.

"Take me to Rizah." Sharia's voice was uninflected, as though only part of her lived within her flesh.

Ine hesitated. "Don't count on Rizah telling you anything out of gratitude if you heal her. Za'arain. She wants to die."

"Of course. But there's one thing she wants more. Revenge. I can promise that—in the *then* and the *now* and the *always*."

Neither man spoke as Sharia walked to the door. The soul-eater condensed at her left hand, ice-pale and glowing like dawn. She looked back over her shoulder at Ine. When she spoke her words were, like the azir, ice-pale.

"Hurry. We are dying."

Ine stared, then went quickly to lead Sharia. She followed him through Beoy's darkening residential streets, streets too narrow to accept the ship's transport. The azir matched her stride for stride. Her feet made soft, almost secretive sounds on the synstone walkway. The soul-eater's feet made no sound at all. Ine looked over his shoulder once. Sweat broke out on his body when he saw the luminous Za'arain and the deadly beast following him. There was a chilling similarity in movement and purpose between the two life-forms. All but running, Ine led Sharia deeper into the lurid, lawless quarters where pirate crews lived between raids.

As Beoy's denizens saw the woman and the azir, silence spread out in expanding rings; conversations were stopped in mid-sentence and forgotten. Raiders renowned for both courage and viciousness saw the cloud of unbound, translucent hair seething out from the woman and the powerful, translucent soul-eater pacing by her side, and decided that they had business elsewhere in Beoy, urgent business. They faded quietly into the condensing night.

Ine wished that he could join them.

Sharia said nothing when the Jiddirit led her into a multi-leveled structure suspended from a central pole. Lights burned throughout the building, but they did not burn half so clearly in the dusk as did Sharia's violet eyes. The upshaft was empty. Word had preceded both Za'arain and azir. The Dust raiders of Doursone knew that Sharia was going to Rizah. And the Dust wanted nothing to do with that confrontation.

"To the right," said Ine. His voice vibrated with the fear he felt and was fighting to control. "The blue door. There are no locks, no traps. The other raiders know that she's always under the protection of her Wolfin ship."

Sharia turned and looked at Ine with violet eyes. "Go back to the ship," she said softly. "Kane may need your skills while he hunts down SaDyne."

The master trader hesitated. He felt strangely bound to the Za'arain woman who had chosen to let him live. "If it would help you, I'll stay."

"No. But thank you."

A tendril of silver hair touched Ine, sending a feeling of joy shivering through his timeshadow and body. He bowed swiftly to Sharia in the Jiddirit manner and then left, for he knew that he could help her no more.

Sharia turned and looked at the black-eyed azir glowing by her side. She did not know if she could communicate with the Fifth Evolution creature. She knew she had to try.

Azir.

The soul-eater tilted its head up toward her and murmured musically.

The woman inside is mine. Don't interfere until you're sure that I would die otherwise. Even then, don't kill her. No matter what happens to me, Kane might be able to use her mind.

The azir hummed soothingly, twin voices in perfect harmony.

Sharia and the soul-eater glided into Rizah's darkened suite. The raider lay quietly on a furred pallet. Nothing was alive about her but her eyes and the hungry rage that her slowly dying mind radiated. She saw Sharia's violet eyes—eyes like SaDyne's. With no warning Rizah attacked Sharia's mind, caring nothing for the azir glowing by the Za'arain's side.

The first instants of Rizah's aggression staggered Sharia. Desperately she shut down her mind, trying to evade the awful pain as Rizah fought to tear her mind from her body. Sharia had never been exposed to psi-attack before, not like this, not in this lifetime. There had been other lives, though—many, many of them. Survival imperatives released the controls she had placed on her mind. Levels opened up that she had never before acknowledged. Energy flowed into her, understanding racing through her mind as lives and times flowed together into a potent whole.

With a surge of power Sharia swept aside the raider's mental onslaught. She could go no deeper into Rizah's mind, however. Not without killing her. For a moment the two women simply stared at one another, stalemated. More knowledge crystallized in Sharia, techniques for moving among the interstices of another's mind without destroying it.

She flowed into Rizah's mind like an azir flowing into time. She held the raider's writhing awareness even as she rode her seething timeshadow, searching for the damage that SaDyne had done. She found it. There was a raggedness in the recent currents of time/then, as though the timeshadow had been shredded in more than linear time, shredded and then left to dissipate its energies slowly into the *other*. Sharia did not know how to heal Rizah's torn timeshadow. None of her other lives had encountered this aftermath of exquisitely controlled savagery. Kiri psi-hunters killed, yes, but they drank the blood and ate the flesh and bathed in the last cascading moments of their prey's timeshadow energies. Psi-hunters did not subtly maim and then abandon their prey, leaving the intricate synergy of life and energy to leak away among all the manifestations of time.

Rizah would never be born again, and she knew it. So did Sharia. The knowledge of SaDyne's wanton cruelty unleashed a fury that fed on all the primal power of Sharia's frustrated lias'tri need. Between one instant and the next she became as exquisitely controlled as SaDyne had been. And as cruel.

Listen to me, raider, Sharia breathed seductively into Rizah's mind. *I'm here to bring you your dream.*

With Sharia's words came a torrent of Kiri savagery, an outpouring of the feral psi-hunter from which Za'arain had sprung and from which it might die. The lash of unexpected bloodlust both appalled and fascinated Rizah; it was like her own need for revenge, hot and deep and infinite, stronger than the desire for life itself.

Rizah listened.

If you help me, I will kill SaDyne in all lives, all times, or I will die in all lives, all times. Do you believe me?

For moments out of time the raider felt the raw power and white-hot savagery of Sharia's Kiri atavism. The raider believed.

Whether I live or I die the last death, SaDyne will never be born again. My azir will hunt him through every life and every time that he ever was or will be. SaDyne will die again and again until he has no more lives, no more deaths but the final death. Za'ar death. He will live all his lives knowing that he is azir bait. And he will die knowing that it is the last time. Will that satisfy you, raider?

Yes!

The soul-eater's triumphant howl echoed the primitive blaze of Sharia's Kiri eyes.

Do you know where SaDyne is? Sharia's question was barely a whisper in Rizah's mind.

He lives on Skire. In the ice mountains. I saw it in his mind when he tried to kill me. All he could think about was getting there to his psi-stones and taking up the Eyes of Za'ar. He was obsessed with them. Rizah's pouring thoughts paused. *He's Za'arain, isn't he? And so are you.*

Does it matter?

An echo of bitter laughter turned within Rizah's mind. *It would take one to kill one. If I'm still alive, send SaDyne's ashes to me and pour them into my hands.*

If I'm still alive, I will. Give me what you know about SaDyne.

A stream of images poured into Sharia's mind, years of raider knowledge compressed into a few instants of time by the skill of a vengeful Jhoramon psi-master. Memories of ancient artifacts condensed within Sharia's mind. With them came Rizah's certainty that these artifacts had been handled by psis of various races for thousands upon thousands of years. The objects fairly pulsed with psi energies. Yet still SaDyne had demanded more objects of her, and more, obsession without end or surcease.

He was looking for something to equal lias'tri, whispered Sharia within Rizah's mind.

He hated Za'arain. The thought was Rizah's, cool and utterly certain.

Yes.

He'll try to rule or destroy it.

In SaDyne's case it comes to the same thing. Sharia's mind raced through new information, old lives, condensing possibilities. *Did he find anything as powerful as the Eyes?*

Rizah shuddered as she remembered again the tearing instant when the Eyes had been unbridled in SaDyne's room. *No single thing. But all taken together, who can say? When he left here he expected to control the Eyes using whatever he had on Skire.*

Beneath Rizah's thoughts Sharia sensed the weakness spreading, the hollowness as timeshadow energies leaked inexorably into the *other.* She took the coordinates of Skire from Rizah's mind and left in their place a timeless promise of revenge. As she withdrew from the raider's mind and timeshadow, Sharia left as much peace as she could. With a long, trembling breath, Rizah slept.

Sharia went quickly to the ship, knowing what had to be done. She also knew that she did not have to go physically to the ship; she could tell Jode from here whatever he had to do, what Kane had to do. Yet she could not bring herself to let Kane go without seeing him once more.

For she knew that she could not go with him to Skire. With every new level of her mind touched, with every past life flowing into her, with every pulse of blood through her body, she knew that her self-control was leaking away as surely as Rizah's timeshadow energies.

If Kane were within reach Sharia would touch him. It was as simple and as final as that.

The ship rose above the synstone apron. The personnel ramp was down, the door open. Kane was waiting at the top, his lias'tri stone blazing like a clear sun rising through colored rain. Sharia opened her mouth to speak, afraid to touch Kane's mind. Even as the impulse to speak came, it died. There was no need. He knew what had happened, what she had done, what he needed to do—just as he had known that he could not leave without seeing her once more, her beautiful Darien hair unbound, her eyes both savage and serene. He would have spoken to her, told her that she was his only light, his only color, his only dream burning through all his lives, all his times. But there was no need. The truths they shared were lias'tri truths, as old as life and linear time combined.

Jode came to stand beside Kane. The psi-master sensed the currents of communication both new and old, swift and slow, awareness overlapping all boundaries. Fear came to him then, fear that it was too late, that the lias'tris would touch and incendiary psi would burn through all the layers of time and life, destroying intelligence, leaving only mindless life behind. It had happened before apparently; legends had come down through the ages of cities and planets where intelligence had vanished overnight. Had it happened to other evolutions of life, First or Third or Fifth? Had wildfire psi like the two Za'arains' taken whole evolutions and reduced them to protoplasm oozing over muddy shores?

Was it going to happen to the Fourth Evolution right now, right here?

Jode felt Dani come to life around him, vibrating with a surge of power that presaged a violent leap toward the stars. Neither Kane nor Sharia moved. The azir flowed up the ramp and stopped at a point equally distant from each Za'arain. Eyes as deep as time looked from Sharia to Kane. The soul-eater's muzzle lifted and extraordinary regret poured out, a song composed of every might-have-been from all times, all lives. The Za'arains wept and agreed . . . but they did not move toward each other. Colors poured from each lias'tri stone to its mate, colors arching over the azir to make a rainbow of shattered light, shards of time glittering openly. The brilliant fragments poured into the azir's open mouth until time overflowed, concealing the soul-eater in a tide of shimmering energy. Song and light dissolved, leaving nothing. The soul-eater was gone.

Jode thought that its companion's grief had killed the azir. And then the skin on his body stirred in primal fear. He had been wrong. It was creation he had just witnessed, not destruction.

An azir stood by Sharia.

An azir also stood by Kane.

As one, the Za'arains covered their lias'tri stones with cruel, trembling hands. Sharia and the azir moved swiftly away from the ship. The personnel ramp retracted, but not until Sharia was out of sight did Kane permit the ship's door to iris shut. Despite Jode's assurances that the immediate danger was past, Dani clawed for the nearest za' node with a desperation only intelligent life could achieve. When Jode tried to deflect her panicked flight, he encountered Za'arain determination and a soul-eater's translucent smile. Both speed and destination were out of the pilot's control.

"Are we going through a gold node again?" asked Jode wearily, unable to get through the barrier of Kane's mind.

Is that the fastest way to Skire?

Kane's sardonic question cut like a whip across the psimaster's mind.

"If speed is all that matters, let me help Dani."

Though Kane said nothing, Jode felt the ship open to him once again. He spread through Dani soothingly, gathering her for the leap into chaos. Za'replacement nodes condensed in his mind, showing him the way to Skire. Eight replacements if the planet were approached sanely. Three replacements—gold replacements—if it were not.

Jode cursed and settled in for a wretched trip.

When Dani went through the first gold node, Sharia and the azir screamed as one. With lias'tri so close to completion, separation in space was difficult enough. Separation in time was unendurable. Yet it had to be endured until Kane found the Eyes of Za'ar and brought them to her. And he would bring them to her rather than take them up himself, for they both knew that she had the better chance of surviving the Eyes. She was a rider of living timeshadows, and in most ways the Eyes were very much alive. Kane had sensed that in the Jorke's sullen gloom. So had she.

The Eyes were not Fourth Evolution life. They might have been First, with one of the many lithic races living among their flawless crystal lattices. The Eyes could have been Third Evolution. Construct. Life constructed deliberately by other intelligent life. Or were the Eyes born of the Fifth Evolution, like the azirs, creatures of time?

Sharia did not know. She suspected that it might be the last thing she found out before she died.

Cool, silky tendrils from the azir's ruff fanned over her hand, wrapping her in comfort. In the descending night the transparent ruff was invisible but for the fugitive glide of light deep within the tendrils. The rest of the soul-eater glowed, though, uncanny radiance emanating from its ice-pale body. Sharia did not notice that her own body was luminous with more than its Za'arain heritage, and that her hair shivered, trying to comb through aspects of time that had once been beyond even Kiri, Darien and five. Her living hair became a silver corona shimmering out from her, seeking the life that was more than her own, pouring out her own life in a need not to lose the subtle presence of Kane.

The second gold replacement brought Sharia to her knees in a firestorm of pain, separation in time and space increasing, more of herself draining out in lias'tri desperation.

The azir lifted its slender muzzle to the distant stars and poured out a long ululation of warning and despair. There was only one voice in the soul-eater's cry and no music at all. The sound exploded through Sharia's mind, setting up terrible resonances that made her want to scream, telling her that she had to get up, she had to search, she had to . . . *touch Kane.* But she could not. He had gone out to the stars, sliding among space and times, further away with each breath. She was stranded in Beoy's alien streets with a half-mad soul-eater crying by her side.

Sharia glowed a little more brightly now. A nimbus of pale, uncanny light surrounded her. Azir light; light out of time. Energy poured from her as she fought not to lose the contact with Kane that had become as necessary to her life as her own heartbeat. Her hair quested wildly, seeking currents of time and life that must exist, dimensions and paths leading toward Kane. She found them one by one, tendril by tendril, her Darien hair quivering as it sought purchase among times and energies that Fourth Evolution life had not been meant to inhabit.

The third gold replacement nearly destroyed Sharia. Her lias'tri stone flared wildly, unevenly, silent echo of the screams tearing apart Sharia's throat. She fought fiercely to master her agony, to ride the myriad expressions of time and life, to reach through za' itself and *touch Kane.* Her silver hair combed ceaselessly, seeking the deeply familiar energies of her lias'tri. She found . . . something. A haunting wisp of color, a distant quiver of pain and desire, a fading echo of Kane's torrential, living timeshadow. She clung to the forlorn remains of what had been richness, pouring her own colors and desires into the few channels that she had clawed out of time to connect herself to . . . herself. For that was what Kane had become. He was an extension in all dimensions of herself; and she was the same to him. They were a whole being torn apart in every time, every life.

And they would die of it.

A negative coursed through Sharia, an immense determination to survive that sprang both from Kiri atavism and the immeasurable tenacity of lias'tri. Blindly she struggled to her feet, knowing only that she had to move because movement was a characteristic of life and she was *alive*.

The soul-eater howled, sending a single-voiced song through Beoy's dank night. With the grace of a creature uninhibited by time, the azir condensed beneath Sharia's hand, subtly supporting her. Its ruff flowed up like transparent black water, opening currents of time to her touch. Not too many currents, for that would kill the azir's Fourth Evolution companion as surely and more quickly than thwarted lias'tri. A few currents, though. A transparency to match the radiant Darien hair. An alien exchange of time energies and life, an exchange to equal the dimensional shimmers emanating from Sharia's body.

Sharia was no longer wholly of the Fourth Evolution. Like the azir, she was bathed in uncanny light. Like the azir's ruff, her energy-combing Darien hair had become transparent rather than translucent. Like the azir, part of her now lived outside of linear time. The changes would have killed any Fourth Evolution life other than Kiri, Darien, five, lias'tri. Eventually the changes would kill her too, kill him, kill them. But eventually was not time/now, and that was where Kiri, Darien and five had evolved. Lias'tri could not revoke linear time, but it could steal from other times to buy time/now.

The cost of that theft was a slow draining of life energies as Kane and Sharia reached through unnamed dimensions in order to survive separation in time/now. That was why they glowed.

The *other* was leaking through their intertwined timeshadow energies into time/now, bathing them in imminence. And their energies, the life of linear time, was slowly dissipating into the *other*. When the last of the light leaked through, when they became wholly transparent, Kane and Sharia would be dead. Unlike Fifth Evolution life, they could not draw sustenance from time to balance the energy they gave to it in order to remain connected one to the other.

Jode watched Kane's radiant body. With each passage through a gold node, the changes had become more distinct. The Za'arain's black hair was like the azir's ruff, transparent, restless, riding currents of time no Fourth Evolution person could name. His body was ice-pale and glowing. And his thoughts. . . . Thoughts that could not have been his own formed within his mind, the wisdom of other lives, other times, lias'tri reaching in desperation back down to a place and moment where life itself had begun, lias'tri tearing apart all times in order to find a single one that would allow it to survive.

Kane and Sharia had separated too late. Their minds had taken root within one another. To divide them was to condemn them to an excruciating death. Yet to put them together was to condemn every psi within their unimaginable reach to death.

The soul-eater howled. Its supple, single voice lifted in warning and despair.

Abruptly, decision crystallized within Jode, resonating through his powerful, highly trained mind. He held the ship softly, inexorably, in his grasp. They would go down to Skire and seek the Eyes of Za'ar because Kane had built that imperative into Dani's living mind. But soon, very soon, Jode would take Kane back through time and space to Sharia, to life. If that meant wildfire psi, so be it. All living things died somewhere, somewhen. There were many worse ways to leap into eternity than on the incandescent outpouring of lias'tri united.

Dani exploded out of the final gold node. A huge planet filled Jode's awareness, for he was seeing as Dani saw, completely. They were all but on top of Skire, atmosphere burning violently around the ship. Neither Jode nor Dani flinched. They had only to feel the *other* radiating from Kane to know that there were far worse things than dying quickly in time/now.

For the first time in his life, Jode took a hot lightship screaming down a planet's gravity well.

Nineteen

Sonic thunder hammered across continents, shattering land and buildings alike. Distantly Jode sensed Kane trying to slow the awful descent. Jode fought back swiftly, powerfully, deflecting Kane's attempt with a psi-master's trained skill. As long as he worked within the imperative Kane had given Dani, Jode could control the ship with a finesse that Kane could not defeat.

Even so, Kane fought until Jode gently, inexorably, shut down the currents of energy by turning them back on their own source. With a searing curse, Kane gave in and allowed Jode to ride Dani down on the breakpoint of annihilation.

Perhaps it's just as well I didn't have time to train you, Captain. Even stretched across the universe, your mind is hardly docile.

Jode's sardonic thought shivered through Kane's wide-open mind, leaving behind a wake of affection and regret.

You'll kill us before we get to Skire's surface.

No I won't, Za'arain. Watch me. Watch how delicate a Jhoramon psi-master can be.

Dani blasted across Skire's deserted surface with a speed that turned land into a blur. Then the ship slowed, hovered and drifted down to a perfect landing among the ice mountains. Choosing a landing site was not difficult. The only life on the whole planet was concentrated in a single city.

Kane stared at the outside displays. There was one glass building where faceted windows shone. Inside the glass, colors shimmered and twisted and flowed like a river running down to the sea. The rest of the city's buildings were ragged and ugly, comprising little more than a sprawling, squalid camp astride the ruins of an ancient city. Kane could sense the subtle emanation of za' from deep within the ruins; it was the psi-signature of artifacts that had been used by Fourth Evolution psis to evade the restrictions of linear time. Huge machines crouched amid the excavations. Myriad paths wound among the machines and the rude buildings, paths made by thousands of slaves as they had dug through Skire's frigid days to the alien treasure beneath. But no one moved now. The random bundles scattered over ice and excavation were lifeless bodies.

Kane looked away, fastening his attention on Jode. The psimaster flinched visibly as he saw Kiri atavism, uncanny azir and lias'tri determination combined within changing Za'arain eyes.

"SaDyne is still alive," said Kane. His fingers clenched around the headcloth that he had taken from SaDyne's rooms above the Jorke. "His timeshadow is closed to me. I don't think he's wearing the Eyes now. I think he tried to, but. . . ." Kane shrugged and gestured as though the violent backlash of psi surrounding the ship were visible and tangible. "He survived the Eyes, but I don't think he can control them yet. He'll need more za' artifacts."

"Or more minds," Jode said grimly. "Can't you feel it? He stripped minds from living bodies and then he used those minds the way Dani uses atoms—for power, destroying them in the process."

"I know. I can feel the new wakes. SaDyne must have burned out every available mind."

"Or sucked them into his own, increasing his own power. Like the Kiriy. Do you sense the Eyes?"

"It is not like Za'arain," Kane said. His hand lifted slowly as he pointed to the glass walls where colors lived. "SaDyne will be there."

Jode wanted to order Dani to melt the beautiful Za'arain building through to the core of the planet. The temptation was nearly overwhelming; but without the Eyes, Za'arain was lost. And without Za'arain, the Joining was lost.

Yes. Kane's thought was ragged. He stood slowly, like a man balancing on a very fine wire.

Jode came out of the pilot's chair in a controlled rush, prepared to catch Kane if he fell. The azir condensed beneath Kane's left hand. The soul-eater's ruff curled almost invisibly around Kane's fingers, becoming a dark transparency that subtly inhibited the exchange of energy between its companion and the *other.* The azir could not entirely prevent the exchange. Although the alien transference of energy was slowly killing Kane, it was also the only thing keeping him alive. Without it, he would no longer be able to reach his lias'tri in any dimension of time. Then he would die as quickly and surely as though his living timeshadow had been ripped from linear time.

Jode sensed the slight easing of Kane's battle with aspects of time no Fourth Evolution creature should have to face. The psi-master sighed deeply; apparently soul-eaters could do something other than destroy. He turned his attention to the ship.

Dani. Ship transport for Kane, the Xtians and me. Include traveling cocoons. Once we're downside, lift and hover over us. If I holler, come in hot. The cocoons should protect us. Understand?

Dani understood very well. There came to Jode the distinct feeling that the cocoons would not protect them if the ship came in hot. The thought was both Jode's and, subtly, not Jode's. It was Dani's, too. Her trips through gold nodes were condensing intelligence from the tension within her Za'arain and Wolfin mind. She had extrapolated SaDyne's potentialities with and without the Eyes of Za'ar. She was worried about Jode. She wanted to protect his mind as well as his body, but she did not know how.

Only another psi could do that, Jode told her.

Dani waited patiently for Jode to realize that she had an idea to share. When Jode did not understand, she reached out very, very gently to his mind.

The ship's alien, untrained touch went through the psi-master like lightning. Energy, raw energy, enough to take a lightship across the universe. All Jode had to do was figure out how to tap that energy without killing himself in the process. He doubted that it could be done. Then he had a better idea.

If you sense me or Kane going down beneath SaDyne's mind, reach out to SaDyne like you just did to me. Only don't hold back, Dani. Burn him out to the last level of his mind. Burn him down through every level of time. Can you do that?

SaDyne did not wait for the ship to agree or disagree. He struck.

Jode felt no more than the overwhelming instant of attack. With a survival reflex passed down through his part-Za'arain mother, his mind recoiled upon itself in a desperate attempt to survive the psi-hunter tearing at him. Kane screamed and his mind writhed violently, trying to evade psi-hunter attack in linear time without losing his grip on all the complex, subtle energies connecting him to Sharia, to life. But no matter how he struggled, Kane could barely deflect SaDyne's raging mind, much less attack in return.

For a crucial instant the azir wavered, caught in a trap that knew no timely solutions. Fifth Evolution creatures were not omnipresent. They could not simultaneously occupy two places within linear time. If the azir's energy-rich ruff let go of Kane in order to comb SaDyne out of his many lives and times, Kane would die in several dimensions of time, including the one most important to Fourth Evolution life—linear time. Azir vengeance would instantly cost Kane his life. Azir patience would prolong Kane's life for a few more instants of linear time.

Helpless, seething with icy light, the azir waited for its companion to die and free the soul-eater for revenge.

Dani was not restricted by the niceties of balancing lives from one instant to the next among several manifestations of time. As soon as Jode's mind vanished from her awareness, she poured a stream of raw energy toward the only unfamiliar mind within reach—SaDyne's.

Establishing contact with SaDyne was not as easy as touching Jode. Dani spent a long time sorting out ways and means of penetrating SaDyne's energies to the mind beneath. Whole seconds sped by while she grappled with the special, elusive connections among times and psi. When she finally saw the possibility of an opening, she ripped into it with a savagery that she had learned from Kane. But she had also learned intelligence from him. Even before she attacked, she fled, stripping atmosphere to vacuum, using energy at an awesome rate. Her flight left behind a series of sonic blasts that sent shock waves through the building, fracturing thick glass walls. Dani could have turned SaDyne's headquarters into slag, but did not, because that had been expressly forbidden to her.

By the time SaDyne discovered that he had been ambushed by a quasi-living mind, it was too late for him to counterattack. Dani exploded through the gold node at full power, tearing her living cargo through dimensions where SaDyne could not follow.

SaDyne's attack ended as suddenly as it had begun. Kane and Jode slumped to the floor. Tenderly Dani wrapped them both in cocoons, examined her programming, and found herself free for the first time in her intelligent life. No orders, no imperatives, not even a suggestion. For a few split instants she wondered what she would do.

Azir light expanded through the ship, found Dani's brain centers, and focused on them for less than a billionth of an instant of linear time. It was enough. Dani oriented herself on Doursone, found the nearest gold node, and tore through it at speeds possible only to a Wolfin ship under the lash of raw terror.

The soul-eater lay beside Kane's cocoon, still supporting its companion in the *other,* and smiling with black transparency.

The azir pacing beside Sharia also smiled, sensing possibilities of life within the odd confines of linear time once again. No one noticed the soul-eater's smile or the transparent ruff caressing and reinforcing Sharia's body.

Sharia herself was too lost within the conflicts of time and

Fourth Evolution life to realize that the azir smiled. For the entire time that Kane had been gone, she had wandered the streets of Beoy, radiant with imminence. Hardened pirates had fled from the alien with the transparent hair and the ice-pale, nearly translucent body, as though she were a soul-eater herself. The only color about her was the lias'tri stone, like a sunrise viewed through a thick sheet of ice, of color without warmth.

The first passage through the gold node on the flight back from Skire had reduced the tension in Sharia between time/now and the *other*. She shivered subtly, seeking a better hold on time/now as the *other* faded from her through dimensions she could not name.

The second gold node was a firestorm of pleasure racing through her. Kane's healing presence coursing within her mind. The azir lifted its graceful muzzle to Doursone's blank sky and sang triumphantly. For a moment out of time Sharia stood utterly still, listening to the soul-eater's pouring song. Then she turned and ran toward the spaceport. Part of her tried to quench her headlong rush, to reason with lias'tri obsession, to warn her of times overlapping until za' leaked out and destroyed life.

It was no longer possible for her to listen to all the words boiling out of a rational time/then. Time/now was upon her, and the future had a siren call more beautiful than the azir's song. The warnings of the past were vaporizing in the anticipation burning in her blood and in her mind, lias'tri reaching toward itself across time.

Sharia felt Dani burst out of the last gold node, Dani clawing down through Doursone's empty sky. Shock waves pealed over Beoy. Sharia stood on the spaceports apron, laughing and holding up her arms, letting the violence of Kane's return drench her senses. Between her breasts the lias'tri stone blazed with a triumph to equal the azir's ascending cry.

Kane awoke completely as the wine of Sharia's presence in time/now swept through him. Beside him the azir sang in scales and times that were no longer wholly alien to the Za'arain. He looked over at Jode. The psi-master opened eyes that were al-

most as dark as a soul-eater's. Jode looked at the incredible fire
of Kane's stone and knew that lias'tri could no longer be denied.
He also knew the potential cost of lias'tri unity. He tried to
touch Kane's mind, to warn him that Doursone could be stripped
of intelligent life by wildfire psi just as SaDyne's Skire had
been.

And it was possible that even worse could happen. Kane and
Sharia were Kiri, Darien, five. Timeshadow riders. They could
strip minds from time/then as well as from time/now, their incendiary psi burning through all of Fourth Evolution time.

*We know. We don't want that. We want only what is ours.
Lias'tri.*

The mindtouch was neither like Kane's alone nor Sharia's
alone. And they had heard the psi-master even though he had
spoken only within the deepest fears of his own mind.

*Get off the ship, Jode. Take everyone with you. We will try
not to touch until we are in the center of an uninhabited area
of the Dust, where there will be no minds for us to sweep up.*

Za'arain regret washed over Jode, Za'arain sorrow that the
parting was necessary. But harder and deeper than regret was
Kane's determination. Neither he nor Sharia could deflect
lias'tri consummation any longer. Neither wanted to.

Wordlessly, Jode prepared to leave the ship.

Dani settled onto the apron as lightly as a drifting petal. Jode
sensed the electric pleasure racing through Kane, the impatience—and the fear that what had been so long sought would
somehow elude him. Lias'tri. Ecstasy.

Or five touching five. Catastrophe.

Dani dumped the crew onto the spaceport's seething apron
with neither ceremony nor explanation, but simply a command
to get to cover and to do it quickly. The crew hesitated until
they saw the violet-eyed Za'arain woman waiting with the soul-
eater by her side. Then the crew ran, knowing only that something was happening that was beyond their ability to understand.
Only Szarth held back, sensing that Kane and Sharia were in
danger. He hesitated until a Jhoramon psi-master spoke chill-

ingly in his mind about a planet called Skire. Szarth ran very quickly then, following his steel-scaled symbionts to the safety of synstone tunnels beyond the apron.

The psi-master approached Sharia with gliding Jhoramon strides. Deliberately he touched her, letting his timeshadow tangle with hers, wanting her to know beyond doubt that what he was telling her was true to the bottom of his mind.

I want to go with Kane, with you. I may be able to help.

Or you may die the final death. Can you risk that? Can you strand your lias'tri in the rest of her times and lives as her death stranded you in time/now?

Jode's hand dropped from Sharia's arm. For a moment her healing hair caressed him. Then she turned toward the waiting ship and Jode knew just the edge of the raging impatience that consumed her. He ran for the synstone shields as though an azir pursued him. He did not want Dani's takeoff to be delayed one instant merely to ensure the safety of his skin. As he ran, he wondered how much linear distance in space it would take to preserve him from wildfire psi. Deep inside his tightly held mind, he doubted that there was enough distance in the universe to keep him safe from minds that could reach through azir dimensions.

Wildfire psi would be hungry for other minds, other lives, all times, everything.

Dani. Jode's curt thought brought the ship to full alert. *The instant that Sharia is aboard, get through that gold node. Don't worry about hurting the Za'arains. That healing hair of hers will take care of both of them. Just get them as far as you can from any inhabited planet, and do it as fast as you can. Understand?*

The answer came as a shudder of nearly uncontrolled energy vibrating through the ship. Jode dove for the opening of one of the synstone tunnels beneath the apron. Dani waited on her stabilizers, poised for another rending flight through a gold node. She sensed Sharia and the azir running along the still-hot apron, up the personnel ramp, through the open iris—

Dani slammed shut the door and exploded into Doursone's blank sky. The thinness of the atmosphere was all that prevented her from leaving a sonic backlash that would have leveled the city. Even so, Beoy shuddered. Synstone shifted and cracked as Dani ripped a tunnel through Doursone's sky.

Almost casually Sharia reached for strength from her other lives, letting times/then ripple through her as her nearly transparent hair combed from her own timeshadow the effects of Dani's brutal takeoff. As she healed, so did Kane, a healing so reflexive that neither felt more than an instant of pain. It did not slow them down. Nothing could. When Sharia reached the core shaft it refused to lift her to the control cabin. She laughed, understanding Dani's strategy of delay even as she defeated it by climbing swiftly up the hand and footholds that studded the shaft's curved surfaces.

The ship stripped matter into plasma and then used that raw energy recklessly, exploding through gravity's chains to the dubious safety of the gold node.

Kane swung into the core shaft and climbed down to meet Sharia, moving even more swiftly than she was. Strength expanded in him with each breath, each step, each marvelous instant of feeling her shimmer though his mind again. Pathways of life and time that had been as barren as Doursone's skies now pulsed with torrential energy. Their minds quested through each other more smoothly than azirs through nonlinear time.

Time/now stretched as their minds interlocked, power growing incrementally as they rediscovered all of their recent time/then, healed the tenuous years of separation with a soundless rush of color, reached back to their years when Sharia was a child five. With each shared moment, each doubled experience, each vivid Darien memory and dream, their minds linked more completely until they filled all the time/now and time/then of this life. For a timeless instant they were motionless, examining the power and perfection of their interlocking awareness.

Together they reached for the life before this one, a shared time/then on another planet, two people born to another race, psi-masters who sang to alien stars of times and places unknown to Joining, Dust or Za'arain. Memories were soft implosions within their minds, tangerine sunrises and midnights luminous with the stately dance of galaxies, the perfume of golden flowers bathing their senses as he lay beside her, reaching for her with laughter and hunger tightening his body. The flesh was different, rich brown rather than gold or silver, and the eyes were a blue as dark as Jhoramon's autumn sky; but the minds coursing through the bodies were familiar and the lias'tri crystal each wore was a potent seduction in every color known to man.

Kane and Sharia's newly remembered life washed over them like a gentle rain, soaking into minds and bodies thirsty for the unity that had been known in other lives and had been denied for so long in this one. They reached eagerly for the next life, letting its scarlet days and moon-streaked nights pour through their minds. Music quivered throughout, music to make an azir weep, a man and a woman in magical duet while a world listened and learned things for which neither Joining nor Za'arain had words. The two people were alive with music and their pleasure in one another; it was one and the same thing, music and sensual consummation, and they sang more beautifully than any legend could describe. As they sang, lias'tri crystals burned.

There was a world of water, turquoise waves endlessly breaking. He and she swam below the waves, gliding with subtle undulations of their sleek bodies, chasing and catching one another in a game as old as man and woman and desire. When they surfaced it was to catch the creamy edge of a surging wave, to ride that wave forever in a wild tangle of laughter and powerful limbs and minds that interlocked as inevitably as the waves and the sea itself. Other minds rode with them, laughed with them, loved with them, sharing and learning from the sweeping beauty of two beings perfectly balanced within themselves and one another.

A desert world, black sand dunes rippling toward a maroon horizon. Amethyst springs breathed water into the dry air, and plants of metallic gold arched against the flawless sky. She sat alone, letting the dawn seep warmly into her, knowing that he finally had been born into her time/now. It was a song inside her, its sounds as pure as the nightbird calling to the rising moon. Together they would make the dunes walk, the waters flow, the harvest ripen.

Lightning arched all around him, around her, and they gloried in it, drinking its fierce energies. Hand in hand they called down a storm upon a planet that had rocks like shattered rainbows. Under lemon-colored sky and with the taste of spring, they were dying as they had lived, together. Cloud-streaked, grey autumn on plains that had no end; she gave birth to their children while he held her mind and body. Pale green ice, music as clear as light; their mind partners gathered around, planning reunions in other times, other lives.

The rain of lives came more quickly now, less gently, cloud-bursts of music and memory, scents and tastes, textures and powers long forgotten. They were lightship pilots and the inhabitants of a newly discovered planet, children of mortal enemies and the offspring of families united for thousands of years, psi-masters and prophets, hermits and leaders, witches and sacrifices. Through it all, every life, each life, lias'tri crystals shimmered and beckoned, condensations of a hunger that was composed equally of the sensual and the immaterial.

They had been every color, every size, every race, known every circumstance at least once. They had been alive through so many times/then, lives without number, times/then reaching backward and inward in an endless, vastly accelerating implosion. Kane and Sharia reached for all of it, greedy for all the memories/realities of lias'tri united, two lovers perfectly matched in mind and body and times, burning with a flame that bowed neither to death nor to the confinements of linear time. Lias'tri, a condensation of the *always* expressed through the medium of Fourth Evolution's linear time.

And soon, this life, this time. Soon the last steps would be taken, the last rungs climbed, Kane's cabin opening out before them. Soon there would be nothing between five and five but hunger.

Dani had sensed the psi currents increasing arithmetically, a few lives added one to the other. In a few seconds the increase had become geometric, a sudden outpouring of power as each life remembered others, and then others, lives crystallizing out of supersaturated time around the catalyst of lias'tri imperative. Now the ship sensed the next increase in power crystallizing out with a rapidity only a Wolfin machine could follow, a logarithmic increase of psi power that would reverberate through times accessible only to Fifth Evolution azirs—and to Fourth Evolution Za'arains whose minds had slowly evolved through Kiri, Darien, five. Fourth Evolution minds able to touch other times.

That was the danger Jode had foreseen. Wildfire psi burning down through all times. Kane and Sharia might not want to precipitate that immense, overlapping psi-awareness; but if they lost control of the speed with which their lives crystallized out of time, they would do just that.

Dani calculated the speed of psi increase against the distance to the gold node. For the first time in her intelligent life, Dani knew despair. There was too little time. The node was too far for her to reach before lias'tri went to its shattering completion. The ship howled in frustration and fear.

The soul-eaters heard and understood. They did not intervene. Their companions wanted unity. The azirs sat on their translucent haunches and waited for the final seconds between now and consummation of their companions' desires.

The parts of Kane and Sharia that lived in linear time/now felt the vast powers of their shared lives pouring into time/now, making each of them more complete, more whole. At the same instant they realized that they did not have to limit their completion to past lives, past times/then. All of time was available to them. All of Fourth Evolution life. All they had to do was reach out along azir pathways and then they would experience what no life had ever experienced. True unity. They would know everything, do everything, be everything in all times, and the universe would be a gem with countless facets spinning brightly in their minds.

And it would spin only for them, only in their joined minds, for no other Fourth Evolution intelligence would survive the incendiary moment of uncontrolled psi.

No.

They shifted uneasily, not wanting any but their own shared lives, their own interlocking minds. They tried to slow down the process, to control the past lives pouring over them, threatening to drown them. But the vast crystallization of lives did not slow. Kane and Sharia had lived together so many times, in so many ways, with so many things learned—and lias'tri demanded each one. All at once.

Now.

No!

Together Kane and Sharia fought against the doom they sensed racing toward them from every side, all times. They did not want to remember their countless lives only to rage helplessly through other lives and other times, burning out of control, burning through time. They did not want the boundless, inhuman *always*. They wanted to live in just one life and time, this one. They wanted the mental and sensual consummations possible only in linear time.

Kane and Sharia took the atavistic strength of their Kiri heritage and shaped it with the sweeping intelligence of their Darienfive minds. To that they added Jode's teachings, Jhoramon psi-master's finesse. Then came the azir's Fifth Evolution understanding of time's endless permeability to intelligence. Time and life could be, were and would always be whatever intelligence could conceive of. It only remained for the Za'arains to form a single, clear conception before they were overwhelmed by their own wild hunger for all of their lives, all of their times.

The two Za'arains struggled to formulate a concept that would express everything they wanted and could be. It was not easy, not when lives kept crystallizing out, seducing and distracting them, murmuring to them of worlds long gone to dust, cultures forgotten, music quivering compellingly—and of lias'tri surviving through time. Even as they fought to concentrate, to seek among their countless lives the solutions to a single life, Kane and Sharia knew that there was not enough linear time in which to learn how to control what they were becoming. They could feel alien lives being drawn into the vortex of lias'tri unity. They could sense minds opening to them, minds that were not theirs and never had been, minds igniting and feeding their own lias'tri desire.

Wildfire psi, burning through time.

No!

Dani howled and overloaded every quivering nerve in her ship's body, racing through space to a gold node that seemed to retreat before her. The soul-eaters stood restlessly, looking at themselves and their companions who were only instants from touching physically as well as mentally, timeshadows and lives tangling irrevocably, freeing what few restraints their minds had managed to put on lias'tri obsession. The azirs weighed their companions' desires against the confinements of linear time.

Azir light bloomed through the ship in an expanding wave. The azirs' song poured in rainbow shards from transparent mouths, linear time slowing as the *other* flowed in between gaps in time/now. But the *other* did not take over, not completely, and not for long. Not long enough for Fourth Evolution companions to leak among the cracks in time. But long enough for a Wolfin construct to act. Just as Sharia's long hair swept toward Kane, Dani screamed into the gold node.

And stayed there.

The *always* and the *other* burst through Kane and Sharia. The alien minds that had been drawn to them were peeled away by the presence of time states that were both incomprehensible and inimical to Fourth Evolution life. But Kane and Sharia were Kiri, Darien, five. Their minds and bodies had evolved toward something that was neither Fourth nor yet Fifth. Their flesh and awareness could survive a brush with the *always* and the *other*.

For a time, that is.

They did not ask how much time, or of what kind. They simply opened themselves and let all their lives pour through them, for in this instant out of linear time they were no longer afraid of dragging other minds into incendiary psi. A maelstrom of sensation battered the two Za'arains as their past lives burst into awareness. Instinctively they clung to each other, seeking safety as they always had, in the power of their joined minds. With skills learned among cultures long forgotten, Kane and Sharia subtly channeled the cataracts of energy. They did not try to understand their lives. They simply accepted them and then let them stream outward from Za'arain timeshadows like an endless dance of rainbow fire. The knowledge and experiences of those cascading lives were there, a part of each of them—but not in time/now. In time/now there were only Kane and Sharia, culmination of uncountable lives and a million years of Za'arain evolution.

Whimpering quietly, Dani released her grip on a dimension and a force she had not been designed to understand. Simultaneously the azirs sucked the glistening *always* and the *other* back into their black mouths. The ship reappeared in linear time, Fourth Evolution space; and then Dani hung motionless, radiating away a dazzling display of colors, scintillant backlash of unnamed times.

Sharia's hair was like time itself, cool and gliding, yet burning with a hot core of life that called to all of Kane's senses. There was no injury to comb from his timeshadow or her own, yet her hair caressed him, bringing exquisite pleasure, the same pleasure that coursed through her when she buried her fingers in his seething, shimmering, nearly transparent black hair. Their timeshadows flowed together through all colors and dimensions, interlocking as surely as their minds. For a long moment of linear time they looked at one another. Then he sank deeply into her and she flowed hotly around him, and they knew nothing but the sweet, torrential ecstasy that had been so long denied.

Twenty

DANI.

The ship quailed, protesting the huge voice that spoke to and within every particle of her Wolfin/Za'arain mind.

We're frightening her.

Kane and Sharia took their newfound strength, their pouring lives and times, and combed them all further back into their mutual time/then, letting cataracts of energy dance harmlessly in other times. Azir light bloomed softly around them, helping the two Za'arains balance among time/then and time/now, the *always* and the *other*. One day they would be able to manage the delicate balance themselves, when they had the linear time to sift among their countless lives. But in the time/now of Za'arain and the Joining, only one thing in linear time mattered—recovering the Eyes of Za'ar.

Dani?

The ship's relief was almost tangible as the Za'arains' mindspeech whispered delicately at the borders of her awareness.

The wordless query waited at the edges of their joined minds.

Take us to Za'arain. When you come out of the final gold node, be prepared for SaDyne to attack.

!

Fear shivered visibly through the ship. She had barely eluded his searing mind on Skire.

We'll be able to protect you this time.

For all the confidence of their thought, the two Za'arains had not been able to prevent the multi-leveled inner dialog that had occurred even as the first level of their minds had engaged Dani in gentle mindspeech. *Will we be able to protect her and ourselves? What if SaDyne has time to use the Eyes on Za'arain, to suck up Kiri minds, savage atavism, Darien power—and then to use those terrible Za'arain energies against us? Will we be able to help Dani then? Will we even be able to help ourselves?*

The thought had not seeped out to the ship. They needed Dani confident, for Kane's mind was too turbulent beneath their careful control for him to mesh well with Dani. But the ship trusted her Za'arain gods. Power flowed smoothly through her as she raced toward the next gold node.

A smooth coil of Sharia's hair shimmered over Kane's naked arm. He smiled and lifted a nearly transparent tendril to his lips. "We could send the azirs after SaDyne," he breathed, making her hair shift like clear silver flame in a tiny breeze.

"Could we?" she asked softly, leaning against his strength, letting his warmth surround her as sweetly as her hair surrounded him.

Kane hesitated. Even as he spoke he sensed the interchange of ideas, objections, agreements, extrapolations deep within the interlocking levels of their minds. Yet he used words anyway, because he knew that she took as much pleasure from his voice as he did from hers. Sensory communication was another name for lias'tri.

"We could try, sv'arri," he said wryly. "But azirs are their own creatures."

"They're helping us to control the *always* and the *other*. Maybe they can't leave us yet and hunt down SaDyne."

Pity. I'd much rather give SaDyne to a hungry soul-eater than lose in this and all lives what I have just found. You. Lias'tri.

The thought was his, hers, theirs. It ached and soothed at once, like his Darien hair both hot and cool between her seeking, caressing fingers.

"Maybe we'll get to Za'arain before SaDyne does, before he can suck Kiri and Darien minds into the vortex of the Eyes.

Dani is very fast, v'orri," offered Sharia, her lips brushing over his.

"So are raider ships."

"But the gold nodes. . . ."

"The Eyes will take SaDyne anywhere he wants to go in time," said Kane.

Just as the Eyes will tear us from all our times.

"Maybe he will restore Za'arain."

But even as the wistful words left Sharia's lips, she knew that it would not happen. SaDyne wanted power, not creation. He had coerced rather than partnered the Eyes of Za'ar. He was a destroyer rather than restorer. Lias'tri thwarted. He had stripped one planet of intelligence merely to wear the Eyes for a moment of linear time. He would strip Za'arain in order to rule the Eyes, to wear them to the end of his own linear time.

Maybe the Eyes will kill him on Za'arain.

Yet neither Sharia nor Kane believed that. If the Eyes could have killed SaDyne, they would have. He would find greater strength on Za'arain, not greater weakness. All those psi-hunter minds to burn, raw life-energy fueling him in his battle to fill his own emptiness, an emptiness that could never be filled for his lias'tri no longer existed in this or any other time. SaDyne would be a cruel god bent only on wreaking the final death.

We can't let psi-hunter atavism rage through Fourth Evolution lives, Fourth Evolution dreams, linear time.

And we can't hope to defeat the Eyes of Za'ar. Dani is taking us to the final death, and we've only begun to live.

Kane touched Sharia's lips lightly with his tongue, enjoying the instant shiver of her response.

"He wasn't born to wear the Eyes," she whispered, touching Kane in turn.

"No," agreed Kane, fitting his mouth over hers, filling her senses even as she filled his.

But SaDyne does wear the Eyes, if only for moments at a time, and we'll have so few moments together before our last death. Come to me. Let us learn about each other and ourselves,

*five joined to five. We have turned our backs on the secrets of
the* always *and the unexpected powers of the* other. *Let us know
the consummate joys of time/now.*

Lias'tri stones were a sunburst of every color, of overlapping
times, cascading lives. Azir harmonies celebrated emotions
Fifth Evolution would never know, consummations impossible
beyond linear time. The songs were like the air the Za'arains
breathed, glistening with Fourth Evolution sensuality.

A gold node burst around Kane and Sharia, suspending them
timelessly within their incandescent ecstasy. The soul-eaters radiated through the *always* and the *other,* and their music was a
cascade of glittering rainbows that filled all times, all lives.

Dani listened and wept and fled through the space between
gold nodes, knowing that she was bringing her Za'arain pas-
sengers closer to death with each instant. She examined her
programming in the light of knowledge both old and new, certain and possible; and she found no crack in the structure of
logic and imperative. For a time she considered ignoring her
clear instructions and then pretending never to have received
them. Finally she rejected the temptation. That was a child's
solution, useful for only the most brief moments of linear time,
and she was no longer a child.

Cursing her Wolfin creators and her Za'arain gods, Dani
plunged into the last gold node.

Za'aral reverberated with the thunder of a Wolfin lightship
riding its own incandescent star wake down onto the planet.
Dani had done it before. She had hoped never to do it again,
glass buildings cracking and shattering and finally flowing
hotly beneath her. She did not know why Kane and Sharia
counted each instant of delay as an enemy; she only knew that
she had committed herself to the Za'arains.

Kane and Sharia lay within her healing cloud of hair, combing the crushing effects of Dani's descent from their joined
timeshadows. Their minds were tightly shielded with only a
single bright current of mindtouch extended to comfort Dani,
for she remembered SaDyne's strength with awful clarity. The

azirs stood at either side of the Za'arains, exuding the dangerous Fifth Evolution protection of the *other* as they subtly continued to help their companions bridle the seething energies of their countless lives.

Where is he? The question was repeated many times, a silent litany of fear and anticipation.

The answer came as SaDyne struck at Dani's quasi-living mind. She had surprised him once. She would not do so again.

The ship screamed. Even as Kane and Sharia poured themselves into deflecting the attack, Dani threw herself back into the gold node. Once again she stayed within the sleeting, unknowable energies. Yet the safety that she sought eluded her. SaDyne's power was diminished but not overcome.

Kane and Sharia attacked the raw hatred they sensed raking over Dani's unprotected mind. A Fourth person would have died under SaDyne's attack and been grateful for the chance—but Dani was not alive. Not quite. She knew pain, though. She shrieked it from every brain center.

Kane and Sharia struggled with the outpouring of atavistic savagery. At first it was all they could do to deflect the worst of it, preserving Dani's sanity. Then, gradually, they sensed a thinning of SaDyne's power. Their concealment within the gold za'replacement node had not stopped him, but it had affected him. What had once seemed like a raw cataract of undifferentiated energy could now be separated into some of its components.

There, the violet-carmine-indigo currents. They aren't his, not wholly. If we could touch him, we could comb out some of the living Kiri minds.

The knowledge of SaDyne's energies came from Sharia, rider of living timeshadows. It was matched by Kane's wake rider skills, for he saw the deep shivering of lives shearing away from SaDyne's time/now, sliding back into time/then and rooting irrevocably in the *then*. The dead Kiris' energies were still available to SaDyne, but differently.

If we could land on Za'arain, we could take those wakes and twist SaDyne like hot glass.

We could take Dani in and melt all of Za'aral. But then we would destroy even more than SaDyne—the Eyes of Za'ar.

The smooth, pale chill of the *other* lapped warningly at the edges of the Za'arains' awareness. They opened their glowing violet-silver eyes and saw an exhalation of azir light surrounding them. The soul-eaters' bottomless glances pleaded silently with their companions to recognize . . . something. Music the color of all times poured from their transparent muzzles. Kane and Sharia did not have much more living time in which to hide. They could choose to die the last death amid the cascading hues of all times or they could go back to fight and succumb to Za'ar death beneath the silver skies of their planet.

Or live. There is always that chance, one among thousands.

Protected by her Za'arain gods, Dani gathered herself and burst back out of the gold node. She shrieked down to Za'arain's surface riding an expanding shock wave which she hoped would at least rock SaDyne's concentration, if not the ground beneath his feet. Instantly SaDyne attacked the ship, but this time Kane and Sharia were prepared. They were deeply inside every particle of Dani's brain centers, shielding her even as the azirs shielded them from incursions of the *other*. There was nothing the Za'arains could do as a counterattack against SaDyne, however. Caught among the confines of linear time once more, they were lucky simply to hang on to Dani's sanity, to keep her from losing control and crashing spectacularly on the planet's unforgiving surface.

Dani chose the time and the place of her landing. She had discovered SaDyne's ship, determined that he was not aboard, and had made her plans with a pragmatism that Jode would have approved. She came downside hot and hard, vaporizing much of the Kiriy's sacred fountain and melting SaDyne's ship to slag. A shattering blast of steam raced outward in all directions, cooking any Kiris foolish enough to be waiting in ambush among the artesian fountain's concealing veils. The deaths ripped through SaDyne's mind, through Kane's and Sharia's minds, through the Kiri psi-packs SaDyne could not yet control. It was then that the two Za'arains realized that SaDyne had landed on the planet only a few minutes before. As fast as raider ships were, Dani was faster still, for she had experience with—and a near-Za'arain understanding of—gold za'replacements.

Yet with every second, every heartbeat, SaDyne was calling more minds to him, and then more. Neither Kane nor Sharia knew when the lives pouring into the renegade Kiriy would go from arithmetic increase to geometric to logarithmic. They only knew that the increase would happen as inevitably as one second replaced another within linear time. If they were to have any chance of defeating SaDyne it had to be soon, very soon, before he ignited Kiri atavism and began to burn up through time/then into time/now, and then perhaps burning all times one by one. Once begun, SaDyne's incendiary psi would blaze until there were no minds left within his reach. Kane and Sharia did not know what SaDyne's reach through time and space was. They did not want to know. He was Kiri, Darien, five.

Dani snapped a triple cocoon around Kane and Sharia, spat them far out onto the scorched pavement and clawed for the gold node once again. The ship knew that protecting her was costing the Za'arains too much of their energy. Using every particle of power and fear within her Wolfin-created body, Dani fled for the dubious safety of Jode and Doursone. Neither Kane nor Sharia objected; they had given Dani the idea themselves. If SaDyne's reach did not now extend beyond Za'arain's surface, they did not want to give him the immediate means of attacking the Joining by riding a captive Dani.

The cocoon measured the outside temperature, adjusted for the curiously resilient physiology of the Za'arains within and waited for Dani's signal. There was a long hammering of sonic thunder, then a deafening silence as Dani escaped into the gold node. Even as the artesian mists returned, cooling the once-white stones surrounding the sacred fountain, Sharia and Kane stepped out of the cocoon, their five-fingered hands intertwined. Light rippled subtly through her flying silver hair, energy that was not wholly of linear time. It was the same for Kane's shorter, darker hair. The imminence of the *other* radiated from him. Identical azirs paced at either side of the Za'arains. In them, the light of the *other* was not subtle, it was a beautiful, ghostly radiance that warned of states of being and times deadly to Fourth Evolution life.

SaDyne attacked. He found no seam in Kane and Sharia's unity, no crack for him to pry apart their defenses. With Dani's troubling, half-living mind gone, Kane and Sharia were able to hold SaDyne at bay.

Not enough. We still can't attack him without opening our own minds for attack.

An image of Sharia's healing, deadly hair floated deep within their minds.

Yes. Closer. Touch him.

Slowly, carefully, deeply aware of one another and the seething psi energies surrounding them, Kane and Sharia walked through the fountain's diamond mists. Each forward step was a small battle in itself. SaDyne sensed what their strategy was. He did not know if a timeshadow rider could destroy him. Nor did he intend to put the question to a test. He relented in his attack somewhat, turning part of his energies back to the Kiri minds burning so brightly around him. He took the minds as he found them, absorbing the surging power of Kiri atavism. Some of the Kiris died beneath his burning demands. Others did not. Those were a source of increasing strength to SaDyne, minds piling one upon the other, reaching toward the moment when his powers would increase geometrically.

Step by step, Kane and Sharia came closer to the shattered Kiriy corridors. Neither one needed to ask where SaDyne was. The Eyes of Za'ar called to them as surely as they called to every other intelligent Fourth Evolution person. But unlike the inhabitants of Skire, the natives of Za'arain were infused with both potent psi and a violent atavism that raged against being ruled by anyone or anything. Where Skire's people had gone helplessly to their psychic and then their physical deaths, the people of Za'arain fought back with a savagery and determination that was unparalleled in any race of the Joining or Dust.

Psi-hunter packs swirled through the brilliant mist. Some of the hunters were SaDyne's. Some were not. Both kinds demanded SaDyne's attention. The packs he had called to him were unruly, rebellious, constantly seeking a way out from under the control of the Eyes. The wild packs hunted SaDyne with a predatory determination that sent flickers of atavistic hunger streaming through Kane's mind. Memories rose of his last time on Za'arain, of bending over a dead psi-hunter, of being eager to drink blood and shred flesh with clawless hands. Only the clean, hard fire of his lias'tri crystal had stopped him from sliding into mindless atavism.

Kane flinched from the memory, withdrawing his hand and mind from Sharia's, not wanting her to know how close he had been to succumbing to a Kiri's sickening bloodlust. In the instant of withdrawal came the opening that SaDyne had sought. Separated, they were simply very powerful, very vulnerable Darien fives. Pain shattered through them at the same time that the Eyes of Za'ar poured their siren song of incandescent psi directly into Kane's and Sharia's minds. Screaming, driven to their knees, they fought to protect themselves from SaDyne's lethal, predatory mind—and from the Eyes' seductive promises.

All times, all lives, everything. Burning.

Even as Sharia fought against SaDyne and the Eyes, she sensed deep within herself what had happened to Kane, atavism and bloodlust, revulsion and withdrawal. She accepted it, all of it, and caressed him with a streamer of Darien hair, joining them once again. Whatever he was, whatever he might be, was also a part of her. Kiri, Darien, five. All their lives. All their deaths. Everything.

Sharia's acceptance went through Kane like a benediction. Pain receded instantly, as did the murmurous seductions of the Eyes. United, he and she came to their feet again. The soul-eaters sang softly, relief and worry equally mingled. The chill luminos-

ity of the *other* was dangerously thick around their companions.
It had been all the azirs could do to protect the Za'arains from
themselves while SaDyne's attack raged. The soul-eaters did not
understand why their companions had separated, but knew that
it could not happen again if the Za'arains hoped to retain their
grasp on linear time.

With every passing second more minds were being swept
into SaDyne's, like debris to a black hole. Psi-packs still struggled against him, but not as many and not as powerfully. One
by one they bowed to their cruel master, accepting what they
could not defeat. Packs blended together, gorged themselves on
dying psi, and then sought new prey. SaDyne's hunters concentrated on the unbridled packs, for those hunters physically
threatened him. But soon the wild psi-packs would be broken.
When that moment came SaDyne would loose his psi-hunters
on the two powerful Za'arains.

And then SaDyne would have the strength to tear Kane and
Sharia from this life, from all lives.

Kane knew it, sensed it as surely as he sensed Sharia's silky
Darien hair caressing him. The thought of losing her in this and
every life made rage explode within him, rage burning wildly
through time/now to the potent, deadly time/then of untrammeled atavism. Kane's Kiri eyelids flicked down, stayed down,
reflecting the chemical storm sweeping through his mind and
body. The pure violet eyes of a psi-hunter measured the world.
There was no silver turning in their depths, nothing to detract
from the stark hunter's light limning timeshadow energies. In
the atavistic light, timeshadow wakes gleamed invitingly. The
wakes were thickly layered, beckoning to him, promising the
sweet means of destruction. Sheathed in Sharia's living Darien
hair, Kane called to the multicolored wakes whose static streamers wove throughout the Kiriy compound.

They came to him in a soundless rush that made the ground
tremble. Laughing savagely, Kane rode the dense wakes into
time/then. He wove them into a thick network that both permeated and surrounded the Kiriy's glass rooms. The complex,

deadly manipulation took only an instant of linear time, less than a heartbeat, for Kane was one-half of lias'tri united, a unity older and more potent than SaDyne's psi-packs keening toward him.

Now!

With a flick of his mind, Kane yanked the thickly woven wakes. The Kiriy's glass corridors vibrated, then splintered musically, like crystal shattered by a single reverberating scream. Kane twisted the wakes suddenly, ripping them from time/then closer to time/now. The energies could move but the matter they were rooted in could not. The building buckled and slabs of glass sheared off with a sound like ice breaking.

Abruptly SaDyne stopped trying to collect more minds and concentrated on surviving the unexpected attack. Psi-hunters had come at him before, making the floor crack, but never had even a whole pack been able destroy entire sections of the compound. He was too new to the phenomena of Kiri atavism and the Eyes of Za'ar to anticipate or fully control either one. SaDyne could learn, though. And he did, with deadly speed. He called to the wakes woven through Kane's hands and timeshadow.

Kane stiffened, sensed the danger, and released the wakes with a speed that made the ground leap. Then he snatched up the wakes again, twisting savagely, keeping SaDyne off-balance.

Sharia led Kane forward, closer to SaDyne with each step. As she walked she combed her hair through Kane's timeshadow ceaselessly, reinforcing his atavism with the strength of her own. Her eyes were as violet as his, her body swept up in the chemical storm that Kiris had suppressed for a million years. But no longer. Kane and Sharia gave themselves to the ancient predatory strength with a near-violent joy. They would not die as the people of Skire had died, tamely.

Together Kane and Sharia stepped into the Kiriy compound through a jagged gap in the wall. While Kane and SaDyne grappled for control of the passive wakes of former lives, the Eyes called to Sharia. Glass shivered and shattered and the building shrieked as though it were alive. Deadly shards rained down while SaDyne and Kane fought for control of the wakes permeating the Kiriy compound.

For an instant Sharia was tempted to release Kane and run to the Kiriy's suite where SaDyne sat enthroned on the ruins of Za'arain. She would touch him then, ride his timeshadow with the ruthless skill of Kiri, Darien and five—and the combined, terrible strength of lias'tri. With her own skills she would comb SaDyne from time/then and time/now. And then with Kane's skills she would do what only the Eyes of Za'ar had done—she would tear a life from the *then* and the *now* and the *always,* dispersing SaDyne's energies into the *other.* Za'ar death. Death without rebirth. Soul-eaters waiting, shining with imminence.

Azirs warned her not to let go of Kane, azir song surrounding her, holding her fingers locked in his.

Psi-hunters attacked, controlled by SaDyne. Even as Sharia's hair licked out hungrily, tearing Kiris from time/now, Kane wrenched savagely at the wakes, using everything he had learned from a living timeshadow rider and two deadly soul-eaters.

The wakes shattered like ribbons of glass. They shattered in time/then, time/now, the *then* and the *now* and the *always.* Shards of color glittered, vanished and then reappeared from the azirs' muzzles as they threw back their transparent heads and howled in all the colors of time. Ice-pale light bloomed, energy that shed the consequences of time/now as easily as Jhora fur shed water drops. A sense of becoming, of imminent time, condensed thickly, both chilling and protecting Kane and Sharia, deflecting for a few crucial instants of linear time the lethal glass explosion.

SaDyne had no such protection. Nor was he a living timeshadow rider able to heal himself. He had the Eyes, though, protection of another sort. He saw the coming explosion, knew that he could not prevent it, and reached out for the numbing safety of the *other.* The aspect of time known as the *other* was difficult to control, as difficult as the Eyes themselves. It poured over him in an icy, shimmering cataract. As soon as it touched him, he began to throw it away frantically, keeping as little as he could. It was enough. Glass rained around him harmlessly, cutting him only lightly, for his flesh was not a part of time/now. Not quite.

The azirs sucked the *other* back into themselves, freeing their deeply chilled companions. As Kane and Sharia staggered into the Kiriy's audience room, they saw a nearly transparent SaDyne glowing with imminent time. For a instant they hoped that he had finally succumbed to the Eyes. The instant passed, bringing with it something close to despair. SaDyne was not losing control of the Eyes; he had discovered the *other,* and was surviving it. With it he would be able to subdue the Eyes, for they were partially rooted in the *other* even as the azirs were.

Kane reached for wakes to manipulate—and found only the reverberations of recent explosion. There was nothing left of the thickly layered timeshadow wakes but echoes rapidly fading. New wakes were condensing around him, psi-hunters dying in the slicing instant of exploding glass raining down, wakes still quivering with their sudden release from the life of time/now. But he could not use those wakes yet, not for a few moments of linear time, not until they no longer resonated with recent life and violent death.

Too long. SaDyne will control the Eyes by then. There is no linear time in the other.

Sharia and Kane ran toward SaDyne. He wore a crown of alien crystals that seethed with psi- and time-energy, artifacts from cultures that had learned to tap dimensions and aspects of time. The Eyes of Za'ar glowed a pale lavender, a mere shadow of what they could be when worn by a true Kiriy. Yet even as Kane and Sharia ran toward SaDyne, the Eyes' color became more intense, more brilliant, crystals catching fire, blazing, reaching toward all minds, all times, consuming everything they touched.

The deadliness of condensed time began to fade from around SaDyne even as the Eyes of Za'ar flashed with violet energy.

The words of command condensed slowly in SaDyne's mind, the command that would send Za'arain irretrievably into an endless night of the soul, driven by the mind of lias'tri thwarted.

I AM—

The two Za'arains threw themselves at SaDyne. Sharia's terrible Darien hair raked through SaDyne's living timeshadow, tearing each color from linear time. SaDyne screamed and retreated into the *other* as he had once before, sliding among the interstices of Fourth Evolution time. Sharia pursued his writhing, tormented timeshadow with all the savagery of her psi-hunter ancestry and the energy of her countless other lives. She hunted SaDyne even into the *other.* And then she loosed all her skill, all her atavistic rage, tearing SaDyne from every life, every time, while Kane poured his strength into her, burying his hands in her lashing hair, giving everything of himself through all his own lives and times.

The deadly light of the *other* bloomed, wrapping the three Za'arains. Inside that icy illumination colors churned violently, lias'tri crystals blazing through all shared times and all shared lives, drawing energy recklessly because the only alternative was death for lias'tri in the *then* and the *now* and the *always.* SaDyne screamed and twisted, seeking escape within the cascading, searing, unsuspected times of the Eyes of Za'ar. Sharia followed, stripping away his life one color at a time, peeling him of lives and times until there was nothing left and he was naked within her incandescent hair.

The azirs closed around SaDyne; and then he died in all of his lives, all of his times, everything. The soul-eaters sang, drinking his colors, drinking him, and when they were done there not even a fading echo of life remained.

The azirs glowed, replete with Fourth Evolution energy.

Sharia clung to Kane, staring at what had once been SaDyne and now was merely flesh clothed in a soiled robe and cracked, dulled crown. The Eyes of Za'ar had a sullen lavender cast, as though they resented being worn by a corpse. In that moment Sharia feared the Eyes more than she had ever feared anything,

even the final death. Yet there was no choice. Za'arain needed
the Eyes. The Joining needed Za'arain. She must try to wear
the Eyes of Za'ar.

NO!

But there was no alternative. They both knew it. Even now
the psi-packs were beginning to form again. For a million years
Kiriys wearing the Eyes of Za'ar had shaped that savage psychic
energy into one of the most constructive civilizations ever
known to the Fourth Evolution.

There must be a Kiriy. Someone must take up the Eyes.

. . . yes . . . but . . .

As one, Kane and Sharia bent down, reaching for the Eyes
of Za'ar.

An eerie light blossomed through SaDyne's corpse. The dead
flesh changed before their eyes, brown to grey, weightless, drifting . . . ashes sifting on currents even a timeshadow rider could
barely sense. A soul-eater sang beguilingly. The ashes spiraled
upward into the beast's translucent mouth.

Nothing was left.

Not even the Eyes of Za'ar.

The stunning realization broke over Kane and Sharia in the
same instant. They had saved Za'arain from a renegade Kiriy,
but they had not saved it from the azirs' inexplicable need to
give its companions that which they most desired.

Sharia and Kane suddenly understood that while their rational
minds had accepted the probable cost of her taking up the Eyes,
the deepest levels of their minds had not. She would have taken
up the Eyes, but it was Kane she wanted. He would have taken
up the Eyes in hopes of sparing her, but it was Sharia he wanted,
not the title of Kiriy. They wanted the extraordinary, demanding,
exquisite reality of lias'tri, not the world-ruling Eyes of Za'ar.

And the azirs had known it, so they had simply removed the
Eyes of Za'ar—and in doing so the azirs had killed Za'arain
and the Joining. The Eyes of Za'ar would never again open in
Fourth Evolution linear time.

Twenty-one

A psi-pack's atavistic howl shivered through the ruined audience room.

Kane and Sharia heard it, heard Za'arain's future prowling closer on predatory feet. Their minds wept as an azir once had, in scales and times unknown to Fourth Evolution life. They had not wanted this for their people. They had not wanted savagery and futile death. They had wanted the boundless creations of lias'tri, of life. There was no limit to the possibilities of time and life combined. The seething energy of Kiri atavism could build as well as raze, renew as well as destroy, celebrate as well as annihilate.

Psi-packs condensed and glided through shattered hallways, broken lives, recent death.

The soul-eaters moved soundlessly forward, standing between their companions and the approaching hunters.

No. We have killed enough. Too much. We will remember how it was and dream how it might have been.

And then we will die.

The azirs found neither conflict nor regret in their companions' desires. Both Za'arains would rather die in linear time than kill again. Helplessly the soul-eaters lifted their muzzles to the broken ceiling and sang of inhuman regret and the inexplicable desires of Fourth Evolution companions.

Alien harmonies poured through Kane and Sharia as they held one another and waited to die; and while they waited they remembered deeply, dreaming as only lias'tris united could, dreaming to the boundaries of time. They remembered Za'arain's glory, its rainbow cities glistening beneath silver skies, its people living freely, seeking new answers and daring to ask new questions, Za'arain bathed in the luminous serenity and potency of the Kiriy's mind, a serenity and excitement shared and reinforced by Za'arain minds, Kiri hopes, Darien strengths.

There had not been perfection, even under the Kiriy and the Eyes of Za'ar. Kane and Sharia remembered that. They also knew that perfection was neither attainable nor desirable. Perfection was of the *always*. Fourth Evolution life was not; it changed, like Kiris slowly evolving into Dariens, and Dariens into fives.

If not perfection, though, creation was possible to the changing people of Za'arain. It was this of which Kane and Sharia dreamed, Fourth Evolution minds radiating through time and space, the endless human colors of curiosity and emotion, poetry and pragmatism, striving and attainment—all of it was waiting for Za'arain's children. Life expressed in countless ways, time without end, a universe of glittering possibilities waiting.

Creation, not annihilation.

Lias'tri stones ignited with the force of Darien five dreams. The crystals scintillated with blinding light. Neither Kane nor Sharia saw. They were as deeply embedded in their potent dreaming as life was within linear time. With each moment, each heartbeat, lias'tri crystals blazed higher, brighter, infusing time with all the colors of life.

Psi-packs glided unnoticed into the room, drawn by the ineluctable power of two fives touching, of Darien dreaming, of lias'tri consummation. A cataract of colors claimed the Kiris, all the possibilities of creation coruscating around them, inside them, mind and body, caressing them as sweetly as a lover. Where SaDyne had demanded and coerced, lias'tri dream simply offered and suggested. Savagery melded its wild potency willingly with the dream, for Kane and Sharia had accepted rather than denied the Kiri atavism that surged within all of them.

Kiri after Kiri silently came to the dreaming lias'tris, stood within the shattering and renewing beauty of their dream, added to that dream, and withdrew as quietly as they had come. The dream grew slowly, mind touching mind; and then the dream expanded more and more rapidly as new minds added more shades and hues and tones of creation. The shared dream over-flowed the room, the compound, Za'aral. The potent dream lapped over from mind to mind, city to city, continent to con-tinent, a sunrise of joined minds shimmering with the infinite possibilities of creation. . . .

Within the renewed compound Sharia stirred slightly, like a swimmer floating within one of Za'arain's warm seas. But it was not water that supported and caressed her, it was Kane. She smiled up at him, and her eyes were a brilliance to equal the crystal resting between her breasts. He buried his hands in her rippling Darien hair, and smiled as she delicately touched all the aspects of his timeshadow. Then he laughed richly, a sound as beautiful as a soul-eater's song. Lias'tri crystals resonated with a music that could only be felt, not heard.

"Well," said Jode quietly, "it's about time you woke up." He slanted a black glance at the azirs glowing by his friends' side. "Your, er, pets wouldn't even let me get a thought in sideways," he added. "And it was such a marvelous dream." He sighed and touched his dimmed lias'tri crystal unconsciously. "I don't sup-pose you'd want to tell me what happened between the time that Dani left Doursone and the moment when one of your azirs appeared to Rizah?"

Kane smoothed his palm down the length of Sharia's body, savoring the warmth and life he had never thought to touch again. She curled against him even as the meaning of Jode's words sank in. "An azir?" asked Kane. "On Doursone? When?"

"Three days ago. Two days after Dani reappeared. But I'm

not sure my time measurements mean anything. Dani glowed with azir light when she landed on Doursone. She had been in times that she refuses even to think about. And she brought me here in less than a day. I wonder how long it took the azir to get to Doursone," added the psi-master thoughtfully. Then he saw that neither Sharia nor Kane understood. He swore with odd wistfulness. "I'd hoped that you would be able to explain at least what happened on Doursone. Rizah was dying. I stayed with her, doing what I could because she was fighting so hard to hold onto life. Then out of nowhere one of your azirs just . . . condensed. Rizah held up her hands. It opened its mouth and an eerie pale dust poured out. Rizah laughed and laughed. When she could laugh no more, she died."

"SaDyne's ashes poured into her hands," whispered Sharia. "The soul-eater kept my promise."

"That answers another question," said Jode. "He's dead?"

"Yes. Always. In all times."

"The azirs killed him?" asked Jode curiously.

"No."

"The Eyes of Za'ar?"

"No."

Jode hesitated, reading the answer in the violet shadows turning deeply within Kane's and Sharia's silver eyes. "I see. And the Eyes themselves?"

As dead as SaDyne. Always. In all times.

Jode looked baffled. He waved a hand to indicate the compound and the rebuilt city of Za'aral itself. "But the psi-packs are gone. Did you kill them even as you killed SaDyne?"

Kane smiled and smoothed Sharia's living hair. "They're all around you, Jhoramon. Kiri and Darien, fours and sixes—and soon there will be fives, many fives. Za'arain's people are changing as all life changes."

Jode circled back to the one thing that interested him. "How did you control the psi-packs without the Eyes?"

"We didn't," Kane said. "They sensed our dream. They wanted it. You see, the Eyes of Za'ar had coped with Kiri savagery by burying it far back in our racial time. SaDyne dealt with Kiri atavism by trying to force it into his own channels."

"And lias'tri?" asked Jode quietly. "How did it deal with this atavistic aspect of the Kiri mind?"

"We accepted it, all of it. We are Kiri atavism and Darien timeshadow rider combined."

Jode drew a deep breath and almost smiled. "I should have guessed. Lias'tri's solution is always unity." He stood quietly, watching the two people whom he loved and hardly knew. "What of the Joining? Are we safe from Kiri psi-packs now?"

"Psi-packs belong to time/then. We live in time/now. There will be no more lias'tri exiles to make the name of Za'arain and timeshadow rider synonymous with obscenity," promised Sharia.

Her voice faded and then was reborn in haunting duet, Kane and Sharia speaking clearly of lias'tri and a death that knew no end.

"There will be no more Kiri, Darien, and fives born and then divided from their lias'tris. Like SaDyne. ZaDyneen. The dead Kiriy was his other half. He didn't know that. He thought that the unity he *hungered* for waited within the Eyes of Za'ar. To attain that unity he created the virus of the winnowing, knowing that eventually it would ravage even Za'arain, even the Kiriy herself. He knew that no one could heal her, for the only living timeshadow rider on Za'arain was also a five.

"And then he felt the Eyes of Za'ar close. At least he thought that what rent his mind with rage and sorrow was the closing of the Eyes. It was not. It was his lias'tri's death in the *then* and the *now* and the *always*. She poured herself through all times trying to control the doom she sensed closing over Za'arain. Like SaDyne, the dead Kiriy will not be born again.

"Nor will we speak of them again. Ever."

Jode closed his eyes and listened to the azirs sing softly of times only translucent soul-eaters knew. They shimmered with music and energy, ice-pale light, ghostly exhalation of the *other*.

"Za'arain is no longer a closed planet, afraid of the atavism burning deeply in our mind," Kane said, looking at his other half smiling at him with pleasure. "Whoever wants to come to Za'arain is welcome. Whoever wants to leave is also blessed. We are the Joining and the Dust, the past and the future. We will be one. We will build a civilization where life can evolve freely, create joyously. It has already begun, called by lias'tri dreams."

Kane and Sharia rose as one and walked toward Jode, wrapped in colored light flowing through healed glass walls.

"Za'arain no longer needs us, Kiris accept and control themselves, freeing everyone. We will go out with you to the stars of the Joining and the Dust, bringing exiles home, uniting that which no longer needs to be separate."

Then Sharia spoke alone, sending a nearly transparent tendril of hair out to touch Jode's lips. "But you don't have to go with us if you don't want to. You're free to do whatever you want, just as Dani is free."

"Dani would be lost without her Za'arain gods," said Jode dryly.

"There are no Za'arain gods. There are only people who dream. Whoever wants to join us may also dream. Even Dani."

Jode started to ask another question but found he had no words. Even the thought was inchoate. But the Za'arains heard him, sensed the thought he could not quite form.

Yes, in the immensity of time we will come together and dream again, the Dust and the Joining and Za'arain, dreaming through all, our lives and times, becoming . . . what?

Is there anything that man cannot dream?

Epilog

If there is an answer to the Za'arain Question, it has not come down to us through the immensity of time. All Cycles, all civilizations, all races of the Fourth Evolution, have asked that question. As an answer we have only hints, fragments, tantalizing clues:

We know that life evolves.

We know that the Za'arain Cycle endured longer than any Cycle known to any Evolution, millions of years and then millions more, creation like a radiant tide rising throughout the galaxy.

We know that the dreamers of Za'arain vanished between one instant and the next.

We do not know why or where or when or what they became.

And we know that azirs have begun to sing in our dreams from time to time.

Or is it we who have begun to sing in theirs . . . ?